SHE TALKS TO FISH

By
Brian Hester &
Barbara Beam

CUZINS ENTERTAINMENT

Copyright © 2024 by Brian Hester and Barbara Beam

All rights reserved

This book is a work of fiction. Names, characters, places, and incidents are either a product of the authors' imaginations or are used fictitiously. Any resemblance to actual people living or dead, events, or locales are entirely coincidental. No reproduction without written permission.

For booking information, events, and all inquiries, please see our website: shetalkstofish.com

Published by Cuzins Entertainment
Printed in the United States of America
Paperback book: ISBN: 979-8-218-47245-0
eBook: ISBN: 979-8-218-47683-0

FOREWORD

Dear Reader,

What you're holding in your hand is a unique love letter that is crafted with delicate hands, and made perfect with every metaphor, plot twist, i-dotted and t-crossed. With Maya's journey, we explore a different kind of passion—a love for something unexpected—fly fishing.

As you read, you'll begin to understand the sport as more than just a hobby: It's a lifestyle. One that Brian and Barbara have so carefully brought to life through the eyes of our brilliant (and feisty) heroine— Maya. When I started working on this novel, (as an editor,) I said it was a beach read... something leisurely and entertaining that you could pick up under sun-soaked umbrellas and digest next to saltwater pools. But as they continued to refine and reframe this, what became clear is this work would be much more than that. They've taken this book from casual to profound and, by extension, elevated the sport of fly fishing.

We often refer to fly fishing as the great equalizer. It's the one sport whose spectators (fish) don't care who you are or where you come from; all that matters when you're knee-deep in the water, preparing to cast your line, is you. It's about how you court your catch, how delicate your cast is, how attentive you are to the world around you, and if you do it right, you'll likely find yourself in a similar position to Maya. She is at peace and confident in her place in the world. This is the potential for personal growth that fly fishing offers.

So before you turn the page and immerse yourself in the world of Maya, Ed, and Will, please remember that this is a love letter to the characters, the sport, and the world of possibilities that can exist when you try your hand at experiencing the wonder of fly fishing. This story will inspire connection and discovery among those who may be established and those who are new to the sport. Fly fishing may not be the most popular sport in America, but if Brian and Barbara have anything to say about it, it will be.

Happy Reading,
Malin Curry

A copywriter and writing coach in a past life, Malin is an aspiring marathoner, book connoisseur and marketing junkie. Following the onset of the pandemic in 2020, he picked up blogging and racked up bylines in Medium, TVGuide, Better Marketing, and more all within a year. Today, he's excited to grow his love for reading by helping the next generation of writers shape their stories for diverse audiences and working on his debut novel.

*An ounce of experience is better than a ton of theory simply because it is only in experience that any theory has any vital and verifiable significance… We do not learn simply from experience... We learn from **reflecting** on that experience.*

--- John Dewey

PREFACE by Brian Hester

Being a public school visual arts educator for thirty years can drive any human to drink. Fly fishing has been and will always be a better choice than the bottle… although some might think that both are a must for the total experience of a full day on the water. This is where my backstory takes hold.

I will never forget a warm, late May Saturday morning. I had just turned fourteen and was high-stepping cow patties through the pasture near my house to get down to the New River as fast as I could. I followed my mentor's protocol and caught my first Brown Trout on the fly. There was no one around to hear me scream, witness my dancing, or see my permanent smile. I knew I had done something special all by myself. I also knew I was one of few, if not the only, kid who did what I did. I recall thinking, "Why the hell doesn't everyone do this? This shit is unreal!"

Fly fishing saved my life, which is why I pay it forward every chance I get. For as long as I can remember, even at my lowest points, it gave me an outlet to cope and grow and heal. Aside from being outside, in tune with nature, and focused on solving all the problems in the universe, the sport simply makes better human beings void of a cell phone.

I started a Fly Anglers club at the high school where I taught in order to reach as many kids as possible and introduce them to something they might never be exposed to otherwise. Right out of the gate there was a major discrepancy in the ratio of white males versus any other participants. I wanted that to change because fly fishing is a gift **everyone** should experience. As more young women bought into our Angler's Club, I began to push even harder for more women of color. In the span of seven years, women, including women of color, held every officer's seat. This was something I had advocated for so long, and it was finally coming to fruition.

The young women in the Angler's Club were the catalysts and inspiration to write this novel. Along with their inspiration, I was also driven to find answers to the many questions that I raised as I considered the facts.

Roughly eight million people in the US say they fly fish: 73% are white, 27% are women, and only 2% of those women are black. Why is this? Why don't more women of color fly fish? How can I influence these statistics to change?

What else can I do to introduce more people to these magnificent creatures of the current through the extension of a fly rod? How do I increase the size of my audience? I decided to write a novel with a compelling message of belonging, adversity, empowerment, and encouragement to reform this narrative. Fly fishing has never been about degrees of melanin, socioeconomics, or gender identity. My vision for this story was built on respect, conscientious research, and illuminating the profound perseverance summoned as the human spirit always triumphs over the human condition.

Hopefully, when you read Maya's story, many of you will explore the wonders of fly fishing too. Everyone deserves the opportunity to be happy and learn the valuable lessons fly fishing can teach us all. Sometimes just a taste can summon an insatiable hunger. You don't know what you don't know until you bite.

Prologue

Bozeman, MT, 1978

"Daddy, why is mommy sleeping on the bathroom floor?" their three-year-old son asked. Ed was getting breakfast ready for his family, but he raced to the bathroom before Will even finished the question.

Sarah's pregnancy was turbulent. During the first trimester, her morning sickness was out of control, and she was bedridden for days. She made it through those difficult months but faced more complications and had started a regime of labetalol to combat her high blood pressure. Throughout the second and third terms, she dealt with gestational diabetes and hypertension.

Ed found her on the floor unconscious. He checked for a pulse. It was weak. Unwilling to call 911 and wait for the EMTs, he gathered her unconscious body, side-stepped through the hallway and frantically loaded everyone in his truck. Will held her hand saying, "Mommy. Wake up, Mommy." Ed sped out of their short driveway and raced down the street. Will said, "Why is your arm bleeding, Daddy?"

Ed glanced at his arm and punched the gas even harder. Sarah began softly moaning as Ed dodged car after car. Her water had broken, and she was bleeding. As they arrived at the emergency wing of the hospital, Ed jammed the truck in park and ran to the passenger door catching Sarah as she poured from her seat. As he carried her through the automatic doors, he cried for help and was met by two nurses with a gurney.

Covered in her blood, he watched the love of his life disappear through the ER doors. Unable to comprehend the admission nurse's barrage of questions, he finally shook from his trance, remembering Will was still in the truck. Feverishly, he sprinted back to find his son engaged in a conversation with an old man wearing an Army baseball hat. The man assured him, "Saw you run in... hope your wife's okay. When I noticed you had a little one, I took it upon myself to watch him." Ed thanked the man, grabbed Will, and raced back inside. He stared at Sarah through the glass window and watched joy slip from his grasp.

The pandemonium of doctors and nurses and the beeping and buzzing of alarms saturated the ER room. Too many things needed to happen at once. One nurse shouted, "BP is 150 over 95," and another nurse began fastening leads on Sarah's chest to the EKG monitor; yet another was trying to find a vein for an IV line.

To make matters worse, the baby was breech. The lead nurse had immediately paged Sarah's obstetrician, who was already there finishing another delivery.

While the attending ER doctor tried to rotate the baby's head down, Sarah flat-lined. The doctor couldn't wait any longer and barked, "Scalpel dammit! We need to deliver this baby, now!"

One of the nurses started chest compressions. The entire medical team had specific roles and executed them to perfection. The defibrillator was wheeled over as the OB moved in to cut the umbilical cord and take the baby girl. She wasn't wiggling or crying. The OB began CPR right in front of the window where Ed stared helplessly. Will stood quietly, holding his father's hand. The attending physician seized the AED paddles shouting, "Charge to 150. Clear!"

Everyone stepped back with their hands up. Sarah's chest flexed and bowed, then dropped back to the bed with a thump. The heart rate alarm was shrill and cruel… and flat. He roared again, "Charge to 200. Clear!"

PART ONE

1

BOONE, NC April, 1987

For me, being different was never about making a statement, fighting to swim upstream, or finding myself situated in a place where I didn't belong, or even doing something I wasn't supposed to do. I just did me. It's what my Daddy and Momma preached, so that's what I did. I did me.

Normally, this time of year I would play with caterpillars, but today I found the famed Chartreuse Cruiser praying mantis.

He was crawling across the desk. I put my pencil down, and he'd crawl up it like an on-ramp, legs alternating in a wobbly, jerky type of movement. Then, I rotated and tilted the pencil back down like a seesaw, watching intensely as he strutted and carefully paused to stare at me with his big beady eyes. I held him up and teased him with my finger, prompting him to extend his long prickly, praying arms to shadow box with me. Then I would let him crawl back down to the desk again in that same rocking, staggering motion.

It wasn't exactly thrilling, but it was better than doing math, and I needed some form of entertainment. I had already grasped the principle of fractions and three-quarters of the class was still stuck back in basic division and multiplication. I was bored, so I took it upon myself to study the cadence of my partner's stride and tendencies.

Now THAT intrigued me, and, for whatever reason, held my attention.

Today, I was focused on two things: NOT doing math and playing with my little friend. My friend, Annie, saw me playing with him and started laughing. She knew I've always had a special relationship with bugs. She mouthed to me, "You're gonna get in trouble." I smiled and shrugged.

Once Annie said something, Jenny, the girl in front of me turned around and saw it. She yelled, "STICK BUG...Oh my goodness! STICK BUG!"

Then other kids followed, gasping, and sucking all the air out of the classroom. Eventually Warren, my arch nemesis, and his friend, Cash, saw me and REALLY laid into me.

"Look at the cricket playing with a cricket," Warren sneered.

"It's a praying mantis, dumbass."

"What did you call me?"

I ignored him. I knew Warren wasn't right in the head. We were all completely convinced he had been dropped on his head when he was a baby. By this time, Mrs. Martin, who was leaning over a student's shoulder on the other side of the room, finally perked up to see what was going on. If any other horrendous thing was going to happen at that moment to bring even more attention to me, now was the perfect time. Cue the swarming commotion.

The gawking stir around my Green Glider agitated him enough to take flight-- straight into Mrs. Martin's hair clear across the room.

Complete chaos ensued as Mrs. Martin screamed and ran around the classroom while thrashing and swatting her head. Like cockroaches in the light, everyone in the class started taking cover, ducking and diving under desks, causing total mayhem. I stood still in amazement, not at the bedlam consuming the room, but at the glorious aeronautical tour my friend was taking. First stop, Mrs. Martin's hair. Second stop, the bookcase across the room. And last stop, directly on the hairbrush that Jenny had left on her desk when she dove for cover. It was simply captivating. I leaned forward and scooped him up, carefully cupping him in my hands. And of course, I was the one who got in trouble. Mrs. Martin could barely catch her breath, as I saw a tear roll off her mascara-smeared cheek. I surveyed the room in its now deafening silence. One by one, each student slowly and cautiously peered out from under the desk, making sure the coast was clear.

Mrs. Martin in a half-whimpering cry, shouted, "Maya, what in the world? Are you playing with a grasshopper?"

"No ma'am. That's a praying mantis I named Langston after my favorite poet."

"Oh no, Maya! A praying mantis?" She began to twitch a little. Her right eye and cheek pulsed uncontrollably.

"Yes ma'am."

"Well… kill it and put it in the trash can."

"No! I can't just kill him!"

The kids all sneered at me, pointing, and mocking my words. I quickly shut them up by lunging at them, pretending to send Langston back into flight in their direction. It was like Moses parting the Red Sea. Almost everyone backed away, except for Warren. He didn't block my path exactly, but he wasn't going to move either.

"Then take him outside, and let him go…and for heaven's sake, do it now!"

"Yes ma'am."

As I walked past Warren, he tried to slap my hand to shake my friend loose. There's no doubt he would have stepped on him just to watch his green blood spurt out. Like I said... he was messed up in the head.

Luckily for him, and Langston, I knew he'd try something stupid, so I gracefully dodged him and continued outside...glad to leave.

I remember thinking, as I played with my buddy, "I don't know why other people don't enjoy insects like I do. Do other girls think of anything other than their hair, gossiping or trying to be popular? Do boys ever think about things like the gravity defying flight of a praying mantis or the life cycle of a caterpillar and the magnificent transformation that awaits?"

I doubted it. I knew I was different then, and I know I'm still different now. It's almost twenty years since that incident in my class, but it's time for me to tell my story. Not because I have more to say than anyone else... but because I've never met anyone who has traveled the same road as I have... Well, it's not a road, exactly. It's a river.

I have always lived my life by the three F's: Faith, Family and Fishing. There's no place I'd rather be than on the river: the sun warming my face, a light breeze making it easier to breathe, the river carrying my stress and sorrow downstream, and hooking a big ol' Rainbow Trout.

Fishing is what keeps me healthy: mentally, spiritually, physically...all the "ly's" really. There's no doubt in my mind that the world would be a better place if there were more fishermen. That's why I decided to tell my story.

This story didn't materialize because someone told me I couldn't, shouldn't or can't... I didn't become a fly fisherman because I'm a rebel, although I guess I am. I fell in love with those beautiful creatures that inhabit that space beneath the water's surface. The sad thing is that there are millions and millions of people on this earth who look like me who will never experience the peace, beauty, and exhilaration of fly fishing. How sad is that? But without exposure, there is no interest. Without interest, there is no pursuance. Without pursuance, there is no true understanding or sustained hunger. Without parents, mentors, teachers, and other role models teaching us…guiding our efforts…molding and sculpting our lives…we will devolve into uneducated individuals with no community and no purpose. The human condition always favors the void.

Throughout my life, I have been blessed by so many wonderful people. My mentors told me that I didn't need to worry about being different, so I didn't worry about what other people thought or why I was different. Sure, I got teased and picked on, and most everyone I know called me "weirdo," "worm girl," and things much worse, but I didn't care. Say what you want. The haters just don't understand the serenity of becoming one with nature and the joy of having fish as your friends. I felt sorry for those haters, bless their hearts. They simply didn't know what they were missing.

As I reveled in the memory of Langston's graceful aerial ascent around our class that day, I thought about how lucky I was to see things very few people could see… to learn things from nature that other people wouldn't take the time or care to learn. When your passion becomes your way of life, the game changes completely.

I was named after Maya Angelou, the great American poet, who once said, "*You are only free when you realize you belong no place – you belong every place – no place at all. The price is high. The reward is great.*"

Maya Angelou knew, as I do, that at some point you have to be okay with who you are…which is a tough ask for anyone, let alone a kid. Being comfortable in your own skin helps filter the outside noise, so even as a child, I was prepared to shut out that noise. Most encounters of vulnerability or shame rolled off me like water off duck feathers. Once you accept who you are – then you belong. If more and more people stepped outside their proverbial comfort zones, consciously immune to the difficult the task, then sympathy and common ground would flourish.

My mind traveled back to that day when Langston and I were outside together and what Ms. Pearce, my principal, said when she found me outside at the end of the school day.

"Maya!" It was Ms. Pearce, our principal.

"Yes, ma'am."

"What are you doing out here by yourself?"

I wanted to say, I'd rather be out here than inside, but I was raised better than that, so I said, "Ms. Martin asked me to take a praying mantis outside, so I was just making sure he got into the forest safely."

"Good for you, Maya. He will be grateful. You are always very kind to all of God's creatures. You could grow up to be a vet or an entomologist or something! You have a unique gift…But, right now, you need to go back to class and get your things because the bell is about to ring."

"Yes ma'am," and, taking one last look to be sure Langston was safe and sound, I headed back to class. When I walked through the classroom door, I noticed a trashcan propping it open. As I entered, I couldn't help but notice Jenny's hairbrush sitting right there on top of the other trash. I grinned. Life was funny to me.

Everyone experiences highs and lows and challenges in life. That's how life works. But no one could have fathomed the obstacles that were strategically positioned on the water waiting to wreck me.

2

Boone, 1989

We lived off Brookshire Road which ran parallel to the New River. The second oldest river in the world was literally out my back door about three hundred yards away. I remember asking why we didn't live in Junaluska, just behind King Street, with the rest of the Black community. We went to church there. Daddy said my granddaddy, back in the early 1900's, had worked out a deal with a neighboring family for a couple of tracks of land. Both were riverside about a half a mile apart. We lived on one and the other was on a floodplain, which was the access to our favorite fishing hole just below the Stapleton pasture. He was also quick to mention there were a bunch of families tied together that worked the land who all got along with one another. So, choosing to live away from the Junaluska was a good fit for us. The Robinson and Johnson families were a part of that deal on Brookshire and collectively built homes that have been handed down one generation to the next.

We had a long, gravel drive that was shared by the three homes. There was only one-way in and one-way out. Daddy's little red Datsun pickup was...well... a piece of crap, but it was a 4-wheel drive, so we were good and could pretty much get anywhere we wanted. Winters in Boone, North Carolina, could occasionally dump a foot of snow on us before we could get home from church.

Our house was a modest two bedroom and one bath, but it had a front AND back porch and that's where we spent a lot of our time...when we weren't down the hill at the river. From the house it was a short walk through the field straight down to the New River. It seemed like there were miles and miles of solid fishing anywhere you went up or down the New. Our favorite fishing hole, just past the pasture and down the ravine, was water that always produced healthy smallies and the occasional trout. That's where the second plot of land is. It's really not good for anything other than fishing and swimming, but what else is there?

Back then, I never really liked to fish. I mean, I would be so bored sitting there with Daddy. Being quiet. I always said I wanted to go with him, but not necessarily to fish. I just liked spending time with him. as he hummed country tunes like, "Let a little Love Come In" by Charley Pride. Daddy loved Charley Pride. One day I asked him why he loved Charley Pride so much.

"He's just like you, baby girl." I thought about that for a minute. He's a man. He's old. He sings. Nah. I didn't get it. Finally, I said, "Why do you think he's like me, Daddy?"

Daddy laughed. "'Cuz, baby girl. He doin' somethin' ain't no one else doin' right now. He singin' that country music. That's the music of farmers and country folk. White people buy his music. Ain't that somethin'? They buy that music 'cuz he be preachin' it!"

I thought for a little while longer. "I still don't understand. I don't sing country music."

"Charley a trailblazer. You a trailblazer. You a Black girl...fishin'!"

I had no clue as to what he was talking about. I knew lots of black girls who fished. Entire families would be fishing. Later on, I realized he wasn't talking about just fishing...he was talking about fishing being my passion and my first great love...besides my Daddy, of course.

My dad was about six feet tall, with dark skin, dark brown eyes, and a stunning smile. His hands were rough and calloused, but he used Momma's lotion all the time. He didn't like to be ashy. He wore jeans and flannel shirts most days and great big, steel-toed boots. He drove trucks, forklifts, and did other stuff at the New River Building Supply, and when we weren't fishing, as a side hustle, he also did some framing for Mr. Remmey Myers Construction Company. During those warm summer days, he would wear cut-off shorts and a t-shirt. When he dressed up to go to church or take Momma on a rare date to The Peddler Steakhouse, he wore either his gray or blue Kangol hat. He was cool. He was strong and athletic. His voice sounded like hot honey whiskey with about three extra scoops of honey. I thought he was the greatest man on earth.

Fishing took me a little while longer to fall in love with. But bugs? I loved them from the get-go. I was the kid in class who found a grasshopper or caterpillar at recess and picked it up. Luckily, in Boone, there was always a plethora of them crawling around in the spring. They were everywhere, traversing from one side of the street to the other. The kids always liked riding their bikes over them to watch their guts spurt out. Not me. I kept them as pets...at least for the day.

Momma read me *Their Eyes Were Watching God* even before I really could read. She wanted me to be strong like Janie. Caterpillars reminded me of Janie. They were not always the prettiest of creatures, but wise people like me could see the beautiful butterfly just waiting for the opportunity to be dazzling and soar. I always thought it was cool that these caterpillars were painted with the same colors as Appalachian State: banded with black and canary gold. I thought it was funny the university had its own caterpillar.

Milkweed would line the banks of the New River in early spring and the Monarch caterpillar would latch on for its transformation and eventually for a long migration to the west. Unbeknownst to me, I would end up just like the Monarch, maturing into a journey west myself.

When a random snake, spider, or cricket got into the classroom, my teacher would always yell out with her predictable scream. So did all the girls. Screaming just because someone else did was stupid. Anyway, the boys would try to act cool, but that depended on how big the spider was. Almost always, I got called in for the extraction. I didn't kill snakes, either. Most are harmless and are good for the ecosystem. You just have to know what you're dealing with. And everyone knows it's bad luck to kill a cricket.

Depending on the insect, like a spider, I would usually just trap it in a cup or let it crawl on to a piece of paper or a stick and move it to a wooded area as quickly as possible. This always gave it a fighting chance before it got smashed or stepped on. I liked spiders usually, and I was fascinated by the intricacies of their webs. And I loved how determined they are to rebuild those webs even after I swept them down every day. (Our front porch attracted lots of spiders. Momma made me sweep them down every day. And every night they would rebuild them. Such determined creatures!)

I was the "go to" kid who helped the teacher by getting rid of the unwanted visitors. I loved the insects, but I also loved that once I grabbed one, I could walk outside and spend like five minutes out there in the fresh air watching the cricket or whatever get away. Unfortunately, my track record and a few previous classroom incidents usually prohibited me from enjoying my quality time with my multi-legged friends. News traveled fast through the teachers' lounge about my fascination with my little creature companions and inevitably, I would be pulled aside at the start of each school year and told, under no circumstances, would I be allowed to have any "pets" during class. My interests somehow always kept everyone at bay, and I was okay with that. The girls stayed away. The boys would, too, although some acted like they weren't scared…and would talk big and bad, but I knew better, and "prior events" had proven it. They learned to keep their distance.

Truth be told, I didn't really want to be friends with many people. I always thought girls cared about stupid stuff like shoes, clothes, and hair and boys made flatulent noises with their armpits.

Fishing was a slow-growing interest. It combined bugs, being outside, and Daddy. All of those things were fun.

Daddy would talk about things that I didn't really understand at the time, but I remember most of his advice to this day. One day, we were cleaning fish, and he gave me one life lesson I have always remembered, "Fishin' is God's equalizer, baby girl," as he expertly cleaned the fish. I cut the heads off. I was only eight, but I was good at it. Daddy had to do the hard part.

"What does that mean, Daddy?"

"See fishin' don't care 'bout nothin'...how rich or poor you are, how ugly or pretty you are, how you dress, if you're black, white, red, green, blue, boy or a girl, skinny or fat, or where you worship. Only thing fishin' care 'bout is your attitude and your effort." He stops what he's doing and turns and looks me in the eye. He holds up his index finger. One. "Attitude." He holds up his middle finger. Two. "Effort. As long as you have a good attitude and good work ethic...or effort...nothin' can stop you." Finished with his philosophy lesson, he turned back and gutted his last fish as I started packing up.

"My teacher said I can do anything I want."

Daddy chuckled. "Nah, baby. You can't do ANYTHING."

I was indignant about this response. "Whatchoo mean? You don't think so?"

"Course not, Maya! You can't be no ballerina. You gonna be too tall."

"Well, I don't wanna be a ballerina."

"That's right. God creates you to be unique in your own way. And he don't make mistakes. So he didn't give you a ballerina body because he don't want you to turn into a ballerina. You can't do anything... but you can do EVERYTHING you are supposed to do."

"How will I know what I am supposed to do?"

"Fishin'."

"Fishin'?"

"Fishin'." He laughed. "When you fishin', you at peace... you quiet...and one with creation. Just you and this beautiful world. Then you'll know."

3

Boone, 1989

I remember the day I caught more fish than Daddy. It was Saturday, April 13, 1989. It was a few months before my 10th birthday. We got up while it was still dark. My toast had way too much jelly, but Daddy didn't fuss at me. He packed our bologna sandwiches while I got our gear together and then we tip-toed out the door, so we didn't wake up Momma.

The night before, I caught like fifty nightcrawlers. I looked for one of the small ones, and I baited my hook with it. "Baby girl," Daddy said, "this time try putting the hook through his head and wrapping it a few times on the shank of the hook."

"Like this?"

"Great job! Now leave about two inches of its tail to float and drift freely."

As the clear, Carolina sky turned pink with the approaching dawn, I launched the perfect cast and let the line swing to a stop at the perfect spot. Then BAM! Not two minutes in and I was in a nice fight with a sixteen-inch brown. I caught a 'bow, too, and it put up a nasty little fight as well.

Meanwhile, poor, ol' Daddy caught a tiny little suckerfish. He said it was because he wanted me to cast in the deep while he stayed in the shallows. Still not sure if he really did it on purpose.

My confidence was steadily climbing, and after that day it was clear that I had a knack for the sport, and it was growing on me. I began to think of myself as a fisherman. Fisherwoman. Fisherperson. Fisherqueen. All of the above. I was developing a rapport with the fish and that amplified my desire to be on the water. Even when Daddy had to work late, I would wait in anticipation of his arrival so we could get a line wet right before dinner, even if it was only for an hour or so.

"Sounds like them fish got the hook in you, girl!" His laughter always made me laugh, too. I didn't even have to know what was funny. He wasn't always happy, though. Sometimes he'd get quiet and look sad. I wasn't sure what he had gone through in his younger days, before I knew him, but life had wounded him somehow.

On rare occasions, Momma came with us to fish. She was funny. Momma, Daddy, and I walked down the hill to the river. Momma wasn't sure-footed, but I was a mountain goat, so she made me hold her hand. She was slow, and I was impatient, but I was glad she was there with us…so I went slowly, too, and guided her down the slope. When we got to the bank where we fished all the time, Momma just stopped at stared at the river.

"Wha'choo looking at, Momma?" I asked her.

She threw a rock into the river. "Look at those ripples. They go on and on."

"Yeah," I answered. "They do. That's pretty cool."

"It's better than 'cool.' It's a miracle."

"Why do you think that, Momma?"

"Because… one tiny little pebble affects everything it touches. EVERYTHING. Imagine how much more power we have than a little pebble?"

I threw a pebble in the river, too and smiled at Momma.

"Maya, come over here and put that cricket on my hook."

I sighed as loudly as I could. "Why can't you do it yourself, Momma?" Daddy, who had already made a cast, tried to stifle a guffaw.

"Hush up now, Zeke.

"No, ma'am." Daddy said, still grinning.

"Humph. Maya, come on now."

I rolled my eyes (without Momma seeing of course), walked over and put the cricket on. I was embarrassed for her.

"Don't be mad at me, girl. Ya best be glad I'm down here fishin' with the two of you."

She smiled. When Momma smiled, you knew everything was going to be okay. No matter what she was wearing or what she was doing, she was beautiful. I think it was in the way she carried herself. I wanted to be like her...except I didn't want anyone else ever baiting my hook. I loved my Momma. Everyone said we could be sisters. I looked just like her, except I was about five inches taller and thirty pounds heavier. Her skin was smooth and soft. Her hair had a slight auburn color, and her eyes were light brown. Sometimes her eyes were weary, but, after a good meal and time with Daddy and me, they'd be dancing again. She didn't have many friends, but those she did have were loyal and devoted. She had grown up in Avery County but moved to Boone when she was fourteen. Her parents worked as custodians at Appalachian State, and they both died before I really got to know them. Daddy's parents died young, too. Maybe that's why they both worked so hard to be good parents...they appreciated the value of time which they instilled in me. And they always made sure I was loved and prepared for life. They didn't pave my road for me, but they gave me the greatest road map any kid ever got. Everyone in town loved my parents.

I guess I get my love of reading from Momma. And probably my teaching skills as well. Some people say teaching is a gift. You either got it, or you don't. I got it. Momma had it, too. It's just something that allows you to read a class and know what to pay attention to. Or look into someone's eyes and know what they need you to say or do. Whether you teach in Sunday School like Momma, or in college like me, students are the same. It's a hard job for every teacher but having the "knack" makes it much easier. Momma helped kids learn to love coming to church.

Daddy and I tried to help her learn to love to fish. I don't think she ever did, but she loved us enough to go with us now and then just to spend time with us.

Later on, I learned to appreciate Momma doing that for us. But back then, I just thought she was silly... probably the way my daughter thinks about me when I try to play tea party with her. I never had a tea party in my life. But that's what she likes, so I spend time with her. A tea party isn't as tough as learning how to fish. That's what made my Momma so awesome.

She didn't start fishing 'til she was grown, so insects were something she just swatted at or stepped on. Momma wouldn't take the fish off the line either. Daddy said she wasn't a real fisherman. But he said I was. I could bait my own hook, catch a fish, and take the fish off the hook. It wasn't until I was older that daddy showed me the proper mechanics of preparing our catch. He would put his rough, big hand on mine, and methodically coach me through each step.

Momma would only go fishing when she was caught up with all the housework and had her Sunday School lesson ready to teach. She worked in the Appalachian State cafeteria during the breakfast and lunch shifts. Every morning, she was gone before it even got light outside, and she got home in the afternoon. She never went to college, but she was as smart as Daddy because she read so much. We had all kinds of books in our house.

And boy could she cook! I mean, of course, she could fry up some fish. But she was such a good cook, even the buttered brussel sprouts were delicious. Who knew anyone could make brussel sprouts good? Momma could.

She didn't really ever teach me to cook, though. When we were boiling potatoes, she told me to "check on them." I didn't know what that meant... check on them doing what? Escaping? But I didn't want to look ignorant, so I lifted the lid and looked into the pot. Then, I noticed some water dripping onto the counter. I looked up at the ceiling to see where the leak was coming from.

"That water's coming from the lid, girl. Oh lordy."

She wouldn't let me "help" her in the kitchen much after that.

On my 10th birthday, June 2nd, 1989, Momma had me close my eyes as she brought the cake over and put it in front of me. "Open your eyes, baby girl!"

I was expecting my usual birthday confetti cake...but no! Momma baked me a cake that was in the shape of a fish. A beautiful, colorful rainbow trout. It had blue and pink icing. It had all colors in fact. It was the prettiest rainbow trout I had ever seen. (And the sweetest!) I thought that was my only gift, and it was a great gift! Then, as Daddy and I were smiling at each other with that colorful icing turning our teeth blue, Momma went to her purse and got out a tiny felt box.

"Happy birthday, sweet girl."

"Momma! You got me a present?"

Daddy said, "Whatcha mean? We get ya a gift every year. Remember that bike?"

"Yeah, I love my bike."

"You'll love this even more," Momma said.

I opened the box. It was the most beautiful necklace I'd ever seen. The silver was so shiny and as bright as a full moon. And it was a fish. A fish! I didn't know they made a necklace with a fish on it.

"You found a fish necklace? Where did you find this, Momma?"

"It's an Ichthys."

"An ick – the- us? What's that mean?"

"An ichthys was what the Christians used to identify each other back in the day. When the Romans were killing Christians, they had to come up with a secret symbol. Some historians believe it was a fish because the disciples were 'fishers of men.'"

"And fishermen!" Daddy interjected.

Momma smiled and continued, "Yes. And fishermen. So, this necklace represents your Christian heritage, but for you, it's even more. It represents you and your connection to them fish and to your family."

Daddy took the necklace from me and turned me away from him as he fastened it around my neck. "It also represents your family heritage because WE are also fishermen. Don't think for a second, baby girl, that I can't hear ya over there talkin' to them fish when we're on the river. Sounds to me like you're talkin' to ya best friends about all sorts of mess." I laughed and turned it over and it even had my name engraved on it.

"Maya," I said it aloud. "Maya." I kept rubbing my fingers over my necklace. It was my best gift ever.

4

Boone, 1989

My 10th birthday was also about the time I started to go fishing on my own. I still didn't quite get why Daddy thought it was so necessary in life, but he encouraged my independence without supervision when it came to this particular life skill. At first, I was kinda scared to go by myself. I was a good swimmer, so I knew I would be okay if I fell in. But being out there by myself was a lot different than going with Daddy. Maybe I thought I was just too young or subconsciously assumed I needed him there as a security blanket.

Once I got there and got settled, though, I got more comfortable. I enjoyed the outdoors. I knew I was always protected by the mountains. I loved the warm sun and the blue sky with a cool breeze. I never relaxed like I did with Daddy. I always heard things. Sometimes nature was so loud. Even when I was with Daddy, I heard things. There would be rustling behind us, and I'd turn quickly and be ready to fight off the Bigfoot or whatever was getting ready to attack us.

"What are you jumpin' at, baby girl?"

"Didn't you hear that?"

"I did hear it, but you don't need to worry. I got you."

I wished I could be more like my Daddy.

I don't know what happened to change my mind about fishing. Or why. But it changed. Maybe it's because I learned to appreciate the mental aspects of it. Daddy taught me how to build a Carolina Rig. It's what we always fished with if we were slow jigging live bait or just letting it bottom bounce with the current across deep water. The days when I would head down river by myself are when I truly started talking to the fish...and they started talking back.

After a heavy rain, the water table was high and nothing I tried was working. I stopped and assessed my surroundings, and that's when I started trying to think like Daddy. Am I going to slowly reel this live bait against the river's pressure, or am I going to stay artificial with a popper and dead drift it on the surface and follow it down river? What would be optimal in these conditions?

I asked the fish, "What do you need so you can see what I'm offering, and where do you want me to put it?" I listened carefully and studied the water closely. If I speed up my retrieval, the bill on this crankbait will force a lower ride in the water column. Or should I use a heavier spinnerbait that naturally rides low and only needs a gradual recovery?

I tied on a chartreuse Rooster Tail based on the clarity and pace of the water. Most of the Rooster Tails I used had a small reflective spoon at the head. The faster the recovery of my cast, the faster the strobe of that little reflective plate and vice versa. I began to let the fish tell me the speed my crank should be simply by the strike. I would purposely direct my casts so my line would shift right through the sunspots peppering the water, hoping the light would catch that metal leaf just enough to pop off a little flash and entice a smallie, 'bow, brown, or brookie into a chase.

Figuring all of this out didn't come without some trial and error. I remember thinking one day after a crushing downpour, the water looked like a Yoohoo chocolate drink. I was fishing a Rapala mini river shad crank bait. Cast after cast I would target the opposing riverbank, and it would swing down river, across the current lightning quick, with no luck whatsoever. I changed the angle of my cast. I changed the holes I was fishing in. I stopped, exhaled, and dissected what mother nature was giving me. The variables she posed had an answer I had to reverse engineer. I began to anticipate their processes, tendencies, their response to weather, what and where to pitch my lures. Cloudy or muddy water meant using something that creates vibration or sound as well as flash to attract them. Heavier or stronger currents meant I needed to work my baits closer to the slower water near the river's edges. Fish don't have to work as hard in calmer water to forage. Clear and low water forced me to stay back and make longer casts, so I didn't spook them...I asked the fish constantly what they needed, where they needed it, and most of the time, if I tweaked my delivery, they told me.

I knew that this day was gonna be a quick day. The grey awning of clouds broke with seams of blue and rays of sunshine. Momma had told me repeatedly to be home, clean, dressed and ready to leave by three, otherwise my fishing excursions would come to a screeching halt. We had a fish fry to get to. Making momma and daddy late for anything wasn't tolerated. Besides, I loved our fish fries. I told myself that I would change up and sling it a couple more times, and then head back to the house.

In my last-ditch effort to try and master my fate, I tied on a single hook, White Worden's Rooster Tail. That tiny adjustment in color and size was the turning point and pretty much when I learned how to speak to the fish and crack their secret code. Initially my conversations were one-sided, but as I fine-tuned my efforts, the fish started responding. I started piecing together aspects of their language in correspondence to the conditions, and though my fluency was choppy at times, I was still able to hook up often. I realized the slightest of alterations for the fish's benefit was the difference in being a bench warmer or getting in the game. Just going through the motions wasn't ever going to afford any playing time. I landed a beautiful creature, thanked him for the fight, and released him for the next aquatic battle.

The Isley Brothers played on Mr. Robinson's boom box and the smell of fish and grease wafting across the neighborhood was our dinner bell calling us all to enjoy the late summer community bonding of our fish fry at Mrs. Jackson's house. She was a teacher at Hardin Park and the matriarch of the Junaluska community. A fish fry wasn't just about the gathering of the masses, it was a time where the community bonded over the fortunes of sharing a good life.

Daddy and Mr. Robinson fried the fish. After letting them soak for about two hours, Mr. Robinson grabbed them out of the buttermilk and tossed them into a cornmeal tub full of spices for a complete coating. Meanwhile, Daddy would flick the flour into the grease bath. When the flour sizzled and dissipated immediately, it was all-systems go. As soon as the fillets hit the grease, the bubbling was violent and quickly settled to a nervous ripple. Once the planks began to float, they were done, and it was dinner time.

Earlier, Mrs. Jackson and her loved ones had gathered all the chairs that "belonged outdoors" and set them around her backyard in preparation for all the folks who would soon swarm the yard. Now, every chair was occupied, and several people stood in groups and talked. Loud eruptions of laughter flooded the air as the men talked about the weather, work, sports, and had spirited discussions about last week's game of spades or the size of bass that was caught without an eyewitness to support the claim.

Meanwhile, the women gossiped about the men, people at church, and the children who needed a whipping before they got too big for their britches. The feast spread out on the serving table seemed endless to me. On this night, there was a whole buffet: fish and sausage, collard greens, mac-and-cheese, black eyed peas, and cornbread. Some people only put hot sauce on their fish. Not me. I sprinkled it on my entire plate. Everything tasted better with hot sauce.

I played hula hoop and blew bubbles for the younger kids to chase, but my favorite part of the night, besides eating, was watching the different games of spades. No one could pop his fingers on the table louder than Mr. Robinson. When he cut a book with a spade, he slammed that card down with so much force, the crack of his knuckles sounded like the boom of a firecracker. He crushed people's feelings.

After dinner, when all of us had our to-go plates labeled and shoved anywhere they would fit in Mrs. Jackson's refrigerator, the line dancing began. The sounds of Earth, Wind, and Fire's "September," got all of us, from the most arthritic grandmother to the youngest toddler, out on the dance floor.

Later in the night, the grown-ups made us go inside, and we'd drift off to sleep wherever we fell and dream the impossible dreams that only children can. The world would be a better place if there were more fish fries.

One day, we were running errands for Momma, and we stopped by the butcher shop. We talked and waited for our turn at the counter. The grocery store was faster, but Momma said the pork chops straight from the butcher were better. Daddy didn't argue, so off we went.

When we finally got to the counter, Mr. Pettis, the butcher, looked at Daddy, but then looked over at Ms. Beam and asked her what she wanted. She was a teacher at Watauga High School. Everyone said she was crazy, but she was a good teacher.

I don't know how long she had been standing over at that side of the counter, but I was pretty sure we were there first. It gave me time to look at all the different cheeses behind the glass: goat cheese, feta, limburger, blue cheese... I read about a few of them but had no idea how they tasted. As I leaned in closer to examine them, even from behind the glass, I could tell there was a distinct odor. Trying not to gag, I took a couple of steps back. I couldn't pinch my nose fast enough. The scent left me squinting just to keep from crying and made me question, why in the world would anyone eat cheese that smelled like that?

"I think Mr. Jones was here first, Mr. Pettis," Ms. Beam said.

"He can wait."

"That's right, Ms. Beam," Daddy said. "Thank you for thinking of me, but ladies first."

"Thank you, kindly, Mr. Jones," and she sort of curtsied to him. She was crazy.

Mr. Pettis looked over at Daddy, annoyed, and then looked back at Ms. Beam and smiled sweetly. She ordered two ribeyes. Mr. Pettis weighed them, wrapped them up and took her money. She thanked him and looked over at us. "Y'all have a great weekend."

Daddy smiled and looked back at Mr. Pettis.

Then, finally, Mr. Pettis looked at Daddy.

"Ok, Zeke. Wha'cha need, boy?"

I looked up at Daddy. He didn't flinch. I knew he was mad, but he hid it well. Mr. Pettis probably knew he was mad, too, because he gave Daddy a sly little grin. Daddy took a deep breath and said politely, "I'd like three pork chops, please."

"Oh, sorry there, Zeke. They's all been spoken fer today. I got some chitlins though. Don't y'all like them?"

Again, Daddy didn't react. At least, his face didn't. "No, thank you. My family don't eat chitlins. How about some lamb chops? Lemme have some of those, please."

"Well, dadgum, Zeke, I swear if you ain't pickin' all the cuts that's been spoken fer already."

"Who spoke for them?" Daddy looked around and raised his hands indicating the fact that they were alone in the shop.

Mr. Pettis, never one to be accused of being quick on his feet, struggled to come up with a lie. After shuffling back and forth on his feet, he came up with something. "I can't tell ya that now, boy. Butcher-client confidentiality and all." Mr. Pettis grinned. We didn't.

"Okay then, why don't you recommend something."

The bell on the door dinged and Mr. Remmey Myers walked in. Daddy occasionally worked with Mr. Myers on his construction sites. They grew up playing sports and fishing together and were buddies.

"Hey there, Zeke, my man. Hi Maya. How are y'all doing this afternoon?" He shook hands with Daddy.

"I'm doing great, Remmey," Daddy said. "Just livin' life. Tryin' to get some pork chops for supper tonight."

"Millie is a great cook. I need to invite myself and Jen over to your house again soon. She still hasn't stopped talking about Millie's mac-n-cheese!"

Daddy laughed, so I laughed. "Yes, sir. She do make the best mac-n-cheese. Just let me know when y'all can come and ya know you're always welcome."

"Thanks, man. I'll talk to the chief and letcha know." He turned to Mr. Pettis. "Bill, how are ya?"

"Doing fine Mr. Myers. How can I help you today?" Mr. Pettis asked politely. "I bet Zeke ordered pork chops, right, Zeke? Go on and get that while we catch up. I can wait." Mr. Pettis looked at Daddy. Then looked back at Mr. Myers, and looked at Daddy again, shook his head and went to get the chops ready for us.

I don't know what kind of secret revenge plan Daddy was thinking about in his mind, but he was quiet the whole way home. He got quiet sometimes.

But most of the time, Daddy talked A LOT. Especially at home with just me and Momma. "Look here," Daddy said during one of my life lessons as we were in the shed replacing our lures and adding fresh worms and crickets. Daddy had an old metal tackle box that was his father's. It squeaked when he opened it. It was olive green and had rust in the corners. The compartments were all full of different lures and bait, extra hooks, split shot, extra line, a knife, and a scaler. I loved that tackle box because Daddy loved it. I loved the treasures it held.

"Look here," he said again and there was a long pause as he sorted his thoughts. "Our experiences give us knowledge. Knowledge is power, and no one can take that away. No experiences, no education, think you know every damn thing... well, all you get is ignorance. And ignorance...well, that just leads to bad ideas. My pops told me: Before you judge, you must experience. You gotta listen to others. And you gotta at least try to understand others... just like you try to understand fish. Once you get it... well, that knowledge you get from being quiet...well, that'll keep people from being so ignorant.

"You know how much you love fishin' in all? You can do it for the rest of your life. That goes for everything. You love it, you go do it for the rest of your life—you don't let anyone ever tell you different, ya hear? NO ONE."

We headed down the river then, waiting for the fish before Daddy spoke again. "Fishin's in your blood now, and you good at it. You'll always have it. Whenever life starts weighin' on you... and you know it will. It gets to us all from time-to-time. And when it does, that's when you come down here to the river. Get right with fish and get right with God." He took another deep breath and looked at me. I probably had a confused look on my face because then, he asked, "You understand what I'm talkin' 'bout?"

"I think so, Daddy."

He musta read my mind. "It's okay, baby girl. I know I run on and get caught up on myself. But there's so much I wanna tell you so you grow up as smart as me." He winked at me and we both chuckled. "Let's pack on up and get home."

I blinked and our time on the water was over, and we headed home. We walked past our closest neighbor's house and Mr. Robinson was in his old rocking chair on the porch, just like he was every time we went past. He seemed like he was a hundred years old, but, in reality, he was probably only in his late sixties. He laughed a lot. I guess that's why Daddy liked him. "Zeke, where ya catchin' all them fish?" Mr. Robinson asked.

Daddy shook his head and said, "No sir…Wouldn't tell the preacher, so ya know I ain't tellin' you."

I stood up straighter and said proudly, "I caught all those fish, Mr. Robinson."

Daddy flicked my hair. "Maya, don't be lyin' like that to our neighbors."

"Oh yeah. Daddy caught a small sucker fish," I added.

"Well next time I see y'all walking pass here wit ya gear, I'm gonna spy on ya."

Daddy said, "You know you never been up that early before."

"Well, I got an alarm clock."

"Maya got the gift, Robbie." Daddy threw his arm around my shoulders and squeezed me next to him. "This girl…I tell you, no one can get'em talkin' like she can."

Mr. Robinson smiled and said, "You keep right on talking to them fish, Maya. It's a good thing fishin.' Everybody be better off if we all got a line wet. You keep on fishin', girl."

"Yes, sir."

"Don't you be following us, Robbie."

Mr. Robinson slapped his leg and threw his head back and kept on rocking. Everyone liked my daddy.

5

Boone, 1990

Daddy would come with me whenever he could. He taught me everything he knew about the river. His knowledge made sense when you could actually see what he was talking about.

"Look here..." he said and pointed out to where there was a break in the current. "See that? That means there's something like a rock or log just below the surface, so beware."

Then he pointed to another spot and said, "See that choppy water?" I nodded. "That choppiness usually leads into deeper pools. See where the water changes from emerald green to forest green?"

I nodded again and he continued. "That's where fish can be holdin', so pay attention."

I soaked it all in. Hours and hours, we'd talk and laugh. And fish.

Langston Hughes wrote, "My soul has grown deep like the rivers." That's what happened to Daddy. The more he was on the river, the deeper he got. Sometimes I didn't have any idea what he was talking about. But I tried very hard to listen. I knew Daddy was smart.

"Fishin' is life, Maya. It's not just the thrill of the chase. Or the challenge. It's all of it. It's the Peace. Jesus. Joy. Friendship. Everythin' ya ever need is right on this river. Everything."

I was skeptical as I cocked my head to the side like a dog does when he hears a sound he doesn't recognize. He just grinned.

I never paid much attention to race. Neither did Daddy. But one day, in school, I overheard someone call me the "N" word, and I wasn't sure I heard him right. And if I did, what should I do about it? So I went to ask the smartest man I knew. I asked Daddy.

"Daddy, has anyone ever called you the N- word?"

"If they did, they only did once," he laughed.

"What did you do to them, Daddy?"

"Nothing, baby. I was just kiddin'. Ya caint just go around beatin' on people who say mean things. That's just ignorance. I always kinda felt sorry for folks like that. Think of all the good stuff people miss when they don't bother gettin' to know someone for who they really are? It's their loss, and I don't worry about it."

"But doesn't it hurt your feelings?"

"Emerson once wrote, 'Win the respect of intelligent people.' Ya know what that means? That means you think about who's sayin' it. Ask yourself: Are they intelligent people? If they ain't, then forget it. If they knuckleheads, then they ain't worth sweatin'."

My Daddy was just like that. He quoted Emerson, Twain, Shakespeare. As I write this, I'm thinking that I've been a college professor for seven years now, and I don't think I've ever quoted authors as often as my Daddy did.

I'll never forget one afternoon in early June. It was a great day. The school year was ending, and my 6th grade class was having "Field Day" which consisted of simply being outside playing for the whole day. The day was packed with various track and field events, dodgeball, a grade level kickball tournament, tug of war, and then a picnic lunch. I knew when it was lunch time, the day was almost over. Best day of the year...and not just for us kids. You could always tell the school year was wrapping up because of the "Thank God! It's almost over-exhausted smile" on each teacher's face.

I remember doing the mile run. I knew I could run because I couldn't be caught even while playing tag during recess. I was a little taller than most in my class, had a decent stride, and I never got tired. Mrs. Dishman put me in a heat with the boys. I guess she wanted to see what I could do. I smoked 'em all. It wasn't even close.

I finished my lunch with a few girls from class and slipped away by myself. I quietly began my inspection of the various terrestrials inhabiting the tall grass outlining our playground.

I became so engrossed with my search, I had blocked out all of the screams, water balloons, and beach balls that cannoned and twirled in the air. Unintentionally, I found myself right behind Mrs. Dishman and Mrs. Green who never knew I was there as they chatted while they supervised the pandemonium. I remember Mrs. Dishman looking to the sky as she ran both hands through her hair saying softly, "All we need's a tent, and we'd have a circus. Only four more days...we can do this...Right? We can do it."

"I need a beer," Mrs. Green replied.

I snickered and both women turned, eyes wide open, surprised that I was there. Mrs. Green sternly put her index finger over her mouth warning me not to repeat what I just heard. I mimicked back the zipping of my own lips, assuring them that what I heard would stay in the vault.

Not three seconds later, I got called to the office and was asked to bring all my belongings. Reluctant and confused, I made my way to the main office, and Daddy was standing there. My mind was racing with all the "why's" he would be picking me up at school. I started check-listing everything that it could be. He never had to come to school for anything. I was thinking whatever it was, it couldn't be good. Death in the family, no way! Early vacation, no chance! Lunch, I just ate! Car issues, maybe? He was always having to fix his truck for some reason.

As we walked out of the school building, Daddy asked me about my field day. I let him know how I ran the mile with the boys, handled them all, and wasn't even tired. He laughed while shaking his head. "You mean to tell me you can fish and run? Well girl, ain't gonna lie, you got that from me, too. Back in my day, I could run. Yes-sirree, I could run all day long."

When we got closer to the truck, I caught a glimpse of our rod tips peeking out of the back corner of the truck bed. Cupping my hands over my eyebrows to block out the sun, I looked up. Daddy was grinning ear to ear. "Are we goin' fishin', Daddy?"

"Yes, ma'am! We are. Imma put you on some new water and see how you do. I got you somethin'…it's sittin' in the front seat."

I threw all my school junk in the bed of the truck and threw the passenger door open so hard it ricocheted, slamming me into the truck. He had bought me my own set of hip waders. I couldn't wait to try 'em on and give 'em a test run.

"Where are we goin' today, Daddy?"

"Up 105 towards Foscoe, there is a stretch of water, the Watauga, everybody been talkin' 'bout at work, downstream from Old Shulls Mill Road. You know, the Hound Ears Club. I helped Mr. Myers dry-in a couple of A-frame homes he built up in there. I been starin' at that water for years and ain't done nothin' about it. Mr. Myers himself told me to get some waders and go down there and give it a try. He even said to take you cause he knows you fish, too. I got us both a pair and we gonna hop in and give it a try if all those stupid college kids ain't jumpin' off the dam, drinkin' beer, and makin' a bunch of racket."

We pulled into a gravel lot, off 105, at the top of Old Shulls Mill and there were ten cars lined up. Daddy sat there mumbling under his breath.

"What'd'ya say?" I asked.

"Nothing sweetheart," but I had heard him. "Crazy-ass white folks." I giggled.

We put on our waders and grabbed our rods and tackle box. A few crushed beer cans peppered the lot, and everyone was dressed in bathing suits. They all seemed to know one another, a fact apparent from how closely they stood together and how animated they were when they talked. Their heads were thrown back so far when they laughed, you'd think they'd break their necks. But no one said a word to us, which was fine by me.

There was a small trail leading to the river's edge just down from the parking lot, and halfway down the trail, I heard a high-pitched squeal followed by a massive splash. I looked back at the college kids, "Daddy! Look Daddy! Those kids are jumping off that dam!"

"I know Maya. Just ignore all that for now…we got fish to catch."

I peered downstream. Gigantic rocks jutted out from both sides of the river creating gorgeous pockets of soft, pooling water. It was incredible. There must have been hundreds of fish there. We carefully walked downstream far enough away from the party at the dam. Daddy stood over me and said, "These pockets are tight, so you can't cast like you in the front of the house. Cast it over there in that deep pool and be careful of your distance." He had already tied me on a chartreuse Rooster Tail, so I let it rip. My first cast was straight into the bank, my second, third, fourth...twentieth cast went everywhere but the river. I had no direction or depth perception to my casts.

The river was shaped like an hourglass: cramped, then forgiving. No matter what section I was in, I stayed hung up the whole day and lost four lures. If I wasn't in the rough on the bank, I was snagged on a submerged tree limb or wedged deep in the rocks. After a few more failed attempts, that was it. I was done for the day. I tight roped, leapt, and lunged to a perch twenty yards upriver from Daddy. There, I watched his silhouette against the rolling tree line and dimming blue sky. He was a maestro as he manipulated the river, gently lofting each cast with precision. His lure rode the current effortlessly. Like a conductor with his baton and fish as his orchestra, they followed his lead. He directed one symphony after the other with each cast. With graceful motions, he guided each crescendo and decrescendo of the rivers' drifts, creating perfect harmony between conductor and orchestra; between man and nature. It was hypnotic. I was lost in his rhythmic command. He caught nine that day in less than four hours.

As he walked back up to me, I asked, "Why do you keep throwing those fish back, Daddy?"

He looked at me and said, "Baby girl, it's Delayed Harvest right now. Law says we can't keep any until next weekend... about the time you are gettin' out of school, right? I wanted us to give these waders a try, test out some different water and give you a break from school."

"What's Delayed Harvest?"

"It means we can't keep any fish until the top of June, and we can't use any live bait. When the summertime hits, we can keep up to seven a day, per person. Then, at the top of October it starts all over again."

I didn't understand, so I dropped it and changed the subject. "Daddy, when did you learn to fish?"

"When I was a kid, my pops taught me. That's why I'm teachin' you. It's the secret of life."

I gave him my skeptical look. "Fishing is the secret of life? *Fishing*?"

He always laughed when I made that face. "Sure is. You'll figure it out if you don't quit."

"Well," I shrugged, "it's fun…if you're catchin' fish."

"It's more than fun, Maya. It's so much more. That's why it's called fishin' and not catchin'. This ain't Burger King… you can't always have it your way. You can let this be a lesson, or you can continue to pout and quit. What's it gonna be?"

I flashed back and replayed that defining day a year earlier, when I consciously altered my approach in an effort to instigate some dialogue with my fish friends. It was my respect and strategy within the chess match that got their attention and a response with a Worden's Rooster Tail. Sadly, on this day, my complacency had gotten the better of me. My surroundings and my coaches effectively communicated: it was time I have a seat on the bench and regroup.

That was a wake-up call. Learning the fish's language didn't mean a thing if my line wasn't in the water and lures presented properly. Different aspects of fishing required me to adapt, not only to the environment, but the ever-changing elements within that environment. No one river, creek, or stream was ever going be the same, and I needed an attitude and effort check. I had only been exposed to easy conditions up to this point, so if I wanted to engage, I needed to up my game. I had a new pair of hip waders, so quitting wasn't going to be an option. I was not going to quit. Ever.

6

Boone, 1991

I attended Hardin Park Elementary. It was a K-8 school that fed directly into one county high school, Watauga High. I had a few friends that I got along with pretty well. They got me, and me them. If I had at least one of them in my class, I was happy. They didn't judge, and never talked out of both sides of their mouths. My friends and I always hated it when someone would say something one way and then turn around and say the opposite. It would be one way or the other. Never both. I remember one day coming back from the cafeteria after lunch, we were in a single file line and had stopped to gather the stragglers who couldn't clean up after themselves. In the blink of an eye, Melissa, who was standing in front of me, had Robert Smith's shirt twisted up in her fist and wedged under his chin. Robert looked just like Bert from Sesame Street with a cone shaped head and an amazing uni-brow, so we all called him Bert. Melissa had him jacked up on top of the water fountain yelling at him, "After school I'm gonna whoop your ass for saying that! And you know what, Bert? I will choke you down, til' your head pops clean off!"

Bert had said something awful about her mom and then mumbled some lie to try and cover it up. She had lost her two years earlier to a weird virus. She was raised by her dad, who was a retired Marine. He had taught her a thing or two about standing up for herself. She had Bert pressed so hard up against the fountain his right leg was straddling the scoop on the water dispenser but was also resting on the push button causing a perfect rainbow of water to land on his crotch. When she let him go, he fell to the floor like a wet noodle. Bert had to walk around the rest of the day being called "pee-pee boy." He had it coming.

Most of my classmates were nice, but Warren Boeling and Cash Martin didn't get the memo. I don't know exactly why they didn't like me, but they just didn't. When I threw the softball farther than Cash did, they called me an Amazon. When I knew the answer to a question that no one else in class knew, they called me Einstein. Mostly though, I'm pretty sure they just didn't like me because I was black, and they weren't. They were jealous.

Daddy told me to ignore people like them. He said they were ignorant, and it was their loss if they didn't want to be my friend. He reminded me of Emerson's quote. But sometimes, they still hurt my feelings.

One of those days was in math class. I raised my hand like ten times, and Mr. Haynes would never call on me. I tried to pretend he already knew that I knew the answers, so he wanted to check on what the other kids knew.

After a few minutes of being overlooked, however, I started to lose my faith in that theory.

He called Warren to the board to solve a problem. He was a big, strong guy with wiry, sandy blonde hair. He had rosy-red pimples on his cheeks. When he opened his mouth, his teeth looked like Calico Indian corn, and he always looked like he slept in his clothes. He fumbled around, wrote some numbers, but gave up and sat down. I raised my hand again.

Finally, Mr. Haynes called on me, so I went to the board and tried to pretend like it was hard for me to work the problem, too. I acted like I was thinking, but the truth was, I knew the answer before I even stood up. I just figured the rest of the class could wait a while.

Once I solved the problem, Mr. Haynes said I was right and acted all surprised even though I almost always got it right. As I walked back to my desk, I had to walk past Warren's best friend, Cash. Cash was a skinny kid who could not sit still and sported an untamable cow lick at the top of his forehead. He relentlessly gnawed his fingernails, and his eyes blinked like bat wings in flight. He always looked like he was up to something, which reminded me of the would-be purse snatcher in the short story, "Thank you, Ma'am," except he was white. I don't think Cash was a bad kid per se, he was just easily led astray, and craved attention from whomever would give it to him. He stuck his leg out and tried to trip me. I just stopped and looked at him. He and Warren and a couple of their friends begin to giggle. I know if I just step over him, he'll raise his leg up and trip me anyway. So, I did what I always do, crossed my arms and waited.

Mr. Haynes says, "Maya, please return to your seat. A penchant for arithmetic does not excuse disruptive behavior." He couldn't see Cash's leg.

I was still standing there waiting. I kept waiting for Mr. Haynes to say something to Cash, but instead, he fussed at me again.

"Maya. I'm not going to tell you again. Please. Sit. Down."

I pretended to trip over Cash's leg, but I kicked him with everything I had. Cash yelped like a chihuahua, but he moved his leg. I pretended to regain my balance and got to my seat.

"Maya! I saw that. You need to apologize to Cash. Or you can go ahead and pack your desk up and make your way to the office. I mean it, young lady."

Trying not to cry, Cash just wobbled like a little Bobblehead doll.

"Maya!" Mr. Haynes yelled.

With a straight face I said, "I'm sorry you were trying to trip me, and I accidentally kicked you." My friends, who were good girls and never got in trouble, tried hard not to laugh.

One of my favorite classes was Mrs. Holt's. She was a great teacher and understood how disruptive I could be when I was bored. And I was bored A LOT, but not in her class.

Mrs. Holt loved NC history and made us love it also. She allowed us to write a story theorizing what we suspected happened to The Lost Colony. We spent forever learning about those early settlers. We learned why North Carolina license plates had the motto "First in Freedom" on them.

When I walked in one day and saw that 800-pound TV strapped to that cart and that top-loading VCR that took up almost as much room as the TV, I jumped for joy. I loved videos and remembered everything in them.

One of the videos I really loved was about the Cherokee Indians. Mrs. Holt always stopped the video and let us ask questions and discuss some of the things we saw. One thing that captured my attention was when they showed us how to build a travois which the Cherokee used for their dogs and horses to help them transport supplies. It was a great class.

I also enjoyed my science class...especially when the teacher allowed us to do projects. One time, we were doing a project on animals, and, of course, I picked the brown trout. I liked science. Not just because of the bugs, animals, and learning about things I thought were cool, but also because Mrs. Elliott was an excellent teacher because she made learning interesting. She did a lot of "hands-on" projects. She knew how to ignite the fire within me and make me want to learn more. This project was like that. I would have done it even if she wasn't going to grade it.

She called on me to go to the front and present my project to the class. I talked for WAY longer than any of the other kids did. I told my classmates all about the trout's habitat including how their eyes worked (Monocular vision where their eyes work independently instead of binocular like the way humans see) and the other stuff science teachers like for you to talk about, but I took it further. I added the best places to cast after surveying the river flow, the best lures to use to catch them, and what trout tasted like. My visual aid wasn't just a picture I drew. It was a sculpture I made. I was proud of my brown trout masterpiece.

The class applauded when I was finished. Mrs. Elliott told me I had done a great job. "Does anyone have any questions for Maya?" I had already started walking back to my seat when Warren raised his hand.

"I have a question for Maya. How do ya know what lures to use when ya know you ain't never caught no brown trout?"

Some people in class laughed, and I stopped at his desk, leaned in, and whispered just loud enough to be heard by Warren, but not Ms. Elliott. Warren had his knees up on his desk, balancing on the back two legs of his chair.

"Hey Limburger, I can out fish your hillbilly ass any day of the week."

Warren dropped the front two legs of his chair and shot up right into my face. "Watch yer mouth, Cricket. You don't know shit about fishin'."

"Ok Limburger, you know what?"

"What?"

"I just realized we shouldn't be having this conversation right now."

"Why?"

"You do the math… since you failed the 1st and 3rd grade, you're two years older than anyone in here." I sat down and began packing up.

"Why do you keep calling me Limburger?"

"Well,…it's a type of cheese and like you, it's white, crumbly, and smells like ass." The few students sitting around us couldn't contain themselves and erupted with belly laughter. Warren was visibly shaken but could do nothing… at least, not right then.

7

Boone, August, 1991

One day in August, I went to Daddy's favorite fishin' hole. I caught a couple of decent size smallies and started on home.

I could almost taste the fried fish and buttered cabbage as I turned the corner into my neighborhood. I got ready to wave to Mr. Robinson, but he wasn't there. I hoped he was okay.

Our pastor, Reverend Smithfield's shiny black Cadillac was in our driveway. And a police car. I was scared to walk in, but I knew I didn't have a choice. I walked inside slowly, and it started getting hard to breathe. Like I was underwater.

Reverend James Smithfield sat beside on the couch beside Momma with his hand on her shoulder. His wife, Sister Michelle, was in the kitchen doing something...Sheriff Martin was in Daddy's chair. Mr. and Mrs. Myers were standing solemnly in the corner.

I dropped my fish and tackle box right on the den floor. Momma was crying and rocking back and forth with her arms folded over her stomach as if she would be sick. "Momma. What's wrong?" I fell at her feet and put my hands on her knees.

"Oh, baby." She stopped rocking and put her hands in her face.

"Maya. Sit down here," Smithfield said and patted the couch next to him. I didn't move.

"Reverend Smithfield," I asked with imploring eyes, "what's goin' on?"

He looked over at Momma and saw there was no way she was going to be able to talk. I looked at Momma. I had seen her cry a few times like when I rode my bike without training wheels or when Daddy gave her a diamond necklace for their anniversary. But I'd never seen her cry like this. My stomach was in my chest. I felt like I was going to suffocate.

"Maya," Reverend Smithfield said. He had tears in his eyes, too. Oh, no. He took a deep breath and exhaled slowly. I didn't say anything. I didn't know what to say. My eyes were already full of tears.

Mrs. Myers walked to me and sat down on the floor beside me at Momma's feet. "Maya. There's been an accident," she said.

"What you mean? What kind of accident?" I wondered.

"Your father. I'm so sorry, Maya. Your father was killed in a car accident...."

Noise faded to silence. I could see her mouth moving, but the words fell from her lips and onto the floor silently. Her voice faded into what sounded like river cascades in my head. I couldn't catch my breath. I don't think I was crying. I just felt like one of the boys at school had kicked me in my stomach. I was going to be sick. I was already kneeling at Momma's feet, but I kind of tipped over and then I was lying on the floor. Rapids rushed over me. Cold rapids. I was locked in a state of incomprehension. It wasn't registering in my brain as real. It was a dream. It had to be. And Daddy always chased away the monsters in my dreams. But if he was truly gone, who would rescue me now?

Mrs. Myers moved closer to me, lifted my head and shoulders, and rested me against her. But she couldn't lift me up from the surge of the undertow. I was drowning. So, we just sat there. Momma was crying and someone was talking, but the only sound I heard was the repeated pounding from the crashing waves.

Boone Missionary Baptist Church was a small church surrounded by its members in Junaluska. It had little to no parking because almost everyone who attended lived right there. Church Street was one road in and out. People made parking spaces between the "SLOW

FUNERAL" signs and wherever they could fit their cars as people came from everywhere to pay their respects.

It was standing room only and the gospel choir shook the walls with their version of "It Is Well." Many who came gave accounts of my father's smile, his work ethic, his kindness, generosity, willingness to help anyone, anytime, with anything he could. They described his passion for fishing and the genuine love he had for everyone he met. He always greeted people with a handshake and smile. Sniffles and tears flooded the room. I still felt like I couldn't breathe. I tried to distract myself with other thoughts. I was about to implode. I stared at a spider web swaying back and forth in an air duct over the organist's head. Rev. Smithfield delivered the sermon as cries of "Amen," and "All right now," bounced from one person to the next elevating the intensity of his message.

As the service was ending, there was a big commotion outside the front steps of the church. The incessant honking and thunderous rumble of a truck with no muffler drowned out the words from the pulpit and momentarily stopped the service.

Mr. Myers, his wife, and daughters were part of the standing room only crowd. He quickly turned, glanced out the window of the double doors and bolted out of the church. About four folks followed him as he jetted down the steps chasing after them.

Even though he was on foot, he almost caught them as their loud, muddy truck raced away. After he gave up the chase, he calmly walked back into the church. His teeth were clinched, and his face was red as he motioned from Rev. Smithfield to continue.

"Jesus said in Matthew 4:19, 'The kingdom of heaven is like a dragnet catching fish of every kind.' That's how our dear brother, Zeke, was. Not only was Zeke an avid fisherman, just like his daughter, Maya..." He looked at me and smiled sympathetically. I didn't look at him. I could only vaguely hear him anyway. All I could think about was that the symphony my Daddy conducted a few days ago turned out to be his final opus.

Rev. Smithfield continued, "But Zeke, like our Lord, was a fisher of men. Everyone of all races was drawn to him. And he treated everyone the same. Whether he was talking to a stranger on the street, a co-worker, or a supervisor at the mill, he was always the same. We should all strive to be like brother Zeke."

As he wrapped up the service, I tried to be somewhere else in my mind. On the river. No. That made me think about Daddy. Not the river. The spider web over the organist's head. I'd be that spider for a few more minutes.

A soft sob escaped Momma's mouth. That day, I heard a lot of sobbing. Not from me though. No one can hear you cry when you're underwater.

After the funeral, Mr. Myers stood alone at his truck, head down, hands in his pockets, teeth still clinched, and face still red. Momma and I held hands as we walked up to him.

He grabbed Momma and hugged her tightly, then released her but kept his hands on both of her shoulders. "Millie, I don't have words. I'm so sorry."

"Thank you, Remmey. And thank you for what you did today."

"Millie, Maya," he left one hand on Momma's shoulder and put one hand on mine. "Zeke was a brother of mine and I'm going to miss him. He was a great friend. I'm sorry those idiots disrupted Zeke's service like that. I'm gonna find out who---"

"Remmey let me stop you right there."

"No Millie, with all due respect, this is Boone...That kind of foolishness doesn't happen here. It shouldn't EVER happen."

"Remmey, I appreciate you and I understand we all handle things in our way. You go do what you gotta do but please don't do anything on account of us. I'm gonna handle it by praying for those young men and then we'll move on. And Remmey--" This time it was Momma's turn to put her hand on his shoulder.

"It isn't about Boone, Remmey. It's about cancer and chemo."

"Cancer and chemo?"

"See, cancer is just like that deep-seeded hate. It'll spread and take over if you let it. Chemo is the mindset each of us carry as we choose how to get rid of that cancer. Yeah, it's a personal struggle that you gotta endure...physically, emotionally, and mentally. But when you got a bunch of folks workin' with ya, doin' the right things to make it go away, the percentages to rid yourself of the cancer go way up. There is strength in numbers, Remmey. As one or two change their hearts, others will join in and pretty soon, the whole world is cancer free."

Remmey thought for a minute about what Momma said. Then he said, "That reminds me of something Zeke told me back in high school. He said you don't make people stop being racist by beating them with sticks..." Momma joined in as they said the last part together, "you gotta change their hearts...."

As I remembered Daddy telling me that too, I smiled through my sorrow. It wasn't just me and Momma who would miss my father. Everyone he ever knew would miss him. But that didn't stop the air from leaving my lungs as I slipped further and further under the current.

8

Boone, 1991

"Come on, Maya," Momma said while she packed our lunches. "We're going fishing."

"What?"

"You heard me, girl. Come on, now."

"But why, Momma? I don't wanna go."

She came over and sat beside me. She took my hands and looked deep into my eyes. "Maya. Honey, I know you're still missing your Daddy. I understand. Believe me." She spoke slowly the way that counselors talk when they think you're dangerous and don't want to make any sudden moves. "But your father wouldn't want you to quit fishing. He knows how much you love it. And didn't he tell you that when life gets hard, fishing always helps? Well, life is pretty tough right now, I'd say, so it's a good time to get to the river."

I kept looking down. I couldn't look at her. In my heart, I knew she was right, but I also knew it would hurt way too much to go back to our special spot. I felt myself fighting the current. Losing. "What if I can't do it, Momma. What if it makes me sad?"

Momma pulled me closer. "Oh, baby. It's definitely gonna make you sad. This time. And maybe the next couple more times, too. But one day, you'll be standing there, and the river will soothe you. The fish will speak to you as they always have. The sun will dry up your tears. And you'll have fun again."

"I just want to forget him, Momma. I know it's wrong, but it just hurts so much. I can't even think about him. Fishing will bring him back. But not really. He won't really be back. Not ever." I slipped under.

"Let's go fish. You feel however you feel. If you feel like crying, cry. If you feel like yellin', then yell. If you feel like laughin', laugh. The Good Lord already knows what's on in your heart, so there ain't no sense tryin' to hide it. However you handle it is fine. But let's just go."

"No, Momma. No. I'm sorry. I can't go. I can't."

I kicked Daddy's old metal tackle box and the top broke off from one of the hinges, but I didn't care. I ran to my room, as I slowly sunk, hoping all the while that when I made it to the bottom, I'd stay there.

A few weeks later, Mr. and Mrs. Myers came by the house to bring us some Kentucky Fried Chicken for lunch. Mrs. Myers used to work in the App State cafeteria with Momma. She acted like she and Momma were the same. And it wasn't an act either. Even if they were nice and never said anything mean, with some white people, you could just tell that they didn't want anything to do with you. They just didn't know many Black folks and weren't quite sure what to make of us. But some white people were like Mr. and Mrs. Myers. I don't know what made them different, but I liked them.

After lunch, Mr. Myers said, "Come on, Maya. Let's get outta here before they start cleaning up." He winked at me, and it reminded me of Daddy. I got sad for a minute, but he grabbed my hand and led me outside. We stopped in front of Daddy's shed, and Mr. Myers opened the door and walked right in. He walked right in my father's shed! I felt some kind of way about that. I liked Mr. Myers, but I didn't like that. No one ever went in there but me and Daddy. It was *ours*.

"Show me your favorite lure, Maya." I guess I could show him. I never saw him with very many fish. Maybe he needed some help. I wasn't ever going to use it again, anyway, right? So, I pulled out my favorite. It looked exactly like a minnow. Shiny, skinny, jelly-like, and it wiggled as you pulled it slowly across through the water.

"And what kind of fish do you catch with this one?"

"Whatever I want," I said without enthusiasm.

"Well, it seems to me like that wouldn't work at all. I think you need this one." He pulled out a pumpkin seed worm. It was a burnt orange with dark flecks that sparkled. I never used that one.

"That's not one I use very much, Mr. Myers."

"I'll betcha $10 I can catch more fish than you!" I stared at him. He knew that I knew what he was up to. Still. I appreciated his effort. I didn't want to go. But Momma wanted me to. And I knew Daddy did, too. Plus, I could use ten dollars. So, we went down to the river behind the house.

I can't say I felt very much. I tried to concentrate on beating Mr. Myers and not to think about anything else.

After just a few minutes, I started to feel a little better. Mr. Myers was just close enough to me and could hear me talking.

"Maya, are you talking to me? Who are you talking to?"

I simply stopped and pointed to the river in three different spots. He pointed at himself. I shook my head,

He said, "The water?"

Again, I shook my head.

"The fish?"

I grinned.

He raised his eyebrows and cupped his bottom lip. "Do they ever talk back?"

I couldn't help but smirk. "Kinda. I mean, you know, I'll think about Yeats's poem, 'The Fisherman,' and some Bible verses about peace and stuff, but mostly, I think about what Daddy..."

I stopped abruptly and began to fight back the tears.

Mr. Myers brought me back to the task at hand: kicking his butt on the water and winning ten dollars. "Well then, you do your thing...but you're still not gonna beat me, no matter what you say to those fish."

I smirked. We fished long enough for me to land three smallies. He watched me thank each fish for their fight and for giving me the opportunity to catch 'em before I sent 'em back home. Mr. Myers stood in awe of my skills, and I heard him deliver a 'dadgum, Maya,' when I pulled in my second smallie. The third one was just an exclamation point. We headed back to the house and made small talk for a few minutes. Mr. Myers said I cheated. He said I could just talk to the fish and make them take the bait. I couldn't help but grin, even though I felt like I owed it to Daddy not to have had fun.

We put everything back in the shed and went back inside the house. Jen stood up and headed toward the door. Remmey and Jen gave us both hugs. Momma looked really happy and thanked them for lunch as she walked them to the door. Mr. Myers said he wanted a rematch soon...double or nothing he said. I smiled, "Okay," because I knew I'd have twenty dollars.

I didn't say anything to Momma, and she didn't ask. I locked the front door and continued to stand there. It was then I started to sob. Momma came up behind me and wrapped her arms around me and let me cry. I missed Daddy. But I had gone fishing again.

9

Bozeman, MT, 1992

Ed took off his reading glasses, scribbled an 85 on the paper he was grading, threw it on a stack on the end of the desk, stood up and stretched. He walked over to the tall bookcase and picked up an old picture of two boys with their shirts off and fishing poles in their hands. It was 1956 and they were in Boone, NC, fishing on the New River. Ed was ten, and Remmey was eight. It was a beautiful day in the high country. The breeze was as cold as the mountain water, but the sun was hot. People don't call the mountains of North Carolina, "God's Country," for nothing.

Ed said, "You know where I'm going when I'm eighteen?"

"Where?" Remmey answered.

"Montana."

Remmey laughed. "Montana? Why?"

"Shut up, Rem. You don't even know where Montana is."

"Don't havta know. I know you ain't goin' nowhere that far. You're a mountain boy."

"They got mountains out there. And if the fishing is good, I ain't never comin' back. Never."

"Well, I ain't goin'. And mom and dad ain't goin'. So, I suspect you'll be real lonely."

They both made another cast.

"I won't be too lonely. I'll make friends."

"But you'll never have another brother!"

"Thank GOD for that!" He reached down and scooped up as much water as he could and threw a wave on Remmey. Remmey said, "Man!" and splashed him back.

As they walked home drenched, Remmey asked, "Why Montana, anyway?"

"Mr. Jackson, you know, my English teacher, said when he got back from the war in 1951, he was all shot up and he ended up in Montana. He found a job writing articles for a newspaper and said the fishing out there was unbelievable. The fish were fat, and they fought real hard. He said his boss at the newspaper showed him how to catch fish on the surface of the water with little hooks that looked like insects."

"That's kinda what we do, ain't it?" said Ed.

"Nah. He said what he does is fly fishing. It's different from the fishing we do. It's more fun and more of a fight. You're constantly thinking and moving. He said these trout eat bugs on the surface like we got here. Then he showed me the fishing rod he used.

The fishin' reel sits low at the bottom of the rod, and the fishing line is real light so you can whip the bug back and forth. Suddenly, these huge trout look at it and come to the surface and swallow it. Then he showed me pictures of these trout and they are huge."

"It would be sweet if we could get a job fishin' all day." Remmey said.

The phone rings and jolts Ed out of his memory. Ed sits back down and answers.

"Myers." Pause. "Yeah, come on. I'm here."

He clicks his computer back on. The thing is massive, taking up most of his desk. He hits the return button about nine times and cusses at the computer, "Return! Dammit! Return! Return! Return!"

James Withers sticks his head in the door. "You ok?"

"Withers, get in here. This stupid ass computer…"

"What's going on?"

"I'm trying to send a message on this stupid Campus Bulletin Board thing that admin said we had to start using."

"Yeah Ed. It's called electronic mail…or e-mail."

"I call it a pain in my ass. It's stupid." He hits enter a few more times and gives up. He laces his fingers behind his head and leans back. "So boss, what can I do for you?"

"Remember the grant you got for proposed degree programs?" Ed nods and Withers continues. "You're up! And guess where you're going?"

Ed looks bored. "Tell me."

"Remember that fly fishing advocacy curriculum grant you got a while back?"

"Yeah." Still bored.

"The one where you would panel as third party for course accreditation with Ecology degrees?"

"Yeah, so?" Ed asked.

"Well, the HEA (Higher Education Act) has your number and you, my friend, will be on a peer review committee checking standards down South."

"Great" Ed said without enthusiasm. "Where am I going?"

Withers lowers his readers and looks down at a folded sheet of paper in his hands. He runs his index finger down the page. "Looks like…Ah, here it is, Appalayshun State University."

"What? You've got to be kidding."

"Nope says right here, Appalayshun State Uni---"

Ed cuts him off. "Yeah, I heard you, and it's Appa-latch-an, like a latch on a door!" Withers continues, "whatever…it's in Boone, North Carolina."

Ed shook his head and put his head in his hands. "This cannot be happening."

"Aren't you from North Carolina, Ed? I heard there are good fisheries down that way. My wife's cousin's brother lives in East Tennessee and swears by the…"

"Withers, I know the water. I grew up there."

"Well then, it will be a homecoming for you."

Ed mumbles under his breath, "You cannot be serious."

Withers replies, "I'm as serious as a heart attack. Look says right here…" Withers points to the paper in his hand, trying to show Ed what it says. "This is how you cover that grant money, and you leave in about two and half weeks."

Ed gets up and puts the papers into his file cabinet. "Two and a half weeks? I can't do that. Who's gonna watch my shop?"

Withers thought for a second and then said, "Will's like eighteen or nineteen, right? He can do it."

"He's gone," Ed said flatly.

"Gone? Where'd he go?"

"He left after he graduated."

"Huh! I didn't know that. Oh, that's right," Withers waves his index finger in the air while he pretends to search for the words. "Ah yes…you don't tell anybody anything," he says.

"Whatever. I can't be gone that long."

"Betty is good, right? She'll be fine holding down the fort while you're gone. Plus, I'm not asking you if you'd like to go. I'm telling you that you are going," Withers says.

"Look, Withers," Ed softens his volume to try to help his boss understand his situation. "I appreciate the opportunity, but Will was my best guide and he's gone. I can't be gone, too. You know what I get paid to teach here."

Withers grunts and Ed continues, "Don't get me wrong, boss. I love teaching and I love MSU. But I make much more from the shop."

Withers puts the picture back and looks at Ed. "I know, Ed. It's hard to balance the demands of life, but you'll figure it out. You always do."

"It's not just that, James. I grew up in Boone. Those mountains are my old stomping grounds. When I left, I left for good. I only went back at Christmas a couple of times, and I quit doing that after my folks died. It's been years since I've been back."

"Well, looks like you're going back now. Have fun and do us all proud here at MSU."

Withers smiles, smacks Ed's shoulder, and walks out waving the paper he's holding. Ed crosses his arms, takes a breath, and exhales.

Ed wanders into the kitchen and scans his frozen dinners. He shakes his head, grabs the one on top, and sticks it in the microwave. He staggers to his refuge in the den where his old recliner is waiting to embrace him again. He grabs the phone and dials.

"Remmey, how the hell are ya, buddy? It's Ed."

"Yeah, I know my brother's voice. What's wrong?"

"Don't sound excited or anything…"

"Come on, Ed. It's been forever. You didn't just call to chat."

Remmey had called him a thousand times to check on him, to give him someone to talk to, and just to be sure he knew he wasn't alone. Sometimes Ed picked up, but usually, he just let it ring. Over the last few years, he called less and less, and Ed couldn't blame him. Their relationship was deeper than talking, but still. Soon it had been years since they'd last talked. Christmases, birthdays, and even a few family members had passed until all that was left was time. Time lost and spent. But mostly lost.

Remmey listens to the silence and finally says, "So what's up, Ed? You in jail?"

Ed laughs. "Not this time, Rem. I'm coming back to Boone."

"Really? Don't bullshit me man. When? Wait, why?"

"I'm gonna be on a special grant that requires me to sit on an advisory board for universities wanting to accredit undergrad programs. I wrote a grant for schools that had the resources to add fly fishing programs."

"And App State is gonna add yours?"

"Looks like it," Ed sighs.

"Good for them. When you comin'?" Remmey asks.

"End of May through June, maybe into a bit of July."

"Isn't that your busiest season?"

"Yeah, that's what I'm concerned about...having the shop covered. Betty is my store clerk, but I guess now she's gettin' ready to be my manager until I get back. I'm gonna have to hire some grad students to fill in. I'm hopin' we'll be all right."

"That's good. I'm looking forward to it. Jen and the girls will love to have you here."

"Well, they're gonna put me up in a hotel there, so you don't have to worry about that."

"Hey, jackass. You know you gotta stay here. Jen will kill you and me both! She'll be happy to have someone else to fuss over since the girls are so busy, and I'm so ungrateful."

"How are my nieces anyway?"

"Teenage girls...so insane. Sam's at App, and Annie is a tennis star, and she practices twice a day and then comes home and eats more than we ever did."

Ed laughs, "She must have inherited Jen's athletic ability."

Even though Ed knew Remmey was a great athlete, he had to give him a hard time. Brothers.

"I guess she did," Remmey laughs. "She really is good! How's Will?"

"I wish I knew. I get a postcard every month or so letting me know where he is...I guess that alone lets me know he's alive. After he graduated, he bolted. I thought he just needed time away, and then he'd be back. He was working in the shop and was guiding clients a few times a week. He knew the water 'round here better than anyone. Seems like he never had a bad day on the water. He is a damn good fisherman. But, looking back, I feel like such a bad father. Between teaching and the Fly shop, all I did was work. I should have been there more."

Remmey offers him as much comfort as he can. "Aw, Ed. You're a great father, and Will is a great kid. It's hard to tell an eighteen-year-old much of anything. He's smart and savvy, and everything will be okay."

"I hope you're right about Will. I miss the kid."

"I'm always right. Remember, I was always the voice of reason. It will be nice having you here--- finally...even if you do stay longer than either of us can stand."

"I hear you, Rem. The hotel is still an option," Ed says.

"Yeah. I'll keep it on speed dial. Oh, and by the way, I still have your old Chevy truck for you to kick around in while you're here."

"You still have that old thing?"

"Yep. And it's running pretty well even though it looks like shit." Ed chuckles.

"That's great, Rem. It must take a lot of work to keep it running."

"It does. But some things are just worth it. She runs like a Ferrari... sucks up the gas, though. She is a tank. I put a newer engine in her, new belts, new plugs, a new battery, so she'll probably go another 100,000 miles."

"That's amazing. Why would you keep that old thing?" Ed asks.

"When you left, she was falling apart, and someone had to fix her up... that is, if I wanted to drive. Dad wasn't gonna fix it, and Mom started getting sick little by little. It was up to me if I wanted transportation, so I figured it out, started tinkering with it, and learned a lot about replacing worn out parts. Now, she's running like a champ."

"I can't wait to see it... and you, Rem."

"Me too, man. Safe travels, bro."

"See you soon." Ed hangs up with a long exhale.

10

Boone, May, 1992

By the time Daddy had been dead long enough for me to go through most of the "first" milestones without him, I was fishing pretty much every afternoon. Momma was right. The river, fish, and sun did help me heal. But other days, I felt miserable and numb. Some days, I felt like I was going to be okay. Other days, I still heard the rapids and couldn't take a deep breath. Mostly though, I had at least started to heal.

One afternoon, I was having a good day. I had caught five fish already, and it had only been a couple of hours. I wasn't in my usual "go to" spots. I had decided to try a different stretch of water down Bamboo Road, which was still relatively close to the house. I had set my rod down, walked up stream about ten yards, and began inspecting the bank for a few earthworms. Suddenly, out of nowhere, Warren and Cash came crashing through the bushes that lined the riverbank. It startled me, but I wasn't scared of them. I was just incredibly annoyed that somehow, they had found my refuge.

Both boys were standing between my fishing gear and me. Before I could get to my rod, Warren reached down, grabbed my line, rolled it around his meaty fingers, and then suddenly cut my line with his knife. For extra insult, he promptly bent down, grabbed my rod and snapped it over his knee. I was stunned and couldn't move.

"Stop it!"

Warren laughed. "Shut up, coon! I aint gonna forget that bullshit you dropped on me in class a couple of years back. This is me, making things right for calling me out like that."

"Are you kidding me? That was like two years ago!"

"Better watch yer mouth, shadow."

A red rage clouded my eyes. My vision was laser-focused on Warren, so I didn't notice Cash sneaking up on me from behind. Both my fists were clinched and ready to punch Warren's teeth in when Cash's spindly little ass grabbed both my wrists and held me roughly. I tried to break free, but he was too strong.

Warren slowly walked to my tackle box, opened it, and began dumping all my gear at the river's edge. He went as far as to chuck a few spinner baits downstream so there would be no way I could retrieve them.

Cash tightened his grip with each lunge I made at Warren. My mind was racing. How was I going to get out of this? I stopped struggling and pleaded with Cash.

"Cash, this ain't like you. Why are you doin' this to me?"

Cash said with his screechy, whiney voice, "Come on, Warren, we did what we came to do. Let's let her go 'cuz we got fish to catch ourselves."

Warren piped in, "No way, man. She hasta be taught a lesson 'bout bein' som'ere she ain't wanted."

Cash continued, "Okay, here's what we're gonna do. He'll let you go if you promise not ta come 'round yere no more."

I shook my head. "I can't do that. The way I see it, fellas, this is a public river and it belongs to anyone in the state of North Carolina."

"Nuh- Uuuuhhhh...not for your cricket ass."

"I'm tired of you calling me cricket."

I made one last jerking surge to free myself from Cash's bonds. This time, he couldn't hold me back. I exploded at Warren, and Cash fell to the ground. I was seething and got in two solid swings at his chest and jaw which stopped him for a split second. I pushed him as hard as I could, sending him face first into the water. As I grabbed my tackle box, I swung at Cash, too, clipping him just above his left eye.

"Cash, you're a little punk ass, too." I walked away. I was so mad that I wished they would start some more with me. They didn't. So, I kept walking.

A few days later, I went back to the river to check for the remains of my lures, hooks, and split shot. I loaded up what I could find and headed upstream about two hundred yards. I had put my little pocketknife in Daddy's fishing vest in case I ran into asshole one and two again. I wasn't worried. I was more ticked off than anything. Having my pocketknife wasn't going to do much, but it was enough security for me. I never told Momma about what happened that day. I knew she would lose her mind, and probably forbid me from fishing by myself again.

I got set up and made a perfect cast. I looked up at the sky to see clouds rolling in. I may have to cut this short today. Out of the corner of my eye, I got a glimpse of something coming at me. Then I heard the boys laughing.

"What's wrong with y'all? You have got to be dumb as hell! Both y'all come down here to start with me, again?! Why can't you just Leave. Me. Alone?" as I stomped my right foot three times on the ground to emphasize each word. I reeled in my line as fast as I could and grabbed my gear to head home. I didn't feel like fighting today.

I tried to find the pocketknife, but I was too slow, and the boys flanked me. I tried to show I was not afraid, so I walked between them with my head held high.

Warren grabbed my arm. "Seem laick we got a little score to settle... you pushing me in the river and all." I ripped my arm away from him and kept moving up the bank. Cash scrambled up ahead of me, and Warren closed in behind. I was trapped.

"Cash," I implored, "this isn't like you. What's your dad gonna say when he finds out what you two are doin' to me?"

Cash looked guilty, but he didn't move. Warren kept inching up behind me. "Shut up, Cash, you dumb ass. Don't say a word! Your dad ain't gonna find out shit. I'm gonna teach little girl here a lesson on how to behave."

He was right behind me now and shoved me hard. My fishing gear went flying, and I turned to run. He was right behind me and then pinned me up against a monster oak tree. His breath was rank. I could feel his forearm driving my shoulders upward. My chest and neck were embedded in the bark making it impossible to turn my head or rotate my body. I couldn't move anything, and my vision started to blur as stars dotting at the corner of my eyes.

I could see Cash out of the corner of my eye standing there looking surprised. "Cash! Help me!" I yelled at him. I knew that he knew better, but he was just a follower. After a long beat, finally he said, "Warren, come on, man. This ain't cool. I thought we were just gonna scare her. Come on. Let's go."

"Oh my god, Cash! Shut the hell up! I'm not gonna kill her. I just wanna be sure she knows... she knows she don't need to be fishin' in my river. You hear me, girl? MY river!"

I could feel my shirt rip against the jagged grip of the tree each time I would try and break free. I was running out of options. I told them, "You do realize you're going to jail for this, and Cash, your dad has the key to it."

In the skirmish, the silver Ichthys necklace that Momma and Daddy gave me twisted and rotated 180-degrees to my back. The last gift my Daddy would ever give me was staring Warren right in the face.

He grabbed the hair on the back of my head and raked my chin across the tree bark. "What do we have here?" Warren grabbed my necklace and pulled the chain tight around my throat.

Cash finally blurted out, "Warren, this is crazy man! We gotta go!"

Warren grabbed my necklace, and I felt it pop loose on my throat. He held it up in my face, laughed, and sneered, "Wonder how much I can get for this at the pawn shop." He kept laughing. I wanted to cry, but I couldn't give him the satisfaction, so I gritted my teeth harder.

"What's goin' on here?" We were all startled as a loud bass voice roared from the bushes. Warren jumped back and stepped back all in one motion, shoving my necklace in his pocket. Horrified, I fell to the ground like a rag doll. Warren tried to turn and run but couldn't. The overgrowth of brush and barbed wire fencing up the bank cut off his escape.

The stranger was about six feet tall, muscular, and had short light brown hair with wisps of gray under his ball cap and a voice that commanded your attention. With one quick movement, he took his fishing rod and pinned it against Warren's shoulders daring him to move. In the same breath, he called out to Cash without even turning to look at him. "No, son, you don't wanna run, and if you do run, I will find you and you won't like what happens when I do. Now, get your ass over here!"

Cash obeyed. "Now, you." He turned to Warren. "Don't you move, either."

He stared at Warren until Warren was suitably intimidated.

The old man looked me up and down to make sure I was okay, and he gently leaned his rod up against the fence.

This time he spoke slowly but forcefully, with loud whisper of gravel that made him sound hoarse. "If you boys know what's good for you, you'll tell me exactly what the hell you're doin' here. Right now."

Neither responded, but both looked whipped.

The old man barked at Cash first, "What's your name son?"

"Cash, sir."

"You're Sheriff Martin's boy?"

"Yes sir, that's my dad."

Cash and Warren were frozen with fear. For a second, I even thought Cash was going to cry. The old man moved closer to Warren and put his finger in his chest. "I don't know you… but I have a pretty good idea what you're doing. I'm gonna tell you right now if you ever mess with this young lady or any young lady again, there'll be severe consequences. Y'all hear me? As God is my witness, it won't end well for you," he said. He turned to Warren then, whipping to face him like an errant sprinkler. "Either of you!"

As I sat up a little straighter, I thanked God and Daddy for watching over me. I watched as the old man adjusted his fishing vest, revealing a .38 Special locked firmly to his hip. He was softly tapping it while delivering a message on how these boys could avoid going to jail. They slowly backed away as he was still rolling his fingers on the handle of the revolver. "Any questions?"

"No, sir," Cash mumbled.

"Then get the hell outta here." Their feet wouldn't move…until the old man reached for his holster and snapped off the thumb break.

Warren and Cash looked at each other, and like rabbits, they hopped the fence into the thicket and took off.

I just laid there, still in shock from the attack and mad that Warren stole my necklace.

The old man approached me, grabbed a bandana from his pocket, and gently wiped the blood from my chin. "You all right?"

As he helped me to my feet, I said, "Yeah, I'm good. Just a little shaken up is all."

"Those boys won't bother you no more. And if they do, you come find me, and I'll take care of it for you."

"That's okay mister. I can handle myself. Th-thank you for helping me though. Was nice of you."

I don't know why I was nervous, but I could feel it there, clawing at my throat like a mouse caught in a trap. There was something about this man. Maybe it was the gun or the adrenaline from the past few seconds, but I could feel it nonetheless.

If he suspected my nerves, he didn't show it as he looked me dead in the eye, put on a wide smile and said, "I'm Ed Myers. You might know my brother, Remmey Myers."

11

Boone, 1992

"It's okay. You're okay now," Ed Myers said. "Don't worry. I don't think they'll bother you again. At least not any time soon."

I never did cry. This man was nice and knew I didn't want to talk just now, so he didn't ask me any questions. After a few minutes, I told him, "That kid, Warren, took my necklace."

"He did? Don't you worry about that. I'll see what I can do to get it back for you. What does it look like?"

"It was a silver Ichthys with my name on it."

"What's your name?"

"Maya Jones."

"Maya Jones? Well, I'll be damned, young lady. I heard you talk to fish!" I was proud. Even this old white man knew who I was.

"Where'd you hear that?"

"My brother. Sorry about what happened to your dad."

"Thanks. Did you grow up with my dad?"

"Yes ma'am! I grew up here, but I moved to Montana a long time ago."

"Montana? That's a long way away, isn't it?"

"It is indeed. But it's a little like this place. It's quiet and peaceful. But Montana has the most beautiful rivers and mountains in the world."

"Really?"

"Yeah. And the fishin'? Girl. Now THAT is worth moving for."

"Is it different from fishin' here?"

"Kinda. Most everyone who lives there, or even passes through, fly fishes." We continued walking down the winding trail that led back to my house. I wanted to ask what fly fishing was, but I couldn't really concentrate. I looked down at his left hand where he held something that looked like a weird fishing rod. "What happened to your rod?"

Ed chuckled. "This is a fly rod. They're different from regular fishing rods. The reel sits down at the base for balance. The concept is to use lighter terminal tackle to get the job done, and there is never a dull moment. You're constantly thinking and moving."

"Terminal tackle?"

"Yes ma'am. Like your strike indicator, split shot, flies, leader, tippet. Basically anything on your leader that can be cast."

"I get the split shot, but flies, strike indicator... and what's a leader and a tippet?"

"Look, I'm gonna be here for a few weeks. Maybe you and I go fishin' sometime. I can teach you how it's done, and you teach me how to talk to fish," he grinned.

I still wasn't sure about this old man, but he had saved me and made me laugh; so maybe I could give him a chance. And now that I saw him up close, he was probably not super old.

"Okay, Mr. Myers. I'd love to learn how to fish like that."

"You can just call me Ed."

"Okay, Ed." I giggled because it felt weird to call him Ed. We walked a little farther and I continued, "What do you do as a job?"

Ed replied, "I'm a professor at Montana State University."

"What do you teach?"

"Fish and Wildlife Ecology and Entomology. I'm here helping Appalachian State get a fly fishing program."

"What does that mean?"

"I help evaluate the courses to ensure the course standards are where they need to be so students can get credit for the class."

"You mean students can get credit for taking a fishing class in college, FISHING?"

"That's what I'm hopin' for."

"That's way cool. I love insects, too."

"Well, young lady, that's a fine hobby to have. Entomologists make quite the living out here with all these creepy crawlers around."

I didn't know what to say then. I felt like he was on to me, like if I said more about the bugs, I might scare him away or he'd think I was weird like so like many others did. I forced myself to continue. "I spend lots of time by myself cause most of my friends don't go fishin' and definitely have no interest in bugs."

"Most people don't," Ed said, "but I do. I guess that makes me weird, too. Or maybe THEY are the weird ones, and we're the smart ones." Had he read my mind?

I laughed. He was nice. He walked me all the way back to my house. I started up the front porch steps and then turned back to him.

"Nice to meet you, Mr. My—I mean Ed." We shook hands formally. "And thank you for your help back there."

He smiled at me. "And it's nice to meet you too, Miss. Jon—I mean, Maya."

We just stood and stared at each other for a second. Momma wasn't home yet, so I didn't want to invite him in. But I didn't want to be alone either.

"Ed, would you sit on the steps with me and wait with me 'til Momma gets home?"

"Of course, happy to. And I'll teach you more about my fly rod." We sat down in the rocking chairs together, rocking and talking about fishing, the weather, and bugs.

I didn't know it then, but my whole life was about to change.

12

Boone, 1992

Ed was nice. I'm glad he walked me all the way home. As we sat on the porch rocking slowly, I wanted to go in and change clothes so Momma wouldn't notice the rips in my shirt, but I didn't want him to leave until Momma got home. I tugged on my shirt so it would lay without the rips being obvious.

Finally, Momma drove up. She saw Ed sitting there with me and jumped out of that car so fast I was surprised she had time to put it in park.

"What in the blue blazes is going on here?"

"It's okay, Momma." I said trying to reassure her. "This is Ed Myers."

Ed stood up and extended his hand. "Hey Millie," he said.

Momma didn't even look at him, so I continued. "He saved me from…uh… something that happened by the river."

Momma frowned and narrowed her eyes. She was intimidating when she wanted to be. "What kind of something?"

"Nothing, Momma. Just some stupid boys from my class messin' with me."

Momma got right in my face, grabbed my hands and pulled me out of the chair. "Explain what 'messin'' would cause you to have your shirt ripped."

I pulled away from her. I could never hide anything from her. She was like a bloodhound on a scent. "I was in the thicket down by the river that picked my shirt. I was in some tight spots climbing up the bank. I'm FINE. Anyway, Momma, this is Mr. Myers."

Momma still wasn't paying attention to him. She kept looking me over to see if I was telling the truth.

"Good to see you again, Millie. How ya doin'?"

Momma finally looked over at Ed. A spark of recognition came to her eyes. "Ed Myers? Well good gracious, son! Wha'cha doin' back 'ere in North Carolina?"

"I'm just here visiting Remmey and his family for a few weeks and hangin' out at the University doin' some curriculum stuff for the Ecology Department."

"Well, welcome home, prodigal!

She moved closer to him, and Ed stuck out his hand. Momma was having none of that. She enveloped him in a big bear hug. I even heard him let out a little humph. "Dr. Ed Myers, back in Boone!"

"How you been, Millie? You're looking beautiful as always."

"You always were a charmer jes like your brother."

"No, ma'am. Remmey's the charmer. I'm the smart, good-looking one," Ed said with a smirk. Momma cackled a big laugh that was good to hear. Ed continued, "Millie, I was so sorry to hear about Zeke. If you need anything at all, let me know. I know what you're going through."

"I know you do, Ed. And thank you." Momma's eyes welled up, but she took a deep breath and asked, "And what about you? I know it was a long time ago, but I was so sorry to hear about your wife and daughter."

"Thank you. That was a long time ago," Ed said.

"And Will? How is Will?"

"He's a know-it-all pain in the butt, but he's fine." Ed turned to me and nudged my shoulder. "He's not nearly as good a fisherman as your girl here."

Momma turned and looked at me and hugged me tightly. "Maya, tell me what happened."

She turned and started walking me in the house. "Ed, you come on in here, too, and have some supper with us."

We trailed in behind Momma, but Ed said, "No ma'am. I wouldn't dream of imposing on y'all that like. I was just waiting with Maya 'til you got home. I'll be heading on back to Remmey's. He'll be wondering what happened to me."

"Maya, it was a pleasure to meet you. Don't worry," he lifted up my chin so that I was looking him in the eye, and he whispered, "I'll get your necklace back." Ed turned back toward the door.

"Thank you again, Mr. Myers," I said.

"You're welcome. But you need to call me Ed."

"Can't. Momma would lose it if she heard me calling an adult by their first name." Ed grinned. "Good to see you again, Millie. I'll stop in and visit again before I head back to Montana."

"You better! Tell Remmey and Jen we said hello." Momma still hadn't gotten used to using a singular pronoun. It had taken her a while to switch from "I" and "me" to "we" and "us" after she got married, and she wouldn't go back to singular for a while. If Ed noticed, he didn't mention it and kept walking down the stairs and back toward the river trail.

"I'll do it. Y'all have a good evenin'."

Later that night, I was in my bedroom drawing pictures of a praying mantis. His face was a little scary looking, but I was trying to soften his eyes, so he didn't look so evil. I couldn't get it right.

Momma knocked softly and came in. She looked over my shoulder to see my picture of the praying mantis and sat down on the bed. She took a breath before she started talking. That meant that it was going to be a TALK...not just chit chat like we did all the time. A TALK meant that she was going to tell me something serious...something I probably didn't want to hear. Something that made me grow up a little more and lose a little more of my innocence. I hate those talks.

"Maya. Tell me what happened today. I saw your shirt in the washroom when I got home, and you're all bruised up."

"I don't wanna talk about it. Besides, it was no big deal."

"Good. Then you shouldn't mind telling me. You can just gimme the short version." I could see this was not going to be a fight I could win. So, I put my pencil down and turned to face her so she could see my eyes.

"These mean boys, Cash and Warren, tried to run me out of my fishin' spot down by the river where me and Daddy used to go fishin'. They said I didn't have the right to be there because I was black, and I was a girl, and I was on their river."

From the look on her face, I could tell that Momma had already predicted what I was saying. She didn't look surprised or even sad, really. That face told a thousand truths all at once. This is the way of the world. This was how we lived. And I wondered if she had ever faced a Cash and Warren of her own.

Most white people seemed okay. But there were always a few. Daddy said there would always be a few. He also said that you can't change people's minds by hitting them over the head. You had to change their minds by changing their hearts. He never got to the part about how to actually do that.

Momma asked, "What about your necklace? Why did Ed say he'd get it back for you?" I looked down sheepishly.

"I was hoping you hadn't heard him say that. It went missing after the tussle and Ed said he would keep an eye out for it, especially if he was fishing that same stretch of water. I'm gonna look for it tomorrow when I go fishin'."

"No, ma'am. You not going to the river on your own anymore. I will take you."

I made my skeptical face.

"Okay, maybe Dr. Myers can take you when he goes," Momma conceded.

I frowned, "Who is Dr. Myers?"

"That's Ed. The man who was just here. You didn't hear me call him Doctor Myers?"

"He said he was a teacher. Not a doctor."

"He teaches in college. They call them doctors. He's not a medical doctor. He's just been to school a long time like doctors have to."

I shrugged whatever and continued. "There's nothing you need to be worried about. The only time I'm ever gonna see Cash and Warren again is at school. They definitely won't be at the river anymore."

"How so?"

"Ed, err, Mr. Myers made it clear to 'em, you don't come up on someone's fishin' spot and think you move in and just take over. Before he walked up on us, I was standing my ground and things got a little heated."

I knew if Momma thought I was in danger, my opportunity to fish by myself was over. My heart was broken, and I was incensed that Warren had taken my necklace, but I had a feeling if anyone could get it back for me, it would be Ed.

13

Boone, 1992

A few days later, Ed was enjoying his late breakfast and the *Watauga Democrat* newspaper in a corner booth at Boone Drug. The diner is situated on King Street in the middle of downtown. Warren and Cash were pulling up in Warren's old, beat up, black Ford Ranger that looked like it had hit more than one deer in its life, and the clear coat wasn't clear anymore...like it had a nasty rash from the creeping boils of red rust that engulfed the undercarriage of the cab and wheel wells. Ed watches as the boys walk in, sauntering around like they own the place. Ed is annoyed at the ruckus...especially when he looks over and sees Hal Martin, the Sheriff, sitting and laughing with some locals.

The waitress is annoyed too. She is behind the bar, and she walks over in front of Hal and whispers to him, "You need to get a hold of these boys, Hal. They're being loud and disturbing my customers. I've already had a couple of complaints. I don't want that in my diner."

"Relax, Bea. They're just young'un's all hyped up 'cause it's summer. They ain't hurtin' nobody. Besides, they'll settle down once their food comes." Bea rolls her eyes. She is about sixty-five, and one of those people who loves her job. Her orange and white uniform is pressed and spotless; her smile is easy and friendly, and her hair is just a touch too high. This isn't just a job to pay the bills. It is her career, and she enjoys it.

Bea takes the milkshakes over to the boys and asks them politely to hush up. They don't. In fact, they get worse. They laugh louder, cuss more, and make obnoxious bubbly, crackling sounds as they suck their milkshakes through their straws.

Ed can't take it anymore. He has to do something. He keeps it friendly, though, as he walks over to Hal's spot at the counter where there was an empty seat.

"How ya doing, Hal?" Ed asks and extends his hand.

"Well, I'll be damned! I heard a rumor you was back in town." Ed shakes Hal's hand and sits down beside him. "What brings ya back to these parts?"

"I'm on a peer review. App State wants to add a fly fishing program. It's all about standardizing courses for accreditation." Hal grunts his approval and Bea smiles proudly while refilling Ed's coffee.

"Well, we sure are glad to welcome your Royal Highness back to our small lil' town."

"It's nice bein' back."

The boys make a rude comment about a passerby and all the customers hear them. Ed makes his case. "So, Hal, ya see those boys over there? Bea asked you to go over and have 'em tone it down. Ain't no need for them to cause such a ruckus."

"Don't I know it," Hal said, laughing. "The brown-haired, handsome one's mine."

"Uh-huh. And would that be the one who doesn't know he's supposed to take his hat off inside or the one who doesn't know he needs to wipe the cow shit off his boots?"

Bea busts out laughing, but Ed keeps staring at Hal without so much as a smirk. "Boys will be boys... am I right, Eddie?"

"Well, Hal, I gotta tell ya. I think those boys are actin' like they need a lesson in manners." Bea's smile fades fast as she scurries away to restock the napkins on the opposite end of the counter. Hal bristles, sits up as tall as possible, and puts his fork down. "Wha'cha mean by that?"

"Well, ya see, Hal, I came up on an incident that I can't make heads or tails of. I was on my way down to fish a few days ago, and I walked up on your boy and Warren cornering that young girl, Maya Jones...that'd be Zeke's daughter. When he saw me, Warren backed away real quick like and stuffed something in his pocket. Come to find out, he snapped a necklace off Maya's neck."

"Now wait a minute! Neither them boys, would hurt anyone. I know they ain't perfect and raise a little hell here and there, but I'm sure they wouldn't go an' do sumthin' like 'at. It's just a misunderstandin'."

"I don't think so. I hate to think what woulda happen'd if I hadn'ta walked up on 'em." Ed lets that concept sink in a little, put a ten-dollar bill on the counter and continues. "I don't think I need to bring the law into it though, Hal. I think I'll just talk to the boys myself." Ed gets up, slaps Hal on the shoulder, and makes his way over to the boys' booth.

"Don't mind, do ya, Hal?"

Hal just sits there trying to figure out what to do. If he gets up and tries to stop him, Ed may decide to press charges. If he doesn't stop him, his son might get a good "come-to-Jesus" speech. Hal decides his son probably needs a "come-to-Jesus" speech, and he'd rather Ed do it. He tries to be a good father, but that boy needs a lesson every now and then.

The boys don't notice as Ed makes his way up to them and borrows a chair from a nearby table. He sits with his chest facing the back of the chair and blocks their path to dissuade them from trying to escape. "Hi again, fellas. Cash, do you always pick your nose at the table?"

They sit speechless and the diner goes mute, quieting down to turn its attention to Ed and the boys. "Fellas, I was just thinkin'…I know you go to school with that girl, Maya, and I know you're planning to return that necklace you stole."

Warren makes a move to leave, but Ed leans in and jams his fists in the seat cushion. Ed continues, "Or you can magically make her necklace reappear in my hand right now, and I'll be on my way, or I can just find you later and we can discuss how the juvie system works here in North Carolina."

Ed leans over toward Cash. "That goes for you, too, runt. You're an accomplice, which makes you just as guilty." Ed is quiet for a minute and lets the boys think…as though that were possible. Then he continues, "You see that man sitting over there?" and he points over to Hal.

Both boys nod yes. Hal is like a squirrel facing an oncoming car not knowing where to turn or what to do.

"That's Sheriff Martin…you know him, right, Cash?"

Cash whimpers a "Yes, sir."

"Maya and I will file full reports of assault and battery with intent to commit bodily harm charges against the two of you. That's a felony. And just so you know, this will be on your permanent record. That means, it will follow you wherever you go for the rest of your life. Unless you two figure this out in about three seconds, I'm going to go get Maya right now," He turned to look at Hal who was circling right behind him with his head down.

"We'll be in your office in forty-five minutes, Sheriff."

Warren blurts out in a last-ditch effort to save face, "Look Mister, we don't know what you're talkin' 'bout. You oughta be more careful about accusing folks of things that ain't true. All of what you're sayin' is a bunch of bullshit. And you don't scare me."

Ed chuckles. With the quickness of a flea catching a ride on a running dog, he thumps Warren dead in his throat. Warren is suddenly gasping for breath, and, like a Sears Roebuck tent, he folds clutching his neck. Ed continues calmly, "You got quite a mouth on you, son. Better be careful. Someday, you may run into someone who isn't as calm as I am."

Cash leans back in his seat and decides he was no longer willing to spiral deeper in the hole Warren was digging for the two of them. He whispered, "Come on, Warren...just give it to him."

"You better listen to your buddy here." Ed gives Warren another couple of seconds to consider it. Warren doesn't budge.

"Suit yourself, boys."

Ed hops up and walks out of the diner, straight to Warren's truck.

The boys, along with everyone in the restaurant, watch intently. No one had ever shut them down before. Ed reaches into the truck bed and grabs one of the rods before cracking it over his knee. The boys jump up and run out to the truck. "You're gonna pay for that!" Warren yells.

"Am I? How much you think that necklace is worth compared to these rods?" Ed grabs another rod, smiles at them, and smashes that one too.

"Hey, you old bastard!" Warren lunges for Ed, but Ed pushes him back. Warren stumbles back far enough to know there was not much he could do about this situation. By now, everyone inside the diner is plastered up against the front window, gawking at the scene.

"I'm gonna keep breaking this shit until one of you starts talkin'."

"Dammit, Ed. Stop!" Hal hollers.

"If you'd do your damn job, as a father and as a law man, your boy would stand up to an asshole like Warren Boeling."

Warren musters up all his courage and charges Ed. Hal grabs him at the last second to try to calm him down.

"Easy, Warren. Now. Simmer down, boy." Ed doesn't want to smash the expensive rods... not that he respected the boys or their parents' money, but he does respect fishing. Instead, he walks around to the front of the truck and slings the front driver's side door open. He finds a bag of Red Man and shoots it into the trash can. "That shit will kill ya, boys. Don't be chewin' that."

When he looks back again in the cab, he sees the necklace shining in the ashtray. "Well, well. Look at this." He holds it up and the sun reflects off the shiny silver glimmering in the light.

"I don't know where that came from," Warren says.

"Me neither, but it ain't mine," says Cash.

"Cash, seriously? Did you get up this morning and take a stupid pill? You just sat there urging Warren to 'give it to me.' Hal, your boy needs help! It says MAYA right on it," Ed holds it up closer to Cash's face. "Now who do we know whose name is Maya?" Ed strokes his chin like he was really contemplating all the many possibilities. "Hummm… could it be that girl y'all assaulted down by the river the other day?"

"Assaulted? Don't say assaulted, Ed." Hal says clearly worried about the implications.

Cash jumps in, "We found that necklace."

"You found it? I think you found it on Maya's neck when you had her pinned up against the tree."

Now, Cash is scared. He isn't going to grow up to solve the question of nuclear fusion, but he was smart enough to know he was in serious trouble. Warren, however, may not quite be as quick on the uptake…and he also may be still ticked off about the whole thump to the throat thing.

"We didn't do nothin' to that little girl," Warren protests.

Ed grabs Warren and jacks him up against the side of his old truck. Hal and Cash both try to get between them, but Ed is strong and has a good grip on Warren's tattered "Def Leppard Hysteria Tour" t-shirt. Ed is one and a half inches from Warren's face...noses practically touching at this point. He snarls through clinched teeth.

"Listen here, I'm gonna say this one more time, and then let you go. You are not to go anywhere near Maya Jones. Ever. You open your mouth again with an insult or anything racially offensive toward her, I'll make sure you meet my brother and he'll drive you to Watauga County Hospital himself. Don't even breathe near her and you damn sure better not go near her while she's fishing, in school, 'round town, movies, nowhere! Do you understand me?" Now, his nose is actually touching Warren's nose. "I said, do you understand me?"

Warren tries to nod but can't since he is literally nose to nose with Ed, so instead he mumbles in the affirmative. Unsatisfied, Ed takes a step back, but keeps his grip tight and asks, "What'd you just say?"

"Yes, sir."

Ed releases his grip and takes a small step back. Hal and Cash let Ed go, but they all stand still in their tight little circle. No one dares to move until Ed says they can.

"All right then. You boys grow up already. You're too old to be actin' like ten-year olds. And do NOT forget what I said. Don't mess with girls. Especially not Maya Jones. She's gonna be fishing on that river any time she wants. You read me?"

Cash answers quickly, "Yes, sir." Warren looks down and nods.

"Ok guys, why don't you go ahead and head out," says Hal, finally jumping in after the mayhem subsides. The two boys give Ed one more look and then a nod, before jumping into the car. They're almost free, but not before Ed manages to wedge his head in the open window.

"Oh, and I'll tell Maya you gentlemen found her necklace for her."

They drive off leaving Ed and Hal standing on the curb and some patrons of Boone Drug crowded at the store window to get a glimpse of the show.

"Ed, I'm sure they didn't mean to hurt nobody. They're good boys, really," says Hal as Ed turns to walk toward his own car.

"Good boys don't pin girls against trees, steal their necklace, and then threaten 'em with slurs, Hal."

They walk a few more feet.

"Warren isn't always a good kid, but Cash is pretty good usually."

"Whatever you say. Just make sure those boys never go within twenty feet of Maya, and we are good. I hear different, and I'll be soliciting all these fine citizens of Boone and Watauga County to have your job if anything goes sideways."

"That sounds like a threat, Ed. You're not threatening an officer of the law, are you?"

"Oh no, Hal, it's not a threat. It's about having parameters to work in. A reminder if you will, to uphold the law and do what's right for everyone here in my hometown. They stay away, everything will be just fine."

Ed got in his truck, and Hal turned around and walked back into the diner.

14

Boone, 1992

Momma made me take a little break from fishing to let things calm down. I thought twenty-four hours was long enough. It was six a.m., and I was wide awake, counting the minutes until Momma left for work. She quietly entered my room, and I faked sleep. Momma bent over me and said, "I love you, baby… fresh strawberry jelly is on the kitchen counter."

I was plowing through my chore list to avoid the tongue lashing I would get if I got caught fishing alone and too soon for Momma's liking. My room was already clean…all I had left was to make my bed, sweep the front porch, and shine the kitchen counters. Momma and Daddy were always big about the action of "leave no trace." So I made things look like I was never there.

I headed out to the shed to grab what I needed for the day. I inventoried Daddy's—I mean, MY tackle box with a bunch of old hooks and lures. I added some new miniature rainbow trout crankbait that I picked up at the local Roses Discount Store. I hadn't used them before, but now, they were about to get a workout. Not taking any chances, I slipped my pocket-knife into my shorts for quick and easy access, just in case. I crammed my waders into my backpack with my lunch. I was in a hurry, so I just grabbed a spinning rod and accidentally picked up Daddy's. I realized it immediately because it felt heavier than mine. I paused and sighed. Would fishing ever be as much fun as it had been?

The morning air in early June was still crisp. I knew it would give way to a quick warming as soon as the sun crested the Blue Ridge. Dew covered the green grass with a soft frosting. Winter stuck around a bit longer than usual and was still wandering aimlessly through our spring in the high country. Daffodils dotted their yellow on the hillsides. All of it was a beautiful gift.

But the river? The river is always more than a gift. It is therapy.

The New River was settling to a mellow drift. It had rained for an hour or so the day before. Kudzu was starting its summer migration up the majestic oak trees that lined the trail to my hot spot through the Stapleton pasture. As soon as I crested the knoll down to the river, I spotted some movement and crouched down. I scanned the area a hundred yards up and a hundred yards down.

Someone was in the river. This couldn't be. Who was in my fishin' hole?

I reached for my knife and realized it was a grown man wading. Not Warren or Cash. Thank goodness. All I could make out was a blue ball cap. Stealthily, I crept closer, careful not to make any noise. I stayed tucked behind a row of pine trees hugging the riverbank. Then I saw Ed.

Careful not to interrupt his concentration and process, I watched him from afar for a while. Ed effortlessly rocked his fishing pole side-to-side aiming each cast and landing line with accuracy and purpose.

For a moment, I thought we'd stay like that forever. Me, enraptured by his precise casts and expert moves in the river, and him none the wiser.

"You know I can see you, right?" he said, suddenly breaking my reverie though I said nothing. "I'm a fisherman. Fishermen see everything. We are trained to see everything. All fishermen have eyes in the back of their heads."

I slid out of my hiding place and said, "That's crazy, Dr. Myers. I was just thinking that."

Ed said, "Yes ma'am, it's a thing. And just so you know, I grew up fishing these waters, but is it okay that I'm here?"

"I suppose so, given your lifetime status and all, and you don't have to call me ma'am."

Ed grinned at me. "And you don't have to call me doctor...some habits die hard."

"Fishermen pay attention to everything about their surroundings... water flow, depth, what bugs are comin' off, trees, changes in the weather. So young lady, are you gonna just stand there or put your waders on and get a line wet?"

"Yes sir!" I said and put on my hip waders. "Dr. Myers," he shot me a dirty look. "Oh, uh...Ed, as I was watching you back there, is this what you said you were gonna show me? You know, when we were walkin' back to my house talkin' about terminal tackle and all?"

"Yes ma'am, and it's Ed," he said firmly.

"You don't have to call me ma'am, DOCTOR Myers," I said firmly as he shrugged. "You said you're originally from here in Boone. What made you go to Montana? That's a long way away."

"I love Boone. It's home... but I got it in my mind there was more to see than just the mountains of North Carolina. I read books about fishing in the West. I loved fishing just like you, so I made up my mind to go. Mr. Jackson, my English teacher, had a lot to do with that."

"Why Montana?" I asked, and he proceeded to tell me more than I thought I needed to know.

"Mr. Jackson lit that fire under me, talking about the landscape, the beauty, and all the opportunities to fish and to hunt out in Montana. He talked about the BIG SKY country where you could see forever past the prairies, rivers, and mountain ranges, that seemed like they never ended. He said everything was wide open.

"Check this out. Here's a little fun fact-connection that sealed the deal for me to head out after I graduated. In class we had to read some excerpts from A.B. Guthrie Jr.'s novel, *The Big Sky*.

"It was the first in a series that talked about the Oregon Trail and how Montana came to be. One of the characters was a fella by the name of Boone Caudill who was from Kentucky. Well, that character got his name from Daniel Boone, the militiaman, and our mascot at Watauga High.

"You see just over that mountain ridge over there." Ed pointed due west. "Just over the Appalachian Chain into East Tennessee, he blazed a path called the Cumberland Gap which became a gateway for travelers to head west. Also, another fun fact, that massive gap was created by a meteorite that slammed into the earth about 250 million years ago. Cool, huh? Mr. Jackson really helped change my outlook on what could be. I needed to leave Boone and see the west for myself."

I interrupted, "Wait. Militiaman and meteorite? I had no idea I was gonna get an American History and an Astronomy lesson today."

Ed laughed out loud. "Once an educator, always an educator. It's a curse and a blessing." He threw out another cast, and I was still hypnotized. "So, you're into bugs, right?"

My head was still spinning from the whole lecture. "Uhhh…yes, sir. They don't bother me one bit."

"Me too. Are you ready to catch some fish on the fly?"

I was apprehensive but inched a little closer to him to observe. His demonstration was graceful as his body stood still, and he shifted his arm back and forth methodically, never moving his elbow at his side. He handed me the rod.

"Just hold the fly line tight in your left hand and try it until you get the rhythm. I'll coach you through it."

I began whipping the rod high above my head as though I were Indiana Jones. The fly line cracked and snapped behind my ear. Nothing about what I was doing felt comfortable. I was swaying my body left and right and twisting my hips with each toss of the line. I lost my grip and successfully launched the entire rod six feet in front of me.

Ed stood there, unaffected. I looked at him and he looked at me under the brim of his Braves baseball cap with one eyebrow raised and the other one lowered. I still had the fly line in my left hand clutched in a death grip."

"You're gonna go get that rod you just threw, right?"

I started retrieving line hand-over-hand as if I was in a game of tug-of-war.

"Here, lemme help you," Ed grinned. He walked downstream, grabbed the rod from the water, and shook it a few times to drain the reel.

"Let's try this again. Be sensitive to your grip, not too loose, not too tight, just enough to know you're in control. Let the line's movement in front and behind you tell you how much pressure you need here on your grip."

He handed the rod back to me. Defeated, I shook my head with angst. My mind was telling me, I can't do this, but I didn't want to disappoint Ed. I exhaled and this time he stepped up and steadily held my wrist, not allowing it to bend. He was focused on teaching me to cast, and I listened intently and let him guide me.

I held the fly line lightly in my left hand and, from the elbow up, he moved my arm in a smooth cadence. His voice was calm, and his words were simple.

"Don't twist your body. Relax. Let the cast tell you what you need to do. Pay attention to the tension the line creates in the front and the back."

Keeping the rod angled up at forty-five degrees the entire time, he was making a sweeping motion. I was standing there stuck, cautiously watching the line uncoil at the end of each forward drive. He continued teaching, "Now, when you switch to your back cast, wait, and give the line time to roll behind you. If you hear that cracking noise again, then you're breaking your wrist and rushing the cast. Don't tilt your wrist."

I was in a trance as I tried to put into practice everything he was telling me to do. Was I doing it right? It felt like I was.

Just then he said, "You're doing it, young lady!" His voice sounded faint like he was a mile away. As I turned my head to him for affirmation, he was literally twenty feet away. I didn't even feel him let go of my wrist and step back. Immediately, I lost my focus, and my repetition turned to a jerky swing that abandoned the elegance of my initial attempts.

Ed spent the rest of the morning and through lunch walking me through small tips to work on: tying about twenty-five feet of line to the very top of a broomstick or tree limb, holding the broom or limb at its base, and casting until there was no cracking or popping behind my head. Snapping meant the rod tip wasn't up, my wrist was bent, or I was too fast in my back cast, so the line didn't have time to uncoil. It was one o'clock, and Ed said he needed to leave for a meeting. Without hesitation, I said I was ready to go, too, because my arm was unbelievably sore. We gathered our gear, and he offered me a ride back home.

I told him Daddy and I fished the Watauga down from Old Shulls Mill Road. He said, "That's good water. Any luck?"

"No. It sucked. I spent more time fishin' on the bank than in the river. I didn't catch a blessed thing! I did have one break me off though. The hen had to have been at least eighteen inches."

Ed gave me a funny look and mumbled, "Sure she was...she was thiiisss big." He mirrored his hands, close then wide, close then wide, as if he was playing an accordion. "Seriously, that's something my dad used to say: no proof means it didn't happen."

"So do you think I'm lying?" I asked.

Ed looked me dead in my eyes and said, "Maya, all anglers are liars." And then laughed out loud. "My wife used to do to me what I just did to you. She would pretend to clap in slow motion with her hands never touching, asking was it this big? No, this big? How about this big? It's okay. It's all part of the experience. That is tight water below the dam. If you figure out how to use a fly rod, you'll crush 'em in there. That's really good water, but it demands precision casting. If you get that part down and learn the bite, you'll own that stretch of water."

"Daddy tried to explain Delayed Harvest, but I had no clue what he was talkin' about."

Ed took my admission as an opportunity to educate me further. "North Carolina Wildlife Resources has designated lakes, rivers, and creeks where it stocks with brownies, 'bows, and brookies. By stocking these trout in the fall and spring, numbers increase, and they will start spreading out to occupy not only the deep holes, but some of the healthier intermittent runs between those pockets. So, from the first Saturday in June through September, you can keep up to seven fish each time you go fishing. The thing is, October to May, you gotta put 'em back. Wildlife Resources wants you to keep 'em June through September or they will die due to the water temps rising too high. The idea is to wait for summer months to take 'em home. Delayed Harvest is great for getting people out to fish. It supplements the fish populations and supports the ecological cycle that our waters need."

"What cycle?"

"Picture this—"

"Oh brother," I thought, "here it comes, another lesson," but I didn't say anything.

Ed continued, "You already know vegetation like trees and bushes line our rivers, lakes, and stuff, right? That coverage does a lot. It holds banks up, which slows erosion and keeps those areas cooler for fish to spawn. Fish gotta eat, right?"

"Yes, sir."

"Well, tons of terrestrial invertebrates... those bugs that we love... come from that vegetation and provide food for fish. That's the short version."

"That's the short version?" I said with a smirk.

Ed chuckled. "That's a three-hour lecture in my college classes."

"All right... here we are. I had a blast. Wanna meet tomorrow, same place?"

"Yes sir. I'll be there. Eight-ish?"

"Yes ma'am, with bells and whistles on."

As we pulled up to the house, I saw her car and realized Momma had already gotten home. Crap! I mumbled, "She's gonna lose her religion now."

"Why?" Ed said.

"Because I didn't tell her I was going fishin,' and she told me not to go for a while. I figured missing one day was a while, but I'm startin' to think one day isn't enough for my mom."

Ed laughed, "I'm not sticking around for those fireworks. You're on your own with this one, young lady."

"Thanks a lot." I took a deep breath, got out, and slammed the heavy truck door. I grabbed my gear out of the back bed, headed straight to the shed, and tried to slink into the kitchen.

Momma was standing at the stove cooking two pork chops. My mouth was watering. I was starving. She didn't look up. "This is becoming a recurring theme. Why would Dr. Myers be bringing you home...again?"

"Before you ground me, let me explain please."

"The floor is yours."

"Momma, I wanted to fish. I needed to fish. It's one of the only things I can think of that keeps me close to Daddy. It's a routine I can't shake—and I don't want to! Dad did say once or twice, 'Sometimes it's better to ask for forgiveness than for permission.'"

Momma stood there, leaning with one hand on the kitchen counter and one on her hip with a damp rag in her hand. She still hadn't looked at me yet.

"Dr. Myers was at the river today, and he taught me how to fish a different way, and it was really cool."

She flipped the pork chops. "You mean to tell me, just by coincidence, Dr. Myers was fishing where you like to fish."

"Think about it Momma. He is from here, right? He has to know these waters 'round here 'cause he showed up outta the blue when Warren and Cash were messin' with me. He lives in Montana, teaches at Montana State University and is here for some fly fishin' class credit thing...something about course accreditation so App State can add a fly fishing curriculum."

"You're telling me he fishes for flies?"

"Ugh, no Momma. I was trying to tell you. It's a different style of fishing. It made my arm sore. You never stop moving and pay attention to what's around you. It's nothing like how Daddy taught me. That way was more cast and wait. This way, you're constantly castin' and lookin' for your next spot. The rod is much lighter, too.

Almost too light. When he was teachin' me to cast today, I accidentally threw his rod in the river."

"Well, I'm glad you had sense enough not to go alone."

"I'm okay. I promise."

After I narrowly avoided my premature funeral and Momma's feelings seemed assuaged, we sat down for dinner. I said the blessing, and as we ate those delicious pork chops, mashed potatoes, and greens, I told her the reason my arms ached, and I told her about fly fishing. Wouldn't you know, the whole while I told her about it, she smiled.

When I was finally finished and came up for air, she was still smiling. She asked me all kinds of questions. One time, when I paused long enough to take a breath, she started laughing and squeezed my arm.

"What's so funny?"

"Nothin', baby. It's just so good to see you happy again."

Then I got quiet and reflective. Daddy. Was I betraying Daddy by enjoying fishing again?

Momma took my hand and waited until I looked her in the eye.

"Your Daddy would be glad that you were having so much fun fishing again. It's okay to enjoy life again." Although her eyes were misty, she smiled and patted my hand. Then, she looked back at her plate and cut the last bit of meat off the bone.

"How long is Dr. Myers going to be in town? Did he tell you?"

"I don't know. He said he would see me again tomorrow."

"Okay, honey. Just please be careful. Now, go get us those Rice Krispy Treats I made and tell me some more about them flies."

15

Boone, 1992

It was another early morning, and I was about to explode with anticipation of what was to come. My arm was still incredibly sore, but I didn't care. I thought what I was learning was beyond cool, and Ed was a great instructor. His appetite for this thing called fly fishing was infectious.

Like every great educator, Ed picked up right where he left off, reiterating the fundamentals of the cast. I noticed he had brought two rods down with him because he held one in each hand. Everything he did was fluid.

"See what I'm doing with my rod in accordance with my body position?" I was captivated by how little he had to do to get so much out of each cast. He never moved his lower body and gradually allowed his shoulders to follow the tempo every time. He was instructing the whole time he was casting. Every word was sequenced to explain what was happening right in front of me. He asked a series of questions and paused between each cast to give me time to answer.

"What's my left hand doing?" He waited for me to answer and then kept asking me question after question. "What's my right hand doing? Where am I casting? How am I opening up more line with each cast? See, it's kind of like a clock. All the gears and pullies work in harmony to keep the right rhythm, and you're the spring. The spring controls the force or energy that's needed to make the gears, pullies, and levers keep time. For example, if I wanna extend more line to reach a certain spot, I use my left hand to pull line from the reel right as I moved into my back cast. My arm is like a lever, pulling that line out, and the inertia established will increase or decrease the amount of line you use to reach your desired spots."

I watched first. I answered his questions. Then I tried to make the same motions with my invisible rod, mimicking his every move. My mechanisms—right hand, left hand, arms, shoulders, line, rod, reel—all had to work in synchronization.

"It's not hard if you can listen to the tick-tock of a clock in your head." I gave him my "I'm doubtful of the accuracy of your last statement" look that always made Daddy laugh at me. Ed laughed, just like Daddy always did, and continued.

"I know it seems like a lot. You know what I mean...tick-tock, tick-tock..." he said as he moved his fly rod back and forth through the air like a grandfather clock pendulum. He stopped and put his rod under his armpit. "You see that fly rod?" He pointed to the rod at our feet.

"I want you to give it a test drive."

I picked up the rod apprehensively. Ed reassured me. "I'm gonna help for the first few casts, and then you're gonna take the wheel." He firmly held my wrist again and initiated the first deliberate lift.

After about four or five "tick-tocks," I was rolling, and he let go. I only had about fifteen feet of line out, but I was sustaining what I thought were pretty good shots of line. My first lesson was only yesterday, and already I was crushing it. I told my fish friends that they were giving me comfort today and that I appreciated their encouragement. I don't think Ed heard me say it, though.

I went for another perfect cast, and just like that, spooled out the line like a bird's nest not only in the reel but managed to snag about four tree branches. It was like watching a pair of Chuck Taylor's tied together by the laces twist themselves over a telephone wire. The weight of my terminal tackle just wove a beautiful web of chaos through every leaf and limb imaginable. All the while, Ed was just standing there being all philosophical...babbling about whatever.

"Ya know, fly fishing is an art form. Think of yourself as Michelangelo painting a masterpiece every time you cast. You can't rush perfection. There's more technique to it than when we fish with conventional tackle, spinning rods, bait casters, and so forth. You are constantly moving and thinking about everything: What's behind you? What's in front? Where am I going with this cast? How much line do I need out? Is my strike indicator set at the right depth? Do I need to redress my dry?"

Ed stopped for a second, catching his breath and gazing at my fine tapestry of line in the trees. "Lookie there! You just caught a limb brim, and by the looks of the spaghetti on your reel, you paint more like Jackson Pollock than Michelangelo."

He blew his own mind with the comparison and laughed so hard he doubled over on himself. I knew who Jackson Pollock was because Mr. Hester, my visual arts teacher, had a print of his work hanging in his art classroom. I always wondered how someone could get famous from just randomly slinging different colors of paint in every direction on a canvas. I'm pretty sure I could do that. Anyway, I did my best fake chuckle and rolled my eyes. He reached into his vest and pulled out what looked like a book and broke it open.

"What's that?"

"My Fly Bible. These flies right here are answers to all my prayers. They're like verses to help me get through tough times. Sometimes they work great, and sometimes they don't, depending on the day and what I'm searchin' for."

He was so calm and immune to my challenging situations, maybe even eerily joyful that I was hung up several more times that day. What was visibly daunting to me was losing fly after fly, getting jammed up on tree limbs, caught up in brush on the riverbank, and staying hung up on the river bottom. All of that just rolled right off his back like water off a duck's feathers. He was unflappable. I was very flappable. I was dropping into an abyss of frustration.

"Maya, this is the reason most folks don't pursue this endeavor... because of what is happening to you right now. Don't let it get ya. Inhale and exhale, you can do this. Getting tangled in trees will happen. Get used to it. It's always gonna happen. Still happens to me all the time too. Learn from it. You'll start to figure it out."

That was all the assurance I needed. I went right back at it. Back and forth. Just like the pendulum of the clock. tick... tock...tick... The line flowed effortlessly from the tip of the rod.

He steadied my wrist and backed off.

"Now, go."

It was then I surrendered to the process. I waited in the back cast and could feel the line load in my grip. Forward, my target and pressure commanded more line from the reel. In an instant the algorithm made sense. If I broke my wrist or rushed the cast forwards or backwards at any point, depending on my line length and speed, it wouldn't work. When I added in controlling the extension of line by wisely anticipating what I needed to draw from the reel, my brain exploded.

"Whaaaaat?" I yelled. My mind was racing with the possibilities of what could be done to manipulate this interchangeable system. It was like an endless game of dominoes. Everything was built on a chain reaction.

I told Ed, "This is way more fun than sitting on bank just waiting for the fish to bite!"

"I think so, too," Ed said. "It's fly fishing. You just talk the fish right onto the hook."

"I can definitely do that."

Ed said, "Uh-huh, I've heard that about you. My brother said with you, it's a full-on conversation. He said it was like watching you talk on the phone, just no phone."

Ed and I both howled with laughter.

Even though I started minimizing my hang ups, Ed happily continued to untangle those few incidents where branches would jump in my way and catch my line. I started blaming the trees for my mishaps as if it were their fault interrupting my efforts. Ed was constantly bolstering encouragement, reassuring me that practice will pay off. When he would fish a little, I would stop and watch his presentation. I continued to try to copy his movements with and without holding the rod until my movements felt smooth. He kept talking about muscle memory, and I was hoping my muscles would remember the right things.

We walked upstream, and he said he saw some fish holding. I couldn't see anything. Still, I trusted him.

"Get your rod ready."

He pointed with his rod and said, "Twenty feet—right there! Cast into that run and let it drift through, but you have to be a solid ten feet above the run, so the drift looks organic." He moved to my left so I wouldn't hook him in the head, and I started punching line. Again, wildly unpolished, but I was slowly getting the hang of what he was preaching. Still…no bite. Not even a nibble.

I fussed at him. "You told me to aim for the top of that run. You said fish were holding there."

"You're right. I did." He moved behind me, grabbed my elbow, stabilizing it. "Quit with the chicken wing thing. You're not a bird, and you can't fly. And you almost hit the exact right spot I was talking about. Do it again and keep your elbow from flailing. Two false casts and then lay it down."

"False cast?"

"Yes, ma'am, like I said, it's those casts that allow you to get your distance and direction right. Sometimes, it can help you dry off your fly, and the debate is out still on whether it imitates the flight of a fly but no more than two false casts. More than that, you're wasting time casting and not fishing. Casting allows you to have some control over the things you can control. The fish are what you can't control, so you don't need to worry about that. What you can control is how well you hear what those fish are telling you."

The stars must have been in their proper alignment because I did exactly what he said to do. It was textbook and complete luck. I hoped Ed didn't know that, though. He continued, "If that fly disappears, you'll see the sip. It will be gentle. Then barely lift your rod tip up stream. If you set toward us, you're just pulling the fly out of its mouth. Always set with the current."

In one motion all hell broke loose. I saw the sip but didn't react. The monster took my fly and hooked himself. I kept my rod tip up but forgot to strip in fly line. I started panicking and then time stopped.

Ed slowly and smoothly helped me gather the slack line with my left hand and thread it through my index and middle finger on my right hand where I had a death grip on the cork line.

The rod was bouncing like crazy with the fish's movements.

"You got you one, young lady!"

I snapped back to reality. What a rush!

"Now when he demands line, you give him what he wants, and then you take what he gives."

"Take what he gives?"

"Yes, strip the line through your fingers when you feel him start to surrender. He'll tell you. You dictate the fight. Whatever you do—do NOT, under any circumstances, drop your rod tip. You do that, he'll break you off and the match is over. That's good. You got him! You're a natural girl!"

Just about that time, I dropped my rod tip and...pop! He was gone.

I was mad I failed, but I was also exhilarated that I had come so close. Ed seemed pretty content, too. My line got ensnared in a tree and knotted up again from the recoil, but I got to experience what that tug signified with such light tackle. It was euphoric. He got my line unraveled and kept encouraging me. "Did you see that, Ed? I almost did it!"

"I saw it. Maya, that was fantastic. Great job and please don't drop your rod tip next time."

We stayed outside until it was almost dark. Neither of us caught any fish at all, but I got a taste of why fly fishing was so addicting. I was starting to understand the science of it and getting the essence of what force and tension require to tame it. It wasn't just relaxing and peaceful, it wasn't just art or becoming one with nature...it was science, too: understanding the fish and what made them want certain flies, understanding the river and how not to get your ass kicked by those fantastic creatures. In no uncertain terms that fella that grabbed my hook today told me to my face I needed to up my game if I was to land him or any of his friends.

Ed said I was talented. My head swelled. He said some people were just naturally good cooks, good writers, good athletes…and I was a good fisherman.

"You can always get better though, Maya. Complacency rests in the lap of the apathetic. You will only be as good at this as your interest and inquiry takes you. No matter how gifted you are as a teacher, farmer, doctor, or, in this case, an angler, you can always improve. Everyday try and get better at your craft." He reminded me of Daddy. Both philoso-fishers.

Ed didn't have to spend his time teaching me how to fly fish. It could have been because he was bored. I don't think so, though. I could sense there was a deeper reason why he was compelled to pass on the gift. It could have been my drive and determination that excited him. It could have been his coping with something internally or simply his searching for some obscure purpose.

Whatever it was, we forged a bond through fly fishing and a language only spoken by those who seek out its comforts.

16

Boone, 1992

The next day Ed gave me three mini-tutorials on studying water, the principles behind rod weights, and how to mend my line. He pointed out the riffles, the eddies, and the slower water on the inside edges of a bend and that stronger, heavier paced water stayed out wide. He called it "turbulent flow" and explained it like a NASCAR race. "Fast cars that don't gear down into turns will stay fast and wide. The cars that slow down can hang on through the inside of those turns and give themselves an opportunity to win the race.

"Rocks and structure can cause that water to slow, creating opportunities if you're paying attention to the seams those currents create. If you can ride that sweet spot... right where the slower water catches the faster water... in those curls, you'll find 'em holding. Fish don't have to work as hard to stay stationary in slower water. Those crafty devils will hang out in their spot all day long if they're not disturbed. When sustenance is flowing down low and beating them in the face, they don't have to do much but shift a little right or a little left and maybe rise to a hatch. Most of the time they just stay in their own lane."

We kept moving slowly upstream, and he pointed out a few unseen differences in the river that I don't think my Daddy even noticed or knew about. And he noticed everything. Ed sure was smart.

"This is a 4-weight rod. In theory my reel, line and rod should all be congruent to maximize cast efficiency. Sometimes you can get away with line weight either a point above and or below your rod weight if you really know what you're doin'. Think of it this way, the smaller the rod weight, the smaller the fish. A 3-weight rod is what you need for smaller stream fishing while a 6-weight is a bit more effective for bigger water and potentially some bigger fish."

I nodded, but I thought, "Why wouldn't I always use the heaviest weight to catch the absolute biggest fish I could?"

Ed said, "Knowing how to tango is the whole kit and kaboodle."

I turned my head from side to side, "What?"

He said, "It's a style of dance that has it all. You and your partner can start at a distance or face-to-face. You can move slowly or with tempo. By dancing with a decent-sized fish and an extremely light tackle, you will learn how to connect, how to follow, how to lead, and, if you're lucky, how to embrace in the end. Nothing is ever a given, and sometimes, there is a lot of improvisation. Everything is always a gamble. Rod, reel, line weights, leader, and knots can give you a chance, but how you react and counter-react based on your partner's movements are what destroy probabilities or improve them.

Ed continued, "See right here?" He pointed to a place where the brush was so thick it covered a couple of downed logs cresting the edge of the riverbank causing a soft pooling downstream from the debris.

"Get your line ready. I'm gonna coach you through another aspect of this game. It's called mending. And every fly fisherman needs to learn how to do it. If your fly moves unnaturally, guaranteed it gets ignored. Mending line is used to stay in-line or behind your fly to sustain an unforced and pure presentation of that fly. If the current is forcibly pulling your line or your fly in any direction at any time, it's game over. Recast. By gently lifting your rod tip and purposefully flipping your line behind your strike indicator or fly, it will look natural as they feed low or on the rise."

I was going to need a dictionary to understand all these words, but I don't know if they make a fly fishing dictionary. On the other hand, they do have a Fly Bible, so maybe... I just tried to focus on where he was telling me to cast, and what to do with it as it landed.

"Try practicing it a few times in this run right here. Just kick some line out, land it, and flick the tip of rod above your fly so your fly line follows suit. Do it quickly like a band director."

That analogy made me think of Daddy, but I didn't say anything. It reinforced the fact I thought like he did, and he was a seasoned angler. Maybe I was a seasoned angler, too!

He continued, "Just a quick little twitch and keep your wrist still. Then relax through the drift and follow your fly with your rod tip."

I tried it a few times, and Ed reached over to grab my wrist again. "Snap it with certainty behind the fly."

Like a puppeteer, he lifted my hand keeping the rod tip at forty-five degrees that made a deliberate little arching motion that forced the fly line up six feet behind my fly.

"You're the conductor. Did you feel the stroke? You do it now. Try and emulate that transfer of line."

I tried to repeat the movement, but it was futile. I did it again and again and again, cast after cast, each jab better than the one before.

"Again," I heard. "And again. Good. Again."

It started to click, and just the way Ed described it. I was directing the symphony of line control with my mend. Over and over, he would say, "Mend and manage your line to give yourself a shot. Strip in the excess line and follow your fly with your rod tip. Fish know when things aren't right. If one rolls on it, you have got to be ready. A bunch of excess line out means, if you're lucky enough to hook up, you'll be playing catch up to get tight to the fight, and you don't want that."

There was so much to think about, and a few times my brain wouldn't compute what to do or how to do it. The level of information I had to process was overwhelming.

"This is a lot to remember, Ed. How many kids have you taught to fly fish?"

He said, "One. Will. My son. He's eighteen, and he's a damn fine angler. You're getting it a bit quicker than he did. Aren't you about thirteen?"

"Yeah. I'm thirteen. So how many Black girls do you think fly fish?"

"Huh. Now that I think about it, I think you may be the only one that I've ever met."

I said, "Get outta here, Ed! I might be the only girl like me on the planet doing this? I'm a pioneer like Charlie Pride and Daniel Boone!"

"As far as you know you are… and good for you. You were born to fly fish. I really am impressed."

"I'm impressed that you're such a good teacher. And you tied all of these flies?"

"I did. Exactly what I sell in my shop. I'll teach you to tie a few if you wanna give it try, but for now let's get one on top, and land it."

I took a deep breath, looked around again and started punching line, cast after cast. "Lay it down. Perfect! Now mend. Wait…follow the fly and add another soft mend." I did everything he said waiting for each command. BAM!

"Set. Maya. Set. Set. Set."

I set, and then it was on. I was late but managed to get hooked up anyway. "Let him play and start stripping your line so you're taut."

I did, and just like Ed mentioned, I got my tango dance lesson. This guy was little but fought like he had stolen something, jetting right, then left. Each directional blitz I countered rolling my rod angle in the opposite direction making sure I stayed hooked up. I was going to win this time no matter how badly my arm was hurting.

"Keep your rod tip up. He'll tell you when to strip line."

I felt the force, and that was it. I was hooked... pun intended. It was exhilarating! I was so excited I started bouncing up and down.

"Slow, Maya... stay focused... strip, strip. That's it. He's starting to calm down." Ed kept coaching me. I got the trout closer and closer to me, and Ed got the net ready.

"Wait, Ed. Can I do it?"

Ed shrugged. "Sure. It's your fish. But remember, he's still got some fight in him, so keep it slow and steady."

I tucked my rod under my armpit and slowly took the net from him with my left hand. This beautiful 'bow was perfectly cradled in the bottom of the net as water glistened over his camouflage.

Ed said, "Here. Use my hemostats and pluck that Sulphur out of his mouth so you don't get all tangled up if he starts to bounce."

He handed me what looked like pliers for a surgeon, long and skinny, so it could remove small flies. I clamped the fly carefully and pulled it right out.

"Now, get your hand wet before you grab him so you don't remove the mucus on his body and then gently but securely, grab the middle of his body."

I knelt down and wet my hands. Everything faded into silence. I realized I had arrived at a crossroads of regret and responsibility. From that encounter alone, I had been undone and reassembled with a new infrastructure. My internal compass would have a new design and direction. I realized my past had taken advantage of a privilege, and my jury had acquitted me. Moving forward, there would be only protection, gratitude, and reverence for the fish and the waters that nurtured them. I had fallen in love. I was captivated by the action, infatuated with the fish, hungry for the adventure, and spoiled by its rewards. My eyes were now open.

I knew what a rainbow trout looked like. I had caught a few before, but nothing matched the intensity and thrill of what I just experienced. This little Hercules was special, and in that moment, I observed him completely as though I had never seen a 'bow before! He was painted in an opaque emerald green, centered with a single pale-magenta brush stroke from gill to tail, and covered in tiny freckles so beautiful that if the renowned Mark Rothko had been there, he would have wept with envy.

"Ed, look how beautiful he is!" I screamed.

"That's a great looking rainbow, Maya."

It was one of those times when I was happy and sad at the same time. I hate that. Ed snapped me back into the present. "Stop basking in your own glory and get him back to the river."

I thanked the 'bow, pretended to give him a kiss, and carefully returned him to the river.

After he darted out of sight, I turned to Ed. "I did it!" I yelled, throwing my hands in the sky.

"Yeah, ya did! Now before you think it's always like this, remember: a fisherman's adaptability is the difference between fishin' and catchin'. Never take this for granted. These creatures were put here for us to enjoy. Never abuse the cycle."

"Huh," I thought.

"What's that Maya?" Ed asked.

"Nothing. It's just…that sounds exactly like what my dad would say."

He softly chucked my shoulder and winked at me. I knew this old, white dude wasn't going to replace my Daddy, but I was enjoying myself again. I had almost forgotten the feeling, but I thought, if we spend enough time together, maybe happiness wouldn't be a faraway idea, but my reality.

And then I thought about the end of summer and Ed's inevitable return home. And reality sunk in again, and I swore I could hear the waves rushing in.

I prodded Ed for more information so I could rest for a minute. I was still in my head and needed a distraction, so I turned to Ed. "So, Ed, where do you live in Montana?"

"Bozeman. It's kinda towards the bottom left corner of the state."

"And you knew both my parents growing up?"

"I knew your mom and dad but unfortunately, we didn't get to hang out much. It was the 60's and Watauga County didn't integrate Appalachian High School until 1964, the fall after I graduated. My younger brother, Remmey, got to play football with your dad. Zeke had an arm on him and was quick as a cat. Remmey said he threw him a few nice TDs."

"Really? My dad played quarterback?"

"He sure did…was good. Pretty sure he sang in the choir, too."

"Yeah, he did. Mom was in choir and Dad said he took choir too so he could make the moves on mom."

Ed laughed. "Well, it musta worked."

"But I sure didn't know he played football. Momma and me are going to have a talk tonight. That's crazy."

"Your pops was a great dude."

I changed the subject back to Ed.

"And you teach Fish and Wildlife Ecology and Entomology?"

"Yes ma'am."

I thought about it for a minute. How do you teach a whole class on insects? That seemed fun, but as much as

I loved most of the insect world, I'm pretty sure I couldn't handle more than about eight hours of it.

"Do they teach a class in fish? How they swim, their anatomy, how they eat, what they eat?"

"Montana State has a class where they do. It's called Ichthyology."

I remembered that's what Momma called my necklace. An ichthys. I sure wish I had that necklace.

"Maybe I'll go there and take that class."

"Sounds good to me, but don't tell your mom."

I laughed. "I won't. She would be upset with you for taking me that far away!"

We fished for another hour or so, and Ed said, "Let's go get a bite to eat."

I was starving. "You don't have to ask me twice."

"Hardee's burger good with you?"

"Yes, sir."

We stopped and got a burger and then headed out, but we didn't head toward the house.

"Where are we going, Ed?"

"Up 194 here off Castle Ford Road to the shooting range. If you're going to be a fisherman, out on your own in nature, you need to learn how to use a gun for protection from wild animals or…whatever."

"You're going to teach me how to shoot a gun?"

"Yep. You're gonna learn and get comfortable. Hopefully, you'll never have to use it. But if you need to, you'll be ready."

"Did you ask my mom about this?"

Ed smiled, "Of course I did after a long discussion about the necessity of it and how well-trained you'll be after you practice about a thousand hours."

At the range, the instructor handed me a Smith and Wesson .38 Special air weight revolver. (I didn't know it at the time, but Ed bought it for me.) After my mandatory lessons with the instructor, Ed and I continued to practice.

We talked about the black bears we have in North Carolina, and he told me all about the grizzly bears, plus mountain lions, and angry moose they have in Montana.

"Always shoot as a last resort," he said. "Remember, most animals are scared of you unless they're provoked. Make yourself as big as you can, in a loud, deep voice, tell him to go, and don't ever back him into a corner. If he doesn't run away, slowly reach for the weapon, but don't fire until your life depends on it."

"Look, Ed! I nailed that target right in the bullseye that time."

"Great job!"

He made me go to six more lessons that summer until he was confident I would always handle the gun safely and shoot straight if I ever needed to.

Ed tilted his head down and frowned to accentuate his seriousness. "Maya, this firearm is yours, but it is registered to your mother. Under no circumstance should you use this gun unless she is with you down here at the range. The only request I have is that you practice occasionally to stay sharp and keep your confidence up. Do you understand the terms?"

I replied with a commanding, "Yes, sir."

Ed responded, "Great! Now I'm gonna teach you how to clean it."

17

Boone, 1992

After church on Sunday and Momma's delicious country ham and rice lunch that we shared with Mr.

Robinson, I headed to the river again to meet Ed. Today, he was going to teach me how to tie a fly.

When I got to our spot, Ed was sitting on the tailgate, tying already.

"Maya, what took you so long? Get over here."

"Never been to a Black church, have ya, Ed? We take our time." Ed laughed.

"Yeah, yeah. I've heard. Come up here and sit with me." I walked over to him and climbed up beside him.

"So, where'd ya get this old truck?" I asked him.

Ed snickered and said, "You like it?"

"Yeah, I do! It's got room for everything. Daddy had a truck, but Momma sold it. She said she didn't wanna see it waiting for her every day."

"I get that."

"Yeah. I guess I do, too." We were both quiet for a little while. I stared out at the rock where Daddy and I fished so many times. I missed Daddy.

He snapped me out of my memory and said, "Check this out." He pulled out a wooden briefcase thingy. He opened it and inside were tiny drawers and small bins of beads, hooks of every size imaginable, feathers, deer hair and spools of thread. I had no idea what some of the stuff was, but it was beautiful. Everything had its proper spot. He called it his mobile fly-tying desk.

"I take this everywhere I go. Based on the time of year, I can tie the right size fly with the right color of the fly. It's kinda like flies on demand. If the trout aren't taking what I'm serving, I can head back to my truck to make a few adjustments for what I think might help get the job done."

He opened his Fly Bible, displaying row after row of what were meticulous executions of fly brilliance, perfectly positioned side by side. Each type of fly was precisely ordered by color and size.

He showed me the options and continued, "It also helps when you're teaching a kid how to cast, and she keeps losing your flies in the trees." He nudged my shoulder.

After seeing how much work it took to tie even one, I felt bad that I had lost a few. "I'm just teasin' you, Maya. You're a natural. Do you know how many flies I've lost? Too many to count. That's why I have this travel case! Besides, we've only been doing this for like a week and you're already as good as my son."

"Your son...Will, right?"

He paused to gather his thoughts, and then said softly, "Will... yeah..."

"Is he your only child?"

"I had a daughter named Maggie, but she passed away."

I didn't know what to say, so I just mumbled, "I'm sorry," and then tried to change the subject to something more pleasant. "What about your wife? Is she still in Bozeman?"

"No. She died, too."

Did he mention that when he talked to Momma? He may have, but I was wrapped up in my own stuff and must not have been paying attention. "Oh geesh, Ed. I'm sorry."

His mouth said, "It's okay. It was a long time ago," but his eyes said he was still in mourning. I decided we better talk about Will some more.

"So...I'm already as good as Will?"

"He's a few years older than you. He's been fly fishin' with me for years, so he's very good, but it doesn't come as naturally to him as it does to you."

"He doesn't catch anything?"

"Oh, no. He catches some beauties here and there, but, for him, it's too much like work. He has to concentrate. Not like you. You become one with the river… with the fish."

"They are beautiful creatures. I love the challenge. The fight."

"Me, too. And, because they will win almost as often as we do, let me show you how to tie a couple of these before I head back to Montana."

I had almost forgotten he would be leaving soon.

"Come on. Let's tie a few." He began to talk me through it. First, he just showed me, and then he let me tie some with him.

"It's all about the sequencing," Ed said. "See how you layer those materials left-to-right and right-to-left on the shank of the hook. Just like this…" At first, I couldn't do it, but I stuck my tongue out Michael Jordan style and kept trying.

"Choosing the right material and how you sequence it is the key to mimicking nature's buffet for the fish, and they know. They always know."

I held up my fly for Ed to inspect. Then I studied it and held it above my head the way the fish would see it. "What do you mean, 'they know?' They know what?"

"They can tell if a pattern, color, or proportions are off even a little bit. Or if the size isn't what it's supposed to be. They won't even touch it if any of those things are off in the slightest."

I put that fly down and began tying another one. Well, at least I tried to. "You know, Ed, I've really enjoyed learning all of this." I held up the new one. It wasn't much better than the other one. Ed took it from hand and scrutinized it. "Not bad, young lady. Not bad at all. It's a solid second attempt. What I really want you to remember is: head, thorax, and abdomen. Just those three things. After that, I want you to study each phase of their development. I have a few fly-tying magazines I brought with me you can have. They have some great visuals to reference. If you can capture their stage-appropriate appearance, you will be able to start piecing the puzzle together, and then you'll really be speaking their language. Each new scheme will help blueprint the next. It's pretty cool when the fish start hammering away on your own variations. It's like beating mother nature at her own game."

After that, we spent the whole day tying and talking. When it was time to head back home, I realized I hadn't casted at all that day, but I didn't mind. Ed was leaving soon, and I wanted all the time I could get to learn from him.

Ed closed his mobile fly desk, and I scooted off the tailgate and carefully climbed up into the cab. Ed started up the truck with a bellowing roar, and I listened to George Strait singing something about his exes who live in Texas. I kept asking Ed questions about fly fishing and whether he thought I would be able to do it on my own.

"Of course! You can come out to the river every day and then tie as many as you need to replace all the ones you lose every night." We both laughed about that. I was going to miss him.

"When are you coming back, Ed?"

"I don't know, Maya. I'll probably have to come back soon if App State gets the green light for its fly fishing program. I won't know for a few months. But I'll be back, promise."

We pulled into my driveway, and I climbed out of the truck... well, I kind of fell out, but I was really graceful about it. He put out his hand. I shook it like I was a grown up.

"It's been nice meeting you, young lady. Take care." And he headed back to his truck. I stood on the porch and watched as he backed out. He hollered, "Tell your mom I said hey…" honked, and drove away. I was really going to miss him.

The next morning, I woke up to a loud rumbling. I threw on some sweatpants over my pajamas and ran to the porch to see Ed's familiar truck and my heart raced. He was back! But as I opened the door and the screen door, I saw Ed's truck leaving my street. I looked down on the porch steps, and it was like Christmas. There was a new pair of chest waders that looked like they were actually my size.

A fly rod and reel, leader, tippet, a fly box full of flies, a book with lots of pictures about tying flies, and a sealed cardboard box. There was also a note:

Build them the way you see them. Build them with your vision.
Tight Lines--Ed

Inside the cardboard box there were all sorts of materials and a vise to tie flies. Bobbins, beads, hooks… all sorts of feathers, deer hackle… you name it, and it was in the box. At the bottom of the box was an envelope. I opened the envelope and guess what was inside? My fish necklace. It had been repaired.

"Momma! Momma!" I squealed.

Momma came to the door tying her old, faded blue bathrobe. "Wha'choo doin' all that yellin' for, girl?"

"Look, Momma. Look what Ed left me.!" I held up the necklace so Momma could see it.

"Is that your necklace?"

"Yeah! Ed got it back for me just like he said he would."

"He a nice man."

"Yeah, he is nice. Look at all this stuff he left me!" I held up the fly fishing equipment one-by-one. She didn't know what it was, of course, but she acted happy because she knew I was happy.

"That's nice, honey. I'm so glad you got your Ichthys back," she said and gave me a side hug.

"Me, too!" I sighed and picked up as much as I could while mom grabbed the rest. "I'm gonna miss Ed," I said as we walked inside together.

18

June 7, Boone, 1995

Sam Myers stood up straight as her mom, Jen, fixed the collar on her powder blue Watauga High School graduation gown. Sam fidgeted with the bobby pins holding her square hat. Her reddish hair juxtaposed with her light blue gown made her stand out in the sea of graduates.

"We're gonna be late, y'all know that, right?" Annie said as she sat on the couch, flipping channels.

"Your uncle Ed is supposed to be here any second now," Jen said, but Remmey is more realistic. "We're not waiting on him. We'll go whenever you're ready."

Annie said, "I'm ready," while Sam rolled her eyes and screamed. "Shut up! I'm going to be in front of thousands of people, and I need to look good."

Annie laughed. "Good luck with that."

Jen said, "Girls, stop that."

Jen grabbed Sam's shoulders. "You look beautiful, Sam. And they'll be like four hundred other people graduating. Stop worrying, and let's go."

As they headed down the porch steps, Ed's car rolled up in the driveway. Ed rolled down the window and yelled, "Right on time. Get in! I'm driving so we can all be in the same car."

Remmey got in the front while the ladies all piled in the back. "Hi, Uncle Ed. Thanks for coming!" Sam said.

"Wouldn't miss it...you ready to get this over with?"

"You have no idea."

"Oh... I bet I do. I was your age once," Ed stated.

Remmey said, "Nice ride you got here, Eduardo. Did you actually WANT to rent a minivan for your drive up from Charlotte?"

"Sure did, Rem."

Annie guffawed. "Yeah, right, Uncle Ed. Every fifty-year-old man loves cruising in a minivan."

"I'm not fifty yet!" Ed says and then turns to Remmey. "Is she always this sarcastic?"

"Yeah, she gets that from me. She's smart as a whip!"

Ed laughed and said, "Uh-huh," skeptically.

Remmey looked at Ed and pulled a hair out of the back of his neck.

"Stop it, ass hat!"

Jen broke in, "Boys. Both of you. Stop."

"Yes, dear," they said collectively before falling into a fit of laughter.

Remmey kept talking. "You look good, bro. How was the trip? You look a little haggard."

"Remmey, don't start with me."

"Whoa! Simmer down, I'm just yanking your chain."

"Yeah, Yeah, Yeah, it was a fantastic trip if you like four-hour connector flights to Charlotte and then another two-hour drive to Boone in a Honda Odyssey. Splendid. All to see a kid graduate from high school where she shoulda been the valedictorian and ended up being the salutatorian because she got a B in PE in 9th grade. How is that possible?"

"Uncle Ed!" Sam said. "You were listening? I didn't think you were listening when I told you that."

"Just because I don't have diarrhea of the mouth like your dad doesn't mean I'm not listening," Ed said, and Remmey punched him in the arm.

Jen had had enough. "Will you guys please stop it! This day is about Sam and not about you. Stop being so selfish and think about your daughter and your niece."

This brought the car to a shamed silence. They drove on to the stadium completely stunned for several more minutes.

As they arrived, Ed broke the silence saying, "I'm proud of you, Sam. I'm a college professor and I think I finished like 100th out of 101 in my class."

Remmey took the olive branch of truce and added, "I only got into App State because I was a football player."

"I remember you riding the bench most games," Ed said, slapping him on the back of the head. Remmey was going to punch Ed in the shoulder until Jen threw a Pat Summit death stare at them, and he thought better of it.

At the celebration dinner, Jen invited Ed to the kitchen to fix the salad while she tried to talk to him without Remmey. As Ed peeled and chopped the carrots and cut the tomatoes, she gently approached the subject.

"Ed, tell me how you are doing. Really."

"Oh, I'm fine, most days."

"Uh-huh." Jen agreed.

Ed didn't say anything else. He just kept on cutting.

"Remmey and I would like to go to Montana and visit Sarah and Maggie's graves. I know it's been a long time, but we still need to pay our respects." Ed remained silent. Chop. Chop. Jen didn't press him. She stirred the green beans and kept herself busy to keep the pressure off of him.

Ed said softly, "Sorry I didn't tell you about it until after the funeral." Chop. Chop. "I didn't want y'all to fly up there. It would have made it harder." Chop. Chop. "I can't explain it, Jen. It was just easier for me to put my head down and get through it."

He raked the carrots off the cutting board into the salad bowl. Jen said, "You know, Ed, Remmey loves you...we all do. We could've helped you get through it, but now it's been, what? Like fifteen years? We'd still like to be there for you."

"I figured Remmey was mad that I quit returning his calls."

"Oh, he was mad as a hornet," Jen said. "But he misses you more."

Ed sighed, stood up straight and still with his back to her, whispered, "I'm sorry, Jen. I just... didn't... know..." his voice trailed off. "I'm sorry."

Jen said, "The Myers family is a small group, Ed. We need to take care of each other." She got the salad dressing out of the refrigerator and grabbed Ed by both shoulders and made him face her. He wouldn't look her in the eye. She lifted his chin and forced him to meet her stare.

"Personally, I think you're a selfish asshole," and softened the line with a mischievous smirk and continued. "But you're the only brother Remmey has. You've had plenty of time to yourself. Now, Remmey needs you to be the brother you should have always been."

"Sorry, Jen," he said and walked out as Jen finished prepping dinner.

Sam ate quickly so she could get to a friend's graduation party. It was just a small group of their best friends, but it would be fun... and their last time to hang out together as high school students.

After tonight, they would be adults. Kind of.

After Sam left for the party and Annie said she didn't want dessert, Jen broached what she thought was a safer subject over an even safer dessert...pie.

"It was so good to see Will last month. He's so grown up now."

Ed stopped chewing his pie and stared at Jen. Then he looked at Remmey while dropping his fork. "Will was here? Last month?"

Remmey said, "Sure. He's been here several times since you were here last." Ed tried to hide his shock. It was only for a moment, but Jen noticed.

"I'm guessin' you didn't know," she said.

Ed closed his mouth and took a breath. "No. I haven't seen him since he graduated and took off."

Jen said, "Oh. I'm sorry." Ed looked confused and hurt. Jen and Remmey looked at each other shocked.

There was a better chance of Elvis appearing at their front door to belt out a few lines of "Hound Dog," than for Ed to display any kind of emotion, but hearing this news shook him. Remmey to the rescue again.

"I'll tell you all about it, Ed. Go on and finish that big ol' piece of pie."

Ed, paralyzed for words, stared at Remmey, then at Jen, and back at Remmey. Finally, Ed conceded and finished his pie. They changed the subject to the Braves, the garden, and Remmey told Ed about some of the projects he was working on.

Once Ed finally finished his pie, he patted his stomach and let out a happy sigh. Remmey said, "Come on out to the garage, and I'll show you what I need."

They got up. Ed kissed Jen on the cheek, thanked her for the delicious meal, and followed Remmey outside. Once the screen door closed, Ed said, "So you're still using that trick we used to play on Mom, huh?"

"Yep." Remmey flipped on the light and headed to the little refrigerator that only held Miller Lite in long neck bottles. Remmey handed Ed one as they both twisted off the tops and tossed their caps into the trash can. They both took a long swig. Ed said, "Never too full for a Miller Lite."

"Jen is a tough lady, Remmey. I was just told how selfish I was for my lack of communication."

Remmey chuckled, "Yeah, it's been bothering her that you don't call us much."

"She does know that Sarah and Maggie died a long time ago, right?" Ed asked.

"Wanna know how long she made me sleep on the couch after I accidentally bought a new grill?" Remmey smirked.

Ed grinned, "Accidentally? Hard to pull that one off...And you think Jen doesn't know that you brought me out here just to avoid the dishes?"

Remmey said, "She has no clue! I'm that good."

"Forget it, Rem. She knows and since she just blasted me, she's probably backing off the gas for a bit. She's just letting you have this time just like Mom did."

Remmey shook his head as Ed continued, "So, tell me about Will bein' here."

"You didn't know?" Remmey asked as he took a sip.

"How the hell would I? A few months after graduation, he was gone. I hoped he was figuring things out. Truth is, I thought he was fine. He was working in the shop and was guiding clients a few times a week. He knew the water round Bozeman better than anyone. He scouted and found water I didn't even know existed. Seemed like he never had a bad day. Hell, Remmey, looking back, I feel like such a bad father. Between teaching and the fly shop, all I did was work. I should have been more present. I lost Sarah and Maggie, and now, I've lost Will too. That shit rips at my core."

Ed turned his back to Remmey and pretended to look for something on the shelf. Remmey could see him breathe a couple of deep breaths and take a swig of beer.

Remmey opened the hood of the truck and started messing with the belts. Mostly he was just trying to make noise, so Ed didn't feel like he was being watched. From beneath the hood, Remmey said, "Come on, Ed. You were a good father. Can't tell an eighteen-year-old much of anything. He's a smart kid. He'll be fine and everything will be okay. If he's anything like you, he's stubborn, but he'll come around. Ever thought about seeing a counselor yourself?" Remmey stayed under the hood tightening bolts that were already tight.

"Oh hell, Remmey. Come on." Remmey stuck his head around the hood and faced him. Ed made air quotes, "What's 'talking' going to do? It's been years, and they're not coming back."

"No. They aren't. But Will might if you turn into a human again. You're not the one who died. Maybe you should stop punishing yourself for being a bad father and be a good one. Will's not dead, you know. And he still needs a father."

Remmey stuck his head back under the hood. Ed finished his beer and grabbed an axe from the shed wall. He walked over to the stump of an old Elm tree and started chopping away like a man possessed. Swing after swing, he worked up a sweat. Remmey looked over to check on him once or twice, but he didn't say anything. He knew.

When he slowed down, Remmey got back under the hood. Ed came back into the garage and grabbed another beer for them both. He handed Remmey the beer. In unison, they twisted off the tops and tossed the caps into the trash can just like they did on their first ones. After Ed's breathing returned to normal and they had both taken several more gulps, Ed was ready to hear more.

Remmey shared that he and Will went fishing and worked on the truck together…about Will teaching Sam how to slow dance for prom…about Will and Annie going to the movies.

"How did he seem? Is he okay?"

"He's okay. He misses you, though."

Remmey changed the subject. "He could be a contractor, you know. He helped me out a few times when he was in town."

"That's good. I'm glad you had fun together," Ed said. "Sounds like he's doing okay."

"He seemed fine except that he's wandering. He doesn't have any direction. And, apparently, he doesn't have anyone guiding him."

"There ya go again blasting me as if I didn't already feel like shit."

"You're a grown ass man. Man up and face the music, bro."

"Between you and Jen, I am a deer in the crosshairs."

"Yeah, you had this comin'…you moved to Montana, and you figured everything out on your own right?"

"Come on, Remmey! That was a lifetime ago."

"It's taken a couple of decades for me to find the words, which I still don't have. Yep. You graduated and went to Montana and never looked back. You remember we were partners? We were football players. We got suspended from school together when Angie broke up with you and we disassembled everything in her engine." Ed laughed so hard he choked on his beer.

"Man…I haven't thought about that in forever…She was the only chick in school who had a car…a brand new candy apple red, '63 Chevy Impala, right?" They both broke out laughing at that memory.

"I still don't think we should have been suspended for that," Ed mumbled. "It's not like we tore it up. Everything was in fine working order… after a few days."

"Exactly," Remmey agreed. "The school shoulda known we wouldn't have destroyed '63 Impala no matter how mad we were."

"I'm sorry, Rem." They both stared down at their shoes. Moments like this didn't need to be compounded by eye contact. Ed continued, "Look man, I just didn't see a future here for me. I missed you like crazy, but I thought if I came back here…ever… I would never have the strength to leave again. It was the hardest thing I'd ever done. Well. Second hardest."

Remmey slapped Ed on the back. "You know, Ed, we were all so proud when you got your doctorate. That was a big deal around here."

"Yeah...I guess that was pretty surprising. I was just like a machine trying to get to the next level of my education so I could teach at the university level. I just kept grinding.

"Then I was building up the fly shop and my reputation as a guide for tourists. Lord knows you have to have a side hustle just to survive when you're a teacher. It consumed all my time, and I didn't have time to be a brother... or a husband... or even a father," Ed lamented.

"Remember what I said about you not being dead? That means, it's not too late," Remmey encouraged him.

Ed shrugged. "Maybe."

"Hey man, we're family. We all need each other. The girls love Will, and he said he'd be back soon. I promise it's not too late."

"Do you know where Will was heading?" Ed asked.

"He said something about hiking the Appalachian Trail or something crazy like that," Remmey said.

Ed chuckled, "And he is now walking two thousand miles just for fun."

"Kinda like an ol' country boy like you moving to Montana to find himself," Remmey teased.

Ed laughed again, "Maybe."

19

Boone, 1995

My sixteenth birthday fell just two days after the Watauga seniors graduated from high school. I wasn't expecting any kind of party. Momma and I just always went to a nice restaurant for dinner and then Momma bought me a gift, usually something I really needed like a new church dress or something to add to my fishing collection.

We went to Makoto's Japanese Steak House, and I was shocked to see a crew of my very best friends already waiting at the table. Melissa, Annie, and Jenny from school, Stephanie, Renee, and Robin from church. Momma patted the seat next to her urging me to sit there. Then she pointed at the open seat at the opposite end of the Hibachi grill.

"Who else is coming, Momma?" I asked.

Just then Ed rounded the corner. I lost my mind. It had been two years, and I had missed him every day. I stood up so fast my chair fell over and crashed behind me. I leapt at him and threw my arms around him. "ED!"

He said, "Well, hello there Miss Sweet Sixteen. How's my little fly fisherman?"

"I'm great now!" I shouted.

Ed leaned into Millie, "Does she have her license yet? If so, I'm gonna need a ten-minute head start at the end of dinner to get home. I don't wanna be on the road if she is drivin'."

Millie explained, "She's not a bad driver, but just to be safe, I'll give you a wink, and that'll be your cue to head out." The whole table snickered.

The meal was typically fantastic. I loved Makoto's and I got a free cake. As we were leaving, Ed hugged me and kissed my cheek and said, "Would it be okay if I stopped by tomorrow before I leave town?"

I looked at Momma and she nodded, so I said, "Sure, Ed! Do you have time to fish?"

Ed shook his head sadly, "I'm afraid not... I'll just have time for a quick visit."

"Okay! See you tomorrow!"

The next day, before his flight back to Montana, Ed came over and I showed him all the flies I had tied.

Ed whistled his approval. "They are perfect, Maya! You've done a great job mimicking nature. Those fish will be shocked when they chomp down and realize they haven't eaten an actual fly," Ed encouraged me.

I held up each fly and showed them off proudly. "Check out this Elk Hair Caddis, and the Pheasant Tails are pretty sharp, too. I even reached back and started tying some classics like the Royal Wulff. Hey, Ed, have you ever met Joan Wulff?"

"Ahhhh, the Royal Wulff. It is an oldie and a goodie, and no ma'am, unfortunately, I have not. I know she won a ton of casting titles from the mid 40's into the 60's. But more importantly, she made it cool for young women like yourself to pick up a fly rod and get after it."

I responded, "Well Ed, if it wasn't for you, I wouldn't have picked up a fly rod and gotten after it."

Ed laughed and said, "You're welcome. And it is evident you have been tying." Ed inspected another fly closely. "These are tight and seamless, young lady!" Ed held them even closer to his face, trying to find a flaw.

"Maya, you really have done a great job. If I was a trout, I'd have to take a sip or two and these beauties." Ed's encouragement always made me walk on air.

We spent a couple of hours talking about fishing, school, and my future.

"Maybe I'll apply at MSU and take some of your classes," I told him.

Ed grinned and said, "I would love that, but your mom wouldn't want you to be that far away from her."

"She'd be okay. She has lots of friends."

After Ed left that day, I started thinking about Montana State more and more. He was right, Momma definitely wouldn't want that, but I also knew that Momma would encourage me to pray about it and then follow my heart. As long as I did that, everything would be okay.

20

Boone, 1997

I was a senior in high school and hadn't changed very much. I was still an outcast, but a happy one. Even if I didn't have lots of friends, I had fishing, and I had Momma. Plus, I had the best dad in the world for twelve years.

Momma preached the fact that God created us all with unique gifts. We shouldn't try to hide them or be ashamed that we can do things others can't or that we aren't as good at some things as others are. She said that true happiness lies when we discover those gifts and use them to serve others. My gifts were fishing, being nice, and being happy. My flaws, apparently, included being a little bit messy and being way too independent.

Annie was nice, but we weren't really best friends. She was a tennis star and all she cared about was tennis. I never quite understood that, but she didn't understand why I was all about fishing either. Like Momma said, we all have different gifts. The only class we were in together was advanced English. We always did our projects together. She was an outcast, too, now that I'm thinking about it. We didn't have many tennis enthusiasts in this area. Hard to play tennis in all the snow and ice we have here… and they say clay courts are slippery.

I had gotten really good at fly-fishing. Maybe that was why I've always been so happy. I bet, instead of taking a bunch of pills, if people just spent more time fishing, they'd be okay. Whether it was the peace and quiet, the sun, the challenge of catching a wily trout, or the fresh air, probably all of them together, fishing was my gift and it made me happier than eating lunch at the popular table like so many girls wanted.

Cash and Warren had kept their distance from me. Ed must have really done a number on them. As they got older, Cash got more serious about school and became a pretty decent fella. Warren took a different route. He hardly ever came to school and eventually just dropped out. I heard he had moved to Atlanta, but I never knew if that was true. Whatever. I was just glad they left me alone.

As I was doing my thing on the river, I ripped off a cast and began punching line… tick-tock… no takes. I cast into a bunch of different pockets. Still no takes. A Bluewing Olive (a kind of mayfly) landed on my arm. As I stared at the fly for a while, I started thinking. I know I tied a few BWO's. I went through my Fly Bible examining my inventory and as luck would have it, I did. This is why the term "match the hatch" has so much importance for any fly angler. You have to constantly adapt and pay attention to your surroundings to give yourself a chance at the dance.

I tied it on, dressed it with some gel floatant to keep it high on the water, and made a couple of long casts to the fish rising in the back of an eddy. I followed the drift, mending line repeatedly due to the erratic flow of the river's surface. BAM! A trout immediately crushed it. I was late and missed him. My only thought was, "Okay... you won, friend... but you won't win again."

I re-cast close to the same spot. By now, I was a machine, and I could cast the dot on an "i." My routine was simple: locate my spot, activate the cast, build in two false casts, (maybe three for distance), toward the horizon line above my point of reference, lay it down, and throw in a mend.

My next pitch got pummeled, and my hookset was instant. "Now I got you, my friend," I told him. Sure enough... fish on! I almost lost my footing while I was stripping line to get taut. Even though this felt like the biggest fish I had ever hooked, I remembered what Ed taught me. I took a deep breath and centered myself mentally, physically, and spiritually. I was starting to get my fishing chops. I was so thankful Ed taught me this new way to fish. Some people enrich others' lives regardless of the amount of time you get to spend with them. I wished Ed were here to see this epic battle.

I stripped line and we sparred. If he took, I gave. If he relented, I took. It was a good fight, and he was stubborn. I always welcomed those tenacious engagements. Moments like these were instrumental in my learning curve. Each dance was unique, and I had to make adjustments if I wanted to lead that dance. Ed and my aquatic counsel made it very clear: no contest would ever be the same and I would need to adapt constantly.

This knowledge served me in many areas of my life: fly tying, launching line, and most importantly, navigating being a young woman of color in a space dominated by those who didn't look like me.

Bringing in this gorgeous buttery brown closer to me, I gradually finished stripping line. As I scooped him up in my net, I examined him. His colors were perfect. A design by God with the perfect combination of stealthy ferocity and a camouflage of the river's floor. I held him close to my face and looked him in the eye. I swear he winked at me.

I gently pried the hook from his mouth and thanked him for the intensity of our battle. I told him it was nice to meet him, and I held him under the water for a second before he bolted away into the dark river.

21

Boone and East Tennessee, 1997

Momma was diagnosed with breast cancer. She said they found it early. She'd have a mastectomy, and everything would be fine. I had lost Daddy in a car accident only six years earlier. I didn't want to lose Momma, too, but her prognosis was good.

I was accepted to every college where I applied including Appalachian State, North Carolina State, and even Montana State. My choices of schools revolved around Fish and Wildlife studies, Ecology, Entomology, but selfishly I knew I needed to be somewhere I could fish.

Because of Ed and his influence, MSU was a pipe dream, but I knew I needed to stay close to Momma. So, I decided to live at home and go to App State even though she told me not to. My silver-lining was that I had grown up a Mountaineer fan and was excited to stick around to begin my college career. They had added the fly fishing program that Ed helped panel five years earlier, so I knew that would be a priority when I registered for classes. Staying home with momma and going to school was a good fit. I knew she would need me close after her surgery, plus I would have the comforts of home, and I could still fish on occasion.

The day after graduation Momma threw me a nice party. Ed didn't make it down, but he sent me a nice card and a book about insects that had the coolest pictures ever. A few families and friends from the Junaluska community dropped by to wish me well. I was grateful for the graduation cards filled with cash that I would use for an upcoming fishing excursion I was planning as my graduation gift to myself.

Mr. and Mrs. Myers and Annie even stopped by on their way out of town. A few of my favorite teachers popped in as well. One was Mr. Hester. He was my visual arts teacher in elementary school and moved to Watauga High when I was a sophomore. He fly fished just like me, and we talked about it every day. Mr. Hester was big on hunting new water and if it produced, he would share his findings and we would compare notes on what worked and what didn't. He helped develop my drawing skills as well as my understanding of color theory. He taught me how to observe my surroundings with a completely different mindset. Regularly stepping back and altering my perspective meant I was giving myself a chance to try and understand things in more relatable, unique ways. He was forever preaching to the class about shifting our thought processes, that there was more than one way to see something; we just needed to consider the possibilities. That art class revolutionized the way I conceptualized and enhanced my fly patterns to this day.

A few days later, I packed up all my fishing gear: vest, Fly Bibles, waders, boots, and rods. Then, I packed some camping equipment I had acquired over the last three years and a few changes of clothes. Then I headed to the bus station. Everything I needed was on my back... at least, I hoped it was. Off I went from Boone, the only place I'd ever seen in real life, to embrace new environments and fish foreign water. It was time to put my skills to the test.

Momma cried when she put me on the Greyhound. I promised I'd be back before her surgery. She gave me a credit card and $100 in cash to go with my graduation earnings and told me to bring $50 back when I returned in a month. I hoped she was kidding.

I was sad to leave... my first time away from her and from home, but I was so excited about the adventure I had planned. I took the bus southwest through Asheville, and then down below Cashiers, just shy of Mountain Rest, South Carolina. My destination was Burrell's Ford Campground and the Chattooga River, which divides South Carolina and Georgia.

My campsite was on the Chattooga, which made it easy for me to just wake up and roll out. I tattooed that water from sunup to sundown. It was chuck full of

Brookies, Brownies, and Bows. From there I followed the river trailhead due north until it crossed the East Fork of the Chattooga and got a hold of some fantastic wild brookies. Fishing there was tedious, and if I'm honest, the fish there definitely had the upper hand more than once. It was humbling, but I learned a ton about my presentation to avoid spooking them.

My next trek took me back north just west of Erwin, Tennessee, to fish for smallies on the Nolichucky. I camped at Rivers Edge Campground and the owners, Jerry and Sadie, were very welcoming.

I walked back to Hwy 81 where I found shallows. I had purchased a pair of purple Teva sandals that improved my efforts at rock hopping to reach some slow, fat pockets. I was pretty agile but always paid attention to the water's depth and my distance to the banks. I had tied a few Clouser minnows before I left. Ed gifting me that book on fly tying was instrumental in my success. Mr. Hester's visual art instruction didn't hurt either. I sketched out quite a few patterns I thought would work based on the conditions I might face. I tied several imitations, hoping something would meet the demand. They were made with white and brown bucktail and Krystal flash which was supposed to impersonate a simple baitfish. Some were simple straightforward vanilla, but on others I alternated accents of pink and lime skirts fixed inside the tail for flare. I had no idea if they would work, but all of them did!

The last stop on my radar was Bluff City, Tennessee, which was only an hour from home but held the Holy Grail of both the South Holston River, and eight miles away, the Watauga River, which flowed right in front of my home in Boone.

As I was packing up, Sadie, the campground owner, approached me and asked where I was off to next.

"Bluff City," I said.

"Well, I'll be! I'm fixin' to do some shoppin' over there in Johnson City. You wanna ride?"

I weighed the pros and cons (like always) and then answered, "That would be great!"

Getting to the next stop and getting a line wet quickly was the most important thing. Besides, I had "Blanche" with me, (I named my revolver Blanche, the craziest *Golden Girl*) so if Sadie turned out to be some kind of psychopath, I knew I could handle myself if I had to.

I didn't have to use it, thank goodness. Sadie was very nice, and she dropped me off at Cherokee Trails Campground off Morrell Creek Road and our conversation the whole time was genuinely pleasant, yet some of her questions were cunningly vague. I inferred that she wanted me to arrive at my next destination safe and sound. I was a female, alone, eighteen, camping, and noticeably Black in a region where very few folks shared any of those cosmetic characteristics. I'm always conscious of my surroundings. Like Maya Angelou said, "*You are only free when you realize you belong no place – you belong every place...*" Sadie wasn't acting like a mother hen, she was just concerned and I appreciated her intentions, but told her I would be fine. All I could think about was landing one of those river monsters Ed raved about. As I arrived, I noticed the campground littered with waders, boots, and fly rods out drying in the East Tennessee sun. Sadie turned to me and said, "You should be fine here." I got myself settled in and plotted my route for the next day.

As night fell, two older women who were set up in the space diagonal from me asked if I would like to join them at their fire. My first instinct was to say no. But then I could hear Momma telling me to stop being a loner and go say hello.

I walked over to the ladies and introduced myself.

"Well, hey there, Maya. I'm Mae, and this is my sister, Fae."

Fae added, "Our parents were poets." They both laughed even though I was reasonably certain they had used that joke a million times. Fae continued, "What brings you here to East Tennessee?"

"I'm doing some fly fishing."

"Fly fishin'? No shit!" Mae asked.

"Mae," Fae interjected, "Stop that cussing around a child."

"She's no child. How old are you, Maya? Like twenty-five?" Mae asked.

"No, ma'am. I'm eighteen."

"Ok, well, you know I gotta hear the story of how you came to be a fly fisherman. Hush up now, Fae, and let the lady talk," Mae said.

"You shut up, Mae, you bossy ol' heifer," Fae replied.

"I wouldn't have to be so bossy if you had any damn sense," Mae said.

"The only time I didn't display good sense was when I married my second husband."

"Your first and third husbands were not great ideas, either." Then Mae turned to me and said, "Fae's been married and divorced three times, and she's only sixty. None of them were prizes when she married them, but then, just a few years after the wedding, they each had to be institutionalized."

Fae turned to me and said, "That ol' lady's lying. Don't listen to her."

"You're right. Only one was institutionalized." Mae said.

"And the last one took off quicker than a Baptist minister's wife leaving the liquor store," Fae said.

Mae rolled her eyes, and said, "Now that's pretty darn quick. She's also divorce lawyer—"

"Family attorney, thank you!" Fae interrupted.

"Family attorney," Mae said. "And she hired herself to handle all three of her divorces. She took each one to the cleaners, bless their hearts." Mae reached over and patted Fae on the leg and continued. "Needless to say, she will never have to work again."

"You know it, sister!" Fae slapped her leg as she laughed. "And, since Mae is a financial advisor, I let her handle all the money I made off those husbands, so she got rich, too. Didn't you, Mae?"

"I sure did. Thank you, sister." They exchanged smiles and made me wish I had a sister to be silly with.

Mae continued, "But listen to us still rambling on…we want to hear about you, Maya. Tell us about yourself."

I filled them in on meeting Ed and how he taught me. I shared a little bit about Daddy. Even though it had been many years since he died, I still couldn't talk about him very much. I told them about graduation and Momma's cancer.

"Don't you worry, now," Mae reassured me. "I had that same cancer, too, and I've been in remission for seven years now. That will happen for your mom, too."

A waterfall of emotion pierced my soul, and I decided I needed to hurry up and get home. I missed my Momma. "I sure hope so," I said.

They gave me a list of things we would need after her surgery, some recipes of food that Momma would be able to eat, and how to deal with the side effects that usually accompanies chemo treatments.

But after a few minutes, I was sick of talking, so I asked them about how they got to this random campground in East Tennessee. Mission Accomplished.

Fae said, "We grew up in Morrison, Colorado, just outside of Denver, and we were raised with a fly rod in our hands. Ever heard of Bear Creek? That's where we cut our teeth on fly fishing. It's a tight creek demanding precision, and we have bigger water. We grew up fishing, too, but small stream fishing is where you refine your casting technique and get your chops." What Mae was saying reminded me of how I cut my teeth on the creeks around Boone and the intimate bond I had with the New River.

I said, "Why did y'all come all the way out here to fish in East Tennessee?"

Fae said, "We heard about this Mecca of the Southeast and needed to try it out for ourselves. It also didn't hurt that my third ex-husband graciously paid for this fantastic getaway, which Mae and I desperately needed. As soon as I said, 'I don't,' and signed those divorce papers with numero tres, we were off faster than Mae's dress on prom night," and she giggled again.

Mae rolled her eyes and said, "Listen, Maya, next summer, you come out West and we'll show you how we do it out there."

"That sounds great," I said as I scribbled their phone numbers on an old napkin, and we said our goodnights. "I appreciate y'all talkin' to me. I've learned a lot," I said.

"What could you have possibly learned during the past two hours that's worthwhile?" Mae asked.

I said, "I learned I'm not alone."

I slept with Blanche tucked safely in my backpack near my head with the safety on. I slept a little but as soon as there was some light in the sky, I got ready to leave. I took my time, savoring the last few moments at the campsite. When I finally peeked out from my tent, Mae was sipping coffee around the embers of the night's fire and asked if I wanted a ride down to the river.

She dropped me off at the boat landing off Big Springs Road about three miles away from camp as the crow flies. I was fishing the South Holston River, (SoHo as they call it.) The section I was wading had multiple access points to bounce in and out of the river with ease. Because it was a tailwater, I had to be mindful of the generation schedule. I had four hours before the release would reach the section where I was fishing. In the blink of an eye, the water table would rise three feet and I had to be out, or I would be taking a ride. Based on my window of opportunity, I knew I had to be dialed in if I was to have a chance at finessing any of these dynamos.

The morning was slow, but as soon as the morning mist burned off the river, I began picking apart run after run. I was nymphing, which meant my flies needed to get down as low as possible within the water column quickly. Every drift taught me something new. The variations of the water's surface speed seemed impossible to manage until I settled in to make my own adjustments.

After laying each cast down, the current would push my fly line downstream ahead of my strike indicator, which forced me to mend constantly just to keep my flies in the face of the trout. I got pretty good at kicking that mend as soon as my flies landed; otherwise, they wouldn't give me the time of day.

Ed said if I could fish this water with some success, I could make a go of it anywhere.

Deductive reasoning would take over. It was just me... just like I always liked it. My therapists of the deep weren't going to contribute to the conversations unless I persuaded them to talk. My limited knowledge of this fishery motivated me and concerned me in the same breath. I moved through my progressions on every riffle, eddy, seam, pool, and current. I owned them that day, and for the rest of the week, that water and my aquatic analysts built me up, tore me down, and built me back up again. It was a beautiful give and take. They never stopped talking, and I never stopped listening.

After my two days of successful fishing, I saw an older white couple sitting in lawn chairs on a slope of the river. They were using spinning rods just like how I used to fish with Daddy.

That slope was the only entry point for me to move upstream away from them. My plan was to slip behind them and be on my way. When they looked at me, it was as if they had seen a ghost.

I smiled and kept walking about twenty yards past them and kept fishing. I immediately landed two nice rainbows. I let out a "Whoooo-Hooooo!" I was on fire.

Either I shouted with too much vigor, or the old man took offense that I had just landed two, and I hadn't seen him reel in anything. So naturally, he hollered at me. "Hey! Come on up 'ere, girl."

The old man waved me back over to them. Reluctantly, I trudged toward them.

I approached him with trepidation, not fear exactly, but, caution. I didn't want to be rude, so once I got within earshot, I figured that was close enough.

The old man said, "You a fly-fishin'?"

I said, "Yes, sir."

"You don't look much like a fly-fisherman."

"No," I responded. "I guess not."

"But you doin' sum-thin' we ain't doin'…yer catchin' fish."

He smiled and spit out a long stream of tobacco juice at his feet, which really grossed me out. I looked away and tried not to make a face as he continued, "Saw the big 'un ya just bagged. How long ya been fly-fishin'?"

"About eight years total, but six on the fly. It took a while, but I've gotten pretty good at it." "Wha'cha think 'bout givin' us one-a them fish ya caught?" the man asked.

"Well… uh…," I stammered. "I don't keep the fish I catch any more. I return them to the river, so we both live to fight another day."

The lady said, "Well, we ain't caught a dadgum thing all day, so we ain't got no supper." I thought of the fish I had just caught. What was I supposed to do? They were locals and weren't having the luck I was. Given how they were fishing, I doubted they'd be catching anything today.

So, in that moment, I made my decision and walked back up river just past the spot where I knew fish were holding. Resolute, and filled with regret about sacrificing one of my chameleons of the current, I halfheartedly opted to share what I caught so the couple wouldn't go without.

I caught a fourteen-inch rainbow. After netting him, I quietly thanked him for his service. I thought I was gonna self-destruct from breaking my own code of ethics.

As I walked back down river, I held out the fish. The old man laughed in my face and said, "We don't need nuthin' from you, gurl. Git on outta here and take yer fish with ya."

Suddenly, I had the devil on one shoulder telling me, "Nuhhh-uhhh! Set these red necks straight and whip their asses!" While Daddy sat like a parrot on my other shoulder repeating what he always said: "Rise above it. Where there are no logical people, there will be no logical solutions."

Still, through clinched teeth I began to unload, "Sir. Ma'am. You don't get to talk out of both sides of your mouth and think it's okay. It's not okay! It's not okay to kill a beautiful trout like this for no reason. I'm sorry I caught so many more fish than you did. I'd like to—"

I caught myself mid-sentence and shook my head in disbelief. I looked up to the sky in a silent plea for composure and wisdom. Even though I was beyond incensed, I took a deep breath and regained my cool. It was a conundrum, but Daddy won. I walked away without losing my integrity. I realized that they, as illogical people, would never learn no matter how powerful my lecture or how deep my rage. Fools are like that.

The next morning before the sky turned from light gray to soft pink, I was packing up to leave for Boone. My journey had come to an end, and it was time to head home. Mae and Fae were already up, too, and sipping their coffee. They had one more day before heading back to Denver and had to meet their fishing guide at the Food City Grocery parking lot in Elizabethton, eight miles up the road. They were fishing the Watauga River.

They offered me a lift into town so I could catch the bus home. Thank goodness. I was tired, and I had a strong yearning to get home to Momma. I told them to look me up next time they came to Boone, and they told me to do the same when I made it to Denver so we could all fish together.

"You take care and come see us!" Fae said.

Mae added, "Keep fishin', Maya! Never let that part of your life sit idle."

"Y'all too!" I thanked them again, and waved goodbye until they were out of sight.

22

Boone, 1997

After a winding ride through the beautiful Blue Ridge mountains, I was home. It was a Sunday, so I knew mom would be at church. The bus rolled into the station at about eleven a.m., and I started walking home. As I headed down the road, a family friend drove past me, stopped, and backed up.

"Hey Maya. You headin' home?"

"Yes, sir." It was Jake Cromwell. Everyone called him JC. He was about thirty, and his kids were several years younger than me, but all the Black people in Boone knew each other.

"Well, throw your stuff in the back and get in. I'm heading out past Brookshire, and I'll get ya home."

When I got in, we talked a little bit about the weather.

Then he said, "I saw all your fishing gear but no rods and reels. Where ya been?"

I said, "I decided to go try my hand at some different fishing spots in Western South Carolina and East Tennessee."

"Really? All by yourself? Why?" he asked me incredulously.

I shrugged and responded, "I don't know, really. I just graduated and wanted some time to myself. I thought it would also be a great time to see if my skill sets transferred to some different water."

"I can understand that."

"Ya can?"

"Sure! You're an adult now," JC said. "You wanna spread your wings and make it on your own."

"Maybe so. It was fun, but I started missin' Momma after a few weeks."

"Yeah, I can understand that too. And I'm guessin' yer fishin' rods are in those tubes?"

"Yes sir, it's easier to travel with them that way. I'm a fly fisherman," I said proudly.

"Fly fishing? Seriously? Isn't that for old white men?" he asked. I couldn't help but laugh.

It was a question I had been asked often, and each time it tickled me. I liked JC. "Yeah, I think lots of old white guys fly fish, but it's really fun, so who cares?

JC said, "Yeah, but isn't it a lot more work than sitting along the bank?"

Maybe it was because I knew JC or it could have been his probing, but my whole demeanor changed in a split second. It was time for a quick lesson, and I was just the person to give it. "Yeah. I think that's why I like it. My dad always told me fishing was for everyone. Think about it, fishin' don't care about your skin color, it don't care if you are black, white, red, or green… it don't care if you're rich or poor, skinny or fat. You ever tried fly fishing?"

"Can't say I have," he said.

"See? There you go! The key is exposure and experience and that is what drums up interest."

I continued "the speech" all in one breath. "My dad taught me knowledge is power. Lack of exposure, lack of education, and lack of experience breeds ignorance. People assume all kinds of crap they don't know. That's ignorance at its finest. If you want to learn something, you have pour yourself into it. We don't want something until we really want it, right? Then it becomes a question of: What am I willing to sacrifice to get that thing?

"The self-imposed stigma of fly fishing is that there is no one to blame as to why darker-skinned folks don't do it more. Ask yourself this: is it someone else's responsibility to make you or me become wildly passionate about something? No! That's on the person asking the question. Or how about this? Let's say you're poor as dirt, and you see some guys playing baseball. You think it's cool, and you wanna play. You wanna experience it…to learn the proper techniques on how to catch, swing a bat, or throw a ball, but you don't have a glove, or a bat, or money. Do you walk away and miss out on the exposure and experience to have some fun learning some new skills?"

"I think—" he tried to answer, but I was on a roll and kept right on.

"Or do you borrow a glove and bat until you can save up enough money to buy them so you can continue to work on your game whenever the opportunity arises?"

"Uh, I would—"

"Or do you simply make excuses for the reason why you can't or won't do something? Look, no one told me I shouldn't or couldn't fly fish. It's the fault of the individual on the outside looking in, thinking he can't occupy a certain space because of status or gender or other dumb shit. Pardon my language. If you want something, go get it. Don't be the onlooker and say, 'I can't,' because that's just weak. The majority of the people on this planet who fly fish don't look like me, talk like me or whatever, and, for now, I'm good with that. Stereotypes only exist in spaces where we create them. Why? Because people don't know what they don't know, and they aren't willing to investigate. People only want to know about things they are interested in, and where does that come from?" I rolled out my hand out, indicating that it was time for him to respond.

He looked scared to get it wrong. But he said, "Uh… experiences?"

"Yes. Thank you. Experience. And exposure. If more people would just take the time to experience fly fishin', then more people would be fly fishermen."

I finally took a breath, and we could hear the tires biting chunks of road. Finally, JC got the courage to say, "I was just makin' small talk. I wasn't judgin' you for fly fishing. Got a little chip on your shoulder?"

I felt a little bad about unloading on him. "Sorry," I said, "I've gotten a lot of funny looks, and some mean talk just because I love the sport."

JC said boldly, "I think you should fly fish all you want."

I couldn't help but laugh about that. I had converted one in just a two-minute speech. "I will. And thank you for the ride."

"You're welcome. Tell your Mom I said hi." I nodded, got my stuff out of the back of his truck, and started walking toward my porch.

"Hey, Maya!" He called after me. "If you get a chance to talk to my kids about being your own person, I'd like for you to do that. The world is bigger than Boone, North Carolina. Seems like you learned that. I want them to learn it, too."

"Yes, sir. I'll be happy to."

Just like Daddy said…change the world one person at a time…at least until I get a bigger stage.

23

Boone, 1997

Momma had her surgery and they said it was "successful," but they wanted to do chemotherapy anyway. I told her it would be okay, and I'd be right there. She always told me she didn't want me wasting my life on her, but I think she would have been disappointed if I hadn't. I knew I didn't have a choice. Not really. So, I stayed and helped Momma through the terrible treatments.

Momma got sick from the chemo. We got her a pretty, nice wig that matched her real hair fairly well. One of the good things about her getting sick was that she had to teach me how to cook. She never was one to share the kitchen, but now, she had no choice. She had a lot more patience with me now. Of course, she didn't eat much. I bet she lost thirty pounds. But she ate when she felt like it, and I tried to make sure it was good. I remembered what Mae told me about what she felt like eating and what she didn't.

Although she decided to retire from the cafeteria, she kept going to church every Wednesday and Sunday like it was a job. She would sing along with the choir and pray with the preacher. The really amazing thing was, she never prayed for God to heal her. Never. She prayed for strength and peace. She prayed for God's will to be done. And she prayed for me. She said praying for health was a waste of time. She quoted John 16:33, "In this world, you WILL have trouble. But fear not, for I have overcome the world." She said her health was a temporary trouble. So, even when she had sores on her mouth and hadn't eaten in three days, she still prayed for the lost.

Then there was school. I really liked Appalachian State and I liked my classes. It was a whole new world. The students at App State were nice. It's funny how the things that you got made fun of in high school just didn't matter in college.

Like our looks. In high school, I knew girls who spent over an hour getting ready for school. They curled their hair, put on makeup, and dressed like they were going clubbing. If you didn't do all that, the other girls would make fun of you. But in college, that all changed.

There is an expression used by locals in Boone explaining the weather conditions: "Wait ten minutes!" That idiom is eagerly adopted by all rookie "off-the-mountain" residents starting in the month of November. In Boone, the ingredients for a solid weather forecast consisted of certainty mixed in with a pinch of erratic maybes and a dash of brevity. All it took was one seventy-degree swing to a bitter forty-five with some driving rain and a few gusts of thirty mile an hour winds to learn.

But before the first storm, the girls got all prettied-up and headed to their classes with their umbrellas. They walked down through the football stadium parking lot, past the duck pond, through the tunnel under River Street, and by the time they climbed up the next hill, WOOSH! A huge gust of wind hit them and blew their umbrellas inside out. If their umbrellas made it all the way up to the library or cafeteria, WOOSH! Another gust would hit them. If they had to go all the way to Sanford Hall, bless their hearts, they would see twenty inside-out umbrellas along the way.

The upperclassmen would say you could spot the freshmen because they tried to look cute…at least in the morning before the wind got 'em. All those curls you put in your hair that morning were gone before you even sat down in your first class of the day. By the end of the semester, no one did anything to get ready before class. Everyone went to class in their sweatsuits and down jackets.

I had gotten several scholarships, and I also worked in the cafeteria, so Momma didn't have to pay anything for me to attend. That was good since her treatments were expensive.

Around Christmas time, my report card came in, and I made all A's. Momma was proud of me. Then, we went back to the doctor for her six-month checkup. She was feeling well now and was working again part-time in the cafeteria.

I was scared when we went to the doctor. We were holding hands when he came in. He was a white man, about fifty, with kind eyes. He needed to shave, and his breath smelled of coffee, but as long as he took good care of Momma, I didn't care.

"Hello Millie, hi Maya." We said hello but mostly, we were holding our breath. "I won't make you wait to hear the news any longer. Your margins are clear. I'm going to declare you as cancer free, for now. You are in remission."

Momma let out a deep sigh and said aloud, "Thank you, God." I said, "What do you mean, for now?"

"Well, cancer has a tendency to come back. Especially breast cancer. BUT, we will keep a close eye on everything, and if it does come back, we'll be ready to treat it quickly."

We hugged each other, thanked the doctor, and practically ran to the car. We rarely went out to eat, but since we were in the city, and we were so happy, we did. We went to Makoto's Japanese Steakhouse. It was delicious.

We both needed a fun night out. Between work and studying, I wasn't fishing much because Momma needed me, and I needed to make good grades. Momma reminisced about old times with her parents and with Daddy. That meal out was one of my favorite moments in my life. One I would remember forever.

24

Boone, 1999

Momma still had clear margins the spring of my sophomore year at App State. She was doing well and was thinking she may even go back to working in the cafeteria full time. I was thinking of other things. I went to visit my advisor during his office hours to get someone else's perspective.

I knocked softly on the door which was already opened, and stuck my head inside. "Dr. Simmons, do you have a second?" He seemed young compared to my other professors, but he may have just looked young. He looked like John Denver. He was small and had sandy blonde hair and brown eyes. I'm not sure he had to shave very often. If he had busted out some "Rocky Mountain High," in class, no one would have been surprised.

"Sure. Come on in. Are you Jones?"

"Yes, sir. You're my advisor. I was in your biology class."

"So were about 120 other kids. You know I don't really start 'advising' you until you're a junior."

"I know, but I just wondered if I could get your perspective on something."

"Okay. Shoot."

"Well, Dr. Simmons, I was thinking I may transfer."

"I'm sorry to hear that, Miss Jones. Do you not like it here?"

"Oh, no. It's great. I love it. But I'm from here. I was thinking I may want to go explore new things, but I don't know if that's a good enough reason."

He laughed at me. "Is that the only reason you want to transfer?"

"No, sir." I said. "There's this school that has a Fish and Wildlife Management major and I think that's what I want to do."

He didn't laugh now. He peered over the top of his glasses and studied me. He was trying to figure out if I was being serious. After what seemed like five minutes, he said, "You want to study fish?"

"I do! I love fish. Better yet Ichthyology, and I love to fly fish. I met a man some years back and he taught at Montana State University. He was here to panel the fly fishing program we have now. And now, I just...I think I need to get out of Boone and experience something different."

All he said was "Huh." Then he said, "Well, well, well... Montana State?"

"Yes sir, Montana State, in Bozeman." I said proudly.

"That's a really long way from here. Are you sure you don't wanna stick around in North Carolina? Ya know I think NC State or Virginia Tech has what you're looking for."

"I'm pretty sure I wanna get away from home and see what's happening out West."

"Oh, yeah. So why come to me? I think you need to be talking to your parents."

"Well, I want to know about transferring my credits and stuff."

"We're both state schools, so all your credits will likely transfer. What kind of grades are you making?"

"All A's."

"Well, since you're still in the Gen Ed programs, you'll be fine. And that's a good major right now as we are becoming more environmentally conscious. If you are passionate about it, go for it!"

"Would you write me a recommendation?"

"Sure, I will." I reached in my bookbag and pulled out a file with my information already printed to use as a reference.

"Okay. I'll write it and give it to my TA, and he'll give it to you next class."

"That would be great. Thank you!"

"We hate losing great students like yourself... And don't forget, out-of-state tuition will be more expensive than in-state."

"Yes, sir. I've checked into it."

We both stood, and he shook my hand.

"I never would have guessed you were a fishing enthusiast."

I laughed a little as I headed out the door. "Yeah, I get that a lot." Now, I just had one more person to convince. Momma.

After supper, we were rocking on the porch, drinking our coffee. "Now that you're better, I think I'm ready to go chase my dreams."

"You're not dropping out of college to become the first Black, female professional fisherman, unless you think you're good enough to do that! Then go for it!" She slapped my hand.

"That's not what I dream about...much..." I smirked, "but it does have to do with fish." I took a deep breath.

"Remember Dr. Ed Myers?"

"Yes. What about him?"

"I want to transfer to Montana State and major in Fish and Wildlife Conservation." Now, I held my breath. She hung her head down and sighed. I waited for what seemed like forever, but she still sat there quietly staring at her coffee. When I couldn't stand it anymore, I continued, "I wanna go learn about fish, their habitats, what they eat, when they eat, the environment, maybe even teach people to fish like Daddy and Ed taught me. I want to see more than what's here in Boone."

Momma finally said slowly, "You got your father in you. He was happiest when he was fishin'."

"That's a good thing, Momma. You said we had our gifts and passion, and we had to find out God's purpose for our lives, right?" She agreed. "Well, this is my purpose. I'm gonna learn all about fish and fishing, and then I'm going to teach people to love it like I do."

Momma sighed, "Your Daddy always said, the world would be a better place if we were all fishermen."

"I think he was right, Momma. And I want to be part of that movement." I reached out and took her hand from her coffee mug and held it tight in both of mine. "Momma, I found out that with my grades and the recommendations I have received, I got some great scholarship money. It will cover everything for me, except housing, but I found a nice little place where I can stay that's really cheap."

"Is it safe, baby?" Momma asked.

"Of course! It's a small garage apartment in a residential neighborhood. The landlords are a very nice couple. It's not far from great fishing!"

"Oh Lord, help me. Your daddy always told me that you could talk to them fish." She grabbed both sides of my face and pulled me close to her. "Oh sweetie...just promise you'll come back and visit your mother every now and then."

"I promise, Momma. I will." I hugged her.

In July of 1999, I was watching a *Golden Girls* re-run with Momma when I heard something that sounded like Ed's old truck rumbling up the driveway. I headed to the door to see Mr. and Mrs. Myers walking up beside the house. I called Momma and told her who it was, and she got up and came to the porch, too.

I opened the door right after Remmey rang the doorbell. "Hey, Mr. and Mrs. Myers!"

"Hi, Maya," Remmey said, and Mrs. Myers smiled at me and leaned in and hugged Momma. "How are you, Millie? Are you well?" Jen asked.

"Yes, I am!" Momma said. "Thank you for asking. What brings y'all on by? Come on in now and have some pie."

"No thanks, Millie," Jen said. "We just wanted to drop something off for Maya."

"Really? What's that?" I asked expectantly.

Remmey extended his hand and instinctively, I extended mine. We shook hands, but in his hand was something metal. He put it in my hand. I opened my hand and looked down. It was a set of car keys. I was confused. "What's this?"

"It's car keys." Remmey said and looked at Momma and half-whispered, "I thought you said she was smart..." They all chuckled, and I rolled my eyes.

Mrs. Myers came to my rescue. "It's keys to the truck."

"We heard you were moving to Montana, and we want you to come home without paying $400 for a plane ticket."

I just stared at him with my mouth agape. Momma took her finger and put it on my chin and closed my mouth, and said, "Close your mouth, sweetie, or you'll be swallowing flies like your fish do."

Remmey laughed. Jen patted Momma on her shoulder. I just stood there. Remmey broke my trance by saying, "I know it's a truck, but you said you liked it, right?"

"I love it! But it's Ed's. I can't take his truck."

Remmey cleared his throat, "Correction, it WAS Ed's old truck and I acquired it a long time ago."

I uttered, "But what about Sam and Annie?"

Remmey chuckled, "Let me stop you right there. The girls won't go within ten feet of this truck, much less be seen in it. Personally, I think it's a classic and it runs like a dream. It's their loss. Besides, Ed would want you to have it."

"I don't know what to say, Mr. Myers."

Momma put her arm around my shoulder. "Say thank you," she said.

I said, "Thank you!" and I hugged them both. Then, I hugged Momma, too.

"Besides," Remmey continued, "I don't need this thing taking up space in my driveway anymore. It's time to put it to good use, and what better way than to get you to Bozeman?"

"Thank you so much!" I answered and squelched my urge to jump up and down.

"You're welcome. But remember, you gotta come back at least now and then," Remmey said. "Does your brother know I'm heading that way?" I asked.

"No ma'am. No one has said a word," he answered. I smiled and turned to Momma with tears in my eyes.

I packed that old truck to the brim. I was waving to Momma and crying as I headed to Montana to start the next chapter of my life. I was scared, but excited. Momma didn't cry. At least not right then. I never forgot that image of her waving goodbye to me that hot summer morning. I had no idea how much I would miss her. But she knew I had a new chapter to start and new worlds to conquer. I was twenty and the world was mine.

25

Westward Expansion, 1999

I took my sweet time driving to Montana. I wanted to enjoy every aspect of my journey... see all the wonders of this great nation of mine. I didn't have to be there any time, and I didn't tell Ed I was coming at all. I wanted to surprise him and see if he even still remembered me. I had his old truck, and I wanted him to see how well Remmey and I had taken care of it!

I traveled west over the Appalachian Mountains and headed to the Rockies. As I was orienting myself to the nuances of the radio cassette player, I hit eject and a cassette popped out. *Duran Duran.*

I popped the cassette back in hoping it wouldn't be too bad. I had heard a couple of their songs, and they sounded all right. I figured it would just be me and the radio for the next few days. I let the play list loop over and over. One song in particular resonated with me, "Ordinary World." The chorus: "But I won't cry for yesterday, there's an ordinary world somehow I have to find. And as I try to make my way to the ordinary world, I will learn to survive." After the second chorus, I sang along with them as I kept driving.

When I got close to Denver, I called Mae and Fae to see if they wanted to get a line wet. They both lost their minds when they heard my voice. Two years removed from our introduction in East Tennessee, I would get to fish with them in their territory and learn from two experts. Mae insisted I stay in her guest room until it was time for me to move on. We met up with Fae and fished Bear Creek, just outside of Morrison. Both women grew up on that creek and knew what to do and when to do it, so I followed their lead. The creek was snug but full of brownies, and it warmly reminded me of home.

I stopped to tie on a new fly and looked at both women cutting loops with their line as tight as paperclips. I was in awe. They were in their sixties, successful, independent, silly, and extraordinarily talented fly fishermen. I was so fortunate to have met them and then it dawned on me: they had to have been two of the group of women who did this in the fifties which meant I was literally hanging out with predecessors of the sport. They had to of been at least within a decade of the legend herself, Joan Salvato Wulff. I let my mind wander, and, in a breath, found it deeply fulfilling how our paths had orbited, how I was now on their home turf, catching fish under the blue sky at the doorstep of the Rockies, which were enormous, endless, and majestic.

"Fae," Mae said, "Wouldn't it be great to be twenty again?"

Fae sighed and reminisced, "Ahhhh, I remember when I was twenty, good times."

Mae whipped in, "I know they were good times. You were like Santa Claus at Christmas. You got around!"

They both busted out laughing. "Easy now Maefly. What I was investigating did not constitute 'ho' status. I was simply exploring my options and only swam in a few pools just to check the temperature."

Mae cackled, "A few pools? You ran through little college boys like you did ice cream. You had a new flavor every week."

"You're such a heifer," Fae replied. "Everyone knows you were jealous." She turned to me and added, "I was quite a dish back then."

Mae doted on me the whole time. "Maya, we bought tickets a while back for a concert here in Morrison tomorrow evening. One of our friends that was going canceled on us. We were thinking you would enjoy it with us. Are you good with that?" I had never been to a real concert and said, "Absolutely! Sounds like fun." Mae added, "Excellent. We both have appointments in the morning, but you can fish and then, we'll go to dinner before the concert. You'll just need to be back and ready by four.

I gave them an emphatic "DONE."

"Great," Mae said. "I love it when a plan comes together."

The next day, I headed back to try a few more sections of Bear Creek out Hwy 74 toward Kittredge.

I bounced in and was having another great day. The brownies were riddled with perfect white spots centered with black and red bullseyes. Their torsos were such a deep golden yellow it would make a canary jealous.

I hooked up. "Calm down, buddy," I said. "I'm gonna let you go. Ease up now." The hurricane slowed and unwillingly surrendered. Checkmate. I stripped him in close so I could net him, and as I turned back upstream, I saw a man wading through the shallow current coming toward me. He was carrying a fly rod, so I wasn't on red alert. Most fishermen are friendly, but you never know, especially when you look like me, so I did a self-check on how I would reach for Blanche. As he got closer, I realized he looked like a stereotypical college professor. He was thin, with short hair, sporting a goatee and wire rimmed glasses.

The man congenially said, "Looks like you have a nice one on!"

I didn't make eye contact because I was hooked up. Who is this guy creeping up on me? But I'm nothing if not polite, so I answered, "Yes, sir. This is a nice fish," and smiled without looking at him.

"May I ask you what the bite was?"

"Grey Body, Parachute Adam, size eighteen." As I stripped this gorgeous brown in, I pinched my fly line, so I stayed tight to the fish and switched hands with my rod while still playing the fish. I reached into my chest pack, pulled out my Fly Bible, and handed it to him. I smiled but still didn't look at him as my eyes were on my catch.

The man said, "You're incredibly agile. That's some fine dexterity right there."

"Thank you. Grey Adams are on the top two rows, far right. I also have Black Tricos in there as well if you wanna give one of them a test drive, too."

"Tricos?"

"Third row down, middle, size eighteen or twenty. It's just a really tiny mayfly, and they're hatching in ridiculous numbers right about now."

He took my fly box. "Oh my, what a prolific dry fly assortment. These are exquisite." He waited until I netted and released my little beauty.

"Great game, my friend." I said to the brown.

The stranger said, "Well done, you. You're an excellent angler. Do you always talk to them like they're an opponent?"

"I do. It's a game we play"

I think he had a British accent, but I wasn't sure, so I asked, "Where are you from?"

"Across the pond—England," he answered congenially.

"Yeah," I said. "I figured you weren't from around here."

"No, I'm not. Are you from around here?"

"No, sir. I'm from North Carolina."

"Yeah, I figured you weren't from around here!" he said, trying to imitate my Southern accent. We both laughed. I was going to do a British accent, but I decided I should probably practice first.

"Do you do much fly fishing in England?"

"We do have some solid fly fishing... I have to say though, I have fished all over the world, but I've never seen anyone with your skill sets."

"I get that a lot."

"Well, I love it. You have an exceptional grasp of your craft. I like it when people find their space and blaze their own trails."

"I'm trying to. My name is Maya, by the way."

"I'm Eric." He clasped my hand gently and smiled a disarming smile. I smiled back.

"What do you do for a living, Maya?"

"I'm a college student at Appal— well actually I just transferred to Montana State University. How 'bout you?"

"Well, mostly I travel around, playing the guitar and singing."

"That's awesome!"

He smiled again, adjusted his glasses, and handed me my Fly Bible. "Nice to meet you, Maya, and I am humbled by your generosity with the flies. Listen... You keep changing the world. I love visionaries like you."

"Nice to meet you, Eric. And good luck with your music!"

He chuckled again and waved and headed to the riverbank.

As he climbed up the bank, I hoped he was good at playing the guitar and singing because he definitely wasn't catching any fish... at least not today.

That evening, Mae took me to Red Rocks Amphitheatre for a show just outside of Morrison. The view in the venue was breathtaking. The contrast of the blue sky against the fire orange, pink, and lavender haze was silhouetted by mammoth rock faces on each side of the stage.

As the sun slowly disappeared, it seemed like I could see forever. The layering of tapered peaks faded into what I thought was probably Wyoming. We were center stage, five rows back. I had no idea who we were about to see perform. We were so busy catching up, I never got around to asking.

The guy came out to perform and I immediately recognized him. "Holy Shit," I yelled. "That's the dude I met on the river this morning!" I grabbed Mae's arm and repeated, "That's the guy I met this morning on Bear Creek!"

Mae looked astonished. "Whaaaat?"

"Yeah, that's him. He introduced himself as Eric. Who is he?"

"Maya, seriously? That's Eric Clapton. The 'Tears in Heaven' guy."

I had heard the song before, but I didn't remember ever knowing what the singer looked like and I didn't remember an English accent in that song. I was flabbergasted. Halfway through his first set, he thanked the great people of Denver for their hospitality and then proceeded to dedicate the next song to a girl he met that morning while fly fishing Bear Creek.

He said to the entire amphitheater, "Ladies and gentlemen, my next song is dedicated to a very charismatic young woman I met this morning while I was fly fishing right here in Morrison. She was generous, and though I wasn't having the success she was, she gave me a couple of her flies while simultaneously landing a gorgeous, brown trout. It was a sight to behold. She was kind and took the time to help me when she didn't have to.

"We shared some pleasantries, and she shook my hand and wished me well. I was awestruck at her acumen and the brilliance of her casts. She told me she was going to change the world, and I believed her. What a delightful young soul! It gives me hope for change in the future in a sport that has saved my life. There is no doubt in my mind she will go on to be a light in our universe. I thought it was fitting this song go out to her. Maya, wherever you are, this is for you. Continue to blaze new paths."

He launched into his song, "Change the World."

The three of us just stood there dumbfounded for a minute. Could that have really just happened? I just stood there in shock, trying to make my brain believe something that was illogical.

Fae regained her senses first and shouted, "MAYA??? Eric! This girl is Maya!"

Mae screamed to all the people around us while pointing at me, "Hey everyone! This is Maya! This is the girl he's singing about!"

Folks were giving me high-fives and patting me on the back while singing with Eric Clapton at the top of their lungs. It was magical. I started crying, and time stood still. I saw a new future for me and what brought me to this point, my craft, fly fishing. How could something so small and irrelevant to the rest of the world make such an impact on the human condition?

Until now, I had been sheltered, guarded, and even rescued from aspects of life's true tests. The obstacles I previously braved wouldn't even compare to what was in store for me. I had been protected by the safe bubble of my family, youth, and innocence. My own ignorance was about to be fully exposed and examined. The unforgiving fortunes that followed would shake me to my core and test my resolve by defying stereotypes, bigotry, nature, weather, and even death, with calculated instincts and immeasurable perseverance.

But that night, when time stood still, I bathed in the beauty of that moment...and I became Eric Clapton's biggest fan.

PART TWO

26

BOZEMAN, MT

Ed loved teaching. He had that gift all great teachers possess: he could read people. He could talk to a student once and know exactly how to mine for the diamond that lay within each student. (Sometimes really deep within!) Michelangelo said: "Every block of stone has a statue inside it and it is the task of the sculptor to discover it." Ed had a classification for his students just like the order insects have. He had them divided into two sub classes. Some students were Pterygota (with wings) and ready to fly. The others were Apterygota (wingless). They might still be successful but would have to crawl to get there.

Regardless, Ed believed that every student had a "David" waiting to be revealed. He made it his mission to inspire all his students through the simple joy of learning. In other words, he did his best to make it fun. For example, he would have themed group projects forcing students to act out characteristics certain insects displayed, and have them build costumes portraying certain insects and their life cycles. He knew most of his students didn't share his fervor, but still he played on the interests and talents they might possess outside of his content nonetheless. Some would go on to be zookeepers, forensic scientists, and microbiologists. Some would not, and that was all right, too.

He taught Insect Identification at eight o'clock on Tuesdays and Thursdays because he loved getting those future entomologists out of bed as early as possible.

Then, he had Insect Physiology immediately after, so his teaching-day would be done by one o'clock, which included his office hours. Whenever he met with his Plant and Insect Interaction Master's Seminar students, it was usually out on the Gallatin River west of campus on Mill Street down highway 191, near Gallatin Gateway. When he was fishing, he was the most clear-headed, so that's when he felt he could help them the most.

When he wasn't at school, he was at the fly shop. Myers Fly Shop was a favorite with locals and tourists alike, but the big money came from tourism. Tourists were the ones who rented the boats, hired guides, and loaded up on equipment and gear. The shop sold all kinds of fishing gear, but Ed's greatest profits came through his guide service…especially once he had a few loyal pilots who were responsible, personable, and, of course, great fishermen who knew the water and bite and adjusted to the conditions in heartbeat. During their vacations, tourists would come back day after day, requesting the same guide. When they left, they would tell a friend, and that friend would call and book a trip. When Ed was guiding a single, half-day, or full day float, he would ask the client if they minded if his son tagged along. Usually they didn't mind, and Will would serve as Ed's first mate. This was Ed's way of introducing Will to studying water tendencies, blueprinting holes where fish were holding, and adapting to the clients' needs. Will enjoyed being on the water, but he mostly enjoyed spending time with his dad.

Will became quite proficient at manipulating the rivers around Bozeman: Three Forks and Livingston. Some of Ed's best big fish days came when he let Will be his guide. Will got on-the-job training as a guide as he directed and coached Ed through runs, pockets, and pools. Around mid-April, he would bolt to the shop right after school to check on the stability of the runoff and how the fish were feeding. Around the end of May, when the full runoff started subsiding, he was already dialed in. Not only was Will very knowledgeable about what flies to fish and where, he possessed an extraordinary imagination, too. He was personable with a sarcastic, dry humor, which allowed his client to relax and fish. He was lean and fit, with dirty blonde hair and alert, gray blue eyes: Marlboro Man handsome. He always seemed to be in a good mood and told funny stories...mostly stories he made up about the romantic "Old West" and fishing cowboys, which is where the expression, "Shooting fish in a barrel" came from— according to Will at least. He was clothed in sunshine no matter how cloudy the day.

Ed allowed him to step in and guide when the shop seniority was booked up. Will embraced every opportunity and fed off the challenge to work his way into becoming a full-fledged guide. He was an unknown entity until word started spreading. Although he was young, tourists and locals alike quickly learned how gifted he was at his craft. Even when the day started off badly, he adapted to conditions and increased the odds of getting fish to the boat by shepherding his clients' every move. He always delivered instruction with a positive energy. He could carry on a conversation, manage the boat, watch their flies or strike indicator, and blast out, "SET! SET! SET!" if there was the slightest quiver, sip or take in their lines.

Will never shied away from talking to the like-minded to learn as much as he possibly could. Of course, he never took credit for his customer's successes and would send any form of flattery right back to his patrons.

Guides from all over started to take notice, especially as they slowed to detour around his boat. Most of the time gazing in admiration of his clients fly rod tips, bellied, and bouncing from fish. It got to the point they would want to pick his brain every chance they got, even going as far as calling the shop and asking to speak with him directly. If he was available, he would always take the call and tell them whatever he could. He was a great listener and like a sponge, soaked in everything he could not only from Ed, but from every other guide, too. If he could pass on some of his knowledge, he wouldn't hesitate, especially when someone benefited from his advice.

In Montana, Mother Nature's fickle blend of blizzards and hints of warm afternoons made fishing a gamble in March and April. The fluctuation of the temperature would demand every guide and angler exercise caution. In late spring, the fish bathed in the deeper runs when the water was stable. As soon as those rising temperature swings steadied, the thaw would force guides and enthusiasts alike, if they weren't already ahead of the curve, from freestone rivers to tailwaters like the Missouri and lower Madison.

Freestone Rivers are best described as running water without some structure (like a dam) regulating its water flow rates. When runoff intensifies in the late spring, that water will violently inflate and disturb a riverbed causing rocks to skate and tumble hence the name "freestone." Tailwaters are different because they contain dams or weirs that provide consistent fishing production even in the toughest of weather conditions.

Will and Ed spent hours on end picking apart the Missouri, Jefferson, Madison, Ruby, Gallatin, and Yellowstone. They talked about strategy, and about all of the "what ifs" and then, they attacked those "what ifs" as experiments. Will knew how to handle himself on each section of every river, which made him a sought-after commodity.

When the other kids in class were trying to color inside the lines, Will was adding characters and creatures to his pictures. The other kids' pictures were uniform. The tree was brown, the grass was green, the sky was blue, and the sun was shining. In Will's pictures, what was unrecognizable got chalked up to his delving into Abstract Expressionism. Willem DeKooning would have been so proud.

There was always something exciting going on, and it usually wasn't within the lines. The river was purple, flowed uphill, and spilled off the page...or was it a mountain? The rainbow trout was deep blue with lime green streaks and a flame coming out the back because of how fast they would dart upriver...or was it a car? No one really knew except for Will. Ed couldn't make heads or tails of it but would happily tack it to the refrigerator in homage. Not only was Will's ability to fish extreme, but his visual creativity also left no doubt about the uninhibited concepts he portrayed.

Unlike Will, Ed only had a few close friends, but all things being equal, Ed would rather spend his time with a Bead Head Pheasant Tail Nymph. If he were stranded on a deserted island, he would be fine. He was friendly and kind, but most of the time, he stayed in his own head. He was easy to love, but not easy to live with. He didn't always remember to come home for supper. Will would be waiting for his dad while Ed was busy labelling items in the store. He never looked at the time, and, suddenly, it was dark. He'd come home to find Will had already eaten a sandwich and was playing his video games. Again. Ed would go to Will's room to make amends. He'd sit on Will's bed and watch him play Nintendo video games, but the only sounds emanating from the room were "hut, hut, hut, hut" from Techmo Bowl (Will was always the 49ers) and the "da-ding, da-ding, da-ding," from Super Mario Brothers. Even when Ed did think of something to say, Will would only grunt answers and never took his eyes off the tiny screen. After a few minutes, Ed would give up and trudge back into the den to watch *Jeopardy*.

It wasn't always so dark around the Myers house, though. Ed was generally a good father, and Will was a nice young man. Besides fishing, their other shared interest was baseball. While Will's man was Chipper Jones, Ed said no one could ever replace Hank Aaron. Ed was enthralled by how Aaron made everything seem so easy. In 1966, when Aaron played for the Atlanta Braves, Ed would comb through the FM radio dial just to pick up Milo Hamilton's animated broadcasts of the games. Ed's enthusiasm for the Braves was adopted by Will and in the summers, they would watch Braves games whenever they could.

One late April evening, he was coaching Will's 10-and-under baseball team. Ed got tired of the outfielders running to where the ball was instead of where it would be when they finally caught up with it. When Ed had seen enough, he bounced from the dugout with his hand raised signaling to the umpire that he would like a time out. Both coaches and the umpire agreed to a quick two-minute physics lesson. Or is it geometry? Anyway, he gathered the players from both teams just behind second base. He drew two outfielders in the dirt. Then he drew the ball going between them.

"You guys see how, if the outfielders run straight to the ball, the ball rolls past them?" He drew the straight lines in the dirt. The boys all agreed. He continued, "The ball is moving much faster than we can run. But see what happens if you run to where the ball will be when you get there?" Ed drew the outfielders running diagonally backwards before moving towards the ball at an angle. Both teams confidently proclaimed that they could do that.

As Ed and Mr. Harrison, (the opposing coach,) headed back to home plate before they went to their separate dugouts, Ed said, "Do you ever remember a coach having to actually explain that to you?"

"Hell, no, Ed. We had common sense back then. And just so you know, you interrupted the crossword puzzle I was working on."

Ed chuckled. "Funny, I was thinking about fishing. I don't know what we're teaching kids these days."

"Aren't you a teacher?"

"Sure am…don't tell anyone."

Will was good at baseball, but when Ed consistently started letting Will choose the water they fished, sections they would float, bugs they used, basically guiding Ed, all Will ever wanted to do was be on the river. Fly fishing became Will's sport. Will would be up and dressed and ready before Ed, and as soon as he smelled that coffee brewing, he'd quietly glide out of his bedroom. After bulldozing through four eggs and some toast, his job was to grab the fishing gear from the garage and have it ready to load up when Ed got their lunches packed. No words were uttered as both had a collective system in place for a stealthy exit. Ed would grab some granola bars, peanut butter crackers, a couple of cokes, a big jug of water, and his coffee thermos, and meet Will by the truck.

It wasn't until the boat was launched that Will or Ed broke the silence discussing what flies they would use to open the day. Ed loved taking Will to fish because Ed loved fishing. But it was not just fishing. It was really the only time Ed and Will would talked. It was the only time

Ed was comfortable enough to open up...not about himself, of course. But he would talk about the fish, navigating the river, the boats, the flies, and baseball. All these things added up to life lessons.

Having Ed as a dad meant Will would hear all the scientific jargon on an audio loop every single outing. Ed would unload about complete and incomplete metamorphosis and the stages within each. Will's eyes would glaze over as he heard, "Egg, larva, pupa... nymphing comes from 'nymph,' which are insects that live underwater for most of their lives...blah, blah, blah,...it's the juvenile or larval stage...blah, blah... ditches its protective shell, rises through the water column, blah, blah, blah, blah..." It was the same lecture over-and-over. Maybe Ed had forgotten he already told Will all this stuff, or maybe it was just Ed falling easily into his teacher-mode.

Eventually, after a few years, all the entomological talk actually began to sink in for Will. He had to have listened at some point and just put it away in the back of his brain somewhere. Will had to know what the insects looked like in each stage before they could fly and post flight. All of that came from Ed, and Will was oblivious. Will was only concerned about three things: pattern, size, and color. If he could match it and improve upon it, he would use it, tweak it, refine the tweak, and crush them all day long. He wasn't into all the science mumbo jumbo.

Ed's best worker was an older lady from church named Betty. Her husband had passed a few years back, and she was just pushing sixty. There was something about her demeanor, so jolly and bright, that almost made you forget her life had been turned upside down when husband died. She and her late husband never had children. Ed had always taken a liking to her and Will called her Aunt Betty. She was that person who, even though she jumped into your personal space without asking your permission by enveloping you in a big bear hug, she was her authentic self and people respected that.

She wasn't funny in the sense that she told funny jokes. She was just funny because when you said something funny, she would laugh boisterously and everyone in the shop would laugh, too, because her laugh was so infectious. She was honest and always willing to work whatever shifts Ed scheduled her for, which was pretty much any time Ed had class or wanted to take Will fishing. So mostly, Betty worked in the mornings and Ed would take over in the afternoons. Some mornings, however, Ed would open the shop for the early birds, and Betty would come in about 7:30…just in time for Ed to make it to class. During the spring and summer, the shop was open from dawn 'til dusk. Betty wouldn't ever work on Sundays because, as Betty would say, it was "Breaking the 4th commandment and I'm not about to do that just for some fishermen." So, Ed would usually get one of his older, advanced students to mind the shop, and he would swing by to check on them.

Although Betty wouldn't work on Sundays, many anglers would be on the river because the river was a church all on its own. Most anglers considered fly fishing a religion; therefore, Ed did what he did what was necessary to meet his customers' spiritual demands. Ed felt he was doing the Lord's work and didn't think God would hold it against him.

As Will matured within the sport, his success fueled a greater need for exploration. That visceral search expedited his learning curve and thrust it into high gear. It became a cycle of adaptation vs. nature. Even at an early age, Will could understand why those who pursued fly fishing's ever-evolving rewards got sucked in. Once it was in your blood, you could never escape the flood.

When Will got his guiding license, it didn't hurt he immediately got his outfitters endorsement from none other than Myers Fly Shop. It wasn't long before Will got to the point where he was constantly booked, and fishing with Ed became more and more infrequent. Will enjoyed meeting new people and got excited about creating iconic memories on the water. He was making great money, and he was wise beyond his years when it came to saving it. He had a truck he had paid off, and the rest he banked for gas, insurance, and various other needs. Being shrewd with his finances gave him the freedom to take a day off when he needed a break and to fish for himself when he saw fit.

Will loved the rivers and though he was young, he was considered one of the best guides in Bozeman and the surrounding area. He could just sense where the fish would be. He read the currents, read the clouds, knew the weather, knew the bugs, knew the bite, every boulder, every eddy, every run and every pocket. He just knew what to expect and how to manipulate all of it to his advantage. He slowly became a master at his craft and could thread a needle with his boat by mindfully finding the least invasive way through churning rapids or the treacherous rocky contours many of the rivers in Montana possess. He was in so much demand as a guide, the subject of college was seldom ever broached. And if it was, Will would change the subject. He was doing what he loved, and he was very good at it. Plus, that left him with time to travel in the winter and satisfy his wanderlust.

Healthy communication and interaction in general between Ed and Will dwindled until it was non-existent.

Everything was all business. They rarely saw one another unless it was after seven in the evening and even then, it was to heat up leftovers, then to tie flies for the next day, or off to bed from exhaustion. Some people think that introverts don't talk very much. That's not a true definition of an introvert. That's a quiet person. Introverts have a whole other life in their heads. They are refreshed and energized by their time alone. Ed was an extreme introvert who had to process things quietly by himself. Will wasn't. While Ed was re-charged in his solitude, Will was floundering in his. Will needed to talk. Ed's lack of communication drove Will to retreat to a space Ed couldn't reach, literally or figuratively.

After Sarah and Maggie died, Ed became even more reclusive and withdrawn than he had been before. Ed dealt with his best friend's death the only way he could. He buried it deep down and tried not to think about it. In his mind, Sarah was visiting her sister in Laurel, MT, and would be back any day now. If Maggie crossed his mind, the *what if's* would torture him and bring him to his knees. He and Will rarely talked about Sarah and Maggie. Ed just didn't have the words.

"Daddy, why don't I have a mommy?" Will would ask innocently.

Ed would robotically reply, "You have a mommy, son. She's in heaven so she can be with you and watch over you all the time." But that kind of stock-answer, in addition to the other blanket lines he had memorized, didn't help Will. Eventually, Will just gave up and accepted the fact that he would never know anything about his mom or sister and or what it would be like to have a mom.

Ed never dated again. It was too painful to try. And, truth be told, he was a better hermit than he was a husband.

Will had little memory of his mom at all, so it's hard to say he missed her. All he had were puzzling concepts of what he was missing, especially when watching his friends interact with their moms. Observing those exchanges invoked interrogations Ed struggled to resolve. As Will matured, he began to anticipate Ed's routine responses, so any time those emotions bubbled up, he would cram them in a box, close the lid and move on. Over time, those boxes piled up, so much they created walls to a maze he didn't know how to navigate. He was lost. Broken conversations and Ed's despondency forced and fashioned long corridors with right and left turns, but unfortunately, always led to dead ends. The labyrinth seemed insoluble.

Will couldn't make sense as to why their relationship had gone so stale. It was a slow build, and any appreciation they had for one another was dissolving. Will felt as though he was being neglected and taken for granted. He couldn't make Ed engage and it was expected that Will guide. It was both of their names behind fly shop and its reputation, but it was Will who was in the boat and the chatter that his floats created. This is where a strong level of resentment began to take root.

It got to the point Will could no longer stand the numbing silence. He couldn't stay in Bozeman and guide any longer. He needed a change. Staying would mean leaving Myers Fly Shop and getting a new outfitter to endorse him, which was a long process. He also simply didn't want the headache of competing with his dad. So, one day, he packed up all his belongings, cleaned out his bank account, and headed out of town before Ed got home. He left a tiny sticky note with words cramped against each other, like they were afraid of slipping off the paper:

Dad, I've got to go away for a little while. I don't know how to help ease your pain and you sure aren't trying to help me. I hope you find peace soon. Please don't call the police or send out the cavalry to hunt me down. I'll drop you a note to let you know that I'm safe. I have plenty of money and supplies. I just need time to figure some things out. I'll be okay.
Love, Will.

As soon as Ed read the letter, he ran to Will's room. Flinging the door open, Ed discovered it was empty. Ed ignored Will's request not to try to find him and feverishly combed through every number he had to locate him. He called Will's friends, every guide, every fly shop, and everyone Ed could think of.

The last person he called was Betty at the shop. She informed Ed that Will's boat was locked up and still on the trailer, and she had not seen Will all morning. Ed knew after a few days people would miss Will and the rumor mill would start, and Ed would have to come up with an explanation. He kept telling himself that Will would come home, and they would talk through their issues. This time, he would try really hard to communicate with his son.

Slumped over with his arms crossed and face down, Ed sat in anguish at the kitchen table. He broke down sobbing. His own pain, inability to relate, and Will's leaving compounded and exposed new regrets about his lack of skill as a father. He had finally realized what he had done and what he left undone. He knew he would have to deal with the carnage of his own doing.

Eventually, Will ended up in Boone, NC, to visit Uncle Remmey and Aunt Jen. He had already asked Remmey's family not to let Ed know he was there. Since Remmey told Will that Ed rarely talked to them, it wouldn't be a big deal.

When Will was ready, he would call Ed and they would talk, but time apart was necessary. He also made it clear to Remmey he needed the healthiness of the chaos Sam and Annie provided to feel like he was part of a family. Remmey reinforced the fact that Will was welcome anytime.

Even years after Sarah and Maggie died, Ed was still living like one of T.S. Eliot's "The Hollow Men." He went through the motions of life teaching his classes, running his shop, and fishing. It wasn't the same, but he still found splashes of joy here and there. Betty prayed for Ed, but she never offered some of those Bible verses that people say when they're trying to make you feel better—one of those scriptures that sounds good to the ears but does little to heal what's really hurting—your soul. Betty, having suffered loss herself, knew that, so she just always told Ed to hang in there, or you're not alone. Ed was grateful that Betty understood him.

His friends would ask, "How ya doing, Ed" and he was always reply, "Not bad."

Eventually, his friends gave up trying to get him to talk about his feelings. Like Will, they resigned themselves to the fact that they knew Ed wasn't okay, but they also knew there wasn't much they could do about it.

Some people needed to talk about it to get over grief. Some people did better with grieving inwardly. Those people only got over their pain when they were alone. Ed would only talk about his pain to God, to the trees, insects, fish...but mostly, he'd go to his secret spot and talk to Sarah and Maggie directly. He could tell them how much he missed them and dream about what their lives would have been if they were all four there as a complete family.

27

Bozeman, July, 1999

When I arrived in Bozeman, a new energy came over me. I felt like I was truly on my own and ready to start a new chapter. I rented a small, detached one-bedroom apartment close to campus in a residential neighborhood. I was there to study and finish my degree, and I didn't need to be bothered by parties or constant chaos on campus. I needed quiet, and that's exactly what this was.

The owners' names were Lucy and Dwight Harcum and were in their mid-sixties. They were a lovely couple and were excited to have me as a tenant. They met me outside, handed me the keys, and gave me the lay of the land. They even insisted on my eating dinner with them that first night to get better acquainted.

I had an adrenaline rush going, so I immediately started unpacking. About thirty minutes into my unloading phase, I walked out to the truck and saw a girl staring at it. Just staring. She had on shorts, a t-shirt, and running shoes. I didn't know if she was amazed my old truck still ran, or disappointed that a neighbor with a beat-up truck had moved in.

I cautiously walked up behind her and cleared my throat. I think I surprised her because she jumped a bit when I said, 'Hello, can I help you?'

She spun around, and I was blown away by her striking looks. She had brown skin that was a little lighter than mine and beautiful long, black hair. Her eyes held an intensity that belied her easy-going demeanor. She put her hand out to shake mine.

She said, "I'm Judith Whitehorse."

"Maya Jones. Nice to meet you."

"Welcome Maya! What are you doing here in Bozeman?"

"I'm here at MSU studying Ecology."

"Me too!" she replied. There was a collective pause and evaluative tilt of the head from both of us. I could tell she was sizing me up. It was okay. I was trying to read her mind too. "Can I give you a hand with your stuff?"

"No thanks, Judith. I got it."

"Ok. So what is your field in Ecology?"

"I walk on the wild side—with the fish" I smirked.

She said, "I'm studying Organismal Ecology."

"Which one?" I asked.

"Organismal Ecology."

"Better watch out how you pronounce that!" I giggled.

"Right?" She laughed, too.

She ended up helping me carry a few boxes as our conversation continued. "Where are you from?"

"Maybe I'm from around here…"

"Not with that accent, you're not."

"Are you making fun of my accent?" I asked and pretended to be offended.

"Uh—no," she stammered. "Of course not."

I smiled and tried to put her at ease. "I'm just kidding. It's a pretty one though, right? My accent and all?" I said, really laying on the Southern.

"Yes. It is. Very nice." She giggled then and put another big box down on my den floor.

"I'm from Boone, North Carolina."

"Boone?" Judith said. "I've heard of Boone!"

"You have?" I asked incredulously.

"I believe so. It's on the Appa-lay-shun mountain chain."

"Okay, hang on. Let me help you with that pronunciation. It's LATCH-UN, the word is App-a-LATCH-un. Appalachian like the latch on a door. Spread the word!" I said with a wink.

"Oh, I'm sorry," Judith said, covering her mouth and then repeating it out loud. "Appa-latch-un. Got it!," and there was that laugh again.

"It's okay, guaranteed I'm gonna mispronounce some designations around here soon enough. And I expect to be corrected."

"I'll have you sounding like a local soon," Judith assured me as she gently placed a box marked "FRAGILE KITCHEN" on the kitchen counter. "Maya, it was so nice to meet you, but I'm on a run and need to go. I live about three blocks that way," and pointed to the east.

I walked her out the door and back to my truck to get another load. Not many more boxes left, thank goodness. As we got to the truck, she stopped and said, "My grandfather had a truck just like this. When I was little, he let me ride in the back with the wind blowing through my hair as we drove through different parts of the reservation. I loved it. Sometimes I would hop up front and he would pretend to let me drive. It brings back a lot of great memories. I'm originally from Hardin, about two hours east of here."

Maya chimed in, "I was coming up through Casper on 25 and then picked up 90 and stopped in Hardin to get gas. It was like that dream where you're running to get to something, and it continuously teases you with the game of chase. The closer I thought I was getting to Bozeman and the Rockies, the farther they retreated. I could see them in the distance, jutting above the horizon line with the jaggedness of ripped paper. I was amazed. It was August, and there was snow on those mountains! I had only seen that in books."

Judith laughed and said, "I know, right? It seems like you'll never get there, and then you blink and you crash right into the side of the mountain!"

"It was exactly like that!" I replied. "I saw a few signs marking the reservation. So, do you belong to the Crow Tribe?"

"Yes! And let me reciprocate from earlier. We are the Apsaalooke Tribe. The name refers to descendants of the Large Beaked Bird. Thus, the name, Crow, too. Either title works though. Ap-sah-loo-gah," she sounded it out phonetically just like I had earlier.

I tried to sound it out, "Ab-shaa-low-gul." I butchered it. "I'm so sorry, but I'm going to have to work on that for a bit until I get that right. Thanks again for your help, Judith. It was nice meeting you."

"You, too, Maya. Good luck with your unpacking." She started to jog away, but turned abruptly and said, "Hey, you ought to come to dinner sometime. I live with a couple other master's students, and we're all pretty decent cooks. Maybe tomorrow night?"

For emphasis, I laid on another layer of my Southern dialect just to be silly, "I reckon I'd like that more than a pig loves the mud," with a wink.

She laughed again and jogged away. I liked her immediately. I finished carrying in my boxes and began the task of unpacking so I could get settled in.

I took a moment when I was all unpacked and sat on the bed, relishing the moment. It was all happening for me. Slowly of course, but Momma always said baby steps were better than no steps. I couldn't believe it. I was in school in Montana, in my own place, already making friends. Life was good, and it was about to get better.

28

Bozeman, July, 1999

It had been several years since Ed saw Will. Ed was okay, but mostly still going from one task to the next, checking things off his "to do list." It was noonish and he was tagging a new shipment of fishing line when he heard the bell on the door jingle. Will walked in. At the opposite end of the store, Ed shouted, "Be with you in a sec…"

He walked to the front to greet his customer and saw Will standing there. Will's skin was more tanned than Ed remembered. Will seemed taller somehow and also had a full beard and long hair.

They stood and stared at each other. Ed was speechless for a second. Finally, Will said, "Should I leave?"

"Good God, no, son," and Ed took three quick strides to Will and bear-hugged him. Now it was Will's turn to be speechless. When Ed finally let him go, he stood with his hands on Will's broad shoulders. "Jesus Christ, it's so good to see you, man. In fact, you kinda look like Jesus Christ."

Embarrassed, Will stood there, rubbing the back of his neck, avoiding eye contact with Ed. "You look great! You're a grown MAN, with a beard no less," Ed clarified.

"I'm twenty-four, not completely grown."

"Twenty-four? Holy shit! You ARE a grown man." Ed backed away and soaked in his son's presence.

Finally, Ed said, "I'm glad you're here. And you're alive. And you're HERE! What's it been? I can't count." Ed scratches his head while doing the math, "Geeeez man, five years away from you is too long, son. Where have you been, more importantly, how have you been?"

"I know, Dad. I have done a lot of soul searching over the last few years. To put it bluntly, high school was brutal. We just fought too much and when weren't fighting we were like two ships in the night. I needed a dad, and you needed a guide. It wasn't working. Everything seemed like it was a business transaction, and I felt like you just ignored me and us. Truth is, Dad, I really wanted to know all about mom and the little sister I never met, but you kept them to yourself. It was hard…" his voice trailed off before he sighed and continued, "so, like you did when you turned eighteen, I made a choice to leave. To be honest, I thought I would never come home, but being gone has given me a better perspective on where I want to go."

"Where is that, Will?" Ed asked hopefully.

"Home. With you. Where I belong." Will answered, and Ed started smiling. "What?" Will asked.

"Nothing son, you just…you sound like a man. Not that little boy I used to know."

"Shut up, Dad," Will said and nudged his shoulder with his fist.

Ed said, "I thought you enjoyed being here working in the shop working with me."

"It was fun until it wasn't. You know how much I loved being on the river. But I just needed to get away and not worry about you." He paused and sighed. "Or fight with you."

"Yeah. You're right. I did the same thing when I was eighteen. I fought with my dad all the time. So I guess it runs in the family."

"Except," Will added, "Unlike you, I came back home. Uncle Remmey said he misses you, by the way."

"Yeah, I heard."

Will was surprised. "You went back to Boone?"

"Yeah. For a few weeks." Ed walked over to the cooler. "Do you want a beer? Wait...do you drink beer?"

"Yep. Wha'cha got?"

"Mark Brenner, one of my best guides and graduate students, brews beer. Come to find out he has a whole system set up in one of his bathrooms. Anyway, he samples beer from all over and gave me a couple of jugs from a fella in Hamilton. I wasn't too sure about dark brown beer, but it's not bad."

Will laughed. "Yeah. I'll take a run at it."

Ed poured him a glass. They leaned on the counter in silence and sipped their beer. "What do you think, son?"

"I like Miller Lite better, but it's pretty good."

Again, silence.

Finally, Ed got up the courage to talk. "You know, son, I've had some time to think, too. I'm sorry I wasn't there for you. It's my fault we just lost so many years."

"Dad, you don't—"

"No, no... I've been thinking about this speech for years. What I would say, and how I would say it. Let me get through it." Will smiled and looked at the floor. He knew how hard this was for his dad, so he didn't want to make him even more self-conscious. The regret was palpable as it hung in the air like the aftermath of a bad joke. Neither of them knew what to do other than stare intensely at their beers.

Ed took a deep breath and continued. "I'm sorry I wasn't strong enough to help you get to know your mom. I was a shitty father. I still am, I guess. I was so consumed with my own heartbreak, I just couldn't even think of you." His voice began to crack, and he couldn't go on. Will walked to the wall where their GUIDE CALENDAR hung. He checked the names and the number of bookings they had.

"So it looks like the guide business is still pretty good, huh, dad?" Ed welcomed the subject change.

Ed wearily rubbed his face with his eyes glossed with tears, took a breath, and cleared his throat. "Yep." Thank God that conversation was over. He continued, "Well, we still have folks asking when you're back."

Will blurted out, "Bullshit! Ain't no way after all this time people are still asking for me."

"I'm not gonna lie," Ed said, "I got pretty sick of hearing about what a great guide you were. But yeah, Mark and a couple of new ones do fairly well. Of course, they're not nearly as good as you were."

Ed weighed his next words carefully. He had only gotten through about a fifth of the apology speech he had written in his mind. "You know, Will, we sure could use your help around here, I mean, if you're thinking about staying for a little while." Will kept staring at the calendar.

Ed stumbled along, "I could use your help around the house too. You were always a better cook than me."

Will turned and studied his father. Ed had not aged well since Will had been gone.

He was still a good-looking man, but his eyes were no longer stars. "Dad, I'm planning on staying."

Ed sighed deeply and choked back tears. He walked around behind the counter and pretended he was getting something from behind the register. Will walked to the front to be closer to him, physically and emotionally.

"But I don't know how long I can stay." Ed just grunted, while Will continued looking him in the eye. "I don't want to argue or fight any more. Because all of that shit leads to…"

"Silence," Ed filled in the blank. "One of the guys at work says silence is an unwelcome intruder that lingers like cigarette smoke in a 1970's teacher's lounge."

Will laughed. "Nice analogy."

They both took deep gulps of beer. Ed said, "I will try not to fuss at you and treat you like an adult, but I can't make any promises. You were a kid for a long time."

Will looked at his dad with both love and pity. He knew he'd been gone too long. He put his hand on his dad's shoulder. "That's good enough for me, Dad." Ed finally looked Will in the eye. They smiled at each other.

Ed quickly went back to tagging items, and Will followed to help. "So what brings you back up to Bozeman?"

"You, Dad!" Will clapped him on his back. Ed shot a price tag on Will's forehead. "I always liked it when you did that." Will peeled off the $4.99 sticker and read it aloud. "I always felt so valuable," and they chuckled again.

Ed said, "Tell me more about when you were in the Catskills."

Will said, "Okay, well, I tied flies in the evenings, waited tables, crashed on couches, rented spare bedrooms from late fall to early spring and camped when the weather was favorable. I met a few 'fishheads' bumming around touching all the water they could find."

Ed yowled and slapped his knee. "Fishheads? That's funny! I haven't heard that one before."

"Yeah, the fishheads were a bunch of guys from Penn State. All they talked and thought about was catchin' fish. We all fit together, and they gave me an open invite to crash with them if I ever wanted to fish their water in Pennsylvania. I eventually made my way to State College. Dad, when I tell you there was good water everywhere, I mean it. I had Penns Creek to the right, Clearfield Creek to my left, the Little Juanita River below me and the Black Moshannon Creek and West Branch of the Susquehanna River above me. I scouted all the time and learned a thing or two about catching muskie and smallies on the "Sus" using some of the same streamer patterns we use here for big browns. It was cool adding that method of fly fishing to my game. I had the time of my life.

"Most recently, I was in East Tennessee. I moved there in '96 and got on with a Fly Shop and guided there for a couple of years. Being in Bluff City made it easy for me to hop over the hill to see Uncle Remmey and Aunt Jen if I got lonely and needed to be around family. If you can fish that water and be successful consistently, you can pretty much go anywhere that's fresh water and whip some ass. It's incredibly fruitful but also very unforgiving if you're not in it to win it."

It had been many years since Ed ever heard anyone talk that much to him (except Betty). He was glad to listen. Ed said, "What water was it?" and winked at Will. They both grinned and said together: "The Watauga and The South Holston!"

They both laughed out loud. Ed said, "Yeah, that's some really good water."

"I missed you though, Dad, but it was nice. Especially hangin' out with Uncle Remmey and getting to know the girls and Jen. Did you know Sam is in her senior year at App now?"

Ed answered, "I do, I was at her high school graduation in '95. Wait, shouldn't she be done?"

"She is on the extended plan and Uncle Remmey is over it," Will exclaimed. "He told her to get her shit together and get done! Annie is a junior at NC State and from what I hear, a very good tennis player. Uncle Remmey was a football player at App, right?"

Ed stated, "Yeah, he was and was damn good. Tight End with soft hands and quick as a cat, plus the son-of-gun could block. That's probably why he got so much playing time as a sophomore. I do remember that if the football was thrown anywhere near him, he would catch it."

"Look Dad, I knew it was time to come home and mend fences, and, if you'll have me back, I'll help Betty cover the shop, sweep, tie flies, and can guide for you if you want."

Again, they just stared at each other. Finally, Ed smiled.

"Once you get your credentials and guide license updated, I believe I have spot where I can endorse another guide. Hey, you hungry? Mark doesn't have a trip today, and he'll be here any second now to watch the shop. Let's get outta here and get some lunch."

"Where we gonna go?" Will asked.

"Doesn't matter. We'll get a quick bite and—"

"Go fishin'!" they shouted together. Ed's eyes were stars again.

The next few weeks went by quickly, and Ed found some joy in life again. Ed and Will settled into an easy routine as Will got reacquainted with his old haunts. It was like he never left. Both men didn't really talk much about the past. Instead, they let the water cleanse them of their yesterdays as both kept rowing and moving forward.

As Will went through his checklist of refamiliarizing himself with his old winding wet friends, he carefully checked for any significant changes of water flow from his memory. He reminisced about all the hot spots he took his customers and the occasional local who just wanted to pick Will's brain and hear his colorful stories. He hadn't lost his touch.

One early afternoon Ed and Will were wading the Upper Ruby River just below Twin Bridges. Ed was tying on a Tan Caddis with a size 20 Black Zebra Midge dropper and heard an enormous crash. He looked to his right and saw Will crouched down as if he was kneeling like a catcher in baseball, keeping his left leg out wide for stability. By lowering his body, he was changing the trajectory of the fight to lessen his chances of the juggernaut making a run Will couldn't control. Because of the grassy, root-riddled undercut banks of the Ruby, after a solid hookset, if you were not in a position to stabilize the set, you might get hung up and that's an easy way to get broken off. The best fishermen always make constant and quick adjustments.

Ed stood watching in awe. Will had coaxed the mule out into the water column and was rolling the rod angle right, then left and right, just shy of ninety degrees toward the sky. He kept the butt of the rod locked just above his forearm as the tip curled like a flamingo's neck and vibrated fiercely while he tried to tame the tornado, and coax him off the bank. Ed beamed as he watched Will do his thing. After a short fight, Will reached down to net the fish and held it up for his dad to see. Ed gave his approval, and Will felt like he had never been gone.

While Will displayed his trophy, Ed pointed to a shallow run twenty yards downstream on the same cut of the river. He took his index finger and tapped his lips as if to say, "Hush up young buck, watch the old man do it." Will stopped to watch attentively. Ed drew two false casts and delicately laid it down a few feet above the site line of his torpedo. Three... two... one. Right on cue. Ed raised on him, and it was mayhem.

Will moved downstream and netted the rocket for Ed. Ed asked, "Will, you like apples?"

Will knew what was coming and shook his head. "Come on, son, haaa baat dem apples."

"Nice one, Dad! The fish of course, not your idiom."

"Thanks, son! Just a heads up. That's how that shit is done!"

"Good, solid man-talk there, Dad. Fantastic." And thus, it went. They were no longer ghosts occupying the same space. They were friends who talked about fishing with good natured ribbing to boot. Life was pretty good again, albeit still a little dull, however, it was getting ready to get much more interesting.

29

Bozeman, August, 1999

I stood there pondering how Ed might respond to me showing up unannounced. Hesitating with each lift of my fist and searching for the right words for our re-introduction, I started to knock three times. Other than his surprise appearance at my sixteenth birthday dinner, I hadn't heard from Ed in a while. I had missed him. I wondered how he was. I wanted more time to plan the interaction, but finally, I just knocked. I didn't know what I was going to say, but I had to see him, and maybe that would be enough.

Will sat at the kitchen table tying flies. Ed stood at the stove frying up some Spam. The doorbell rang and interrupted their silence. They both looked at each other. No one had been to their house in years unless it was a UPS driver. They shrugged at each other, and Will got up and headed to the door.

When he answered the door, he was astonished to see a young, pecan-brown, 20-something woman standing at the door. Will was thunderstruck and just stood there and stared with his mouth slightly opened.

I had been caught off guard, thinking I would only be visiting Ed. Will had gotten his hair cut short again and was clean-shaven. He was a nice-looking man with his sandy-blonde hair, blue eyes, about six feet tall with broad, strong shoulders. Finally, I blurted out, "Hi! I'm looking for Dr. Ed Myers. Would you happen to know him?"

This seemed to snap Will out of whatever spell I had accidentally cast on him. He said, "Maybe. Are you a disgruntled college student?"

"No."

Will opened the door all the way and said, "Then, yes. I know him," he flashed a luminescent smile. "He's here. Come on in."

As I stepped through the threshold of the door, he moved aside to hold the door open for me. I don't care what other people say, but I liked that. Chivalry will always be appreciated in my world. He extended his hand and said, "I'm Ed's son, Will." As I moved through the door, I shook his hand. I answered, "I'm Maya." He released my hand, closed the door behind me, and led me through the house to the kitchen.

He called, "Dad, you have a guest. And from her accent, I'd say she was from the mountains of North Carolina."

Ed turned from his frying pan and looked at me. "What the... holy smokes, I cannot believe my eyes. Come here, girl, and let me hug you. How are you doin'? Wha'cha you doin' here?"

Ed enveloped me in a big, safe hug. Seven seconds ago, I was nervous about coming to see Ed and definitely nervous about moving up here. Would I get along with these Westerners? Would they accept me? Is this REALLY what I want to do? But with that one hug, my questions disappeared. "Hi, Dr. Myers."

Ed countered, "What's up with that? You called me Ed when you were twelve. You can still call me Ed. What are you doing here?"

"It's great to see you, Ed. I transferred to Montana State. I'm following my passion."

"Uh-huh. And what would your passion be?" Ed asked.

We stared at each other with Cheshire Cat grins on our faces. Ed knew what my answer would be, and we said it at the same time: "Fishing!"

Will said, "I'm pretty sure they have fishing in North Carolina."

I said, "I'm going to finish my degree here in Bozeman... Fish and Wildlife Ecology. I'm gonna know everything there is to know about fish. I might even take a class in entomology." Ed just stared at me a minute. Then he looked at Will. "Oh, Will...I'm sorry. Maya is from Boone. I met her when she was just a kid. I was working through a grant on an advisory board to qualify the addition of a new Fly-Fishing curriculum App State wanted to offer and our paths happened to cross."

"That's where I transferred from. I stayed home to take care of my mom while she was fighting cancer. She's in remission now, and we decided it was time for me to go."

Will said, "So you're here to study...and to fish?"

"That's what I'm hoping!"

"I'm sorry about your mom," Ed said. "Remmey told me about that. She's okay now, though, right?"

"Yes, sir. Her margins are clear! It was a tough couple of years, but I think she's okay, at least for now. The doctors said it could come back at any time, so we're still cautious, but, for now, at least, she's got a good report and doing well."

"It's hard to lose your mom," Will said.

I felt sorry for him losing his mom. I knew Ed was a widower, and Ed knew my dad died, but we never mentioned it. I answered, "Yeah. It would be really tough. My dad died when I was little, I still think about him every day."

"I never knew my mom or my sister. I was only three when they passed."

Ed had a daughter. I had forgotten that.

We just stood there and thought about our troubles. That was enough of that. I broke the silence, "So, here I am to study fish and learn more about fly fishing. Your dad taught me one summer and I haven't stopped. Matter of fact, I've gotten pretty good, Ed. You should see me tie a fly!"

Will looked skeptical, so I said, "What? You don't think I can tie a fly?"

Ed answered before Will could. "Watch out, son. She can read minds...of people and fish. Here, sit down and have some dinner with us." I sat down in the chair Ed offered me, and I stared at my plate. I missed Momma already, but especially when I saw what Ed served. I had never even heard of Spam. But, I smiled and sat down. We began passing around the salad, which looked better than the Spam.

Ed said, "How was your trip up?"

"It was long, but it was fun." I cut off some Spam and ate a bite. It wasn't as bad as I thought it was going to be. With my mouth full, I busted out, "Oh, Ed. Guess what? Remmey gave me your old truck!"

Ed was shocked. "You drove that 1962 Ford all the way up here? Rem was tinkering with it when I was down for Sam's graduation…Speaking of which, Will, why weren't you at Sam's graduation?"

"The Hex Hatch in Michigan with the 'fishheads.' Too many trout to count! We got really lucky and hit just right. Ridiculous brownies!

I couldn't believe I knew what he was talking about, so I blurted out, "Are y'all talking about the mayfly, Hexagenia Limbata, and what the hell are 'fishheads'?"

"Yes, that's the one!" Will answered, "and it's a nickname I gave some fellas I met traipsing around in the Catskills a while back. They're a group of LUNATIC fly anglers with only one thing on their brain: catchin' fish! So, I coined the name."

"I like it!" I said. "Were you on the Au Sable? I heard it is epic," I said.

"It was! What's your excuse, Dad, for not attending Annie and Maya's graduation?"

"Someone had to watch the shop." Ed said with his mouth full.

Will laughed and said, "Good answer. The old stand-by. Everything revolves around the shop."

Ed shrugged and navigated to safer conversation. "Okay, go back. You say you came all the way up here in my truck... that hunk of junk?"

"It's NOT a hunk of junk. Mr. Myers fixed it up, and it's sweet! He even taught me some tricks to take care of it." I took another bite of my salad. This meal was growing on me. Maybe I was hungrier than I thought. "It guzzles gas, of course, but it's fine." Ed uttered a grunt of disbelief.

Will said, "Hey now, Uncle Remmey showed me a thing or two, and we fixed it up together. It was fun, and I learned a lot. Haven't been to a mechanic in years."

I said, "Well, you did a great job. It runs like a champ most of the time." The boys smiled and kept chowing down on their Spam and salad, so I continued.

"When I graduated from high school, I took a month, traveled, and did some fishing and camping. My last stop prior to heading home was in East Tennessee 'cause it was fairly close to home."

Will piped in, "Seriously? I just spent the last few years guiding there." I studied Will wondering if we shared other similarities besides our love for fishing and being outrageously attractive, obviously.

Ed looked up from his plate and asked, "What were they hitting?"

The question brought me out of my head. I said, "I was dry dropping 18 Sulfurs and an 18 Split Case. It took me a few minutes to get dialed in though. I changed up three times before I got it right."

Ed asked, "No Pheasant Tails or Prince Nymphs?"

"Of course! I fished my version of some Pheasant Tails," I answered.

"That's my girl!" he said proudly.

"I was struggling at first and sat down to re-tie at the edge of the river, and accidentally leaned into a bush and got lit up in a swarm of Sulfur Duns drying out their wings. They were in my hair, my eyes, my nose, up my sleeves. It was crazy. I set 'em into a frenzy of flight and didn't have the match, so I went back to the truck to tie the right size, with a stronger yellow coat and more pronounced hackle for wings. Couple of casts and then BOOM! Like clockwork, they were on it."

Will laughed and almost did a spit-take. "You keep a tying system with you? I feel like I'm in a Twilight Zone in Dad's mind. You guys don't exactly look like fishing buddies, but it seems you're more than that…you share the same brain!"

"It's a long story," Ed said, but I interrupted and proceeded to tell Will a ten-minute story about the mean boys, Ed teaching me to fly-fish, and how much I loved it. Will was either a phenomenal actor, or he really was listening to me.

We were finishing up our dinner, and I started loading my dishes in the dishwasher. "These are dirty, right?"

After the clean-up was done, Will handed me and Ed mugs of coffee. "Want to sit on the porch for a minute?" It wasn't really a question. We followed him out and sat on the porch in Ed's rocking chairs. I knew I was sitting in what should have been Sarah's seat. I was a little uncomfortable about that, but if they were, too, they didn't let on.

We talked a little more about Remmey and my mom. We talked about the weather and the upcoming semester. I told them my apartment was a tiny studio just off the south side of campus.

"You know, Ed. If I hadn't had the chance to meet you, even though the circumstances weren't great, I wouldn't have this." I pulled my Ichthys necklace over my shirt.

"That's pretty," Will said.

"Thanks. It was stolen, and Ed got it back for me." I smiled at Ed.

I continued, "So Ed, you are responsible for this necklace which is the last present my Daddy ever gave me, and that I'm here in Montana going to school at MSU, and that I'm up here chasin' a crazy dream, and I sure wouldn't be obsessed with fly-fishing."

We all took swigs of our coffee. Ed said, "And I wouldn't have a 20-year-old Black girl fishing buddy." Will slapped his knee when he laughed, and Ed and I clinked our mugs together.

I saw Will looking at my "new" truck. "She is a nice one, right?"

Will answered, "Yeah, she is. We put a new engine in it, so it better run well." I tested Will's sarcastic skills. "Maybe I'll let you drive some time, if you're nice to me."

He grinned that crooked grin again. "I think I can do that."

"Good," I said, "You're my first Montana friend."

He smiled again and shook his thumb at Ed. "What about Dad?"

"Nah. Ed was a friend in Boone. You're my first friend FROM Montana," I said. "Except I did meet one of my neighbors earlier. Her name is Judith."

Will answered, "You'll know a lot of people soon. Most people from here never leave. It's the most beautiful place on earth."

"I'll let you know if I agree AFTER I survive the winter," I said and hugged myself with my arms. "Brrrr!" Will and Ed both nodded in agreement.

"Maya," Ed interrupted, "Come by the shop after you get settled in. Classes don't start for another week, right? Come by, and I'll show you around. Then, I'll hire the best guide around to take us fly fishing. You good with that, Will?"

"I think I have some time to do that," Will replied.

I couldn't wait, so I said, "How 'bout tomorrow?"

"Don't you need some help unpacking?" Will said.

"No, thanks. I actually got here on Wednesday and moved in yesterday."

Ed shot me a stern, teacher look. "You've been here two days before you came by?"

I laughed. "Yeah. You know how I am. Work first. Play later."

"But it's even better if you have friends to help you finish your work," Ed reminded me.

"You're right. But I didn't want to see you for the first time in forever and the first thing I say is, 'Help me unpack.' You know my Momma raised me better than that."

"Yeah, she did. You're right," Ed said. I stood up and handed Will my coffee mug. The gentlemen stood, too.

"Thank you for the dinner and coffee," I said. "It was delicious."

"Bullshit," Ed said, "But we didn't know you were coming. Tomorrow, we'll go fishing and get dinner after."

I licked and smacked my lips loudly. "Fishin' and a meal. I can hardly wait!" I headed down the porch steps, and Ed said, "Bright and early in the morning, okay?"

"Even before it's bright" I winked at Ed. "See you tomorrow." I climbed onto the running board and said, "Great to meet you, Will."

"Nice to meet you, too, Maya." He waved. I heard him whisper to Ed, "Are you kidding me?" I smiled and drove away.

In between fishing excursions with Ed and sometimes Will, I wanted to explore more of this new and fascinating place that would be my home for at least while I earned my master's degree.

I did a couple of hikes with Will around Bozeman. The first was the iconic "M Trail" which was close to campus. Northeast of Bozeman, this 250-foot-tall M sits embedded on the mountainside as a monument to MSU and its community. Will said, "You're a Bobcat now. You gotta hike the M."

Will labeled it as an easy mile up and back, with a spectacular view of the Gallatin Valley. I thought to myself, "Easy enough. I'm a mountain girl. How hard can it be?" So I turned to Will and enthusiastically said, "Sure! Sounds fun."

Will said, "UP and back," and what I heard was, "OUT and back." I wasn't prepared. "Up" meant literally straight-the-hell-UP. Like, climbing UP a ladder or taking the elevator UP to the top floor. Trying to reach the summit, I took a lot of breaks, gasping for air and trying not to cuss Will the entire time... at least not out loud.

Will noticed my exhaustion and said, "We need to get you some Montana boots. I'll take you to Schnee's sometime."

"What is Schnee's?"

"It's an iconic boot store. Once you buy boots there, you'll be prepared for these Rocky Mountains... especially once the winter blows in."

"Okay. These mountains are steeper and more rocky than I'm used to."

"Hence the name 'Rocky Mountains.' We may not be creative, but it fits," Will said as we continued to climb.

Once I finally got to the bottom of the "M," all I could think about was, 'How the hell am I getting down? Are we repelling or rolling?"

Will then informed me that there were alternate routes to the top and he was testing me to see how I handled my first hike with him. I thought, "Asshole," but then I asked, "Well, did I pass?"

He wisecracked, "C-."

Jokingly, I threw back, "A 'C'- is passing, and I'll guarantee you, I'll have an 'A' by the end of the semester!"

Once I caught my breath and regrouped, I began to take it all in. I could see forever. The endless panorama was breath-taking and humbling. Where does this end? How far can I see? The vast terrain looked like lime green, velvet mounds, riddled with random clusters of deep green, shag carpet as it engulfed Bozeman, which was just a speck in the distance. I thought to myself, "This is my home for at least the next four years!"

Due west-southwest, past the city, stood the Tobacco Root Mountains and the Madison Range that majestically protected the Gallatin Valley like the Blue Ridge safeguarded my playground. It reminded me of home.

30

Boone, December 1999

I spent Christmas with Momma in Boone. It only snowed a dusting, but it was beautiful.

Church was nice, and we sang old Christmas carols, watched some old Christmas movies, and just tried to get into the Christmas spirit. I was starting to really love

Bozeman, but I missed Momma. I tried to get her to fly back with me.

"Girl, you know I can handle cold. But not that kinda cold. That's where your life is now. My life is here. I have to visit your Daddy every Sunday." She sighed and looked sad.

I knew it was a long shot. Though it had been years since Daddy died, Momma rarely missed a weekly visit to his grave. She still missed him. I didn't want her to be lonely, but she was Daddy's. I sure did miss her, though, and wished she'd could see my life in Bozeman. Momma continued, "Plus, the girls are used to having me back at work in the cafeteria. They'd be lost without me."

I looked skeptical. "Isn't Vivian your boss?"

"Yes, but she leans on me like your Daddy did."

"How 'bout Pearl? Is she still smoking those no-filter Lucky Stripes?" We both laughed.

"Chil' please. They don't make 'em anymore. She takes some scissors and snips those filters right off." We laughed even harder.

After our Christmas celebrations and family reunion, we prepared for Y2K. The millennial New Year's Eve came and went without incident despite all the experts predicting the end of the world. "Experts." Humph. In spite of their Armageddon-esque predictions, I already had my plane ticket back to Bozeman. I liked the old truck, but I didn't want to rack up too many more miles on its engine. Besides, it wasn't the most reliable vehicle. I was having to bum rides all the time when I couldn't get the stupid thing started.

Momma and I rang in the year 2000s by ourselves. We listened to Prince's "1999," and watched the celebrations on TV. That was enough celebration for us. I packed my tiny suitcase and Momma drove me to

Charlotte – Douglas International Airport. It was hard to leave her, but neither one of us cried. We hugged goodbye, said we loved each other, and promised to call every day.

31

Bozeman, 2000

Will picked me up at the airport. And just like that, I was back to this place I was almost ready to call home. We had grown close in just a few months, Will and I. He was a great listener, and he always told the best stories. He treated everyone the same. Whether they were rich tourists who were going to leave him an enormous tip, or they were poor college kids who would leave him a beer, everyone was important, and everyone was worth knowing. I don't know if he had to work at it, if he was raised that way, or if he was just born with an inherent sense of equality, but he treated everyone the same. The mayor, the custodian, the mail carrier, the teacher...they had all the same value to Will. I know lots of people say that, but then they swoon over movie stars, or treat rich people differently than they treat poor people. Will was different.

Growing up Black in a mostly white county in the beautiful mountains of North Carolina, I treated white people differently than I treated Black people. I felt bad about that for a while. Then I realized it wasn't that I treated white people differently; it was that I treated strangers differently. I knew every Black person in the county. We all went to the same church and lived in the same general area. The white folks were everywhere, but the only ones I knew were students, teachers, or people who worked with Momma.

Still, I treated people differently. Not Will, though. He never met a stranger. Literally. If he ever did run across a stranger, they weren't strangers for long. I had spent most of my life on the periphery, and I was okay with that. In fact, I preferred it. I knew there weren't many Black girl fly fishermen, so people thought I was weird. It was okay. I am weird, but it's about perspective. I thought they were weird, too, worrying about their hair, who they sat with at lunch, trying to find a date. Please. My world was much bigger than that. I thought about sunrises, bugs, water conservation, and fishing. I didn't have much in common with anyone I knew.

Then I met Will. He didn't care about who ate at his lunch table. Our similarities were woven through the thread of Ed, the outdoors, angling, loss, respect, equality, and our quiet confidence. We were comfortable in our own skin. We were gravy and mashed potatoes. I was the gravy, of course.

"You doing okay? You look tired," he said as we pulled onto the highway.

"I am tired."

"Well, it's good to have you back," he smiled.

"How old are you again?"

"I just turned twenty-six in October. Why? How old are you?"

"Twenty... But almost twenty-one."

He made a face. "What?" I said.

He laughed a little and said, "Nothing," but I knew what he was thinking. He was trying to decide if twenty was old enough for him. "Will you take me out to dinner before you take me home?" What a little hussy I was. I should be ashamed. I wasn't.

He was startled, but we ate together all the time, usually at his house with Ed. He played it off well, though. "Sure!" he said. "Where do you want to go?"

I said, "You choose. You buy the beers and I'll carefully navigate drinking underage. You're driving, so I'm fine. I can just use my fake ID. You know they say all Black women look alike anyway."

"What?"

Maya laughed out loud. "I'm kidding, lighten up, Sunshine."

"What do you mean? I thought you would just order tea and then complain that it's not SWEET tea. And don't call me sunshine."

I tweaked his cheek and responded, "Don't be so sensitive. You ARE Sunshine! And y'all's tea is crappy. You know the tea I make?"

"Yeah," he answered expectantly.

"Well, THAT is sweet tea. What y'all drink here is like brown water."

Will agreed, "Yours is much better. But no one can fry up Spam like me."

"Okay, big boy. I hear ya." We both laughed as we pulled into a bar off Highway 90.

Will swore the joint had the best wings around and the beer was cold, or maybe it was the flashing neon sign outside that read, "COLD BEER." Either way, I was committed now and starving, just not impressed. I learned in kindergarten not to judge a book by its cover, but...I think we all do that at least a little bit. Based upon the cover of this restaurant, I had my doubts, but I was willing to give it a try. That's probably what we were supposed to learn in kindergarten anyway: We all judge things by their looks, but as long as it doesn't affect the way we ACT, that's all that matters in the long run.

There were lots of cars and trucks occupying the parking lot which made me a little wary. Will sensed my trepidation, gently touched my elbow, and said, "Hey now, don't you go all nerves on me. This place is good, and you," he put his finger close to my face then and directed those eyes at me. If I squinted hard enough, I thought I could see the sky in them, all swirling clouds mixed in a sea of cerulean, "you have to trust me," he said. "Now will you just let me enjoy you being back over a beer and wings?"

I was still doubtful. "Err, I don't know, I'm thinking I would just rather get it to go and eat alone."

He chuckled and said, "Thanks a lot."

I laughed, too, and said, "I meant be alone with you and Ed."

"Uh-huh. Tell you what? We go in, scope it out for a few, and if you don't like it, we leave. Deal?"

"Deal."

Inside, it was dimly lit, and George Strait's "Check Yes or No" was playing. I had been the only Black face many times in Boone, but Montana white people may be different, so I was a little more nervous than I had been before. I needed to lighten the mood so I nudged Will and said, "Awe, they're playing our song."

He burst out laughing. "You don't seem as tired now."

"Must be the company," I said.

"Definitely. You're almost chipper now. I'm gonna call you Chipper Jones."

"I honored, Sunshine! I love him!"

"Who doesn't?"

There was a long bar facing the entrance and at least fifty patrons eating and drinking, which was a good sign. I wasn't going to be the only one leaving this fine establishment with food poisoning tonight. That part was reassuring. Will strategically sought out a table near the end of the bar to minimize attention and traffic. Privacy was not an option.

I told Will I needed to go to the restroom and handed him my fake ID just as the waitress arrived to take our drink order. As she glanced at my driver's license, I smiled over my shoulder and waved giving her a quick glimpse of my face as I hustled away. When I got back, two glasses of beer sat there, and Will was smirking.

"That was very savvy. Nice touch breezing the waitress, Chipper. I guess your theory worked."

"See now, you're getting it, Sunshine." I held my beer up, and Will clinked his to mine. The whole night was like that. We were best friends from the moment we met.

We laughed and talked about our holiday experiences. It had been a long day, and I was fading fast but having fun. We finished up our meals, and Will headed to the bathroom. And just as soon as he left, this incredibly overweight, bearded fella bumped my chair spilling his beer in my hair and down my back. I turned toward him and realized it was no accident. Embroidered on his camo ball cap was a gold hand giving anyone who was paying attention the bird, which only made matters worse for me. I kept it cool and grabbed some napkins to wipe the beer out of my hair and off the back of my neck.

"You should watch where you're going, little Miss Midnight."

"Pardon me?"

"You heard me, girl."

The bar was noisy, and my cool demeanor kept anyone sitting near us from hearing or noticing what had just happened. I had a decision to make. Was I going to set this person straight right here, or was I going to let it go?

I decided, since I may have been the only Black person this man had ever seen, I needed to help him understand manners and what being polite was all about. I didn't want him to make this mistake with anyone less gracious than I was.

I rose to my full 5-10 height, moved nose to nose with him, and cooly said, "I'm sorry you bumped into me, sir. But it's okay. I'm leaving. You can have the space you need now…" I looked him up and down like he was short and continued, "and it looks like you need a lot."

"What the hell did you just say to me?"

I ignored his rebuttal and started to walk past him when he grabbed my elbow and kept me from turning away. He sneered, "You're not from around here," and his breath reeked from cigarettes, beer, and only brushing his teeth twice a year.

I jerked my arm away. Now I was pissed. I can forgive people for being ignorant to a degree. I can even look past some levels of stupidity. Maybe he seriously had never seen a Black person before. BUT, intolerance, belligerence, and handsy? Nope! That is inexcusable.

I angled myself to cover what I was about to say to anyone within earshot. I leaned in at him and spoke slowly and clearly so he wouldn't miss a single word.

"Sir, what I just heard from you sounded derogatory and threatening. So, let me be clear. I get it. Say wha'cha want…think wha'cha want…first amendment, right? It's a free country! But don't ever touch me, or any other woman, again you fat-ass piece of shit, or I'll gut you just like the fish I grew up catching. How does that sound? Now go get a gym membership and some toothpaste. Oh, and do you own a gun?"

"Yeah, why?"

"Get home and pack it away, you don't need it anymore. Your breath could kill anything within six feet of your face. The only reason I'm alive right now is because I can go ten minutes without breathing." I winked at him and again started to leave. He bowed back up at me, and said, "I wish you would."

"ARE WE ALL RIGHT HERE?" the bartender interrupted. The man took a step back to let me pass and he sat back down on his bar stool, lucky for him. I smiled at the bartender, and he nodded at me, and said to the man, "She's right, Bob, your breath is rancid." I laughed and turned to walk to the door and there was Will.

"Everything okay?" he asked me.

"Sure is! Why wouldn't it be?"

"Did that guy do something to you?"

"Nah. We were just reaching an understanding." I patted Will's shoulder. We locked arms. I smiled, and we headed out. "It's all good."

Before we got to the door, Will looked back and saw Mr. Personality give us the finger.

Will broke loose of my arm and headed right back after him to provide more education. The bartender, astute in his bartending prowess, saw us and jumped in front of Will. "It's not worth it man. Just leave, I'll take care of asshole Bob over there. Just go home and enjoy your night."

I grabbed Will's arm again and dragged him outside as he glared at Bob.

When we got outside, Will was still standing there looking mad as hell. He's an emotional man, but I can usually even him out, so I tried to intervene. "Relax, please. It's okay."

"How can you say that? It's not okay."

"No. You're right. It's not okay. But you don't make someone not be hateful by beatin' their asses. You've gotta change their hearts. You gotta educate people. Hopefully, awareness helps establish common ground and over time, their mindsets and hearts change."

Will turned to storm back into the bar, "Dammit, Maya, tell me what he did to you."

I stiff-armed Will in the chest to stop him, "Please calm down. There was a little bit of beer spilt. Bob is definitely educated and aware now. I stood my ground and talked to him about manners and being polite. I handled it. Maybe his heart will change soon."

"He doesn't deserve any grace," Will fumed.

I said, "A beat down isn't gonna fix anything."

Will stood there shaking his head. "You're like a robot. Doesn't that make you mad?"

"Of course it does. I just control my impulses. You will be more successful if you learn how to do that too."

"Shit!" He grunted. I couldn't tell if he was mad at me or at Mr. Personality, but he was quiet the entire ride home.

Will walked me to my door and leaned in for a kiss. Although I had fantasized about this moment since the day we met, I pushed him back. "Will," I stammered, "I think we need to be just friends...let's not make any mistakes right now."

"What do you mean by that? You think kissing me is a mistake?" I shook my head, but the volcano had already erupted. He fumed and became more animated with each sentence. "And that's the second time tonight you've pushed me back. Don't do that again. What's the deal anyway, Maya? I'm not understanding your mixed signals. I know you don't want to friend-zone me."

"You think you know what I want? You have no idea because you are only thinking about what you want. Like you always do. Now, please calm down."

Will backed off and shook his head and sneered. "You know, you really are exactly like Dad. You keep everyone at arm's length and don't let anyone get close to you no matter how much you care about them, or how much they care about you. But you know what, Maya? That has ruined his life. You don't have to be like Dad." He started raising his voice again. "Dad never let anyone in, not me, not mom, not even you. He keeps everyone away. I needed to know my mom. I begged him to tell me about her. I needed him to talk to me and listen to me, and help me and, instead, he ignored me."

That's when I got loud too. "You needed him? YOU? What about what he needed? Maybe he needed time alone? Maybe YOU should have thought about what he needed. Have you ever considered what HE needed? No. You packed up and bolted. And it wasn't for a week or a month to sort through things. It was for a what... like ten years? So what I see is a pattern of you bailing. I've seen you fight with Ed about the stupidest things, and you walk away every time. One bump in the road and you're out. You do realize habitually exiting all the time is a major character flaw? Some things are worth fighting for, Will, but you have to actually be around in order to fight. You don't fight; you disappear. So don't lecture me about pushing people away because you do the same thing. We just do it in different ways."

Will exploded, "Do you hear yourself? You think I'm selfish? That I bail? What was I doing back there at the bar? I didn't bail. I was ready to fight asshole Bob so I could defend you. You think I'm selfish? I didn't leave Dad because I was selfish. I left because he was better off alone and we both knew it. I wanted to stay and have a parent. I didn't have a mom to lean on when I needed to talk. I wanted to know as much as I could about her, but Dad enforced the *no-communication* policy between us. I had a sister, too, and I don't even know why she died. He never, literally never, talked about Maggie."

"So what, Will? You think you're the only one who had a tough childhood? Get over it and grow up. I'm talking about right now, tonight. Stop being so selfish and think about other people sometimes."

Will backed up and turned away from me. "You know Maya, I'm convinced now. Your independence has skewed your sense of reality. Think about it, why would I stick around and fight for normalcy in an unhealthy cycle of co-existence? It's like you are only willing to let me see half of you. You don't ever let me in. You and Dad both have a deep river inside of you, and you shut out anyone who ever tries to explore it. Why would I fight to only know half of you? Or Dad? That kind of existence isn't worth my sanity."

He turned abruptly and clomped back to his truck. I yelled after him, "See? There ya go bailing again."

"That's because you WANT me to leave. You literally pushed me away, and that's fine with me. I should have expected it," he yelled over his shoulder.

"It's fine with me too!" I yelled as I opened my door.

As he got to his truck, he said, "Are you satisfied now? I'm leaving."

"Shocker!" I said as I turned to go inside.

The next few days, I told Ed I was too busy with school, and I didn't go to the shop. When Ed finally came by my house and took me fishing, I didn't tell him anything. He knew Will and I had a heated skirmish, but he never asked about it. We just fished in silence, and he allowed me time to talk to my counsel.

When I finally went back to the shop, Will and I walked past each other three times without speaking. Not that I was counting.

After two days of that, even Ed had had enough. "Maya," he said, "would you please run this thermos out to Will before he leaves for his float today."

"No, Ed. You do it."

"I can't Maya. I'm busy. Get over it. Fights are just a loud and frustrating forms of talking. Don't let it ruin your life. Tell him you're sorry and move on."

"I'm not sorry! He's the one who should be sorry," I said.

"He is sorry, Maya. Have you seen him? He's miserable. Of course, he's sorry. You're both sorry. You're both stubborn as hell, too."

I looked down at my shoes. I wanted to cry, but I took a deep breath and fought it off.

"Look, Maya. You miss him, right? Just tell him that. He'll do the rest," Ed said with a smile.

I smiled back weakly and took the thermos and walked down to the boat access.

When Will saw me coming, he tried not to make eye contact. I took a deep breath and said, "Hey, I thought you might want this," offering the thermos to him. He said nothing. I held it out for what had to be at least ten minutes and prayed the peace offering was enough.

He reached out for the thermos, but I didn't let it go until he looked at me. It took a second, but then he finally met my eyes.

"I miss you, Will. I miss my friend," and I released the thermos.

Will sighed, said nothing, and put the thermos in the boat. I turned to walk back up to the shop as slowly as possible to give him plenty of time to reply. "I miss you, too, Maya," he said, and when I turned, he was right behind me on the porch. We hugged it out, and although there were no apologies, we were still friends. Just friends...at least for now.

32

Bozeman, April, 2000

The next few months flew by. I had fallen in love with Montana. When Daddy and I harmonized so well, we made Marie Osmond and Dan Seals jealous as we sang our version of "Meet Me in Montana" way back in 1985. I never really understood the line that says, "Meet me underneath that big Montana sky." How can Montana's sky be any bigger than North Carolina's? All it took was about a week, and I realized you really could see forever. When I was on I-90, especially traveling west, with the setting sun in my eyes, the sky really did look like it went on forever. Montana license plates read "Big Sky Country" for a reason.

My classes had become increasingly difficult as I was delving deeper into the content area of my major, Fish and Wildlife Ecology with a minor in Entomology. I immersed myself in the outdoors, the environment, and fished when I could with Will or Ed or both. I made a few friends in a couple of my upper-level courses but not too many. Will and Ed were enough for me.

One day, I was in front of the class delivering a system oxygen analysis of energy expulsion through varied phases of turbulent and settled water for trout. Judith Whitehorse, my neighbor, was staring at me awkwardly throughout the entire class, almost as if she were sizing me up. I couldn't quite figure it out. I would catch her studying me intermittently with these very inquisitive looks. I could tell she was perplexed, and it seemed like she had something to say.

My intuition was right. When class was over and the rest of my classmates started filing out, Judith stuck around. She said, "Do you have a sec?"

"Sure," I said. We sat on a bench in the hall, and she told me what was on her mind. "You know, Maya, I love having you in class with me. You're so smart and funny."

I smiled, and she continued, "Hey, would you like to come to a cookout at my house with my family and friends? There will be a bunch of people there, and I know you're interested in our history. Even my grandfather will be there, and he's a tribal elder."

"Sure. When?"

Judith said, "Well, it's tonight. I know I should have asked you sooner, but I didn't know if you'd want to go to a family dinner even though lots of people from the community will be there, my roommates, lots of people who aren't Native Americans, but as you were presenting just now, I got the feeling you would enjoy it."

"I'm free tonight. I'll be there."

"Great! Come on over like 5ish?"

"I'll be there!"

As I turned the corner to Judith's house, I could tell she wasn't lying. There were a ton of cars lining the street on both sides, and I assumed they were all there for the soiree. Music, laughter, and the smell of the grill blazing emanated from her backyard. It reminded me of home and the cookouts and fish fries I enjoyed as a kid. I imagined my dad manning the grill, flipping burgers and hotdogs in the summer. I felt a wave of melancholy come over me as I walked up to the front door. Judith greeted me along with her family and ushered me in. What I wasn't expecting was that her family was a bunch of huggers!

One after the other, her mom, dad, and grandparents, cousins, neighbors, practically everyone I saw welcomed me with a bear hug. I'm not a hugger, especially with people I just met, but I went with it, and it wasn't awful. I kept thinking to myself, "You got this. Breathe and push through."

Popcorn conversation and delicious food made the time fly by. As the event wound down, I found myself deep in conversation with Judith's grandfather, the patriarch of her family and an elder within the Crow Tribe. He was an engaging, articulate man with wavy, light gray hair and a smile as wide as his ten-gallon hat. He was fit, with a jaw as sharp as his wit and the tip of his boots.

We talked about the environment, his early life growing up on the reservation, and the similarities in our trucks. He seemed genuinely interested in where I was from and why I chose Montana State and Bozeman. He asked about my upbringing and how I was adjusting to the obvious dichotomy of social discrepancies.

Then, he began speaking more slowly and softly. "I understand you're pursuing a degree in Fish and Wildlife. I'm guessing that content area is heavily male dominated, am I right?" I agreed and he continued. "I'm glad you and Judith are following your passions. I also heard that you were a fly fisherman, which is beautiful."

I smiled but was not sure where he was going with this.

He continued, "Your knowing how to preserve the environment and aquaculture, two of our land's greatest resources, means our future is in the right hands. I think it's in your hands, Maya."

I still didn't understand, but I encouraged him to continue.

"This may sound a little strange, but I had a remarkable vision of a powerful, confident woman speaking about fish: an image of a thin, dark-skinned woman with heavy, tightly twisted hair— a teacher and a leader who spoke the language of the flowing water's creatures, one of the Booadasha or Fish Catchers, who would be resurrected with enlightenment and would lead a great nation of women who spoke the language of the fish, a woman who would honor the Apsaalooke or my Crow Nation and the gifts beneath the water's surface."

I didn't know what to say, so I just sat there a second. Finally, I said, "You think this vision you had is about me? Why?"

He closed his eyes, nodded, and smiled. "Yes. I do. No other female speaks so fluently and articulately of the Phylum Chordata. Because of your open advocacy and enthusiasm for fly fishing, it is a simple deduction."

Still, I stared at him.

He laughed and said, "Of course, I could be wrong... and sometimes my visions are more like symbols rather than actual events."

"So, what should I do about it?"

"Don't worry about it, Maya. I just thought I needed to tell you to encourage you to stay on the path."

"I will stay on the path for sure, but I don't know about the rest of the stuff you mentioned."

"What will be is what shall be, young one."

"Yes, sir. Thank you."

As I headed home, I thought about what Judith's grandfather had told me. Was I the person in the vision? Would I lead a great nation of women fishermen?

33

Bozeman, May, 2000

When Ed and I fished on the weekends, it was always just the two of us, no customers, no Will, no one except us. No one ever knew where we were. It was during those times that I'm pretty sure it reminded him of happy days in Boone when he proverbially adopted me as his own.

When we were downtown one day, Ed took me to Powder Horn Outfitters to buy more ammunition. As we walked in, I was transported back in time. They opened in 1903 and reminded me of Mast General Store in Boone, which first opened under the name "Mast" in 1913. The wooden floors creaked with every step I took. I didn't buy anything but loved just walking through. It was just like home.

I never knew exactly where we were, but I knew we weren't that far from the hustle and bustle of Bozeman. I started blueprinting his drives, making mental notes of the roads we were on. Ed had scouted a few stretches of water that never got crowded, even from the locals who lived right on top of them. Funny thing is, these spots were hidden gems around Bridger Creek, just up 86 north of town about twenty-five minutes. A couple of turns and you're there, in the middle of nowhere before you can blink. We were definitely off the radar, and no one ever paid enough attention to work Bridger Creek's magic.

But Ed did. Most of the hard-core anglers I knew scouted. Anyone who hunts their own secluded water simply wants to fish whenever they want to fish. That's the beauty of it, you hunt, you discover, then it goes in the vault unless you want someone else to know about it.

Ed found it. It was like a fairy tale. Ed's spots were always isolated, but this one was special. After we parked, curiously, I looked down to see if I had a cell signal. I did, but it registered low. I thought, "I hope I don't need this damn thing out here."

Suddenly, it was like we were in Narnia. We walked into the wardrobe, and... abracadabra! Everything opened up into a magical land: Narnia, Montana. It felt like we walked into another world. It seemed like we were way off the grid, even Will didn't know this spot, and he knew just about every inch of water within a hundred miles of the shop. There's no way he had ever stepped foot into this utopia, and now it was my clandestine legacy.

Ed never spoke about it to anyone, so being exposed to it was a privilege. Ed had let me in.

Could I ever be this open with Will? I don't know. I never wanted to be that dependent on anyone and go through the pain that Momma and I went through when we lost Daddy. She was never quite the same again. I didn't want to depend on someone like that. I know that expression: "It's better to have loved and lost..." blah, blah, but was it really?

On the other hand, I already loved Will even though I didn't let him know that. Maybe it was too late. I would never be the same if I lost Will. It wasn't Momma's fault that Daddy died, but if I made the choice to let Will go and he moved on, which he would, it would be my fault. Would I be able to live with myself?

As we dodged the overgrowth into the clearing, Ed interrupted my thoughts, "Maya, take a look at this. After searching for the last forty years, I finally figured out Ralph DeCamp, the painter, stood right here and painted this scene. And it's twenty-five minutes from the house!"

I was still looking down to avoid getting popped on the ankle by a prairie rattler and wasn't paying attention to what he was showing me. Ed raised his hand and waved his arm from left to right. "All of this...it's literally still the same as God made it completely untouched by man."

I finally looked up and all I could say was, "Wow!" I should have paid more attention when my English teacher taught us vocabulary.

He pointed into the Bridger Mountains. "Two miles that way is unabated, raw nature." He pointed back toward town. "Fifteen miles that way is Bozeman. It's amazing how you can go from bustling and growing city, cross over this imaginary threshold, and walk right into what is primeval. "Pretty neat, huh?" He should have paid more attention in English, too.

He stuck his arms out with both thumbs and index fingers framing the image. "I have the print, you know. It's in my office. I like thinking I'm walking into his painting each time I'm out here. This is the place where time stops."

He held spots like this close to his heart, like a poker player keeps his cards tight to his chest. He said, "This is where I come to talk to Sarah and Maggie, and we solve all of life's problems. I figured you'd enjoy this place, too."

As I continued to look around nervously, I exclaimed, "It's a truly beautiful place, Ed. But, uh...you're not worried about bears, elk, moose, or snakes? I bet not even search and rescue can find us here."

He looked all around him again. "Drink all this in, Maya."

The visual in front of me stopped me dead in my tracks. The picturesque wander of the creek, layered by mountain peaks that outlined a vapor-trailed, sapphire sky, completely caught me off guard. It was magical. We were both in our element. Ed didn't seem to mind that a bear could just waltz out of the wall of trees and bum-rush the fish we were netting, so I surrendered and tried to let his mind-set be mine. That task was basically impossible. Every seven seconds I looked over my shoulder to survey the landscape, expecting to see an angry moose. Ed did have eyes in the back of his head, so I figured if I were on the verge of being attacked by something in the wild, he would get off at least a couple of shots and I would survive. Hopefully.

Instead of jumping right into the river to fish, like Ed did, I stopped and watched him. I studied him. I reflected upon the day Daddy pulled me out of school to fish the Watauga for the first time. It was the same surreal experience.

I watched Ed and took in the moment. This was where he belonged. Right here in his secret garden. He became part of the mountains, sky, river, and fish. As I watched him launch his first cast, three feet of fly line tear dropped from the first eyelet and was cradled softly in his left hand.

Eight feet hung from the reel loosely uncoiled on the undulating glass surrounding his knees. In unison, his left hand gripped the fly line with his thumb and index finger. He deliberately lifted his rod skyward toward the treetops and gently stopped at his ear for the slightest pause. The force of the line accelerated behind his head with a bobby pin, tight curl. He hesitated with a count of "one- one thousand, two- one thousand..." and allowed the wave of line to fully extend behind him. His elbow hovered close to his rib cage, barely moving. I could see him faintly inhale and exhale. Tick...Tock, Tick...Tock.

His eyes were fixated on the horizon, keeping each cast parallel to the water. In slow motion his casting arm dropped to a forty-five-degree angle, fluid and flawless with emphatic purpose, like a gavel falls in a judge's hand. Leader and line surged forward as each coil unfurled in its repetition. Three feet siphoned through each release of line, regulating each false cast with direction, distance, and placement. In anticipation of his third cast, he cut the final punch short, allowing his fly to fall gently at his target.

As I took my place beside him in the river, a gray cloud covered the sun. I gently approached a subject that I knew would be difficult for Ed. But, I figured, if there were any place he would bare his soul, it would be here...in his secret spot.

"Ed, how old was Maggie when she died?"

He took a deep breath and answered, "She was a newborn. Sarah had a hard time during the pregnancy and the doctors told us it would be risky to carry her full-term. Sarah wouldn't have it any other way, even though I argued with her. She did everything in her power to combat each complication as they surfaced. One situation triggered the next. Gestational diabetes fed the hypertension and every symptom in between. She fell one morning in the bathroom and by the time I got her to the ER, her heart was failing. They did a C-section…" Ed took another deep, long breath before he could continue. "They delivered Maggie and she… uh, her heart failed, too, and she— I never even got to hold her."

He tossed another perfect cast.

"I watched Sarah die through an emergency room window, and then I watched Maggie die three hours later in the NICU."

I wiped a tear from my left eye so Ed wouldn't see me cry. As if on cue, the sunglow began peeking through the clouds.

"Talk about a tough day…" Ed said weakly.

"I'm so sorry, Ed."

"It's okay," and he said, offering me a faint smile. "It was a long time ago."

"Still. I appreciate you telling me about it," I said.

"Being here helps. There's just something about this place. I can feel Sarah here with me. She really was my better half." He took another deep breath and cast again. "Maggie would have been two years older than you. I bet you guys would have been best friends."

I smiled at Ed. "I'm sure we would have."

Ed moved farther downstream, and I moved upstream a little to give him more space. I knew what Ed shared was difficult. He was not a man that voluntarily divulged anything personal. In most cases, how we related needed no words, only the presence of our company. This scenario was different. Hopefully, talking about Sarah and Maggie to another single human being meant there was potentially some healing involved for him. Our exchange included a level of trust and care that stretched far beyond DNA. He knew that with me, he was in a safe space and his vulnerability was displayed by teaching me fly fishing, then sharing his conviction for conservation, by revealing this clandestine spot, and ultimately by being willing to open up about Sarah and Maggie.

I stopped again to watch Ed in his element, cast after cast. He slipped deeper and deeper into his DeCamp print as he began to meld with our backdrop. That special place is where time stops, and he can speak freely with Sarah and Maggie and they, in return, try to help mend his broken heart.

It reminded me of the poem, "The Fisherman," by WB Yeats. He writes:

"Imagining a man,
And his sun-freckled face
And gray Connemara cloth,
Climbing up to a place
Where stone is dark with froth,
And the downturn of his wrist
When the flies drop in the stream—"

Yeats uses the fisherman to manifest one who is meditatively aware of the universe and his own place within it. It is in that space where trepidation is met with peace and harmony.

Yeats must have known Ed.

34

Bozeman, June, 2001

Myers Fly Shop was located southwest of town off Highway 191 near Gallatin Gateway. The Gallatin River was always in the back, cruising along, winding its way north up to the Missouri, but the Gallatin was doing more than cruising at times. From late March to June, it could also be swollen and hammering from run-off with a merciless groan but never from what I could see out the back of the shop. My view was always this broad, wide-open, steady and even flow. Will would catch me staring and point out, "Looks are deceiving, Maya. She looks beautiful and serene from the back of the shop here, but she is nasty, and her wrath is unforgiving until after the run off. Don't let this picture fool you."

I loved working in the shop. I "helped out" pretty much every day, but after a few months,

Ed actually put me on the payroll, so I didn't have to work in the MSU cafeteria like I did at ASU. Thank goodness because those Montana winters were no joke. At Appalachian, I enjoyed working the breakfast shift, but here at Montana State, I would not have. As I walked to class, it was so cold, I felt as though my hair would shatter. I knew exactly how Leonardo DeCaprio felt in the movie, *Titanic*, when Kate Winslet kicked him off that door. Montana gave the cold a whole new meaning. Sometimes, when I arrived at the Lewis Hall (which was where all my ecology classes were), I had to wait fifteen minutes for my hand to thaw out before I could take notes…unless I just held my pencil in my fist without straightening my fingers. All of us students called it the RMDG—the rigor mortis death grip. We couldn't pry our fingers from the palms of our hands because rigor mortis had set in, and we were still alive, mostly.

When it was slow at the shop, I sat on the back porch and enjoyed nature. One such time, a female Tiger Swallowtail butterfly landed on the railing. Being an insect expert by now, I knew it was the female because they have iridescent blue on the upper side of their hindwings, and on the underside, they have a row of golden spots. Blue and Gold. Montana State's colors. Just like the black and gold Monarch butterfly of Appalachian State!

This morning, as I gazed at the water's beauty. I was astonished how it forcefully meandered its way through the Gallatin range, only to taper and settle, granting us anglers a chance at its treasures. I pinched myself as a reminder of where I was, what I'd gained, and what I'd lost.

For the first time it really sunk in. I could see what nature's true balance consisted of and how its perfection was so incredibly tenuous. I finally understood the environmental chain, the sequencing of ultimate control, and at the apex of that control, the weather: generous and delicate as the sun rises each day or unforgiving and relentless as night falls. Little did I know, I was going to learn some hard lessons about the weather in a couple months.

It was an hour before dawn that crisp, June morning. I thanked Judith for giving me a ride on her way to her morning workout. Thank goodness she was a fitness freak. I waved as she drove away, and I cursed Will and Ed under my breath for not fixing my truck before they left to scout the Yellowstone River two days earlier. Cell coverage there was spotty at best.

I walked up the steps to get everything ready before the fly shop opened at six. I could hear the phone ringing, so I raced to find the keys and open the door. Since I was in a hurry, I dropped them, and they clattered on the wooden porch. By the time I got inside, it had stopped ringing.

I threw my bookbag on the counter, locked the door behind me, and headed to make the coffee for the morning rush of fishermen. The shop didn't open for another forty-five minutes, and I had a few boxes of inventory to tag and shelve. The phone rang again, I spun on my heels and raced back to the counter to answer it.

"Myers Fly Shop," I answered with more exuberance than I felt.

"Maya? Is that you? It's Remmey."

"Hey Mr. Myers. How are you? Ed won't be in today. He and Will left a couple of days ago to check the water between Big Timber and Billings, hoping to make heads or tails on how to handle the Yellowstone."

"Oh, ok then." His voice sounded weird, kind of nervous like.

"What's going on?" I hadn't started to panic yet, but I knew something was off.

"Well, Maya. I'm sorry to tell you this over the phone. I was hoping Will or Ed would be there with you."

"You're freaking me out, Mr. Myers. What's going on?" I could tell he was reluctant to tell me.

"Well, Maya, it's your mom."

"My Mom? What happened?" I asked beginning to panic.

"She…uh…she didn't want you to know, but you need to know now." He cleared his throat. I could feel the dam breaking and the river flowing over my feet and up to my knees.

"Know what? Please, Mr. Myers, just tell me."

He cleared his throat. "Well, Maya, I'm sorry. She made us promise not to tell you." He took a deep breath. "Her cancer came back." The river was up to my waist now. "She's taken a turn for the worse."

"What? What are you saying? Her cancer came back? Why didn't she tell me?" As the river rose to my shoulders, its weight began to crush my lungs. I fell to the floor of the shop. I could barely catch my breath.

"Maya, just come on home, okay?"

"Why didn't she tell me? I saw her at Christmas, and she seemed fine. She seemed fine." I could hear my voice, but it sounded like I was in a tunnel. I know it was me talking, but it didn't sound like me.

"Everything is going to be okay. Just get to the airport and come home."

"But..." my throat was closing in on me. The water was almost over my head. I could barely breathe. "Mr. Myers," I pleaded with him, "I just talked to her yesterday, and she didn't say anything." Much softer I repeated, "She didn't say anything…"

Remmey said calmly, "Maya, just come on home, okay?"

The river was completely over my head now. I could hear him talking, but nothing he was saying was registering anymore. I threw the cordless phone against the wall, and it shattered into a million pieces.

What happened? Momma was fine at Christmas. We had so much fun, and she was fine. She.Was. FINE!

Was she not fine? Was it all an act? Had she known then? She knew. She had to have known.

I screamed, "Momma! How could you not tell me?" I began shaking, bursting into tears, and gasping for air.

I was not sure how long I laid there, but eventually, I gathered myself and stood up and tried to think. I had to get to Boone. I had to be there for Momma just like she was always there for me. Two thousand miles away.

I needed to get to the airport. I'll catch whatever flight I can and get home. Where was the phone? Did I drop it? Shit. The landline to the shop was in pieces all over the floor. What have I done? Where is my cell?

I felt all my pockets, my bra...nope...my bookbag. Where was my bookbag?

On the counter. There. Right where I left it.

I found my phone, flipped it open, and checked the bars. I never got a signal here. Outside. Sometimes, on the back porch, if the wind was right, I had a signal.

I walked to the porch and held my phone high in the air. Still no bars.

Think. Think. What could I do? My brain was a tumbler of lottery balls. I could run to the nearest neighbor. The folks living around the shop were nice. They would help me even if it was still dark, but the closest one was maybe a mile and half away? So, a fifteen-minute run for me.

Gallatin Gateway was directly behind us, about eighty yards across the river. The Gateway was a combination of residential homes, restaurants, and retail shops, so there was no doubt in my mind someone could help me get to the airport. I looked at the river and then back at the road, trying to decide...running or rowing? The river would be quicker. All I had to do was row across and get help. It wasn't far. I could do it.

I knew Will said it would be too dangerous for another week or two, but before he left, he told Ed that he thought it was settling early this season. It didn't look daunting to me. Plus, it would only take me about three minutes to get across the river and over to Gallatin Gateway. I kept telling myself lots of people there would help me.

Will always left his trailer and boat at the shop toward the edge of the put-in, just shy of the river line. I needed to compartmentalize how I was going to handle getting back home and what was truly happening to Momma. I always did my best thinking on the water, but nothing I was doing was rational.

I surveyed the river. It looked fine to me. In my mind what I saw was a moderately paced flow. Will taught me how to row a few times, and I didn't think twice. I unhooked the boat, threw the oars in the oarlocks, wedged the paddle tips together at the nose of the boat, and pushed it to the river line. I stepped in and through the straps of Ed's chest pack. I was already enraged and tried to kick the pack out of the way. Ed was always leaving stuff wherever. I lifted the tips of the oars and started a diagonal push upstream to compensate for the intensity of the current. I also realized this wasn't a moderately paced flow, but I didn't care.

I was a shell of myself. Hollow…which amplified all my thoughts and feelings in a reverberating continuum. I felt like I was gasping for air, drowning on the air that was flooding my lungs. Not Momma too. Not Momma too. I repeated in my mind over and over, as stroke after stroke, I urged the boat to move faster. My entire body was jittery, and the anxious twitching in my knees was uncontrollable.

I knew how to row better than this. What was happening? Why was this so hard? I was sweating and straining at each revolution of the oars. I'd be there any second, and someone would help get me to the airport.

Suddenly, I got t-boned by a massive log. The battering force belted me back and forth like wiper blades on high-speed blistering the windshield. I was pitched off the seat. My body folded in half as my head met my knees. I lost my grip on the oars, and the left one shot out of my hand and smacked me in the jaw hard. Really hard. My head snapped back like I had eaten an uppercut from a heavy weight boxer.

As I struggled to maintain my consciousness, I fell into a trance-like state trying to make out the shapes the clouds were creating. The cauliflower tufts of white bulging from behind the tree line and mountain range were swiftly changing to an ominous black.

Still, not fully lucid, I stared at the big Montana sky and yelled. "Hey God, why don't you just take me, too, huh? I mean, why not? Since you already have Daddy and now, you're taking Momma. Just go ahead and take me, too!"

My heart rate slowed. I felt thud after thud vibrating through my core. I saw what looked like the wings and profile of a crow. It was eerily peaceful. Even through my lack of coherency, my mind kept replaying the phone call trying to recall what Remmey had said about Momma.

Something about the cancer had spread. Momma had known about it over Christmas. I had just spent a whole month with her, and she hadn't mentioned it. She kept saying she was just tired, that she was old. She wasn't old. She was only fifty-two! I should have noticed something! I should have known! Why didn't I know? I wasn't paying attention. I was talking and talking about Montana and Ed and Will and how much I loved being a part of their family.

But I wasn't a part of their family. I was part of Momma's family. Why did I take her for granted all the time? WHY? Because I'm a dumbass. I just didn't take the time to notice her.

Although I had asked her many times to move up to Montana with me, she always said, "No, baby. That's your path. My place is here." She never even considered it. Why didn't I MAKE her come and at least visit me? She would have loved it here. And we could have had so many more conversations, made so many more memories. Now, it was too late. Momma was going to die and I was too late.

35

Bozeman, 2001

I was jolted out of my stupor and identified the echoing thuds as not my heartbeat but the anchor dragging the river's floor. I was now barreling down a cascade of white foam, and there was absolutely nothing I could do to stop it. I was at least thirty minutes into my daze and had no idea how far down river before I instinctively reached down and grabbed Ed's Fly Pack and threw it over my head and arm. I grabbed the life vest out of the storage box and got one arm though it just before I crashed into the first major rolling swell. I reached for the anchor rope and strained with everything I had to lift the anchor toward the boat. I knew if the anchor lodged on anything, I would go sideways, the boat would tip, and I'd be done. Game Over.

Even if the anchor was up, the outlook was not favorable. I reached for the oar handles and made a few whipping swipes to gain some control, but it was futile. My adrenaline was through the roof, yet my arms weighed a thousand pounds. For a second, I held the oar handles in a death grip chest level with my arms bent as I tried to steady the nose of the boat. I couldn't hold the oars any longer. The pressure was too erratic, so I had to let go. I opened my grip. The oars were like wings flapping independently, twisting and spinning the boat like a teacup carnival ride. I did everything in my power to keep the nose of the boat pointing downstream. The oar in my right hand exploded out of the oar lock, almost breaking my wrist. The paddle had gotten wedged in between two rocks and detonated, swinging the back of the boat around to the lead. The boat slammed into a massive rock causing me to whiplash, almost launching me into the mouth of the rabid beast. The boat swung right, facing downstream again, and I immediately lost the second oar.

The water got bigger, whiter, and more violent with falls and chutes one after the other, creating class IV rapids that I knew I couldn't handle. I grabbed the aluminum frame of the boat and tried to center myself. With each rise and fall of the front of the boat, I would elevate and hover over my seat, losing my stomach every time. The repeated slaps of boulders on the floor of the boat caused me to lift my feet off the floor. If I didn't, it felt like my ankles would shatter. My challenge earlier about, "God taking me, too" became imminent.

The boat was a pinball as it ricocheted off one rock and then the other. Then the inevitable happened. The anchor caught and threw me forward, face first into the bow of the boat. Everything stopped for two seconds as my death grip on the aluminum framing skirted my exit yet again. The snag was just above a wave train that forced the boat sideways driving water underneath and closing it just like a lid on a box. I tried compensating, but it was too late. It was going to capsize and throw me into the chasm of rushing water.

How did I let this happen? I'm smarter than this. As I was thrown into the white water, I couldn't believe this was how I would die.

Now, I was the pinball. Blow after blow, I careened off one rock to the other spinning and combing over logs trapped sub-surface. Their broken branches were like spikes slicing my back and legs. I was hurling into each obstruction like a rag doll. I lost my life vest off my right arm, still fighting with all I could to keep my head above water. I prayed that the water would flatten and calm. If it did, I would have a shot at surviving. It was bleak, but bleak always invites chance to any party.

As I felt another powerful blow to the back of my skull and neck, everything slowed, and I became faint. I expelled the air I had left in my lungs with that booming clap. Facing up, I could barely make out the tree line against the sky and above my face was a small amoeba shaped balloon of air rising off my lips. Fate had not invited chance this time. This was it. I slipped beneath the waves.

In a haze, I saw my father leaning into a cast on the Watauga River carved out of a blue June sky. He was standing hyper-focused, following the drift of his lure, and between each lob of line he would look up at me and smile. I reached for him, but he didn't reach back. I saw my mom urging me to bait her hook standing in the New River, laughing as Daddy teased her. I watched as Remmey coaxed me back into fishing, forcing me past heartache and back into a desire embedded deep in my heart. I sensed Will's energy and how his presence stole my breath the first time I laid eyes on him. I felt Ed's hand firmly stabilize my wrist, swinging it deliberately through his patented Tick Tock motion. They couldn't help me. I was so tired. As I sank to the bottom of the river, I conceded to meet my fate.

Rocking lifeless at the edge of the current, the pounding of drums echoed what was left of my heartbeat. Immobilized and unresponsive, I could see myself through a blurred portal.

Counterclockwise, a group of Native Americans ritually danced and chanted in unison raising their arms to the sky. The ornament of feathers on their headdresses and arms shook with each stomp, creating a storm of dust at their feet. It was the Booadasha clan of the Crow Tribe calling their ancestral spirits.

Inside the pillowing clouds, I saw my counsel, the fish, darting and swirling furiously in every direction. As light beamed down, the strobing flashes off their reflective bodies was blinding, like fireworks in my face, yet so far away. At that moment, I felt my body rise as the Booadasha pleaded their case, and the fish did their bidding.

Then there was enlightenment.

I saw many generations of Crow women fishing for their families, preserving the promise of the next generation of fish catchers. As I hovered between life and death, the swell below me grew increasingly stronger, yet gently pulling me upward. Up, up, up toward the riverbank.

Intuitively, my arms began to flail, but that wasn't causing the tossing. It was something else. My chest filled with air and the deliberate compressions on my chest resounded with each beat of the drum.

Although I was still catatonic, the repetition and noise of the ceremony gradually faded, and I started choking and vomiting involuntarily. The river had collected all the demons and sufferings that had besieged my soul for the last eleven years, and they were pouring out of me in a deluge. Seizing from coughing and still gasping for air, I rolled to my side with the aid of the swaying current. The violent expulsion of water and torments now had me on my stomach navigating the uneven river floor to safety.

I wedged my torso between two rocks near the riverbank where an eddy naturally brewed and shielded me from the heavier current. I laid there, propped up in a conscious coma for what seemed like an eternity, agonizing over my pounding headache.

I was alive and well aware I had cheated death, but it wasn't over. I would have to overcome the looming danger of nightfall. The spirit of the Booadasha and my counsel had resuscitated and resurrected me only to be sadistically tortured again as night fell? My qualified status was now: embattled, orphaned, exposed, and lost. My faith and resolve had been systematically dismantled. I was hopeless.

In that moment of self-loathing, I remembered Momma saying, "The Devil don't chase those already on his team." I yelled out loud, "Not today, Devil, dammit! You're not getting me today!" I defiantly laughed and cried all at once in a fiendish tone, and my headache made me regret it immediately. God had a bigger purpose for why I was still here. Judith's grandfather had told me about the Booadasha for a reason. There was a reason I was still alive.

I realized it was me who chose this path. I left Momma and Boone and came to Montana. I got in the boat. I put myself in that situation and yet, Divine Intervention had saved me. I couldn't quit now. I couldn't do that to Momma.

I was sure I had a concussion, some broken ribs, a dislocated shoulder, a ton of bruises on my back and knees, a couple of lacerations, and my thumb wasn't working right. I did a self-check, making sure most of my hinged joints worked. Both gashes were on my legs, one on my left calf and the other on my right thigh. I could tell those cuts needed attention. Anything else would have to be assessed later. Both of my knees and my left ankle had taken a beating, but I could move…barely.

My breaths were shallow, and each uncovered a new level of pain beyond what the frigid water temperatures disguised. I was numb, so I knew other injuries would only reveal themselves as my body began to thaw.

My priority was getting out of the wet clothes because even though the rapids didn't kill me, hypothermia would. It hadn't rained in over six days and since it was early June, I knew the afternoon would be seventy degrees. Soon, it would drop back down to an unfriendly forty.

I needed heat immediately. I took off Ed's chest pack and for a man who couldn't remember his wallet, it was well-stocked. I found a little two by three-inch waterproof clear box, a ferro rod, and striker, tinder tabs, two water purification tablets, triple antibiotic, a few band aids, and some butterfly bandages.

Carefully, I eased off my jacket, shirt, socks, and shoes. It's hard getting wet socks off when you likely have a dislocated shoulder. Although my body was quaking, I managed to crawl up the bank. I nudged two of the tinder tabs into some dry debris I scooped together. My left thumb hurt like crazy, so I awkwardly gripped the ferro rod with four fingers and jammed it into the pile. With my right hand, I chipped and raked at the rod. I prayed, "God, please don't let me die. Please let me make a fire." The sparks jumped as I repeated my struggle again and again. Finally, the dry mound lit up with a stable flame.

If I could dry my clothes and keep the fire burning, I might make it through the night and my chance of surviving would go way up. If...

I scooted up the bank, collecting more downed limbs and sticks. The trembling from my upper body and arms made this simple task almost impossible. Anything dry within arm's reach was thrown into the flame. Possessed, I kept going until the flame was roaring. Dehydrated and exhausted, I inched my way to the blaze and leaned in. What adrenaline I had was gone. My head was pounding. I closed my eyes and prayed to survive.

I wasn't sure how long I dozed off, but I opened my eyes and peeked up at the sky. I could tell it was after twelve and the sun was bright. Between the fire and the sun's warmth, I was gradually gaining my faculties and motor skills. The clear survival box was at my shoulder. I got to my knees, grabbed the case and one of the aqua tabs. Repeatedly, I filled the case, waiting a few seconds for purification between each round of water. A million questions ran through my mind at once. What if Ed and Will decided to stay on the Yellowstone another night? What if I couldn't find food? What if I got giardia? What if I never made it back to Boone? But all of these questions were all outweighed by the biggest question of all: would I die out here? I staggered over to some downed limbs and dragged them with my good arm to the embankment. I propped both limbs against a tree a few feet away and hung my jacket, shirt, socks, and bra, hoping the blaze would accelerate the drying time.

The hot fire kept me warm while I rested. The fire blazed so hot, my clothes were almost dry when I woke up. I ripped the ointment open and wiped it throughout the inside of my shirt thinking it would find its way to the cuts on my back. Gingerly, I threaded the sleeve over my bad shoulder and on to my body. I winced and gritted my teeth as the ointment stung like a jellyfish. I removed my pants and hung them where my shirt had been. They were shredded and pink from the blood stain gashes on my legs. I applied the rest of the ointment to the cuts on my legs and tried not to pass out.

By late afternoon clouds were rolling in heavily. I checked every fifteen minutes imploring the sun and fire to dry my jacket and pants before nightfall.

After another hour or so of endless regrets and questions, everything dried to a damp touch, and I was able to re-dress. I drank water sparingly from the one purification tablet that was left, hoping I wouldn't get sick. I stumbled around, loading up as much dry foliage as I could find until dark. Then I sat stoking and rousing the flames into a bonfire as night fell. I knew I had to be judicious to make the wood last through the night. I thought, I'm not dead yet, so just keep believing Ed and Will are on their way. My head was still pounding, and I was beyond exhausted.

I knew I had to keep moving to generate body heat and to keep the fire going. It was completely black, except for the glow from the fire. The wild is so incredibly loud, especially when it's dark and you can't see where the noises are coming from. Exposed and vulnerable, I prayed the creatures of the night would not come looking for a meal.

I rubbed my ichthys necklace with the thumb on my right hand and tried to center myself so I could think clearly. Each minute was a hurdle, so I kept myself preoccupied with tending to the fire and thinking positive thoughts of making it out alive. Ed and Will would be looking for me by now. I glanced up at the stars. There weren't any. Plop…plop…plop…There were only rain droplets spattering all around me. I curled into a ball and tried not to bring any more attention to myself other than the blaze of red-orange on a blanket of black.

36

Bozeman, 2001

Ed and Will returned from scouting the Yellowstone as the sun set. They stopped by the house to drop Ed's boat off. Things had been so hectic, they were going to surprise Maya at the shop and take her to dinner. Will walked into the kitchen and grabbed a water. "Dad, the answering machine is blinking." Ed had no clue. Will was the only one who checked it regularly, so he walked over to hit play. They heard Remmey's panicked message. "Ed, dammit, answer the phone! Call me back." They exchanged a worried look.

Ed called him back. "Remmey, what's going on?"

"Where have you been, dammit?" Remmey exclaimed.

"Calm down, Rem. What's wrong?"

Remmey took a breath and said, "It's Maya. Where is she?"

"What do you mean? She opened the shop this morning."

"I know," Remmey responded, "but the phone just keeps beeping that damn busy signal."

"Ok, Remmey, slow down," Ed replied calmly.

Remmey continued, "I called your house, and you didn't answer. Then I called the shop, hoping you were there. I wanted to tell you so that you could talk to Maya, but Maya answered. I just told her. I don't know…I guess I shouldn't have…I didn't know what to do…Oh God, Ed. I messed up."

"It's okay, Rem. I'll fix it. Tell me what happened."

"Millie's cancer came back with a vengeance. She's gotten a death sentence. I told Maya to get on home immediately. I don't know how long Millie has."

"Oh shit. You told Maya that on the phone when she was alone in the shop?" Ed was more animated now.

"Dammit Ed! I was trying to find you! Why didn't you answer the phone?"

Ed regained control and said, "Okay, okay. It's all right. So, you told Maya to come home and then what happened?"

"She just kept saying "What? What?" and then I heard a crash and the line went dead.. I called back over and over, and she didn't answer. I called the shop back a million times, and it's been busy all day."

"Ok, calm down, Rem. Will is with me and we're heading to the shop now."

"I told her to head to the airport. Ed, you gotta find her. She's not thinking clearly."

"Don't worry, Rem. I'll call you when we find her." Ed hung up the phone.

Will was already on red alert and was sitting in the truck, honking the horn, and yelling for Ed to hurry. Ed jumped in, and they were off to the shop to find Maya.

"She has got to be at the shop. She's too rational to do something stupid. Maybe the phone at the shop just stopped working?"

"Dad, that's some pretty awful news, and she is a long way from home. There's no telling what she would have done."

Will had a cell phone, but coverage was spotty at best. He handed the phone to Ed and said, "Hit send and see if she answers. Then, call Mark and see if he went by the shop and noticed anything."

The fifteen-minute trip took less than eight. Even before Will had completely stopped and slammed into park, Ed jumped out and ran into the shop screaming. "Maya! Where are you? Maya!"

Will came running in right on Ed's heels. He found pieces of the phone still on the floor.

Will came out of the office and said, "My boat is gone! Maya, what the hell have you done?" Ed walked to the back and the screen door was ajar. He ran out the back.

"Shit! If she left when Remmey called her about seven, she's been gone ten hours, in two storms, and it's almost dark! We gotta go, Dad! Where would she go?"

Ed interjected. "It's Maya, Will. She'll be fine. She's smart and she's strong. It looks like the landline has been destroyed. She didn't have cell service here, and we haven't fixed her stupid truck yet. Guaranteed, she jumped in the boat and tried to cross and ask a neighbor for a ride."

Will nodded, "Okay. Let's go! We have to find her before it gets dark."

"And die ourselves, Will? You know as well as I do, neither you nor I can handle this water right now. Call Captain Allen from Search and Rescue, now! Time is wasting and with the rain coming in, it's only gonna get worse. We'll follow his lead."

Will ran to the back porch to get cell service and called the Gallatin County Dispatch Center. Captain Scott Allen and his team arrived at the shop within ten minutes.

Ed and Will quickly explained the situation to Captain Allen. The sky was ominous, and rain was coming down hard. Captain Allen explained they would make an attempt, but as it got dark, coupled with the front that was moving through, if they didn't find Maya immediately, they'd have to call off the search until first light.

Captain Allen had one Zodiac rescue boat with him and his team at the shop. He had another Zodiac positioned at Norris Road seven miles north. The Zodiac's were wider for stability in relentless currents and were also equipped with a Mercury 40 horsepower motor, allowing for better manipulation around and through the terrain hidden sub-surface. It was just after dark when they launched the search. Thunder was rumbling continuously, and gusting winds made everyone involved wary.

Night fell quickly. After forty-five minutes and two startling streaks of lightning, Captain Allen called off the search and returned to the landing. Will and Ed waited helplessly as Captain Allen pulled Ed and Will aside.

"I'm sorry, boys. We're going to have to call it off for tonight." Will slammed his fist through the wall before Ed could stop him. Allen, who had dealt with these situations many times, attempted to reassure them. "I know it's difficult, but as soon as the gray dawn comes, we'll get back out there, and we'll find her."

Will lost his mind, and grabbed Captain Allen's coat and slammed him against the wall. He shouted, "As long as she has a chance to survive, Maya will survive, but if we make her stay out there through the night, you're basically letting her die! You're a murderer if you quit now! Is that what you want? Is it?"

Ed tried to get Will off him, but Will's grip was too strong. Allen barked at Will, letting him know in no uncertain terms that he was in charge.

Will let him go and backed up. "Sorry," Will mumbled.

"I understand," Allen said. "But we're not helping her if we die out there. Neither my men nor I are going to dance with a pit viper in the dark just to test death. Trust me, Will. No matter how hard we search right now, we won't find her. If we go out with compromised visibility and if either boat capsizes, then you're looking for four, potentially seven bodies, and your rescue crew is down to three or zero. Searching in the dark, in a blinding storm, with lightning and wind, on a freestone river blown up beyond capacity, right now, is not an option. If we are going to be successful at finding Maya, I'm gonna need your help."

After his speech, Will resigned himself to trust Captain Allen and his team. He was still glued to the floor, when Ed saved him. "Will, go get those maps from in my office, will you, son?"

Will sighed, hung his head and nodded, then headed to the office. Ed said, "Sorry about that, Cap. He's more emotional than he lets on."

"It's okay, Ed. I know it's hard on everyone."

The team was constantly putting itself in harm's way for the survival of others. As the decision maker in situations like these, making a call like that is gut wrenching. Although he knew the implications of waiting, he had to weigh all options for the safety of his crew.

Will came back with the guide maps and put them on the counter.

"Gentlemen, we are checking the weather every minute, and when we know we have a solid window to move and find her, we will," Allen said turning to look directly at Will. "I'm gonna need for you to get your head on straight. Ed tells me no one knows this water better than you. Is that correct?"

Will said, "Yeah, I have a decent grasp on the river."

"Ed told me you know every inch of it from Big Sky north to the Missouri and beyond." Allen unfolded the map of Gallatin County. "I want you to pick apart every boulder, downed log, wave train, pitch and fall you know of, everything you can remember on every bend, and I want you to tell me how shallow and deep the water gets minus the run-off."

Allen raised his voice to the group, "I'm calling the Heli Team in at first light. They will be our Air Ops and eyes in the sky for duration of the search. The Heli Team can pinpoint the lost boat pretty fast. They're in the Bell 206 Long Ranger chopper and the sucker will move so we should be able to cover a lot of ground quickly to find her. I'll start our Zodiac 2 Team from that point and move upstream until they meet me and my crew. Ed, Will, I'm going to leave one of our walkies so you can hear what's happening on our end. Gentlemen, this will be a listening device for you so you can stay in the know. At NO TIME should you occupy our frequency."

Ed was sick with emotion but never let on when around Will. He just kept brewing coffee and brought out snacks trying to keep himself occupied and everyone up and ready with caffeine. He thought of Maya as his daughter, and the thought of losing her caused him to hide in his truck multiple times so he could gather himself without anyone knowing.

Ed called Remmey and filled him in on the latest. All Remmey could do was blame himself for what had happened. If he had just waited, none of this would have occurred. Ed reminded him that Maya would have most certainly strangled him if he kept this a secret, and he promised to call back as soon as the rescue mission was in full force to keep him updated.

Will plotted the complications for both Zodiac boats from the Williams Bridge to the Gateway all the way downstream past Interstate 90 toward Manhattan. Allen looked over the map in amazement. "Will, you wanna job with Search and Rescue? It is unreal how much you know about this water."

Will started welling up, so he cleared his throat and gathered himself. "Please, go find Maya."

Will felt sick knowing in his gut that even people who were trained in beating the odds like this, many times they didn't make it out alive. As he paced the shop expecting the worst, he thought about all the things he never told her.

It was around 3:30 a.m. when Captain Allen got the good news that the storm was passing. Everything was estimated to clear in just a couple of hours. Just before dawn, his team would get in position and wait for the Air Ops response team to guide their hunt. Zodiac 1 Team was Captain Allen's boat and would again search downstream, north from the fly shop; Zodiac 2 would hold tight and wait for a response from Air Ops to either move up or down stream from Norris Road. At exactly 5:42 a.m., Captain Allen initiated the search.

37

Bozeman, 2001

I jerked out of slumber, amazed I had made it through the night alive. I had dozed off waiting to be mauled by a moose or grizzly. My body and mind had just shut down. I was alive. My sudden jolt reminded me of my injuries and hurt like hell. There was no question I needed medical attention. I could barely move, and my blaze had reduced to a light smolder from the rain. I collected myself and made it to my feet to gather more dry brush. The fire had kept me reasonably warm, and I wasn't trembling like I had before. My clothes were still a little damp from the torrential downpour, and I had half of a purification tablet left.

My head was still thumping, but I was functional, and my dizziness had subsided. My back and neck were locked up, preventing me from turning my head in the slightest. I had a piercing pain in the right side of my rib cage. I still couldn't take a full breath. As I dropped the damp tender on the laboring flame, it caught slightly, but created more of a tornado of smoke than flame. I was hungry and thought that was a good sign. I had no food and was uneducated in the art of foraging. I knew you could eat chickweed, dandelions, and clover. There was none of that here. I knew I could eat earthworms, mealworms, ants, and grasshoppers, too. I started seeking out earthworms.

I didn't know if I could actually eat a worm, but the hungrier I got, the more I thought I could. It's amazing how your attitude changes when you feel like you're dying. I kept stoking the fire, egging it on so it could maintain its burn while I figured out what to do next. The earthworms I had amassed laid on the ground beside me causing me to gag just thinking about ingesting them.

Then it dawned on me. Ed had a couple of used and bound tapered leaders, a few spools of tippet, a rat's nest of fly line, two Fly Bibles, some strike indicators.

I grappled with the conflict. Would I have to break my own code again for a second time and use one of my aquatic friends to survive? I hadn't eaten for more than a day, and I needed my strength to get out of here.

I was torn. There was a spiritual bond...a place where my faith collided with the spirit of the land, creating a bridge of mutual admiration and recognized respect from a higher power. But there is a shared balance and understanding that the fish and I would both have to sacrifice a great deal to continue our covenant of helping each other survive. If the Booadasha were right, I'd have to survive.

At that moment there was a calm and a purpose. I explored the perimeter around the fire again, looking for a thin branch to use as rod. I remembered Ed urging me to practice my casting with a broom handle or limb. I found a limb that carried almost the same diameter from top to bottom. I stoked the fire with it for a few minutes to make sure it was dry and strengthened it at the tip. I took the clear survival container lid and shattered it. I took one of the plastic shards and bore a small hole at the top of the limb. I threaded about fifteen of the twenty-five feet of line through the hole and took a couple of practice strokes that hurt like hell, but I didn't have a choice. It worked just like it did years earlier when Ed first taught me, and I practiced in the backyard. After a few more test runs, I tied on one of Ed's size 12, Yellow Sally Stoneflies, and said aloud to my fish friends, "Thank you, in advance, for the sacrifice you're making for me today." I began targeting some slower water pooling where I felt trout would be holding and launched my cast. Less than two minutes into my delivery, I had a fish on. Little did I know another creature noticed I was hooked up as well.

38

Bozeman, 2001

The sun crept out from behind the east bank ridge of the Gallatin. Air Ops was with Zodiac 1 from the fly shop toward Bozeman and Norris Road. The Zodiac 2 Team had slowly headed north from Norris Road toward I-90, covering what the rescue mission deemed logical places for Maya to be. Scouring every bend of the river, Captain Allen and his men had made their way north about four miles. Then the call came in. Air Ops was snaking north above the Gallatin following every curve and had located Will's boat.

"Air Ops to Water Ops, do you copy?"

"We do. Go ahead?"

"Captain Allen, we have located the boat a quarter mile below Norris Road."

"Copy that. We are heading your way."

In a flash, Ed and Will were driving north to Norris Road. The boat was stuck in a wave train, and there was no observable movement or sign of life in that area. The Zodiac 2 Team had been deployed to survey that zone around the boat for confirmation. The pilot then turned his attention to smoke cresting next to the river just a few hundred yards ahead. The Heli-Team was just west of town close to Norris Road. Air Ops came on the radio again, "I have a visual of smoke one mile south of Norris Road. Please stand by." The pilot moved in closer to the small tuft of haze rising from the curvature of the river.

Air Ops blasted, "Zodiac 1, what is your location? We have a situation!"

Captain Allen radioed back, "We are approximately two hundred yards behind you. We have eyes on you."

The pilot spun the Bell 206 chopper to face the Zodiac 1 Team and to pinpoint Maya's location. "I have eyes on what seems to be a female fishing at the shoals right at the bend. And, uh, sir...we have a black bear moving toward our patient."

Allen turned to his crew with a perplexed look, "Repeat that?"

"Bear! Bear! Move in now, Captain!"

Captain Allen shouted at his first mate, "Go! Go! Go! We have a bear." Allen readied his Remington Pump-Action Shotgun with two bean bag rounds. As the Zodiac 1 Team rounded the bend, Allen could see the bear charging the fish Maya hooked, and Allen buried the butt of the shotgun into his shoulder. Boom! Boom! He unloaded two rounds into the bear. The shots echoed as the bear immediately turned and retreated into the woods.

The Zodiac 1Team pulled up to a young woman as she stood there paralyzed. Allen jumped out of the boat and approached the girl. Tears streamed down her cheeks as she dropped her makeshift fly rod. "Maya, I'm Captain Scott Allen of Gallatin County Sheriff Search and Rescue. We've come to take you home. You're going to be okay."

She collapsed into the stranger's arms. "We've got you, young lady, and you're gonna be okay." Maya was cautiously placed on the backboard and carried up the gorge to meet the ambulance at River Road.

As Maya was being brought up the ravine, Ed and Will rushed to her side and explained that she was a part of their family. Allen provided the paramedics with the vitals, and Will jumped in the back of the ambulance as they took off with sirens blaring. The team stopped, sat on the roadside, and gathered themselves.

One of the squad members testified, "That young woman just stared down death twice and won! How the hell did she do it?" The other team members all shrugged in disbelief.

Ed walked up to Allen and sat down beside him, put his arm around him, and said, "Scott, not only did you and your team save her life, but you also saved ours. We can never repay you guys. What you did today was nothing short of a miracle." Ed shook everyone's hand as he fought back tears.

Captain Allen, too, was overcome with emotion but didn't let on. Calmly collected, Allen responded, "Ed, we're right there with you, man. We are just glad we were able to bring her home safely. Now get to the hospital and be with your family."

39

Bozeman, June, 2001

When I was in the hospital, the doctors ordered two CAT scans, a couple of x-rays, gave me IVs, quite a few stiches, and though my shoulder was not actually dislocated, it might as well have been because it hurt like hell. Other than that, I was as good as new except for a few broken ribs that would take a little longer to heal.

The first night I was there...at least, I think it was the first night...it all kind of ran together, Will thought I was asleep. He gently stroked my hair and whispered, "I love you," and kissed me lightly on my cheek. I hoped he didn't notice my smile.

In fact, every single time I woke up, Will was there. Ed was there a lot too. He brought me a flowerpot that held a yellow chrysanthemum that was bigger than my head. Bless his heart, he tried. Betty and Judith came to see me, too, but they were smart enough to know I mostly needed sleep, so they never stayed very long. I talked to Momma at least three times a day on the phone. She still said she didn't need me to come down, and that no matter what happened, everything would be fine. I told her I'd be there just as soon as the overly cautious doctors released me. She said she would be okay until I got there.

One night, as I lay there awake listening to Will snore softly, I remembered how happy Momma and Daddy were together…how much they laughed and loved. I thought of Ed taking me to his secret place and trusting me enough to let me be there with him. I thought of my creatures of the current and how they coaxed me back to the surface. Then, I thought about the future and the door opened. Like Dorothy waking up in Oz, I saw a bright and colorful future. Luckily, instead of munchkins and a green witch, I saw Will. He was my future. I softly called to him and woke him up.

"Will," I said.

He jumped up quickly and came to my bedside. "What? Are you okay? Do I need to call a nurse?"

"No, no. I'm fine. I just need to tell you something."

"What? What's wrong?"

"Nothing. I just wanted to tell you that I love you, too."

He stared at me with his mouth open.

"Will? Are you okay? Do you need to lie down?"

"No. Uh. No. I'm fine… just a little surprised."

I smiled at him and said, "No, you're not."

He returned my smile and said, "No. I'm not. But I'm surprised you finally admitted it."

"It's time."

He shook his head. "No, Chipper. It's way past time."

He leaned in and kissed me gently at first, and then passionately. I enjoyed it, but my broken ribs didn't.

"Not healed!" I said. "Not healed!"

"Sorry."

"No, you're not," I grinned mischievously.

"You're right. I'm not." He said and kissed me again.

When the doctors said I could go home, we moved as quickly as I could (which was, in fact, really slowly) to get to Momma. I was irritated at everything: my headache, my bandages, my scarred body, and the fact that all of this was my fault. The kicker was, I wouldn't be hurting like this if I hadn't gotten into that stupid boat. I'd be in Boone taking care of my Momma. I was so angry I wasn't there already.

40

Boone, 2001

To be safe, my doctors recommended I not fly because of my concussion, so we had to get on the road right away. We piled in Will's truck, and he and Ed took turns driving as I slept in the back seat.

Remmey and Jen waited for us to arrive at Momma's house. They brought over some supper for me and Momma to eat for a few days. When Remmey saw me, he hugged me tight and whispered, "I am sorry for what I caused. I shoulda never told you that over the phone. I'm such a dumbass. Can you forgive me? I'm not letting you go until you forgive me."

"Mr. Myers, none of this was your fault. There is nothing to forgive."

He held me tight as he wept. I hugged him back even tighter…as much as my ribs would allow.

Ed and Will stayed with Remmey, and I stayed with Momma. We all got to spend the last two weeks of Momma's life together as we navigated the Hospice care that was already in place.

Everything from now on was about keeping her comfortable, and her church family had piloted all of that so far. Momma knew Ed already, but now I was able to introduce her to Will. The entire Myers family patiently waited with Momma as she lived out her last days.

We talked constantly when she was awake and lucid, which was about half the time. She explained in detail how I should handle her estate. There were things about her jewelry she wanted me to remember and how to divide her "estate" among the church, the homeless shelter, and me as the beneficiaries. She told me about her funeral and how she didn't want me to give the eulogy.

"Why do people think they gotta do that fo' their loved one? It's hard enough to sit there, much less talk. I ain't puttin' you through that."

"Thank you, Momma. I appreciate that." She was always so thoughtful. Even with her body wracked with pain, she thought of me sitting in there, at her funeral, not wanting to be there, much less speak.

She went through her hats and told me the story about when she wore each one… like the Easter bonnet her grandmother gave her that she hated, but wore anyway.

She went through her souvenirs and told me why they meant so much to her. She gave me her high school class ring and her and Daddy's choir yearbook picture that she had framed. She forbade me from ever throwing away the dried rose she had from her mother's funeral. She kept it in her Bible and told me to keep her Bible and read the notes she had made in the margins. "I'll feel like I'm still teaching you if you read those..." I promised I would.

She gave me the veil she wanted me to wear at my wedding. She told me to give the dress to Goodwill because she was "just a tiny little thing" when she got married and I was bigger than she was, even when I was in high school. I took after Daddy. But she wanted me to wear the veil so she could feel like part of her was there. I dissolved into tears, and she did, too. I hugged her and told her she would always be with me and how much I loved her. We cried a lot. It was a long goodbye, but I sure was glad we had that time together.

I was also glad she got to know Will. I never really told her how close a connection I felt with him. She just knew. Maybe it was the way he would magically appear to help me take care of her. He helped me fix dinner and clean the house and then gracefully disappeared. One evening she insisted on him sitting by her bedside. Just him.

I tried not to eavesdrop, but I couldn't help it. She eased him in by starting with easy things to talk about. "I'm so glad to finally meet you, Will. You've been very helpful to me and Maya. Y'all must be very good friends."

"Yes ma'am. I think we are."

"Well, I'm glad you're here with her to help her through this. Death is always hard, no matter how much you're expecting it."

"Yes, ma'am."

"So you never really knew your mother, right?"

I held my breath outside the door. Will hadn't really talked about his mom with me before.

"That's correct. She died when I was three."

"I'm sorry."

"Me too. But Dad did a pretty good job raising me. And I had Aunt Betty. She taught me how to cook and clean...although I don't enjoy it much."

"You're an outdoorsman like Ed?"

"Yes, ma'am. I am."

Then the unthinkable happened. He got comfortable. He started delving into our family history. And even more shocking, he LISTENED to her stories.

She told him about how she and Daddy met and courted. How they built their life together in Boone. The man never met a stranger, and he loved to laugh. At one point in their private talks, though I couldn't hear what they were saying, I could hear them both laughing uncontrollably. He never did tell me about that story, but I was pretty sure it was about me.

This went on for a while: Will sneaking into Momma's room for hours after supper. Both of them, just hootin' and hollerin' like children all throughout the night. I didn't mind the noise. It was music to my ears to hear Momma laughing.

One night near the end of their talks, I peeked my head in just in time to see Will lean in to kiss Momma on the cheek, and whisper, "This is top secret, ma'am, but would you give me permission—"

Momma weakly held up her hand and touched his cheek, "I already know what you're gonna say, and you have my blessing, and the good Lord's." Will smiled and held her hand as Momma prayed for our future. Just as she finished the short prayer, Hospice softly knocked on the door and brought Momma's meds. Will kissed her cheek again. She winked at Will, and he winked back as he slowly started for the door. I scurried away to the kitchen, wiped the tears from my eyes, and tried to pretend I hadn't been listening.

My talks with Momma changed at the end. Rather than talking about the past she asked me lots of questions about my future. We talked about my professional goals and how I would reach them. We talked about my personal goals, how to be a good wife and mother. We talked about my dream to be a teacher. I wanted to teach people life lessons...not just about fish and bugs, but also about the lessons that Daddy and Ed had taught me through fishing. It wasn't just being on the water catching fish that brought me so much joy and peace. It was the camaraderie shared with those who had parallel pursuits. Probably best of all, I got to spend time with my therapists. All of this made me wonder what was in store for me. I knew there was a swell brewing, urging me to fill a role. I just had no idea what that role would be.

I told Momma some of the things Judith Whitehorse's grandfather told me about the visions regarding my future. I wanted more people to find their peace through fishing, how it heals the soul. She always said I was meant to do great things. Maybe this is what Judith and Momma, too, were talking about. I was meant to encourage people to fish.

We also talked about Will. Of course.

"How long y'all been dating?"

"We haven't really dated."

"Wha'cha mean?"

"Well, we hang out all the time, and I'm literally the only woman in his life except for Betty at the shop, and she's like fifty something."

"Well, he's crazy about you. He's got a job. He's a hard worker. He likes what you like. He comes from a good family. You're cut from the same cloth. But there's one thing you may not have considered…"

I was expecting the hammer to drop eventually. I guess this was the time. I knew she'd find something wrong with him. That's what mothers do, right? No one is good enough for their little girls.

So, I sighed, "What's that, Momma?"

"Well, Maya, I don't know if you realize this, but…Will is white."

I had to look into her eyes to see if she was joking. Her eyes danced as much as they could have with her being as sick as she was. She finally let a smile creep onto her face.

"Momma!" I said like I did when I was twelve, and she would tell me to put on lipstick before Daddy and I went fishing.

"I'm just teasing. But only halfway. It ain't only about skin tone." She stopped talking for a second and got thoughtful. I couldn't tell if she was thinking about how to phrase it without sounding ugly, or how not to offend me or maybe she was just tired. I just waited.

"There will just be some challenges that arise with how people look at you…how people treat you…not most people, mind you. Just some people. But y'all just remember it's a big world out there and there are all kinds of shades walkin' around. We probably all got all different blood in us already. White. Black. Indian. Maybe even some Eskimo." She laughed a little and coughed.

"Remember, if you have children, kids just need a place to belong and feel loved. If you give 'em that, they'll be fine."

"We aren't even close to marriage yet, and you're talking about kids. It's time for your meds and you need to rest."

"Girl, I know what I know. Open your eyes."

"I will, Momma."

"I know you will, baby. Let me rest a minute now." She closed her eyes and fell asleep.

Momma and her doctor decided that the cancer had spread so quickly and aggressively, there wasn't much they could do. Hospice kept a watchful eye and kept her comfortable as she spent her remaining days with us. Some days she whispered as if she were talking to Daddy. Other days were quiet.

I read the Bible to her and talked about all the fish I caught. I explained to her that Ed had taken me to a place right out of a painting. It was a place where he went to speak to Sarah and Maggie, and he thought it was fitting for me to talk to Daddy, and I would talk to her there too. I told her she'd be with me every day. I hope that made her feel better.

Two days later, Hospice said it wouldn't be long now. As I sat by her bedside, I saw a tear make its way out of Momma's left eye, roll slowly over her brown, sunken cheek, and down her chin. She was almost in heaven. I thanked God for eternal life, and that she would be reunited with Daddy soon.

Regardless of the circumstances, Momma could always find the joy that surrounded her. She had taught me to do the same thing. No matter what slings and arrows befall us, God always provided blessings even if we didn't notice them at the time because of our overwhelming grief. Yet, joy is there. In the love we share, in creation, in everlasting life. There is always joy.

41

Boone, 2001

At the funeral, I followed all of Momma's instructions. The children's choir sang "This Little Light of Mine," and held up candles and reminded us of how Millie always let Jesus's light shine through her own life. The adult choir sang Momma's favorite, "It is Well With My Soul." The same song they sang at Daddy's funeral. Momma would be a welcome addition to the heavenly chorus.

Just like Will read to her in her last days, the Brother Smithfield read Psalm 30 verses 1- 5: "I will extol you, O Lord; for you have lifted me up and have not made my foes to rejoice over me. You have rescued me from the grave…Sing and give thanks. For anger endures for a moment, weeping may endure for a night, but joy comes in the morning."

"Millie may not have been healed on this earth," Brother Smithfield said, "But she's healed now and walking in heaven with Zeke on one side and Jesus on the other." I cried several tears picturing that, while lots of "amens" erupted in the congregation. It was easy to be happy for Momma and Daddy, but I was sad for myself. I was beyond sad. I was devastated. I was an orphan now, but Momma had felt terrible for a really long time. I was glad she was out of pain now. I was also comforted by the fact that she got to meet Will. Now she was with Daddy. I was a little jealous about that. I really missed Daddy. Now, I had to miss them both. The hope of heaven eases the sting of death, but sometimes it takes a while to rest in that comfort.

"You are only free when you realize you belong no place —you belong every place —no place at all."

Will, Remmey, Jen and their daughters all sat with me on the family row. My aunts and uncles from Alabama were there too. Ed didn't go into the church for the funeral. I didn't ask him why. I knew why. He missed Sarah and Maggie. He waited at the graveside and escorted me to the tiny little plastic white chair they set out for me, him, and Will. That service was only about ten minutes which was fine with me.

There wasn't anything else to say anyway.

I did all I could to wrap up all the details about Momma's "estate" just like she asked me to. Remmey and Jen said they would take care of everything else. I didn't want the house even though it was mine now. My home was in Montana now. Remmey insisted he take care of the house for me along with my neighbors, the Robinsons and Johnsons. They would work with him to find the right buyer who was worthy of my old house and that special street.

I went through everything I wanted and needed; the rest was labeled as trash or as donations to Mount Vernon Baptist Church for their summer yard sale. Remmey prepped every inch of the house for resale. Given he had his own construction company, he had a crew that took care of any loose ends.

On the ride back to Montana, we each took turns driving Momma's car. That way, I'd have Ed's old, beat-up truck, plus Momma's Buick Renegade as my "luxury" car...just in case I wanted to travel in style, or more likely, when the truck broke down again. When Ed and I were in Will's truck together with Will driving the Renegade, I started thinking too much and tears started falling.

Ed didn't say anything for a while, but then, finally, he asked if I was okay. "No. I'm not. I will be, but for right now, no. I'm not."

"I can understand that."

"I was just thinking, it's just me now. I have no parents. No brothers or sisters. No one to worry about me or text me or pray for me."

"Will and I are your family. And so are Remmey and his family. You know that." I patted his arm and smiled. It wasn't the same. But it was the best he could offer, and it was really sweet. I was lucky.

"Maybe this isn't the greatest time to offer, Maya, but Will and I were talking, and we were wonderin' if you'd like to move in with us."

I died laughing. "Are you serious, Ed? I just got done watchin' you two ants walk circles around one another!"

Ed laughed out loud. "What do you mean?"

"Everything is a balancing act of blending personalities. You guys still haven't figured out how to balance each other. How will you do if I jump into that mix?"

"Awww... we'll be fine. Maybe even better if we have you to buffer us." He was probably right. I was always a bridge builder. "I am willing to help you cook, but I'm NOT doing your nasty laundry, and you're not touching my undergarments."

"Ok, so we each do our own laundry. And you cook twice a week. That's still a good deal for you, living with no bills and with an in-house tutor as you get your master's. It's a win-win."

"Have you talked to Will about this?"

"Of course!"

"I'll think about it."

"Ok. Get some rest. We have a long way to go."

I know he meant that literally, but I couldn't help but think there was a double entendre there, too. Getting over Momma's death would take a while. It would be a long road, but it would be a lot easier now with Will and Ed travelling beside me.

42

Bozeman, 2001

After weighing all the pros and cons of moving in with two men, I decided it wouldn't be a bad move as I could lean on them and them, me. I had made my list of demands clear, and they were met with open arms. My focus was to plow through my master's and then evaluate all my options.

My sights were on obtaining my doctorate, but I wasn't sure if I would take a break after my master's or just bulldoze straight through. I enjoyed what I was studying and stayed in good standing with all my professors in case I needed recommendations for future opportunities at Montana State or elsewhere. I picked up a supervisory role in a Foundations of Ecology Lab all the while, working at the shop.

This schedule didn't afford much time to fish, and I became increasingly stressed and short-tempered. We tried to eat dinner together whenever we could, and Will would talk about all the fish his clients caught. He was trying, in his not-so-subtle way, to badger me about how I needed to make the time to get back on the water. I was busy, but Will didn't see it that way. He just saw (and heard) me getting more and more bitchy, and he knew the solution was for me to go fishing and talk to my therapists.

I exploded one Saturday morning for absolutely no reason. I couldn't even remember why I got angry, but I was SO mad. I was so tired and hadn't slept eight hours in as many nights. Will asked me something innocuous, and I blew his head off. Then, I stormed out. Ed came running after me, steered me into his truck, and took me to the secret DeCamp painting place so I could talk to Momma, Daddy, and fish.

On the way home, after I felt much better and more relaxed, Ed suggested I slow down a little.

"Maya, it's important for you to make the time to fish. It's not just 'fun.' It's also what keeps you healthy and centered. Why don't you take fewer classes this fall? There's no need to rush. Slow down, relax, and remember your WHY."

A few months after I moved in, Will and I finally made it official. Although it did test our compatibility, our patience for one another's space, and our stick-to-itiveness. He knew I got him, and he got me.

We were both still careful and moved very slowly. Sometimes, too slowly, but I was always beyond careful with all of my relationships. I never offered too much of myself until I was sure the person was worthy of my time and effort. Will was worthy. I never considered marriage to anyone until I met Will.

From the moment I stood on Ed's front porch and Will clumsily asked me if I was a disgruntled college student, I knew he was different. When we shook hands... I know it's cliché to say it felt like an electric shock wave traveling throughout my body...but, as a lover of words, I can safely say there is no better description. That electricity never faded; I simply suppressed it until I knew he was worthy.

Then, there were the inevitable obstacles. We were both strong-willed and stubborn. We were both leaders and independent. I was Black, and he was white. I was planning to get my doctorate and, although he was very smart, he barely graduated from high school. He grew up in Montana, and I was a North Carolina mountain girl. I was a candle, but he was the sun.

We shared many of the same ideas. Because Ed was his father, he was raised like a Southerner: polite and chivalrous, so we had similar upbringings. Dinner was important, and we made every effort to be there, with no electronics, because it was family time. We lost a parent, and we shared the same passion for fly fishing.

He was "the one," and I had known it for years. It was time to do something about it.

In the past, Will and I had a few encounters, but nothing like this. All the cards were on the table. Any ambiguity was now gone. Our feelings were clear, exposed, and vulnerable. Our trust, friendship, and history of our bond would be our chaperone for what lay ahead. If any experiences from our past cropped up, we would manage them as a unit and move on. He put his hand on the small of my back and one softly on my cheek and pulled me tight to his waist. I put my arms over his shoulders, and he picked me up. I wrapped my legs around him, and he carried me to his bedroom. What came next left no doubt that we were meant for each other, and we would be in good standing for the rest of our lives together. I knew he loved me, and I loved him more than I ever thought I could love anyone.

My eyes opened the next morning as I felt his hand on my hip. He lovingly pulled me to him, and I willingly rolled on top of him. It was mid-morning, and I was thinking I hadn't stayed in bed this long since I was in high school, but in high school, I didn't have Will.

43

Bozeman, May, 2002

It was May 31st, and Ed made sure none of us were scheduled to work the weekend of my 23rd birthday. Both men decided that I needed a weekend getaway to decompress, get back to the basics, and most importantly, consult with my aquatic brethren. The weekend was going to be all about me, which was refreshing and special. Because it was a three-and-a-half-hour drive from Bozeman to the Big Horn River, Ed had called in a few favors to a buddy who owned a resort in Fort Smith we would use as our base camp.

The morning we left, Will had just finished locking the trailer and boat to his truck when Ed got panicky, which was weird for him. Will and Ed started to bicker about what gear to take and other essentials. I couldn't quite hear them because they were talking in some kind of code, but they both became increasingly upset.

It was too early in the morning to deal with that, and I hadn't had my coffee yet, so I walked inside the house for a to-go cup. I glanced out the kitchen window, and I saw

Will bury his finger in Ed's chest in a heated exchange. Ed didn't back down.

Throwing his arms in the air, Will stormed over to the back of the truck and flung the back door open. He was clawing and tossing our overnight bags around like a dog digging for a bone. I had seen enough and snapped. Thunderously, I leapt through the front storm door grabbing their attention as it smacked against the house with a bang. Sarcastically but with conviction, I yelled, "Hey, thing one and thing two, please remind me who this special weekend is for again? Isn't it someone's birthday?"

They stopped, frozen, mouths wide open and stared at me in astonishment, like two deer caught in the headlights. In unison, I heard, "Sorrrry."

I stood there, coffee in hand, supervising both men as they packed up the remaining gear. I barked again, "Aren't we supposed to be having fun? You know, happy excitement that comes with the anticipation of a planned event. If you donkeys wanna keep squabbling, I'm gonna go to the shop, do some inventory and study. I don't need to listen to y'all's bullshit for a whole weekend!"

Silence saturated the moment and neither one dared to make eye contact with me.

I watched as they walked on eggshells while I sipped my coffee. In an instant I had become a drill sergeant, watching my two ants march around, picking up bags and coolers and setting them down, only to move them again until the Tetris puzzle had been assembled "their way." All of what transpired made me laugh hysterically.

"Ridiculous," I blurted out loud as one last measure of my displeasure.

We finally headed east on Hwy 90 toward Billings. Will broke the silence during the drive because Will couldn't *not* talk. He would explode otherwise. I was proud of him, though; he made it a whopping twelve minutes into the drive before he opened his mouth.

Once we arrived and unpacked, we reloaded with only what we needed for about a five-hour drift that afternoon. It was a perfect day, and I was ready to go. It was a pleasant sixty-five degrees, and the sky was blue. We were serving Pale Morning Duns which is a mayfly and a staple consumption of every Bow and Brown we floated through. Will was at the helm navigating, and Ed and I were on fire right out of the gate.

Will's head was on a swivel, constantly observing and directing our cast placements. All we had to do was put it where he said, and the fish took care of the rest. My timing couldn't have been any better with hookset after hookset. I was in the zone. Four times that day, Ed and I were hooked up on fish at the same time, causing Will to choose whose fish he would net first. It was a beautiful scenario.

Back at base camp, we shared a nice bourbon to cap off the day and reminisced. That's when the trash talking commenced. Ed took a couple of jabs at Will. "We could've had sixty in the boat if our guide hadn't missed a few of those high yielding runs, and, we should've changed the bite when the feeding slowed."

Will quipped without hesitation, "Dad, it wasn't the fly. It was the fisherman. And if your hooksets weren't like a snail on sandpaper, your line would have been taut more often. Excuses are like armpits old man…everybody's got 'em, and they all stink." We all laughed.

Ed made a fire while Will got out the camp chairs, and I changed clothes. When I returned, Ed and Will were seated, eagerly waiting for me. In my chair was a present wrapped in colorful fish print birthday paper.

Will exclaimed, "Dad insisted on wrapping it. I, on the other hand, was trying to go for a more avant-garde approach and have you discover it spontaneously. I wanted a more out-of-the-box approach for surprising you on your birthday, if you will."

Ed chimed in, "The birthday paper is fantastic. It's very festive."

Will fired back, "Dad, Maya isn't six."

"Gentlemen! Are you trying to ruin a perfect day? Well, are ya?"

Collectively they mumbled, "Nooo," Just like little boys do when reprimanded because they can't behave.

I told Ed I loved the wrapping paper and began to tear into the gift. I saw Ed out of the corner of my eye, stick his tongue out at Will. Will rolled his eyes, sighed, and stared up at the few clouds crossing the sky.

I wasn't sure what the gift was until the last layer of the wrapping paper came off. It was my dad's old tackle box. I choked up. Tears fell from my eyes, but my smile sparkled. Was this really Daddy's tackle box that I had broken years ago when Momma tried to make me go fishing for the first time without him? "Ed, how did you get it here without me knowing?"

Ed waved his index finger in the air. "I'm like Houdini. It's all about strategy and deception, Chipper. A little smoke and mirrors and then Bammo! I got her home and fixed her right on up."

Will added, "WE fixed her right up. Dad saw that it was broken, but you wouldn't let him throw it away. Soooo, while we were all packing everything up in Boone, he hid it in his duffle bag and brought it back with us. We thought you'd like to have it."

It was a perfect gift. I smiled, and Will enveloped me in his arms. "Happy birthday," he whispered and kissed my ear. "Go ahead and open it up and see how it works." I did. It was fantastic. I couldn't imagine a better gift. "We repaired the hinges, sanded out the rust spots, and hit it with a few new coats of paint, but we didn't want to bang out the dents. We thought the dents gave it some healthy character and personality, so we left those."

Memories came flooding back one after the other, and my tears increased with each re-lived memory. That tackle box was there when I learned how to fish. It was my dad's, and he handed it down to me. It carried all my innocence and my transgressions during my early years as an angler. If the box could talk, the stories it could tell. It was broken just like me. Now, it was better...still scarred with memories, but beautiful and did the job better than most. "Ed, I can't thank you and Will enough for breathing life back into this memento of my past. What a beautiful gift from both of you. My father's legacy will live on." Ed stood up, and we all hugged.

Then Will, right on cue, cut short the sentimental moment. He said, "All right, all right. Dad, you're in charge of the boat tomorrow. I'm gonna get in on that fun!"

"Yeah, yeah," Ed said, and we all chuckled and headed to bed.

The next day provided more of the same. The men had packed what looked to be a buffet meal for our lunch. We made several stops to wade and pick up some fish from the river's shore. One of those stops would be to eat.

It was about noon, and Ed eased us up to one of the Big Horn's many shoals, announcing it was time for some lunch, and we could fish the shoreline. We stepped out of the boat to work the run a few times. Will handed me one of his Fly Bibles and urged me to try one of his new ties. Then he pretended to drop the caddis fly he was tying. As he knelt, I opened the box. Time stopped.

Inside, was a stunning ring embedded into the hook slot sitting there front and center surrounded by a myriad of beautiful flies. Ed had been prepping our food and rushed over to us and started ripping off picture after picture. It was all a blur. I tried to catch my breath. I looked at Will and back at Ed, and yet again, tears started flooding my eyes.

Ed was beaming. Will stayed down on one knee and tenderly took the fly box from my hand and said, "Maya 'Chipper' Jones, will you make me the happiest man on the planet and marry me?"

I gasped and put my hands over my mouth and nodded yes. When I got my voice back, I said, "Yes, William 'Sunshine' Myers. Of course I will marry you!" I couldn't see through the waterfall blinding me. Will took my left hand and delicately threaded my ring finger. He stood, hugged me, and we kissed. I refused to let him go. He picked me up in the air and swung me around in a 360-degree spin. Out of the corner of my eye, I caught a glimpse of Ed dancing and pumping his fists in the air. Then, Ed walked over and wrapped his arms around Will and me. He whispered, "Today is a great day. Now I have the daughter I always wanted. What a spectacular family this is! What a beautiful day to celebrate! Let me tell you what my father-in-law, Beaux, told me and your mom before we got married. He told us this story about a magic tree the preacher planted in a newlywed's yard. The pastor told them that as long as that tree was alive, their marriage would be, too. The tree grew tall and strong…at first. Then, there was a huge drought in all the land. The tree started to die. One night, the husband crept out of bed to go water the tree. As he carried the bucket of water, he ran into his wife who was also carrying a bucket. Do you think that marriage survived? You just gotta work at it. All the time. Never take it for granted because as soon as you do, it's gone. Now let's eat!"

The whole afternoon I could feel myself glowing brighter than Montana sun dancing off the Big Horn. Through each cast, I would purposefully look down at my left hand as I syphoned the fly line off my reel just to catch a glimpse of my ring's radiance. It was the first time I didn't care if I caught any fish or not. All I thought about was having a family, how much I loved Will, and what was to come. I'm not sure how Ed did it, but he had made cupcakes and lugged them from Bozeman all the way to Fort Smith without being smashed. Will reached into his boat bag and pulled out some candles. He lit them, and I made my wish. My wish hadn't come to fruition yet, but I was hopeful.

44

Bozeman, 2003

Grad school was even better than I expected. Ed was one of my professors, and he was a great teacher but seemed a little scattered sometimes. I figured it was just the stress of teaching and the shop. I made an "A," of course, but better than that, I learned so much that I didn't know about the life cycles of insects through their physiology and morphology. All that knowledge coupled with my own prowess translated nicely into helping customers pick their flies, when to use them, and where to use them.

I poured myself into learning everything I could about running every aspect of the fly shop. I tied flies when needed, I did the purchasing, inventory, and books, I studied my butt off while Will guided, Ed taught, and Betty minded the store and phone. It was a lot of work to balance all my school with all the hours I put in at the shop, but I loved it. I never forgot what Ed told me about making the time to fish, so I scheduled time with my fish therapists at least three times a week and stuck to it as though it was an actual class.

Throughout the years, I still cried about Momma and missed her so much more than I ever thought I would. When Daddy died, I was just a kid, so I knew that would be hard to handle. But, with Momma, I was astounded by the depth of my grief. I was grown. I had lived 2,000 miles away from her for over two years. The hardest part was knowing Momma wasn't there anymore. Before her death, I would call her sometimes three times a day, and then a week would go by before I called her again. But she always answered, always listened, always kept me informed about so-and-so's bunion surgery and Aunt Eugenia's family reunion I was missing.

Now, I didn't have that anymore, and it was truly a lonely feeling. Thank goodness I had Will and Ed. They helped ease my loneliness. It wasn't the same, of course. No one could replace my mom and dad, but I was about to be a Myers, and I accepted that invitation like a Venus Fly Trap welcomes his next bug.

Since I had already been living in the Myers's house for a while, I assumed my roles wouldn't shift that much since everyone had his routine. I was wrong. Life was getting ready to take another hard detour, and there was no way to stop it.

We all still fished, of course, and worked in the shop, but I had also assumed the role of Queen in the house to make sure everything got done. I'd be studying, and I'd look out the window and watch them fight over how to fix my old truck.

Both men would be on either side folded over the engine, under the hood, pointing at whatever and mumbling. Personally, I don't think they had a clue as to what they were looking for. It was a point of pride for Ed to keep it running like his little brother Remmey had for so long. Ed would be ashamed if he hadn't been able to do that, too. Will was always reluctant to help Ed repair anything because of the heated bickering that would ensue. Unfortunately for Will, it was my truck and by default, he felt obligated to work on it.

"Dad, do you remember what Maya told you?" Will said one day while he was under the hood of my car.

Ed said, "About what?"

"The truck, Dad. That's why we are here staring at it?"

Ed was in another world. "She sure is a beauty, isn't she? Now, what about the truck?"

"Maya said it quit running again."

Ed said, "Ahhh Haaa, I found the culprit. You see right there? That's the issue, son."

"Where?" Will replied.

"Here!" Ed puts his finger on it. "The wire harnesses on these spark plugs, they're loose."

"Dad, it's not the engine. The engine runs fine. She said it wouldn't crank."

"Well, if it's the crankshaft, it's an engine issue."

Will ran both hands over his face and through his hair. "Dammit, Dad. No! Maya said it wouldn't crank. It's not the crankshaft. It's not getting any juice."

"Son, I just told you the harnesses were loose." Ed leans in to secure the hoods on each plug.

"Dad, your C.R.S. has gotten worse."

"My C.R.S?"

"Yeah C.R.S. Your 'Can't Remember Shit' is much worse now."

Will threw his wrench down and walked away with his hands on his hips, like vintage John McEnroe when he was mad at the chair umpire over a bad call. He would walk in circles, lips pursed, at the precipice of cussing and staring at Ed in disbelief. Ed usually just stared at him like he didn't know what was going on.

Will and I planned our wedding for just after I finished my master's degree and before I started my PhD program. The wedding was set for mid-July, but the honeymoon wouldn't be 'til after Thanksgiving. Neither of us could afford to take off during the busy season and somewhere warm on the first of December sounded better than Bozeman.

Will and I argued for months about where we would have the ceremony. A big, formal church wedding? A quick, simple Justice of the Peace? There were pros and cons for them all.

Finally, we decided we would just use the long, grassy landing behind the fly shop. It was flat and well-manicured. The backdrop behind the Gallatin was always breathtaking and encompassed what both Will and I embodied as our unified desire. It would be nice to have my fish friends at the service as well.

We invited our families from Boone and local friends like Judith and Betty and our fishing buddies like Mae and

Fae. Will even called the "Fishheads," and they all made it a point to show up, knowing they would get a chance to fish Will's home waters. Will had no clue they would show up three days early to give him an impromptu bachelor's party. Remmey's family came up. Miss Betty, Sam, Annie, and Judith were my bridesmaids. They wore whatever summer sundresses they already had. Remmey and Will's other uncle from his mom's side, John, and Mark, the longest tenured guide, were honored to stand with him. They were dressed in whatever blue jackets they had in their closets, and we bought them deep purple ties. Will had on a blue suit as well, but his was much more elegant and stylish. Will surprised me by wearing my dad's cuff links and tie bar. Momma had given Will these items as heirlooms. He then separated himself from his groomsmen even further by elegantly accenting his ensemble with a lavender tie in honor of my mother because it was her favorite color. He assumed it was the color of the dress she would have worn. Will always put me first and that was his way of bringing them close to us as we said our vows. I really loved how thoughtful he was.

That gesture was emphasized with gold-framed pictures of Sarah and my mom and dad sitting in the family row. It wasn't what we wanted, but we decided to include their presence the only way we knew how.

I was in my dressing room with the girls. My dress was just like me. Beautiful, graceful, elegant, and stylish. Ok, well, maybe not all that much like me, but it was just what I wanted my wedding dress to look like. Momma and I had picked it out, and Momma bought it for me before she died. I wasn't even really into my relationship with Will yet, but Momma said it would be her way to help me on my wedding day.

It was a simple, classic satin wedding dress with a strapless neckline and princess line silhouette. The bodice was embellished with lace, beads, and had a lace up back closure. It was an A-line skirt with a chapel length train. I had no idea what any of that meant, but that's what the sales lady told us. All I knew was it was pretty. Momma's veil was also simple and white and stayed on my head with a tiny tiara. I had often thought of myself as deserving of a tiara. Now, I had one.

Betty said, "Ok, ladies, let's go. It's time!" and the girls squeezed my hand and left me alone in my room for a minute. I looked at myself in the mirror, and I started to cry. Momma and Daddy would be so proud of me right now. I've never read this anywhere in the Bible, but always thought that heaven had some sort of aquarium in it, so folks above could take a good look at everything happening on Earth. The saints who have gone before us wouldn't want to see us all the time, obviously. But every now and then, I think Jesus says, "Hey Zeke, hey Millie, come over here and look at this." And they get to see some of the glorious moments we have. Not many of them are worthy of looking down from heaven, but every now and then, there are moments. This was definitely one of those moments. If there is an aquarium in heaven, Momma and Daddy were there and they were looking at me. Daddy had been gone a long time, but it seemed like just a few weeks ago that Jen told me the news. Momma had only been gone just a few years, but there were times when I forgot she was gone. I'd pick up the phone to ask her how to cook something or hem something or what I should do about a difficult situation with one of my professors. One time, I even started the first couple of digits before I remembered she wouldn't answer.

Now, I was at my wedding, looking like a princess, and I was all alone.

"Hey Maya," Ed was at the door. "You bout ready? This damn suit is getting on my last nerve."

Ed was there in his Sunday best. If he noticed my tears, he didn't mention them. I wiped them, took a deep breath, and threw the tissue away.

"Yes. I'm ready," I smiled at him.

"Not having second thoughts are you 'cause I already moved all my stuff to the basement." He winked at me and nudged my arm.

I laughed. "No. I'm ready." I paused and continued, "You sure I'm old enough to do this?"

"Of course you are. Hard to believe...what was it? Ten or eleven years ago we met and started fishing together. Now you are getting ready to be my daughter-in-law, and all I can think about is how blessed I am to have you and Will in my life as a team. It doesn't get any better than this right here!"

Ed had reorganized and restructured the entire downstairs portion of the fly shop as a staging area for me and my entourage. This would be where the bridesmaids and groomsmen started their processional march through the corridor of the congregation. Will had built a beautiful wedding arch and stage that underscored the majestic mountain range which cradled a flawless cobalt blue sky. It truly was a magnificent backdrop to what I would consider an even more remarkable day.

During the rehearsal, Betty had said, "Don't walk like you're plowing a mule! Slow down! One step, pause. One step, pause. Let everyone see how beautiful you are."

"Thanks, Betty!" Ed said. "I guess I should let people admire my good looks more often." Now that we were doing the real thing, I wanted to run down the aisle. Partly because Will looked so good and so happy! But also, because this all made me very uncomfortable. All these thoughts were running through my mind as I waited for "Clair De Lune" to end and my cue.

I was so nervous. Ed must have sensed it because he held out his index finger to me and whispered, "Pull my finger, Chipper." I started laughing just as Wagner's traditional wedding march began, and Ed and I did our best to walk painfully slowly to the altar. Will and I knew the officiant needed to be Captain Allen; it was only right that the person that once saved me years back be the person to usher me into this new life.

Ed proudly finished escorting me down the aisle, and when I reached my destination in front of Captain Allen, he asked Ed, "Who blesses Maya in her union with Will today?" Ed went off script and choked out, "Zeke Jones, Millie Jones..." He cleared his throat, composed himself, and continued, "Sarah Myers, Maggie Myers, and me, Ed Myers."

45

Bozeman, 2003

I started making subtle adjustments to the living situation. It was a fine house, but very plain. I hung new curtains, added a rug accent to the dark, wooden floors and decluttered the kitchen counter tops. The bathrooms were hopeless, so I let that ride. Neither Ed nor Will ever said anything about any of the changes I made. In fact, I'm pretty sure they didn't even notice or care.

I got to where I didn't mind cooking as long as I didn't have to do it every night. I was a much better cook than they were, but still not as good as Momma. Usually, if I cooked, they said thank you. But, over time, people will begin to take other people for granted. One day, I told Will that I would no longer be cooking supper until he fixed the railing by the front porch steps. He and Ed ate peanut butter sandwiches one night, tuna fish the next night, and the third night, when I came home, Will met me at the door. "Look, Chipper! I fixed the railings!"

Ed shouted from inside the house, "WE fixed the railings."

I leaned on the rail as I walked up the stairs. It was solid and sturdy. I made Will fix it for Ed, but I would have never told either one of them that. Ed was a proud man, but his knees were shot.

Except when he came up to the kitchen to eat, Ed stayed in the basement and gave Will and me our privacy. We watched movies some nights and would invite him up to the den. But he had his own den downstairs, plus a small kitchenette with a bedroom and bathroom.

When I stayed up for my late-night cram sessions in my Ecological Physiology of Aquatic Organisms class, Ed would bring me coffee and then help me study. He was still very quiet, but the stars had come back to his eyes, and most days it looked like he had adjusted to his new normal. He was happy teaching and running the shop. Business was booming. Ed handled all the business aspects from stocking to scheduling. Will was the top guide and handled the website and marketing. I handled all the money and studied to finish my PhD. Betty still worked the counter most days, and I grew to love her as much as Will and Ed did.

I wasn't totally committed to finishing it up, though. I wanted to have kids before I got too old to play football and basketball with them. Will was always supportive of whatever I wanted to do. Ed was, too, but I knew Ed wanted me to finish my degree. So did Momma.

I wanted to finish, too. But I certainly wasn't as driven any more. One of the life lessons Momma and Daddy had instilled in me years and years ago was that you never quit. Momma would quote Jim Valvano, "Don't give up. Don't ever give up." Just like Daddy would quote Langston Hughes.

"Don't you set down on the steps
Cause you find it's kinder hard.
Don't fall now---
For I'se still goin', honey,
I'se still climbin',
And life for me ain't been no crystal stair."

That's the kind of thing I heard my whole life, so quitting wasn't an option. I decided to talk about it with Ed when we were cooking dinner, and Will hadn't come home from the shop yet.

"Have you made a pro and con list?" Ed said.

"Only in my head. But what do you think? Should I take one more year and finish up?"

"What do you have left? Just one more class and your dissertation, right?"

"Yeah. And I really like teaching, too. The undergrads are fun. But... I don't know. What I do know is I'm not fishing as much as I need or want to. I like being in the shop. And, let's face it, I'm probably going to have to move to get a tenure-track job. And if I move, Will will go with me, so it'd just be you and Betty at the shop again. I'm just not sure I want to do that."

"Well, the shop is doing pretty well, but I have to tell you, teaching is not only very rewarding and fun, but it's also pretty consistent. When a recession hits, which it inevitably will from time to time, teaching will be a constant paycheck. Who knows, you may find your way back home to Boone. App State would kill for a professor like you. You'll be able to write your own ticket anywhere you want to go."

"I guess so. But I'm not sure I want to leave."

"Then don't. Life always works out the way it's supposed to. Stop worrying! You worry too much to be a fisherman."

I laughed. He'd been telling me that for twenty years.

46

Bozeman, 2003

After Ed and Will had left for the day, I was cleaning the kitchen. I heard water running downstairs, so I went down to check. Ed left the house with his bathroom sink faucet flowing. I turned it off and didn't say anything to anyone.

The next day, I found Ed's wallet in the refrigerator, right there, front and center, beside the milk, and I knew Will and I had to have a conversation. The next time was my whistle blower moment. Ed and I were both on campus. I went by his classroom and stood outside his door where I could see him addressing his class. He had written, "TRICHOPTERA," on the board and lecturing about the life cycle of the caddis fly. Before I knocked, I could see him pause, like he was searching for words. He didn't know what to say and became visually agitated. He threw his head back, rolled his eyes, and stammered over some words. "Ok, guys, let's go ahead and call it a day. See you next class."

The students looked at each other surprised but eagerly filed out. I overheard one of them say, "He's never let us out early before...much less, thirty minutes early." I continued walking down the hall, and when I passed the Dean's office, he stopped me. "Hi Maya. Have you seen Dr. Myers today?"

"Hey Dr. Vogel. I think he has a class right now."

"Well, he missed his evaluation meeting with me this morning, and last week he missed our department meeting."

"I did ask him about that, and he said he had a headache and just forgot."

Vogel said, "Hhhummm. I see. Well, if he's still in class, I'll just go sit in there and wait for him to wrap it up."

I didn't know what to do. If I said, he's already let his kids go, would he get in trouble? If I didn't say anything, was that lying?

I just said, "Ok. Have a great day."

He turned and said, "You, too," and headed on over to Ed's class.

After school, I headed into the shop and could hear Will and Ed fighting.

"I told you that last week!" Will was shouting.

"No, you did not. You never said we were out." Ed lamented.

"We weren't out when I told you to order more."

"You're supposed to write things down anyway. You know that. I'm too old to remember all of this."

"I did write it on a sticky." Will started looking around the desk. Sure enough, he found the sticky and held it up for Ed to see.

I decided Will didn't need to rub it in, so I interrupted and said, "Guys! I can hear y'all hollering all the way outside. Just relax. It's going to be okay. What are we out of?"

"Cliff bars, water, Gatorade, Miller Lite... All the staples we sell out of practically weekly." Will answered, still miffed.

"Ok, I can make a Sam's run later and pick up all of that to at least keep us in good shape 'til the big order comes in. It's going to be okay. Come here, Ed, help me with this. Will, do you want to make a Sam's run, or do you want me to go?"

Will grabbed his blue MSU ball cap and keys. He kissed my cheek and said, "I'll go."

"Ok, Sunshine. Be careful. And keep your receipt!" I hollered after him. He gave me a thumbs up, but I could tell he was frustrated.

After he was gone and Ed and I were locking the shop, Ed looked at me and earnestly said, "Maya, do you think I'm losing it?"

I laughed a little until I realized he wasn't joking. "No, Ed. You know Will probably put that sticky note on the back of his computer or something and it fell off and you never saw it. Try not to worry."

Of course, I was lying.

A few months later, Will and I were having dinner at one of our favorite restaurants, Montana Ale Works right on Main Street. We loved their homebrews and the vibe, so we ate their all the time. As we sipped our Ross Creek Red and Gallatin Pale and ate our Cowboy Dip, our conversation turned to Ed. I said, "It's not just that he's forgotten a few orders or that he skipped his own class. I'm really worried about what the doctor is going to tell us tomorrow."

Will sighed. "I'm sure it's going to be fine...But it's hard not to worry about it."

"I know. I'm worried, too." I started to say something but then I stopped and turned my mouth up into a smirk.

"What?" Will asked.

"I was going to say we've had a hard couple of years, but then I thought, who hasn't? Life is hard."

Will said, "Yeah, it is. But I don't want it to be, 'Dad has Alzheimer's hard,' you know?"

"Yeah,. I know. I'll take him to the doctor, but I don't want you to sit around worried."

Will said. "I'm going to go fish by myself. No clients. No friends. Just me." He pulled his wallet out and paid our check.

"Okay. Be careful."

"I'm always more careful than you and Dad. I am the careful, cautious one who actually checks the forecasts before I get into the boat." I laughed as he put his credit card back in his wallet, grabbed the keys and flipped them to me. He always did this thing where he tossed them with his right hand and slapped his elbow with his left hand. Good thing I could catch.

47

Bozeman, 2003

Betty took care of the shop, and Will went fishing while Ed and I went to the doctor. I was nervous. I thought Ed's forgetfulness was too severe for someone only 60-ish. The nurse came in and took his blood pressure and said the doctor would be in shortly. I waited a few minutes and then told Ed I was going to the restroom right quick, but I'd be back.

I met Dr. Webb in the hallway. "Hi Dr. Webb, I'm Maya Myers. I'm Ed's daughter-in law.

"Nice to meet you. I was just on my way in to see Ed."

"I wanted to talk to you before you came in. We've had some concerns about Ed. Will and I have both noticed some slippage in his memory—searching for words—things like that. Also, there has been some chatter at the University where the students are unable to follow his lectures, and he is missing meetings. Is there any way you could check on him without him knowing you're checking on him?"

"I see. For someone his age, that's certainly not normal but, of course, we'll run some tests and get to the bottom of it discreetly."

"Thank you so much, Dr. Webb. Can you give me a minute, please, so I can walk in before you?"

Dr. Webb smiled and let me go back in and get settled, then he walked in and headed straight over to Ed to shake his hand.

"Ed! It's been a long time! How are you?"

"Fine, Roy, just fine. How you doing? How's Ruth?"

"We're great!" He looked over at me, and I extended my hand as well.

"Hello, Dr. Webb," I smiled.

"Hello."

Ed said, "Oh, Roy, this is my daughter, Maya."

Dr. Webb just smiled at me. "Well, Ed, you haven't been in here for a while, so we're going to run a whole battery of tests."

"Great. I can hardly wait."

"Life after sixty, Ed. It's not for the weak. You need to stay on top of everything you eat and be sure you're still getting plenty of exercise."

"Whatever you say, doc."

I stepped outside so they could do the "man" stuff. Ed was dressed when I came back in. We were quiet as we sat and waited for the doctor to come back.

He knocked softly and didn't wait for us to respond. "Well, Ed, everything looks pretty good so far. I'll call you next week when we get the lab results back. Cut down on the salt and sugar, like I always tell you. Have you noticed any problems remembering things?"

"Nah. Not really. I'm a little forgetful at times, but it's no big deal."

"Ok. Well, let's keep an eye on that for the next several months. I'm going to give you a prescription for something called Cognex. It will help you focus. We all get a little scattered sometimes and this helps with getting dialed in with your memory and thought processes. I want you to come back in three months, and we'll get a gauge and see how things are going."

Ed said, "I haven't seen you on the water in forever. You need to get back out there and get a line wet. It's good for your soul."

"I would love to! I haven't seen the light of day in months." Ed and I stood up to go. "Oh, and Ed," Dr. Webb said, "don't forget to use sunscreen!" They shook hands. "It was very nice to meet you, Maya."

"Nice to meet you, too, Dr. Webb."

A couple of months later, on our next pretty day when Will didn't have a trip, and I didn't have a class, we fished.

Fishing was our sanctuary. It was where we had most of our serious conversations. I knew he was worried about Ed.

I gently broached the subject. "I don't think the meds are working for Ed. Do you?" I could tell Will was in his own headspace because he was quiet. Will was never quiet. He loaded a few false casts and tagged a couple of nice fish right out of the gate. The question hung in the air, but I didn't press.

We were both so in tune with our marks on the water, we didn't have to think about what we were doing, so I knew he wasn't thinking about fishing. Still, there was silence.

Finally, I asked, "Has he been forgetting more?"

"Yes. He left the shop open all night... didn't close up the register, didn't lock up... nothing."

"It's a good thing Bozeman is such a nice city," I said, and Will smiled sadly. I continued,

"I think he's getting worse, too. He left the water running in his sink, and he left his wallet in the fridge last Thursday."

Will said, "Holy shit, that's a new one." I could see his shoulders rise and fall in a deep exhale as he stared at his mark. Will was worried, and he never got worried about anything, except when I almost died a few times on the Gallatin. Now I was getting worried. "When will the three months be up?" I asked him.

"I think his appointment is next week."

"Ok. Let's try not to worry about it right now. Let's just wait and see what the doctor says."

Will sighed and started wading toward the bank. I said nothing and followed him. Instead of packing up though, he just sat down on the bank. I sat beside him. I knew him well enough to know that words didn't matter at that moment. They would have blown away like a dandelion in the wind anyway. My sitting beside him was all he needed. "You know," Will said as we watched the sunset over the river, my head resting on his shoulder, "you never told me how you and Dad met."

"Really? After all these years? I never told you?" Will shook his head and grabbed a blade of grass and started ripping it into little pieces. I told him how it happened. That day on New River, the stolen necklace, bullies, everything.

"Damn, girl. That's scary! I can't believe you ever fished there again."

"I had my pocketknife with me for protection." I scrunched up my face then and held up a single finger like it was knife.

Will laughed. I said, "Scary, right?"

He said, "I'm shaking in my boots."

"Exactly," I said. "Even with my knife, I was scared."

"But you went anyway," Will said proudly. "That's why I love you. You don't let anything ever get in your way. You just go through shit, never around it. That's a damn good story. No wonder you love him so much."

"Yes, I do. He's saved my life…twice. Once literally and also by introducing me to fly fishing."

Will was adamant, "Actually, three times."

"Three? Oh, because he introduced me to you?" I quipped.

"Yes, you lucky, lucky girl! No…when you took off down the Gallatin like a rookie, I lost my mind. But Dad was steady enough to get the search and rescue team involved. I was hell bent on just taking off down the river to find you. So, I would have to credit him for your rescue."

"Guess I need to thank him for that one, too."

Will nodded. "Yeah, he brags about you all the time. Not just for your ability to talk to fish, but also for your tenacity. You stayed with it no matter how many people looked at you funny."

"They're just jealous of my mad skills and all the fish I catch."

Will got reflective again as he threw a rock into the river. "There really is something about fly fishing that just feeds the soul...the constant movement and being engaged, calculated effort with everything you do just to get hooked up on a nice fish. Some people meditate. Some take drugs. Some drink. But fly fishing is so much healthier for you."

"Yeah," I said. "There's nothing like it."

"I bet that was hard, though," Will said. "I don't know many other women who were fly fishing in the 80s."

"Especially Black women."

"That's true." Will said thoughtfully. "That's why you're so awesome."

"I'm awesome for many, many reasons, and don't you forget it."

48

Spring, 2006

I was getting ready to graduate with my PhD. Ed was still struggling with his memory, but the meds had controlled it to the point where his dementia at least wasn't progressing as quickly as it had been from a year earlier. Yet Will and I became increasingly leery of his issues. One minute, he would be fine and then all of a sudden, he would start searching for words and start talking with his hands, until someone would step in to help him play charades.

It was Will's turn to cook, and he had fixed a pork tenderloin in the crock pot. It was one of his staples. I could tell something was bothering Ed when I sat down to eat that night, but we made small talk for a little while until he felt comfortable enough to tell us what was on his mind.

"Hey, I checked the account yesterday and either Will just made off with someone's salary or we're having a big season with your tours," I said. "I just made our biggest deposit ever!" Will smiled, but Ed didn't say anything.

Will said, "I'm not gonna lie... I'm exhausted, but the uptick in clients this season has been a blessing. What do you think, Dad?"

"Yeah. Nice job, Will."

Ed still wasn't ready to talk, so I kept talking. "If we can keep this up, maybe we can retire early."

"That'd be nice," Will said.

"Speaking of retirement..." Ed cleared his throat. "The University wants to throw me some sort of shindig for my retirement."

Will got ready to say something about how we didn't know he decided to retire, but I kicked him softly under the table.

I said, "Well, you deserve everything they give you and then some." Ed shrugged and smiled. Will added, "Besides, the shop is growing so fast, we need you there full-time."

Ed grinned, but I could tell he wasn't happy. I was debating with myself on what I should say next. If I pushed too hard, he could shut down. If I didn't bring it up, he may never talk to us about it.

Before I could decide, Ed made my decision for me. "I'm ready to retire. I've been a teacher for a long time, and I'm sick of the crap."

"What is it, then, Dad?" Will said.

"I don't know. I'm just...I don't know, uneasy about all of it."

I finally understood what he was talking about, "Wait... Ed, are you talking about the banquet? Is that what you're worried about?"

"Hell yes! Why would I want them to do that? They haven't done it for anyone else who retired," Ed said.

"Sure they have, Dad. You just haven't gone because you're a hermit."

"I don't like banquets."

I couldn't help but laugh. Like that was a newsflash.

"What?" Ed said. "I don't. But when Jerry retired a few years ago, I took him out for dinner to celebrate."

Will started to speak, but I interrupted him before he instigated another fight. I'm a good wife. "That was very nice, Ed. I'm sure Jerry appreciated you taking the time to do that."

"Yeah. He got like a thirty-dollar T-bone, so he better have appreciated it." We got quiet and enjoyed our tasty meal.

"Now listen, y'all," Ed continued, "I'm not retiring because y'all think I can't remember anything. I still don't believe anything is wrong with me that's not wrong with everyone my age." We nodded our heads in alleged agreement, as Ed continued. "I'm fine. That's not why I'm retiring."

"It's okay, Dad. You've worked hard your whole life, and you gave me a great life—"

"And me, too." I added.

Will grabbed my hand and continued, "And Maya, too. We're all so much better off because of you, Dad. If you're ready to retire, do it."

"I'm ready. These kids get younger and whinier every year. I even got an email from a mom telling me a kid didn't plagiarize his paper when I had the site he stole it from word for word. It was like a damn court case, and I was the attorney. I had to submit my findings as evidence to the Dean of Students and the little asshole basically got a slap on the wrist."

I said, "They backed you, though, right?"

"Yes. But I just couldn't believe the university had to get involved," Ed answered. "That is crazy," Will said. "Are you sure you wanna teach for a living, Maya?"

"I don't know… but honestly, I'd like for the shop to be doing so well that I can make a choice and not just teach if I don't want to."

We ate for a little while longer in silence thinking about our futures.

"Oh, Maya, I don't think I told you…" Ed said, "I recommended you replace me." Getting a tenure-track position at any college is a big deal. Getting a position at Montana State University, in the Ecology department is unbelievable. My mouth hung open. It was nepotism, and I knew I would have to formally interview, and I had not ever done that before, but I was confident in my track record, content knowledge, and professionalism. The Ecology department knew I was good. I had glowing evaluations from all my students and the professors with whom I worked. Still, I was shocked.

Ed laughed. "You don't think I'd retire without having someone almost as good as me to take my place, right? Maya, you're the total package, Ichthyology, Entomology, and Aquaculture research at its finest."

Will said, "I'm guessing this is a big deal, huh?"

"It's huge. It means we don't have to move!"

"Seriously? That's awesome!"

Will got up and hugged Ed from behind. He even kissed him on the cheek. Ed pushed him away.

"Stop it! What's wrong with you?" But he was laughing. "It wasn't me anyway. It was Dr. Withers. All I did was recommend you. He's the one that asked about your availability and thought it was a solid fit as long as you don't wreck your interviews. You're young and have been a great ambassador for MSU."

"I never thought he liked me very much."

"He does. I made sure of that." Ed winked at me and said, "Besides, there were quite a few folks in the department who agreed that you were a good fit."

"When did these conversations start?"

"A couple months ago when I told him I was ready to step away. Your name came up, and I asked him to let me float the idea to you. I was going to wait, but I couldn't anymore. I know how you plan like three years in advance."

"I do plan three years in advance, and I won't apologize for that."

"Congratulations, Maya."

This time it was my turn to get up and hug Ed. Will got back up, and we got him in two big bear hugs. He was so uncomfortable. Every time we'd let him go, he'd pick his fork back up, and we would envelop him again.

He laughed, but said, "Will y'all quit? I'm trying to eat my dinner, dammit."

"By the way, Dad. Dinner will be served at your retirement event, right?"

"Yeah. I'm going to go fishing that morning," Ed said.

I said, "That's good. Make it a great day for yourself."

"Will dinner be good?" Will asked earnestly.

I said, "Not as good as this delectable meal, but pretty good. I've crashed more than one MSU banquet and always enjoyed the meals."

This time, it was Ed's turn to laugh. "I agree. Good times. And what time does this ridiculous soiree begin?"

"We should all be there at five for the meet and greet and cocktails."

"So Dad, that means you need to be here at the house cleaned up and ready by 4:30. Her majesty here always takes too long to get ready, you and I'll need to be in the truck waiting on her or so we can blame her for being late."

"Hold up, Sunshine," I said. "When you look as good as I do all the time, it only takes a second to spice all of this up. I'll be ready to go before both of you donkeys even have your clean boxers on."

"You talk a pretty mean game, Chipper."

Ed laughed, "Son, just nod and say, okay. Women are always right. Don't argue."

49

Bozeman, 2006

The morning of the banquet, as expected, Ed went fishing. Will and Betty took care of the shop, and I taught my last class of the semester before stepping into my new role as a tenured track professor. It was all surreal.

Will was sitting on the couch in his Bobcat blue shirt and gold tie, when I walked out in my navy pants suit and jacket. "Where's Ed?" I asked. "We need to go."

"I think he's already there. His truck was gone when I got back."

"I thought he was going to ride with us."

"Me, too," Will shrugged. "But I guess not."

"Should we go?"

"Yeah, let's go on."

At the Strand Union Building, we headed to ballroom B. It was set up with fifty tables and chairs, white linen tablecloths, and full place settings. There was a podium set up at the front but not on the stage. Ed would have never agreed to sit on the stage, but the long table up front with family was okay. Not great, but it was all he would agree to. If they hadn't acquiesced, he may not have shown up for his own banquet.

When we walked in, we were escorted to our table in front. Ed's chair was empty. Uh oh.

Will and I greeted the "dignitaries" at the front and took our seats.

"We should have called his cell before we left," I said.

"I did!" he said. "I called him three times!"

"Okay. It's okay." I tried to sound more reassured than I felt.

Will kept calling, "I called the shop and his cell phone three times."

"Let's call the Sheriff. He knows Ed, and we can just let him know we need him to be on the lookout."

"Good call." Will said, and he stood up and covertly made an exit to go make the call.

50

Bozeman, 2006

Ed had headed north of town to fish Bridger Creek. He called it his gateway to the untouched land. He was going to his happy place where he could talk with Sarah and deal with any troubles that besieged his heart. He got to the river and checked his watch. He had five solid hours of fishing and a couple hours to relax and clean up before the big celebration. A perfect Montana morning turned into an even more marvelous day. The sky stretched on for miles and miles without a cloud impeding its unblemished panorama. The river was cool and clear and as always there wasn't a soul in sight. Just him and his thoughts. Ed was glad he had never told anyone about this place other than Maya. It was their secret.

He was glad he convinced Dr. Withers to start at six instead of five-thirty. Thirty minutes to any fly fisherman could mean the difference in a good day or a great one. All it takes is that one special bout with your opponent to make a memory.

Part of Ed's game was to survey the water table and terrain carefully before pinpointing his casts. He was fishing his favorite set up: dry dropping a size 14, Blue Winged Olive with a size 20 Beadhead Pheasant Tail dropper. It was the middle of May, and the water was remarkably stable given the unseasonably warm temperatures.

Ed walked downstream about three hundred yards. The creek twisted and turned, opening up and bottlenecking through each bend. He studied the water judiciously as he chose his spot. He picked up a few fish, occasionally stopping to relish the moment and then continued to push downstream through sections even he hadn't ever fished before.

Now that he was away from the classroom, he knew better days were ahead. He could do what he wanted, when he wanted, how he wanted. Reading a couple of nice eddies back-to-back, he surveyed the shoal that was twenty-five feet away towards the opposite bank. The Bridger Mountains were steep and rose quickly like a green wall behind him. He checked his flies again, dropped them downstream, and readied himself so he could pinpoint where he wanted his line presentation to ride. He lifted the rod tip to instigate his initial cast.

Five feet of fly line tear-dropped from his reel up to the first eyelet on his rod. He cradled it in his left hand and in unison, pinched the fly line with his thumb and index finger as he deliberately fired his rod skyward and forward to the ten o'clock position. He paused. Back and forth he regulated the tension of line as it unfurled and recoiled with each intentional punch of his wand, always hesitating near his ear to let the distance of the line reload. Tick…Tock. Tick…Tock.

His cadence was flawless. After two false casts and then the third, he lowered his elbow and rod tip with purpose. Three feet of line siphoned like a rocket from his left hand. The leader and line followed, uncoiling from a tight loop to its destination. The flies fell gently ten feet above his mark on the eddie. After two mends, he had a take. His hookset was fast and clean, and in the middle of a nice fight, he heard what he thought was some very loud chirping from a bird.

He was hyper-focused and passed it off unbothered as another noise of nature. After netting his prize he moved further downstream, located at the other end of the horseshoe bend, but still part of the same shallow. He looked around, and in a moment, became extremely disoriented. He stopped and looked at his watch. He looked around again.

"What the...Where the hell am I?" He turned his head from side to side. He knew this place should be familiar, but it wasn't. He contemplated his location some more. "Is my truck this way or that...way? I'm positive I walked downstream, or did I go upstream?"

He shrugged and decided to cast just a few more times and then he would figure out where he was and get back to his truck.

For a man who was astute in his ability to observe his surroundings, he still missed the mule deer carcass that lay fifteen yards behind him. He knelt to net another fish and suddenly sensed it. But by then, it was too late.

Still on his knees, with his back to the beast, he had no chance of standing or even turning around and was bowled over by a mountain lion who had been mirroring him for the last hour. The cat's strike drove Ed's head into a rock, dazing him for a split second. Ed didn't have a clue that he had been in the animal's immediate territory. Ed tried raising both hands to protect his face as the first bite came with a fury to Ed's neck. He kicked and rolled side to side trying to prevent more damage.

The mountain lion continued to shred Ed's neck and shoulders with sweeping tears through his waders, puncturing and carving up his back and legs. He was no match for the ambush and lay lifeless as the brute leapt in for one more gnashing. Then, the cat arrogantly walked away to survey his kill.

Back in the ballroom, Dr. Withers whispered to Will, "I'm going to have to start without him. We have five retirees to honor tonight."

I smiled, and Will nodded and said, "We understand."

Dr. Withers signaled to Dr. Anderson, and the host moved to the mic and called people to order. He began the speeches. "Good evening," he started, "Tonight we'd like to honor several retirees, and first on our agenda is Dr. Malone in Biology. He has been a part of the Bobcat family since 1994," he continued, and my mind went to Ed.

I was sure something was wrong. I knew Ed didn't want to be here, but he respected the University too much to just not show up. I also didn't think his memory was so bad that he would forget the banquet. If he didn't forget and wasn't skipping on purpose, then something must be wrong. "Where are you, Ed?"

Dr. Anderson walked to the mic again, "Our next honoree we would like to celebrate has been with us a long time. Some might say, too long." A few chuckles broke from the crowd. "Dr. Ed Myers has been a part of the Montana State family his entire adult life. After enrolling as a wait-listed freshman in 1964..." (more laughter from the crowd) "He loved it so much that he's been a Bobcat ever since..."

Will looked at his watch and then back to me.

I whispered with intensity, "Do you want me to go call Miss Betty and Sheriff Tatum again?"

"Yes, and call Captain Allen, too. I told Withers that I would give the speech in Dad's place. What should I say?"

I took his hand and squeezed it. I looked at him and whispered, "You know your dad. Keep it short and sweet. I'll meet you outside in three minutes."

"Yeah. Not like these other guys, right?" He smirked.

Dr. Anderson said, "Accepting his award on his behalf is his son, Will."

The crowd applauded and Will walked quickly to the podium.

Will nodded politely and spoke like the expert storyteller he is. "Thank you, all, on behalf of my dad, who apologizes to all of you for not being here today. To the University, to the Ecology Department, and to the community of Bozeman, he thanks you all, and I thank you all for supporting him for all these years. He's been here for forty-one years which isn't bad for a kid who was waitlisted."

Everyone laughed, and Will grinned that beautiful smile. Clothed in sunshine.

"He wanted me to invite you all to fly fish with us. He didn't want me to rub it in your faces, but Dad said he was going to fly fish every day. You're more than welcome to join him... as long as you pay and tip really well. We've got to earn a living somehow." The crowd responded with laughter.

"Thank you for everything you have done for my family through the years. You're all very special to him. We are humbled and blessed to have been in such an amazing place with such a wonderful extended Bobcat family for as long as we have. Thank You!"

He smiled and waved to the applauding crowd. Then, he walked past his seat and hurried out the door.

Will tossed me the keys and told me to drive. He wanted to speak with Sheriff Tatum again and, hopefully, Captain Allen, too. Frantically, he took out his cell phone and started calling. No one had seen or heard anything yet. Will reminded them both that Ed was having some memory problems. Both men said they would send the search teams as soon as they could.

Ed lay motionless creek side, fading slowly at the mercy of time that was running out. He had lost so much blood. The mountain lion hadn't nicked any major arteries, but the gashes were deep, and they were everywhere. Ed was weak and knew he couldn't move, much less walk. If he tried to crawl to safety, where would he go? It would only encourage the monster to accelerate what eventually would be a feeding frenzy.

His mind was everywhere, but nowhere as he drifted in and out of consciousness.

On the way back to the house Will and I decided to divide and conquer. Will had gotten in touch with Betty, and she would head to the fly shop to stay there and wait. Will would head west on 84 to check the Madison River at Bear Trap Canyon. I would go north of town to check Bozeman Creek, and the East Gallatin.

We assumed Ed knew he needed to stay relatively close to home to clean up before the banquet, so we checked areas he would frequent locally.

There was about an hour of daylight left, and we all knew we had to find him quickly. Will met Sheriff Tatum at Bear Trap Canyon Access Road looking for Ed's Truck. The plan was if they didn't see his truck, they would double back. Cell service was spotty, and after the third dropped call, I just gave up. I scoured Bozeman Creek and parts of the East Gallatin looking for his truck. I turned down Frontage Road to check Rocky Creek, and it dawned on me...Holy crap, Bridger Creek! Of course! He's at Bridger Creek.

I made a U-turn and headed back east to pick up Bridger Canyon Road toward the Bridger Mountains. As luck would have it, I called Will and the call went through. I told him about Ed having a secret location where he fished on Bridger Creek.

Will contested my claim and said, "What the hell are you talking about? Bridger Creek? Are you sure? No one fishes Bridger. Dad fished Bridger Creek?"

"Will, stop! Listen. You need to trust me. I'm going that way now. I'll call you back in five minutes but start heading that way."

I was flying up the road racing the sunset. If we could just locate his truck, it would increase our chances of finding him, but time was running out. I had to find him. Ever since Daddy died, Ed was there for me. Saving my life...twice, no, three times. Welcoming me into his family. Teaching me to fly fish. No one matters as much as your parents do. But when they die young, or when they don't do a great job loving you and guiding you, other adults can adopt these special roles, too. That's why mentors, teachers, and coaches are so important. They make such a difference in people's lives. That's what Ed did for me. He made a difference. I couldn't let him down now.

My intuition was right. I followed the mental blueprint from when Ed brought me to Narnia's doorstep. "Yes! I knew it," I said aloud.

As I pulled in, I was staring at the back of his truck. I called Will to let him know I had found the truck and gave him my location. Will relayed the information to Sheriff Tatum and Captain Allen.

Everyone was in route, screaming up Bridger Canyon Road at top speed. I told Will it was a service road on the left just above Stone Creek Road. I gave him directions to follow the trampled brush just left of Ed's truck, and head upstream back towards Bridger Canyon Road. If upstream produced nothing, we would start plotting our course downstream.

I didn't wait for Will to tell me to stay put. I just told him to hurry, and I hung up. I knew Ed was out there, and I needed to find him.

I searched my truck for my flashlight, but I knew I had left my revolver in Will's truck with my waders. I could hear Will's voice chastising me, "Dammit, Maya, you always keep your piece with you. Always!" I did have the knife I always kept in the glove compartment. "That's better than nothing," I thought as I grabbed it.

Then, I raced over to Ed's truck, cupped my hands around my eyes and peeked at both the front and back seat through the windows. His phone and gun were sitting in the back seat of the truck tucked behind a pair of work boots, one of his four fly packs, and an old flannel shirt. The doors were locked.

I climbed into the bed of his truck ready to smash the glass in with a rock. Fortunately, the back window slide was cracked, and it slid open with ease. Thank God!

I reached in and grabbed his flannel and .38 revolver, and I checked the chamber to be sure it was loaded. I jumped from the truck bed, slipped on his flannel, and stomped through the heavy brush, purposely bulldozing my entry point to make it easy for Will and company to follow. I was determined to find Ed alive. I'm not sure what it was, but there was an energy urging me to move downstream, and that's where I went.

Shouting Ed's name as loud as I could, I made it through my first major hurdle, and that was through the massive overgrowth that led to Bridger Creek. There was just under an hour of visibility left.

Worrying about my own safety was now an afterthought. For some people, in situations like this, it's a light switch they can turn on and off at will. For me, it turned into an out-of-body experience, like what happened to me on the Gallatin with the Booadasha. It was a stirring consciousness, compelling me to keep moving forward. I could feel the presence of my counsel directing and imploring me to move faster, step after leaping step. I heard faint whispers grow louder and louder in my mind.

Then, about sixty feet away, I saw him.

"ED!"

He was there, quietly moaning. He had heard my calls, but he was too weak to reply. I could see the blood, scarlet and stark against the blanched dirt and earth surrounding him. I raced over, knelt beside him, and checked his pulse. Then I drew my gun and scanned the woods, thinking that whatever had attacked him could still be close. I ripped off the flannel and began slicing strips out of the arms. I was talking to him the whole time. "Don't worry, Ed. Everything is gonna be fine. Help is on the way."

I tied a tourniquet just above the gashes on his right leg and on both biceps.

I checked my watch. The team was still twenty-five minutes away. I knew the trek back was over four hundred yards. My senses were on high alert. I knew whatever had ravaged his body would be back. Waiting for someone else to rescue us would not be an option.

Trying not to panic, I took a moment to think. "How am I gonna get him out of here?"

Suddenly, I flashed back to what I learned about the Cherokee Indians. Thank goodness for Mrs. Holt! They made that travois thingy...the sled they used to haul essentials.

This was my only choice in getting us out of here. There were plenty of broken branches and downed limbs scattered on the bank. I found two, mostly straight, six-foot sections and crossed them in an elongated X. I knotted the intersection at the top of the X and added two, four-foot cross bars with the remaining flannel strips and made sure it was sturdy.

I laid the travois down and heard a screeching noise like nothing I had ever heard before. I jumped out of my skin, pulled my gun, and scanned the forest, ready to unload at anything that approached. I shouted, "Ed, we're going to get out of here...hang on...we both can do this." I scanned the forest again and saw nothing. I tucked Ed's gun back in my belt.

I knew I had to move fast. Whatever creature that attacked Ed would be back any time to claim his kill. I had to move fast. I knew in my gut we were being surveyed. I repeatedly skimmed the tree line above the creek's embankment as the screeching-howls got louder and more frequent. Quickly, I tied the remaining strips together and threaded them under Ed's armpits, across his chest and crossed them behind his shoulders and dragged him onto the sled. The ground and rocks beneath Ed were stained dark red and pink from the blood loss.

I opened the straps and wove them around the base of the sled and knotted it to keep him from sliding off. I kept repeating out loud, "We're gonna make it! We can do this! Hold on!" I was racing against time, the elements, and the shrieking noise that continued to permeate through the mass of timberland around me. I could see my breath from the chill of dusk setting in as the camouflage of night chased away the light.

I grunted as I lifted the travois above my chest and rested the top of the X on my shoulders and started the long walk back upstream to Ed's truck. I could see skin tissue from raking gouges to the back of Ed's head from the animal's claws. My eyes were fixed on the woods as I backed away across the slick shoal to the opposing bank. The strident shrieks of the creature echoed as it charged.

The mountain lion had to be over a hundred and fifty pounds. I backed out of the sled and reached for my gun so fast that I dropped Ed into the shallows of the creek all in one motion. The mountain lion made two loping strides toward us and vaulted in the air to take back what he thought was his. I steadied my gun and blasted a shot, narrowly missing. The shot alone didn't even faze him. I ripped off another shot that landed at its feet halting the surge for a split second.

Will and the team heard the shots and were immediately frozen. They looked at one another in a heightened panic. Night was on the verge of consuming all of us. Sheriff Tatum radioed for back up, and all three men, with flashlights and guns in hand, ran toward the reverberating booms.

I marked my sight just above the monster's neck as he began his second rush, still unfazed by the shot at his feet. I stepped back and faced the cat, eye-to-eye. He continued toward me and that was it. Shaking, I steadied my grip of the gun with my left hand. My thumbs stacked to the left of the trigger, I fired another shot toward its neck. I landed that one and the monster retreated into the woods. Not knowing the severity of that last round, I held my revolver tight...ready just for insurance in case he came back.

All I heard was silence, so I reached down with both arms and lifted Ed again. This time, I rotated the travois to my back and dragged him like a cargo mule as fast as I could upstream. I glanced back every five seconds, expecting our nemesis to reappear.

The base of the travois was effective in moving Ed up the uneven terrain. "Come on, Ed, we got this. We'll be there soon." I tried to reassure him, but I was starting to pant with each lumbering step I took. Not only was I exhausted, but I was paralyzed by the black Montana night. I couldn't even see the silhouette of my hand in front of my face. I was afraid to even move. If I fell, we'd never get out of there.

Finally, I heard the sirens in the distance blaring, and I faintly heard my name muffled from over the crest that led down to the creek. "Thank God!" I said aloud. "Ed, they're here. They found us!"

I carefully rotated the travois from my shoulders to my chest and delicately set Ed on the ground. I collapsed beside him still on the lookout for the beast. My adrenaline was boiling inside of me. With every fiber of my existence, I gritted my teeth, flexed, and screamed in defiance at the wilderness around me in every direction; but I knew we would be okay.

Search and Rescue arrived first. Their flashlights were blinding. Captain Allen asked me if I had been injured or hurt in any way. I shook my head no and pointed to Ed. Sheriff Tatum rolled his flashlight Ed over and said, "Oh man," as Allen and the team got to work patching his wounds and getting him stable for the drive to the hospital.

Will arrived and ran to Ed's stretcher. "It's going to be okay, Dad. Don't worry." Captain Allen and his crew stabilized Ed and rushed him to Bozeman Deaconess Hospital.

Will picked me up and hugged me so tight I couldn't breathe. "I'm never letting you go! Maya, you just saved Dad's life and you scared the hell outta me again! I don't know if I should be pissed, thankful, or both."

"Probably both…but I like grateful better."

51

Spring, 2016

It is evident we are put into situations on this planet to test us. Daddy always told me about those character-building moments, and our character is what invites others around us to be better…to do better. Sometimes, the obstacles and misfortunes we encounter bend those character values. Our reactions in those situations are nothing more than a microcosm of who we will eventually be. My belief is simply this: there are those who adapt to adversity and overcome, and there are those who break and succumb. In a split second, we decide if we adjust, or we surrender. Those choices create our legacy.

Ed's legacy was evident in the fact that the graduating class of 2016 invited him to be the speaker even though most of them had only heard the stories about Dr. Ed Myers. Much to Will's surprise, Ed agreed.

His disease had progressed, but the different meds they tried slowed the progression so that he was still functional. We wouldn't let him drive anymore, which was a really challenging battle Will and I waged, but in the end, Ed acquiesced. He only needed to go to the shop every day anyway. Betty picked him up some days; Will took him others. I had classes in the morning and usually stopped by afterward.

We rented Ed's house out to tourists who had also booked tours at the shop, and Will and I bought a bigger house with a father-in-law suite for Ed. It was even closer to the shop than before, and it was about a thousand square feet bigger. We needed that extra space when Will and I got two dogs, Langston and Angelou, and welcomed a beautiful baby girl into the world. We named her Mills after my mother. She's a lot like my mother: calm, smart, patient, and funny.

Next came a boy, whom we named Beaux, after Sarah's father, but he was a lot like Ed. He was quiet and thoughtful. Even when he was just out of the womb, his eyes darted from place-to-place absorbing everything. He was only a toddler, but I could tell he wouldn't ever really be much of a talker. With Will as his dad, and Mills as his sister, however, he wouldn't get to talk much anyway.

When pink gently spread across the sky chasing the dark away, Ed was already awake and drinking coffee. He was re-reading his speech. He wrote most of it, and I just tweaked a few things. We printed it out in large font so he could easily see it and wouldn't stumble through. I got the kids prettied-up and Will helped Ed tie his tie. "I'm proud of you, Dad." Ed grabbed both of Will's shoulders and they both smiled.

Dr. Anderson stood at the podium and used several of the same jokes he used at Ed's retirement banquet. It was okay. They were still funny. The students clapped as Ed was introduced.

Ed walked up to the podium, took a deep breath, and smiled at the graduates in their caps and gowns. He missed teaching more than he thought he would, but he also liked the freedom of not being tied down to a steady schedule.

Ed began, "Thank you, Dr. Anderson, to all of my colleagues and to my family. Thank you from the bottom of my heart for asking me to be your guest speaker today. I hope I won't let you down… but, I probably will. Sorry!

"Life has a way of letting you down…often. We all face obstacles and challenges. It's what you do with those trials that determine your legacy and what kind of person you become. When I was asked to speak on this momentous day, I was truly taken aback. I have never been much of a talker… unless I was trying to sell a pair of waders or a fly rod in my own shop, and even then, I was not good at it. That's what I got Will for. Y'all know, he's really good at talking!" Everyone knew and loved Will, so they all agreed.

"After thinking about it for a few days, I couldn't believe my ears when I heard my mouth say, 'Yes! I will be the speaker.' I realized that not only was I grateful for the opportunity, but I actually have something I'd like to say to the class of 2016. I want to talk to you about the MOST important quality successful people have: PERSEVERANCE.

"I know, I know…it seems wildly cliché and super boring…" Ed imitated an enormous yawn and the audience laughed again. "I'm not talking about the perseverance that gets us out of bed in the morning… although some days, that's pretty much all I got. I'm talking about the perseverance of survival. So, I pose this question to you: What is the most difficult obstacle you've ever faced?

"Did you overcome it? Did you RAGE against it? Or did you side-step it, avoid it, or ask your mommy to handle it for you?

"I want to tell you a secret. Ready? Repeat after me: Everyone faces hardships." The audience repeated it. "Now say this with me: I WILL SURVIVE." We said it. "Some of you know that I was diagnosed with early onset of dementia...which is probably the reason I forgot to let Dr. Anderson know I would speak today..." Everyone laughed.

"I want to tell you a story about perseverance that will inspire you. It's not about me, but it's about one of your current professors and my daughter-in-law, Dr. Maya Jones Myers."

Everyone turned to look at me. I was mortified. I hadn't helped him write THIS part of the speech. What the hell Ed? You're off script!

Ed continued, "This is a young woman who has persevered through loss, racism, and bullies...never defaulting to the comfortable or wavering in her aspirations. She faced death head on more than once and refused to surrender, undaunted. She not only survived but thrived under these difficult circumstances. She left her home and her family two thousand miles away to chase a dream and earn a degree that, at the time, fewer than eight percent of women in America occupy. A woman of color which at the time represented fewer than two percent of our student enrollment here at MSU, and ladies and gentlemen, she has been at MSU for almost twenty years. Steadfast.

"Many of you have heard the story of my retirement banquet, but it bears repeating. Ten years ago, I didn't make it to my retirement banquet. I went fishing that morning and was attacked by a hungry mountain lion.

That woman right there, yeah, right there..." Ed pointed right at me, and the crowd gasped. His voice cracked, and he almost choked up. He cleared his throat and continued.

"Dr. Maya Myers saved my life. I would have bled to death. Her selfless act gave me this chance to speak to you. She also saved my son's life by marrying him." Everyone looked at Will now, and he smiled and waved, the sun lighting up the sky.

"She has always been unconventional, not by choice, but by desire. She chose her path and stuck to it regardless of what others said or thought about her. She has earned everything she has been given, not because she's my daughter-in-law..." He winked at me, and everyone laughed.

"But because she earned it. Tonight, she has earned the right to be noticed and seen in a different light. Please take note: she looked past the easy road that many of us walk and chose to blaze her own trail, making it her own road. This is what I mean when I encourage you to persevere.

"Calvin Coolidge once said at a graduation speech in 1925, 'Nothing in the world can take the place of persistence. Talent will not; nothing is more common than unsuccessful men (or women) with talent. Genius will not; unrewarded genius is almost a proverb. Education alone will not; the world is full of educated derelicts. Persistence and determination alone are omnipotent.' This is why the human spirit will always conquer the human condition.

"I want you to listen carefully. Life offers more challenges and trials than you can even imagine. BUT, with resolute perseverance, courage, and a lot of support from your family and friends, you WILL survive. Say it with me again, 'I. Will. Survive.'" We said it with him.

"Finally, class of 2016, I want to encourage you with this final phrase, 'Don't look for excuses to fail; think of reasons to succeed.' Once you remember you have an indomitable spirit, you will survive. Thank you, and go Bobcats!"

Ed got a standing ovation, walked to his seat, and sat down. The crowd stood and continued to applaud. They didn't stop. They weren't going to stop. It kept going until Ed motioned to me to stand up.

Hesitantly, I stood and waved, pointing to the graduating class, all of them. Whistles squealed, and shouts from the crowd howled. Then in unison, a roar of M.S.U., M.S.U., engulfed Brick Breeden Fieldhouse.

As I stand in this river, at this moment, I think of Judith Whitehorse. Her grandfather's premonition had meaning now. I understood my calling. I had a purpose. It would be an assignment for reformation and a pursuit of empowerment for all women, especially women who looked like me.

The price is high... the reward is great.

The key for me was to take my life experiences to enhance future generations' awareness of the possibilities of what could be: exposing, preparing, and encouraging strong, capable women to step into new arenas regardless of gender and color; blowing the glass ceiling away and dancing on the shattered glass.

Fishing has taught me to constantly adjust to challenges, to use my resources, and to withstand whatever comes next. If we all experienced that headspace and connection, fishing would dissolve superficial divisions and drive a commonality this world has yet to embrace. This is what I was saved for. This mission. Now.

I remember Daddy saying that fishing is life's great equalizer. It's interesting how this "equalizer" is a metaphor for life. As human beings, if we don't adapt to our surroundings, aspects of our lives then become the proverbial hamster on the wheel. Fly Fishing is the catalyst for anyone willing to surrender to its power as a means of searching for purpose beyond what is mortal. Thank God I was wise enough to be one of the searchers.

ABOUT THE AUTHORS:

BRIAN HESTER

I grew up in Boone, North Carolina, rich with streams, creeks, and rivers full of fish. Boone is a gift to anyone who touches its soil. Tucked up into the Northwest corner of the state, it is guarded by the Blue Ridge Mountains. The word Appalachia or Appalachian was derived from the Apalachee Indians who were indigenous to Florida's panhandle. As the tribe migrated inland into the mountains of Northwest Georgia, so did a derivation of their name. It is important to mention the word "Appalachian" is a shibboleth. When articulated incorrectly, expect to be corrected. Appalachian is ALWAYS pronounced with a "latch-un," NOT a "lay-shun."

The town of Boone (3,333 feet) was named after Daniel Boone: an explorer, hunter-trapper, and militia officer during the Revolutionary War. He was a pioneer who forged a path called the Cumberland Gap, allowing emigrant settlers to travel east into Kentucky.

From the mid 80's to the early 90's, Boone's population was thriving at ten thousand strong. Appalachian State University, one of the most picturesque and best universities on the east coast, enrolled about ten thousand students as well. In addition to that twenty thousand, another couple thousand vacationers visited each season. Summers provided an escape from the heat, while fall attracted an audience to view its canopy of canary yellow, fire-orange and candy-apple-red leaves. When December hit, winter welcomed snow skiing enthusiasts. Boone was a revolving door of flourishing tourism, industrial development, college kids, and drifters alongside the locals who never wanted to leave. This made for an eclectic group of people with their own ideas, values, and backgrounds, all co-existing in a small, but great town.

When I was eight, I sat barefoot on the bank of Boone Fork Creek on the Blue Ridge Parkway. I watched an older man fly fish the tributary and was enamored at his casts and presentation. He was using the same rod and reel combo I had at home that my father won as a door prize and was still in an unopened box in the basement. When the man landed a fish, I asked if I could see it. He posed the fireball so I could see its colors. It was a small, native Brook Trout with a radiant canvas of emerald green transitioning into a palette of volcanic-orange on its belly. That profile was highlighted with red bullseyes wrapped with white and cobalt blue rings. I was awe-struck. As soon as I got home, I got that rod out, went out to the yard, and tried to mimic his way of casting. I thought, how hard can it be?

Around that same time, I ventured into competitive swimming. When I reached a level of proficiency worthy of my mother's approval, she started allowing me to fish on my own. It was pure magic trying to pick apart water with a fly rod. Mom would drop me off at Winkler's Creek or Howard's Creek and over the next four years, there were just enough, ill-timed hooksets, sips, and peeks at my flies to keep me invested in my quest.

Fortunately, I ran across many anglers willing to impart their knowledge on my lack luster attempts to finally hook up with those elusive ghosts. One aficionado was Mr. Daye, *Jedi-Fly Master, aka Obi-Fly Kenobi*. He was a weekend warrior fly fisherman who doubled as my eight-grade science teacher. He explained to me what to use and when, and drew illustrations of how it worked, why it worked, and how to use it. I was a young *Jedi-Fly Wannabe, aka Luke Flywalker.* I tried to utilize everything he said just to give myself a shot. I still treasure some of the flies he tied and gave me.

My hope is that one day, someone reads this book, and it encourages that someone to be a fly fisherman...to embrace the experience...that its act can transform lives by offering the opportunity to hook up to those remarkable rockets of the river.

BARBARA BEAM

I grew up in Charlotte, NC, and am a proud graduate of Appalachian State University with a B.S. in English Education and M.Ed. from the University of West Florida.

Although my personnel file is filled with many letters of reprimand for insubordination, I'm now in my 32nd year teaching, and I've loved all but about 12 days of it! I've never been one to "follow orders" without asking, "Why is this necessary to help students?" If my administrator couldn't answer that question correctly, I didn't implement the policy. I'm thinking Maya may have a few letters of reprimand in her file, too.

Although I'm not a fisherman, (yet!) I enjoy being outside at the pool or the beach. There is indeed something serene about spending time alone with God, yourself, and nature without distractions. I appreciate Brian helping me remember the value of that quiet, uninterrupted time.

Brian and I are second cousins once removed. (Southerners know things like that!) My great-grandmother was the oldest and Brian's grandfather was the youngest in a family of a whole mess of young'uns. We only saw each other at Thanksgiving when a bunch of

Elliotts got together at my Aunt Eugenia's (Brian's grandmother's) house. When the kids played football in the yard, I remember thinking he was really fast, but his hands were bricks! I'm still mad he dropped that touchdown pass that was right in his breadbasket! If this book becomes a best seller, I will forgive him.

As adults, we both taught in Charlotte for a while, and we spent time together watching Appalachian football games and talking about the joys of teaching. I liked him because he made me laugh. (I only hang out with funny people.) Although we had much in common, we were never close.

All of that changed as he bestowed upon me the honor of helping him write this book. I am so grateful he chose me. Throughout this process, Brian and I talked twenty times a week. I'm a hermit. Not just a loner…a serious, legit hermit. People exhaust me. Brian has never cared. He MADE me talk to him. So, just like I do every day as a teacher, I gritted my teeth and dealt with it, then spent several hours alone in the quiet.

Throughout the process of writing this book, we have discussed, discovered, overcovered, fought, fussed, and figured out so many things about ourselves, each other, and Maya's world. It has been challenging. Because he's an extrovert and thinks out loud, and I'm an introvert and never say anything until I've run it through my French horn of a brain, we struggled to communicate at first. Eventually, we developed a system, and it worked! I became a better writer by working with Brian, and our book got better with each draft we wrote. It's been an incredible journey and I'm grateful he asked me to hop in the boat.

ACKNOWLEDGEMENTS & THANKS

From both of us:

Thank you, reader, for reading our book. We appreciate you and hope that our story lights a fire within you to find a friend and a fly rod and get on some water somewhere. Put those phones down, go outside, and enjoy the tranquility that allows you to tune out the ridiculous noise the world pounds in our heads that turns our brains to mush, and listen to your own inner voice. Enjoy the peace that only comes with silence. For more products or to connect with us, please visit our website: www.shetalkstofish.com. Don't forget to buy the She Talks to Fish Journal! Become a subscriber for updates, events, and other fabulous downloads.

We'd like to thank our students who inspire us, challenge us, and drive us bat shit crazy. Thank you all for allowing us to become part of your high school stories.

To all the past members of the MPAC, one day, I hope you pay it forward. Thank you for your inspiration.

Thank you to all our beta readers who read really rough drafts and helped us shape and mold the story: Pamela, Stacy, Joyce, Tia, Erin, Micheal, Glenda 'Lady Mac', Angela, Tommye, Ami, Moria, and Amber. Your voices and insights helped fashion a truly beautiful, strong Southern voice.

Editors: Jodie Scales, Malin Curry, Joyce Godwin, and Susan Lovelace, because of your care and interest, we have reached new heights. We hope you like how it turned out.

Thank you to my UNC-Charlotte Swimming teammates for always supporting my artistic pursuits.

Dale @grayink - you always make magic happen. Thank you for a brilliant website, spectacular book cover, and all the crucial things you've helped us navigate.

David: Thank you for everything. May the force be with you!

Chris: Thanks for your knowledge of the Bozeman past.

Pat: your instruction, analogies, and acumen have transformed my game on the water and in this novel. I am grateful.

Captain Secor, (Retired) Commander Gallatin County Sheriff Search and Rescue: you were my eyes and ears. Thank you for taking my 911 call and becoming an incredible friend.

Dr. Fleming: Professor-Department of Native American Studies, Montana State University, you saw my vision and guided my efforts with structure, truths, and an attention to detail. Thank you for your interest, kindness, and knowledge.

Shout out to Crow Tribal Nation, and all Indigenous American Nations. We are grateful for your history, lineage, and legacy.

Dr. Hester: what can I say? You're a Hester. Charge to 200…CLEAR!

Thank you, Robin and Cecil, for friendships that reach further than just brother and sister. You shared your lives with us from childhood… answered our questions… and stayed patient with us as we tried to understand. We hope you're proud of this book.

To all our colleagues and friends who have been on this road with us, thank you.

Barbara

Thank you to my parents, Conrad and Rebecca, my siblings, Susan and Jonathan, and my extended Beam & Putnam families! I am grateful for the roots and the wings... and the ability to not only dream but dream BIG and in technicolor. Thank you also my Appalachian roommates, my FAC, my FISH, my DAWGS, my Panther families, and all my church families. Whenever I said, "Hey, y'all, I'm going to write a song...a book...a movie...a play," the response I heard from most of you was something along the lines of "That's great!" I appreciate the love and support even throughout the 467 rejections I've received over twenty-five years. Not that I'm counting.

Brian

Mom and dad, thank you for cultivating what was inside of me. Not bad for a little mountain boy from Boone, right? We all got lucky in 1969!

Boof, thank you for your faithful support. Look who learned how to write now?!?

Kaytlin, Mason and Max, I love you beyond comprehension!

Heather, aka "the Chief," and the love of my life, none of this happens without you. My blessings are: dreaming big with me, fly fishing with me (and you're damn good at it,) your heart, your unwavering support, your ridiculously high tolerance for my artsy brain, antics, and lunatic ventures, your contribution to the novel and being rational when I need you to be.

Barb, thank you for reluctantly saying yes twice and not making me beg too much. You grounded my rabid demeanor and put me in my place. You made me a better writer. You believed in me and my story, and we built a magnificent read. It was a perfect storm. I can't wait for the sequel, Zora Neale.

Made in the USA
Middletown, DE
07 March 2025